Phillip Drown is a writer and music enthusiast. He has worked in an independent record shop for more than ten years, where he first discovered a love of blues music. He lives in Kent.

The Reputation of Booya Carthy is his first novel.

ISBN-13 978-1512381801
ISBN-10 1512381802

Cover design by Spiffing Covers.

Follow Phillip on Twitter:
@phillipdrown

And:
www.facebook.com/phillipdrowncreatingtales

*

Find out more at: **www.phillipdrown.com**

PHILLIP DROWN

THE REPUTATION
~ OF ~
BOOYA CARTHY

For Emily Burton and Emily Clarke

CHAPTER ONE

1

Summer, 1927

The boy looked up into the bright blue sky, his thick crescent eyelashes flickering, eyes moistening. Sweet pear juice dribbled from his chin on to his shirt. There was nothing to disturb the vast blue mass except for the flaming yellow ball, and somewhere beyond that the God that Mammy told him about. If God was that big hot Mississippi sun, he was happy and smiling today.

Standing in an avenue of perfectly pruned fruit trees, the boy put the chewed core of pear in his mouth. Closing his teeth around it, he pulled out only the stem, dropping it in the long grass, wiped his bare forearm across his mouth and licked his lips.

A butterfly was standing still as a leaf on a branch. With his eyes still squinting against the backdrop, the boy found it in a moment, the orange and black wings a giveaway against the blue of the sky. He inched forward on his knees, shimmying through the grass, and twisted a ripening plum from a low branch. Not carefully enough. The butterfly was up in the sky, returning to flight.

The boy jumped to his feet. In two bites the plum was gone, the seed spat out. This time he did not wipe his chin, too involved in following the butterfly to mind the sticky juice.

The butterfly led him out of the orchard towards a high hedge. He stopped. There was a new distraction. Tilting his head to one side, he watched the butterfly disappear over the hedge.

A woman's voice, as sweet as the ripe fruits he had just devoured, travelled through the still air. He had never heard anything like it. When Mammy sang, she sang in a gravelled, low voice, the story songs he adored. This distant voice was as light as a butterfly. It soared like a bird.

With his hand atop the rickety wooden gate that dissected the high hedge, he stopped again to listen. The song was clearer here, even more ravishing.

Though he had seen it from the orchard, he had never been through the gate before. He had skipped past it a hundred times, a thousand even. On occasion he had daringly peered over the gate – as he was doing now – at the manicured garden, the pergolas and the rose arbours, the bushy shrubs and the plants. But he had never dared himself to trespass onto the trouble he could bring to Mammy, Paw and himself if he were to step beyond the gate. He had been forbidden to ever go further than the orchard. Mammy's expression alone warned him of the trouble it would bring upon them all.

Looking around, seeing no one, he lifted the latch.

The song drew him along a paved path, parallel to a perfect rug of green. With each step his conscience awoke a little more, keeping him close to the towering hedge, his hand running along its trimmed edge as if he might be able to vanish into its depth if he were seen.

He had walked the entire length of the lawn. The house was standing over the garden like a proud hunter posing above his kill. He could see an open window from which he was sure the sound was pouring. Like a greedy magpie capturing the smell of apple pie cooling on the window ledge, the magical voice gently wrapped arms around him, easing him nearer to devour the tasty sound. The gravel of a rose-lined pathway crunched beneath his bare feet, though the noise of his step was veiled. The boy's eyes had been set on the open window, but he looked down as his foot touched the bottom of the steep stairs leading up to the veranda. He crept to the top.

An open door leading into the shadows of the house was before him. Without stopping to think, his bare foot stepped on to the polished oak floor. The first thing he noticed was how much cooler it was inside the house. Outside he had barely noticed the drops of sweat that had sprung up on his forehead, but he noticed now that the sweat was turning to ice on his skin.

Through the dark hallway, he slinked past an oak sideboard. He ran his hand along its surface, leaving a sticky, wet trail. The sideboard held the same coolness of the hallway, satiating his clammy palm. As his hand ran from the end of the sideboard, it flapped down to his side, gently slapping his thigh.

A tall grandfather clock was ticking loudly above him, a metronome to his heartbeat. On the wall opposite the clock was a long mirror. He caught his wide eyes looking into it. His reflection didn't appear excited to be so close to finding the source of the beautiful voice. Through the dim light he tried to smile at his reflection, but saw only a bare flicker of his lips.

He stepped away from the mirror and walked to the heavy oak door. Placing his hand against the grain, he could feel the sound trying to burst through the wood. He gripped the door handle. He could not turn it with one hand. He looked down the dark corridor towards the depths of the house, and then over his shoulder to the whispering light of the day.

The beautiful voice called to him.

Gripping with both hands, the handle started to turn.

2

Hanging from the centre of the ceiling was a heavy chandelier, glowing despite the bright morning outside. It certainly appeared to be a dark house, but everything in this room was gold, shining with the reflecting light emanating from the grand centrepiece. Gold picture frames and the frame of the mirror, the wallpaper, gold etching on the mantelpiece – beneath which was an arranged but unlit fire –, gold cherubs and figurines, gold candlesticks holding gold candles, gold lampstands. Even the coalscuttle and fireplace utensils were of shining gold. Golden flecks danced in the boy's dark brown eyes.

And the voice continued to sing.

It was a surprise to the boy that there were not a dozen men gathered in here, playing horns and trumpets and bashing drums. Stranger still, there was no singing lady, only empty chairs, sofas, and objects that were shining like the sun. He noticed an upturned horn by the window – surely the source of the sound. It was as golden as everything else in the room.

In the gold frames were paintings, rich colours depicting military scenes; greys on their hind legs with fearsome men riding, holding swords up to the sky; masses of men in battle, some with desperate looks on their faces, others with deadly intent in their frozen cries. Above the fireplace hung a portrait of a man with a neat line of moustache drawn above his thin upper lip, a brave glint in his eye. Another portrait showed a round-faced woman, startlingly pale, who looked sad and resigned as she stared out of the canvas above her high collar, over the head of the boy and out of the open door. Upon the gold-etched marble mantle, delicate white maternal figurines poised: one stooping to tend to a child at her feet, one cradling a baby, another with her hands pressed to her breast, appealing silently to the sky. Standing on a low bookcase were animals carved from ivory – none as fierce-looking as the men in the paintings, even with their mouths full of teeth wide in a silent roar. Standing alongside the bookcase was a miniature totem, head-upon-head of anguished, contorted expressions. In every otherwise empty space in the massive room were shelves of instruments, wooden carvings and statues from all over the world, all captured in a moment of horror or of calm, an import of challenge or of uninterrupted bliss.

With his palms pressed flat against the wall behind him, the boy began to slowly side-step around the edge of the room, the seat of his pants brushing against the wallpaper. His eyes were wide with a beautiful, dangerous curiosity.

The golden horn was nearly within reach, so huge now it was a wonder that it didn't topple forward with the polished box from which it was spouting. Close as he was, the noise was deafening, thudding deep inside his head and beating in his chest. Each high note tore through him, making him shiver with a deliciously painful warmth.

He peered out of the open window, into the garden. From this perspective it looked even more beautiful outside. Every plant, tree and shrub glittered with golden light from the chandelier of the world. The sweet smells of honeysuckle, lavender and the quilted fragrance of roses found its way in through the open window.

As when he looked into the mirror in the hallway, a smile tried to form at his lips. It twitched his mouth excitedly but still would not come, like one of the little statues trying to come to life after being so many years in suspended animation. All over his body twitched, a tingle of cold kindling trying to light. He placed his fingers on the rim of the table beneath the golden horn and eased up on to the tips of his toes.

A black disc was gently rotating on the box. Beneath the noise he could hear the faint sound of the little needle tracing over the grooves as the disc whirred around. It was of no surprise to him that the arm from which the needle was pointing was golden, shaped at the end like a little paw, the needle a claw protruding from it. He watched the disc spin and the needle skim over its surface, making that delicious sound as it ran.

All of a sudden the noise stopped. It disappeared in a triumphant blare of every instrument that had ever been blown, strummed, plucked, hammered or bashed. The only sound remaining was the gentle whirr of the disc moving and the needle running. It was still pleasing to watch the disc, but the faint, crackly noise that remained could not lure a little boy into a dangerous new world. He thought maybe he could drag the needle away from the centre of the disc and make it start all over again. And lifted his arm to do so.

A new noise in the room startled his spinning eyes from the rotating disc, a sound of papers being shuffled and shaken. He turned his wide eyes, but he could not let loose his one-handed grip on the table.

Such had been the magical lure of the music that he had not noticed that a man had been in the room with him all that time, hidden behind a big mahogany desk and his newspaper. The boy could not move to hide. With one arm still in the air, he could not move at all.

The man folded and placed the paper on the desk. Putting his hands on the arms of his chair, he began to lift himself from the seat. The boy could hear the breath stop in the man's nostrils. The man was looking directly at him.

The stilled expression on the man's face was of stern displeasure.

Glancing quickly towards the portrait, the boy recognised that this was the man in the painting with the smart little line of moustache above his lip. He could not summon a single breath.

The man resumed lifting himself from his chair. His moustache rose as his thin lips parted in a smile. 'Young master, good morning,' he said. He repositioned his chair, stepped from behind the desk, and clasped his hands together behind his back. 'I did not realise that I had company.'

The boy had still not moved, but his palms were moistening.

There was silence in the space between them. Save the harmonious call of the birds in the garden outside, the gentle scratch of the needle on the disc was the only noise to be heard.

'I must apologise if my music was a touch loud,' the man continued. 'I sometimes get a bit lost to the world when I'm listening to opera. I forget just how loud it must seem to everyone else. Ha-ha, "*A racket,*" my wife calls it. Drives her potty! It's not that she isn't as charmed as I by all things classical, but she cares for it to be played at a more . . . moderate level.' He laughed again and positioned himself on the edge of his desk, cupping his hands. The queer little smile returned to his lips.

The boy's fingers finally slipped from the polished table top and he dropped down on to his bare feet.

'Whoopsie,' said the man, followed by another little chuckle. 'That was Puccini's *Tosca* that I was shamelessly blasting out. That's the first ever recording of that particular opera that I was subjecting the world to, with Valentina Bartolomasi as Floria, you know. I have to say, it isn't my most preferred opera, but then who is able to choose a favourite out of so many great works over so many centuries by so many geniuses, eh? Ghastly story though, *Tosca*. A story that contains it all: jealousy, vanity, deceit . . . Frankly, young master, not a story fit for young ears!'

The man crossed his legs, reset his hands. The boy had still not thawed. The man smiled.

'I knew Ms. Bartolomasi. In fact, that is a terrible exaggeration. I did not know her so much as I made her acquaintance, for I only actually met her twice. One time was in Covent Garden – which is back home in London, as I'm sure you know – and the other when my wife and I were fortunate enough to visit La Scala – that's the opera house in Milan, perhaps the finest opera house in the world! Yes, we were terribly fortunate. It was by way of an invitation from an erstwhile client of mine.' Leaning forward, the man clapped his hands together. 'What am I rambling on for? I doubt that all of this is of any interest to you at all.'

Silence filled the space between them once more.

'That cabinet beside you, the one with the gramophone perched on top, is full of recorded music.' The man stood up and began to move across the room towards the boy. 'Is it of interest to you? Is that what brought you in here on this fine morning?'

The boy's unblinking eyes widening as the tall figure of the man approached, his only response was to slowly back up against the wall.

'Please don't be afraid, young master,' said the man, closing the space between him and the boy. 'I'm inviting you to have a look. See?'

5

He opened the doors of the cabinet. It was crammed with records in thick card sleeves, though the boy could not see – he remained pinned against the wall.

'If opera is of interest to you, you'll find that it is mostly what I have gathered in here. Gifts, more than not. Not the collection that I would have necessarily chosen for myself. But one mustn't ever turn down good fortune.'

The man was not looking at the boy, instead he was running his finger along the sleeves, pretending to interest himself. His face lit up as brightly as the glowing room.

'I know what will surely be of interest to you, my young master!' The man had caught him off guard, peering forward, startling him like an animal to thunder. 'Please, do humour me.' The man returned his attention to the cabinet, pulling sleeves forward as he searched.

'Since I have been in your wonderful country, I have become interested in one of your local musical fashions. "The country blues" they are calling it. I think it will become as fashionable as this' – he waved a hand to the room – 'Art Deco style. It has a marvellously energetic rhythm. Have you heard any country blues?'

The man turned and smiled at the boy.

'No? Well, I'm sure that you must have heard it played roundabouts, my young master, even if you weren't aware of the name it goes by. But there is something quite special in hearing it recorded on a tough old piece of shellac and played back through the gramophone.'

The boy had taken half-a-step towards the open cabinet. This time he peered forward, trying to see what the man was clearly willing to show him.

The man muttered into the cabinet. 'I know it was here some place . . . Not that one. Well, I was sure . . . Not that one either, blasted thing – I must palm that off on someone I'm not so fond of, ha-ha, cruel and ungrateful man that I am. Ah! Here you are, you devil!'

He waved the black disc in its sleeve before the boy with triumph. The movement shocked the boy back to the wall. Consumed in his delight, the man did not, this time, even notice the reaction of the boy. He lifted the paw with its needle-claw, dropped *Tosca* on to the window ledge, and placed the record that he had so delighted in finding on to the gramophone. With the boy watching with fascination from his position stuck to the wall, the man lifted the needle and carefully placed it onto the new record, watching the disc, eager for the music to begin. The boy was watching the man's face.

'Please, young master, please do help yourself to a seat. I wish for you to feel completely at ease for such a . . . Ah-ha! Here it comes!' the man cried, a finger pointing in the air. 'The country blues! Oh, I didn't tell you the name of the performer, he's called Blind Lemon Jeff –'

A tap came on the door. The man turned to look.

'Mister Henry,' said the large lady, easing the door further open and walking into the room. 'Everthing fine? Just I see the door was . . .' Her mouth opened. She glared at the boy standing there against the wall, his palms pressed out to each side of him as if he might be able to disappear into the golden wallpaper.

'Mister Calvin Carthy! What you doing in Mister Henry's room? What you doing in this *house*?' She gasped, putting a hand to her lips. 'Mister Henry, I can't understand this behaviour, sir. I is so *sorry*. Uh!' She snapped her fingers, pointing to the floor at her feet. 'You get here now, Calvin Carthy. You lost your mind? What you think you doing, huh?'

The boy spread himself deeper into the wall. The man was looking down at him, to the lady and back, sucking his lips, his forehead wrinkling, eyebrows raised. The country blues was playing on the gramophone.

'You answer me, Calvin Carthy.'

'I heared the music he was playing,' the boy answered. 'And I wannid to see.'

She gasped again. 'You call Mister Henry *sir*, Calvin Carthy.' She turned to face the man, her hands playing nervously in her skirts. 'Mister Henry, I is so sorry for my son. He won't be doing it again, assure you that.' She smiled at the man, scowled at the boy.

'Really, dear Adeline,' said the man, 'it's of no ail to me, not one jot. I did rather invite the young master in by playing my music so loud. Don't be hard on the boy, eh?' he said, patting Calvin's head. 'It was my error, if anyone's. And he's been incredibly polite. Rather, he's a credit to you.'

'Well,' said Adeline, still playing with her skirts, as if ready to curtsey, 'you terrible kind to say, Mister Henry, sir.'

'Not at all,' Mister Henry replied. 'I do rather hope that the young master would indulge me by listening to more of my collection with me sometime. There's no point in owning anything if not to share it with others.'

Mister Henry began to move toward his desk, allowing the boy an escape route. Calvin Carthy had still not yet moved away from the wall, though he did seem less stuck to it than he had.

Standing next to Adeline, having silently entered the room, appeared a small blond-haired boy. Like Adeline, he too gasped. He pointed at Calvin. 'What's *he* doing in here?' he cried. 'He isn't allowed to come into the house. Get out! Get out now!'

'George!' Mister Henry boomed, belying his previously cordial demeanour. 'You aren't to speak like that. Young Calvin is your friend.'

George stamped his foot. 'But he isn't allowed in the house, Daddy. He shouldn't be in here. He's not allowed.'

'Don't yell back at me, young man. It's my house and I decide who comes and goes. Young Calvin is here as my guest.'

'He won't bother you no more, Mister Henry,' said Adeline. 'Come with me now, boy. See the trouble you cause?'

Calvin looked up at Mister Henry. Mister Henry nodded.

'Come, young master. I was taught to always do as my mother says. It's a fine virtue, and you'll do well to abide by it always.'

Mister Henry walked to Calvin. Led by a gentle helping hand on the shoulder, Calvin slowly slid towards his mother. It was strange that he wished he could stay beside the imperious man, Mister Henry, than have to be close to his scowling mother and glaring young companion.

Mister Henry had been right about the music. The country blues. He'd only heard one-and-a-bit songs – most of that interrupted by argument – but Calvin loved what he had heard. And what he could still hear above the sound of George being reprimanded. With his mother's hand on his back (while Mister Henry was twisting one of George's ears), Calvin Carthy was led down the dark hallway, towards the kitchens.

3

Hidden in a faraway corner on the grounds of Mister Henry's mansion, after her day's work was finished, Adeline Carthy sat down in a worn-out armchair and pulled Calvin on to her knee.

'You getting big now, my little man, you know that?'

Looking at his mother, Calvin's eyes were moist.

'You gonna be a mighty big man,' said Adeline. 'That's what I is thinking. My little Mister Calvin Carthy, all growed up. What a thought is that!' She bounced the boy on her knee, as she had done since he was able to sit upright. Though his head bobbed like an apple in a shaken barrel, he kept his eyes fixed firmly on his mother.

'What's wrong, Cally? Normally you laugh like a loon.' She stopped bouncing. A look of terror clouded her face. 'You don't feel a fever, do you? You ain't weak or nothing?'

He shook his head from side-to-side.

'Then what's the matter with you, huh? Why you looking so sad like that for?' She could feel the soft rise and fall of his chest, the little wisp of his staggering breaths on her forearms. 'You can tell your Mammy, my little man.'

'You angry at me,' he whispered.

'Whatever give you that idea, Cally?'

'You angry at me fuh . . .' He sniffed and wiped his hand under his nose. 'You angry at me for being in Mister Henry's house.'

She pulled the boy to her chest and rubbed his sticky back. Snivelling, he rested his head on her shoulder.

'I ain't angry at you, Cal. When I first see you in there with Mister Henry, guess I *was* angry, I have to say. But that was more from the shock of it than anything else. See, we ain't to be in Mister Henry's house unless we is invited in. That's why he give us this little place to live.'

'But you go in there ever day.' His mouth was close to Adeline's ear. She could feel the warm air of his breath in her hair. 'Paw still in there now!'

She continued rubbing a hand up and down his back, feeling the resonance of his sniffles.

'That's where we go to work, honey,' she said. 'You understand that now, don't you? We work for Mister Henry and he keep us here. He good to us.' Rubbing Calvin's back, she listened to his breathing, felt the warm air. He nuzzled in closer to her. She was his big, soft cushion.

'Is we slaves, Mammy?'

With her hand on the nape of Calvin's neck, Adeline slowly turned his head and looked him softly in the eyes.

'We is *servants*, honey – that's the word: *servants*. Servants to Mister Henry and his family,' she said. 'And he pay us good and more than we need, as well as keeping us. Ain't no slaves nowhere no more, Cal. We is luckier than any to be in the keeping of such a good man like Mister Henry. But we sure ain't his slaves. Nuh-uh. *Servants*, honey, that's what we is. You remember that at all times. And remember, ain't nothing wrong being a servant for a good man like Mister Henry. We free as wild horses, don't you never forget that.'

She hugged and rubbed him. Though the heat of the day had still not left the little brick house, with most of the windows open as wide as they could be, they shared each other's warmth. The sound of crickets harping in the woodland behind the house was a symphony almost as deafening as Mister Henry's opera. From somewhere beyond the woodland the sound of a noisy party was drifting through on the wind, though the trees dampened out all but a sough of the hullabaloo.

'What make you ax that, honey?' Adeline asked. 'Is it just being in Mister Henry's house like that today?'

'George say we is,' Calvin replied. 'Say it all the time.'

She lifted the boy out in front of her, no longer playfully exaggerating her struggle with his size. Calvin's head sank into his neck.

'George say *that* to you?'

Calvin nodded.

Adeline shook him by his shoulders. 'He say we slaves?'

Calvin nodded again, his lips screwing together, his eyes remoistening.

'Oh, honey, I don't mean to snipe at you. I know you is tired. Here.' She pulled him close to her shoulder, to listen to his precious breaths. 'Come snuggle to Mammy.'

Adeline looked at the candle on the mantle, flickering gently with the breeze. She curled her fingers lightly into a fist and put it to her mouth, blinking steadily, watching the light dance on the wall. She sighed, then smiled.

'Hey, Cal, you remember that day when we was out walking so you could go look for animals and insects?' she asked, jiggling him.

He sprang up and put his hands on her cheeks. 'We gonna go look for some now?'

'Oh sweetheart, no, honey,' she replied, kissing him on the nose. 'It's dark outside now. The time when we first see Mister Henry? He rolled up in his big shiny motorcar, ax us if we knowed where this place was, remember?'

'Uh-huh.' Calvin nodded.

'Well, he ax us then to come work for him. It was *him* axing *us*. He needed us to help him out, see? Like when we ride with him up here, 'cause he was all lost. What did he say? "Like looking for a seed in a barrel of straw."'

Calvin laughed. 'You sound just like him, Mammy! Do it again!'

'Oh honey, no,' she said. 'We mustn't joke, really. He's a kind, kind man. And we got you to thank for finding him, 'cause it was you who wanted to go out looking. You was probably too young to remember now, but we was living in this little old place on the plantation. *Do* you remember?'

'Hmm, not really,' he replied. 'I remember the white bolls.'

'That's right. And it's been better ever since we find Mister Henry that day and he ax us to be his servants; not slaves, Cally. And ain't nothing wrong with that. If ever anyone say different . . . they just muddled with they words, is all,' she said. 'You must always believe in your little heart your place in this world is as important as the next man. The world belongs to everybody just the same. Even if some got a bigger house, or some got more money and things than the next man, that don't matter none, because we all breathe the air the same, black and white. Inside we all got a heart. Ain't no one can touch that.' She bounced him up and down. He laughed. 'There you go. Now come settle down.'

He wriggled to get comfortable against her chest.

'Mister Henry's kind, Mammy.'

'He sure is sweetheart.'

The breathing in Adeline's ear slowed to a soft, steady rhythm.

Outside, the crickets were harping as gleefully as on any night. Often when Adeline sat in that chair, she thought that they were each trying to be as loud as the next singing cricket. Down past the woodland, all through the night, the men on the old plantation were just the same: trying to be as loud as the next man, much like everything in the animal world. It was by the Lord's grace that little Calvin's Paw hardly ever went down there anymore. She knew that when they had first moved onto Mister Henry's property it had been hard at first for him to shake the old ways out of his skin. She'd watch as he staggered back into their little house, always with a kiss for his boy. "You been kissed by a angel, Boo," he'd say. "You been kissed on the head by a angel." In those days the angel's breath had carried the smell of *Moonshine*

– illegal bootleg liquor.

'Mammy?'

She felt the boy shudder as she jumped. 'Oh, Calvin, sorry! Thought you was asleep. What's it, honey?'

'What if you believe in your heart that your place in the world is more important than anyone else?' he asked.

Gripping him tighter, she rubbed her head against his, breathing a little laugh of contentment through her nostrils. 'In my heart you is the most important person in the world.'

Listening to his breathing, she waited as he absorbed what she had said. She could listen to his soft breaths for every second for the rest of her life. She was in no hurry.

His breaths came slightly quicker as he thought before speaking. 'Mammy?'

'Yes, sweet boy.'

'I believe in my heart that I is quite important,' he said. 'Maybe not as important as Mister Henry or Paw, but . . . I don't know. Just feel in my heart that my place in the world is . . . big.'

'Oh, honey, I know just what you saying, I do.' She gently rocked him. 'Aim for the moon, Cally, and you might just land on a star.'

He chuckled in her ear. She smiled and rocked him.

'Mammy?'

'Yes, honey,' she answered with her eyes closed. The soft, rhythmic breathing in her ear was carrying her towards sleep. Pulling himself from her embrace, he pushed against the back of the chair to look at her. She opened her eyes to see his big, brown eyes looking into hers, so close that they were one beautiful giant planet.

'Why does George and Mister Henry talk funny?'

She raised her eyebrows. 'That's 'cause of where they is from. That's the English talk. They probably think the way we talk is funny to them. It ain't right or wrong, just different. England's a whole other country, far from here. But even if you think he's wrong, it ain't right to ever mention to George the way that he speaks words. Even if he say that *you* is wrong.'

"Cause we is servants, Mammy?'

'Sort of, honey,' she replied, again closing her eyes and pulling him close. 'Mostly it just ain't right to say such things to people. Bite your tongue if you think it; just the way I teach you to.'

4

In the summer months, when days start early and nights run late, flowers grow high and wildlife flourishes, Calvin Carthy always arose with the sun. He pulled on his shirt and his pants – the shirt too tight and the pants too short. The fresh air of the day was breathing through the house, alive and calling to play with birdcall and horses' whinny.

The sun was battering at the door to be let in. Calvin rushed outside to meet it.

It was as bright and fine as a day ever was. To feel the dirt beneath his feet was much more of a pleasure than the feel of the wooden floorboards. For a moment he stood where he was, rolling his toes through the grass and breathing the smell of the morning. With the freshness of the breeze came a faint scent of bacon and sausage. Most days Mammy would come with a plate for him, or he'd have to go to the kitchen in the big house if she was too busy. He didn't care for pig as much as he did for fruit. She had said many times that he wasn't to go helping himself to Mister Henry's fruit straight from the branch without invitation: that was *stealing*.

Calvin didn't see how anyone could tell if any fruit were missing, or why Mister Henry would even miss a few pieces from so many. If the dragonflies were counting, let them tell on him. And if Calvin did ask Mister Henry, he was sure that he would say that it was fine. In his head he could hear Mister Henry saying, "Help yourself, young master. Stuff yourself until you pop! It's of no ail to me."

Chuckling as he took a bite, he thought again of the guitar music. It wasn't as grand a sound as the *opera*, as Mister Henry had called it. But Calvin had heard some of the country blues man's words, as if the man's very soul was trapped in that golden horn, not trying to escape but just accepting, telling what it was like living inside there; his voice resigned and sad, but happy to tell of his troubled situation as the strings of his guitar bounded in the background.

Calvin leaned on the wooden fence of the paddock. The horses were trotting, their heads lifting and waving as they brushed aside the buzzing flies, stopping to pick at the grass or to nuzzle one another. Leaning on the fence to watch the horses was one of the things he loved most. They were so big and powerful, yet majestic and graceful in their movements. Sometimes, if he had a bit of an apple or pear left over, and there was no one else around, he would call a horse over and feed it the core. Sometimes they thanked him in the special way they had: bowing their head, looking at him through their big, pretty, long-lashed eyes, allowing him to stroke their snout.

Mister Henry's wife, Missus Elizabeth, was sometimes out here with them. She would play the horses music – like Mister Henry's but without the singing; and never so loud. With Missus Elizabeth or little daughter Victoria on their backs, the horses moved in time to the music with gentle, careful paces.

They were like servants, the horses.

A horse that Calvin knew to be called Lady walked over to him, allowing him to stroke her snout, gently nodding her thanks for the apple core he had just given her – Calvin had guzzled all but the stem of the pear.

'I love you, Lady,' Calvin said, carefully running his hand over the soft, fine hair. 'Your place on this earth is . . . as important as you believe in your heart.'

Lady slowly closed and opened her long eyelashes.

'We all breathe air the same, you know?'

'That horse doesn't know what you're saying, silly!'

Calvin jumped at the sound of the voice.

'They're stupid and dumb, like you.' It was George. '*And* I saw you give it that piece of fruit,' George said. 'If I think they need to be fed then I shall feed them. Or tell your father to do so.'

The two boys were standing looking at each other. They were the same age and the same height, but George had long blond hair, as straight as Lady's tail; Calvin had coarse, tight dark curls. George's stern, bright blue eyes held imperious scorn over Calvin's big, deep-brown eyes.

'You don't speak much, do you, Calvin?' George said, tilting his head, his eyes narrowing, superior, almost daring Calvin to answer him.

'I only say things after I thought 'bout what I want to say. And whether it can do any good to say it.'

'Good,' George replied. 'Anyway, I've not come out here to talk about horses with the slaves.' He turned his back on Calvin and began to walk away. 'Come on then! Father wants me to show something to you.'

'Mister Henry?'

'Such impertinence,' George muttered to the sky. 'My father has instructed me to come out here and show something to you.' George again began to walk away, his hands linked behind his back – his father's way of carrying himself. 'Something that, for some reason, father thinks might be of interest to you. I'm a busy man, you know. We can't all play about all day. I'll thank you not to loiter.'

Calvin followed George away from the paddock.

'What this, George?'

They had wandered on to a hidden corner of the grounds. The boys were standing and looking at the side of a shed. The roof of the shed was mostly obscured by the huge bonnet of a weeping willow. Nailed vertically to the rear of the shed was a stretch of baling wire, wound tight. Near to the bottom nail, a tin can attached to a piece of wood had been wedged horizontally beneath, tautening the wire. The completed piece looked no more inspiring than a stretch of baling of wire nailed to the side of a shed.

'Please, George,' Calvin repeated, 'what this?'

George was standing with his hands on his hips like an archaeologist who knows precious artefacts are buried somewhere in the land before him, but doesn't know quite where. 'I assume you mean what *is* this. It's a diddly-bow,' George replied. 'That's what father says it's called. It's a kind of instrument that father told me was inspired by African instruments. Anyway, he thought that it would interest you.' George shrugged and raised his eyebrows. After a moment posed, he walked to the diddly-bow and ran his finger down the taut wire. 'Did you know that Africans used to make instruments out of human bones?'

Calvin shook his head.

'They did, you know, the Africans,' George continued. 'They would use bones to beat on skulls, like drums.' His finger slid down the wire. 'They made rattles out of rib cages and tied strings, like this one, along the spine, then strummed it like a guitar – even though it was probably animal hair that they used in those days, not string or wire. Most of the time it was explorers that they would make instruments out of. They would cut them open whilst they were still alive, rip out their innards – their guts – and show them their beating heart.' George demonstrated graphically as he spoke, his teeth peeled back to the gums. 'And then they would put the explorer, his heart still beating, in a big cauldron of boiling water until the human meat fell off the bone. Then they would eat the meat and make instruments out of the bones.'

George looked up to see if Calvin was paying attention to what he was saying. Seeing Calvin's wrinkled nose, George decided that he was.

'It wasn't only explorers and people lost in the jungle that ended up in the pot, though,' George said. 'No, they sometimes ate each other and people from other tribes.'

'They eated they own people?'

'That's right,' answered George. 'But they *ate*, Calvin, not "eated", *their* people. Cannibalism, it's called. And they'd eat every single piece of a person. Even their *eyeballs*.'

George stopped running his finger on the wire and, grinning, stared at

Calvin. 'That was in Africa,' he said.

Calvin stared back at George, the look of repulsion remaining on his face.

'Calvin, you don't suppose that you are African, do you?'

'Don't think,' Calvin replied, shaking his head.

'I mean . . . you look the same as African people look. Identical.'

'Paw tole me we 'cendents from African,' Calvin replied. 'But not *real* African.'

'Well, have you ever eaten a person?' George asked. 'That's the way to tell.'

Calvin put his hands to his mouth. 'No, George, no,' he murmured through his fingers, lowering his chin to his chest.

George plucked the wire. *Tuh-dwwaaang.* Releasing his face, after a moment Calvin chuckled.

George laughed and twanged it again. Both boys laughed. And then again . . . and again . . . more rapidly.

Tuh-dwwaaang; dwwaaang; dwwaaang

Calvin's head nodded uncontrollably in time with each twang, anticipating the next.

George beat a more irregular pattern, one harder for Calvin to keep time to.

Dwwaaaaang . . . Tuh-dwwaaa-dwwaaang

Calvin's head was poised to nod with the next twang. He hardly noticed that his hands were posed like a conductor's, ready to signal a crescendo. But George had stopped twanging. Calvin's eyes moved to George, his head steady, waiting for a signal that George was about to twang the wire again. But's George's hand was nowhere near the wire now. It was down by his side.

'So, do you like the toy that *my* father gave *me*?' George asked.

Calvin nodded.

'You'll like this then.'

George fumbled in the long grass growing up the rear of the shed, searching for something. Calvin watched George, but could also not help looking back to the wonderful toy. Instrument. The diddly-bow. It was such a nice sound that it made, even if it was just a twang. And then, through the silence, he thought of Mister Henry's music again.

'George?'

'Yes,' George replied, still fiddling in the grass. 'What is it?'

'You ever heared your daddy's music?'

'Of course! I *hear* it all the time,' George replied. 'I do live in the same house as my father, remember?'

'You ever heared Blind Lemon Jeff 'fore?' Calvin asked.

'Who? Oh, probably.' George was pulling himself upright. 'Here it is.'

He was holding a green glass bottle with clods of mud and strands of dead grass attached.

'So . . . this is how you *really* play with the diddly-bow.' He wiped the bottle on the grass, removing as much of the mud as he could manage. Then he plugged the bottle with one of his fingers and reached as high up the string of the diddly-bow as he could. 'Are you ready, Calvin?'

Calvin nodded, but spoke with some hesitation, almost a question. 'Yes.'

'Here we go!'

George twanged the wire and was answered by the now familiar sound. Calvin chuckled beneath his breath, helpless not to. He could feel his cheeks tingling with the excitement that his smile brought. As the wire resonated, George carefully held the bottle against the wire. It deadened the sound before killing it completely.

'Wait,' he said to Calvin. 'Just wait.'

Calvin waited with his hands ready by his side.

George twanged the wire. Calvin chuckled again.

'Don't make any noise,' George snapped. 'You're putting me off.'

Calvin swallowed his chuckle. All of his excitement went to his eyes, looking from George to the diddly-bow. George twanged the wire. He wiped the bottle on his khaki shorts and held it to the wire. It deadened the sound once more, but before the sound vanished completely, George hurriedly slid the bottle up and down. The dull tone slurred slightly before again dying away.

'Well,' he said, pulling the bottle from his finger, 'it's clearly broken. Stupid thing.'

Calvin drummed his fingers on his thighs.

'George?'

George glared at Calvin. 'What?'

'Please can I play?'

George dropped the bottle on the floor. 'If you wish. But don't say I didn't tell you it's broken.'

Calvin picked up the bottle from where George had dropped it in the grass. The bottle was loose on his finger – unlike George, whom he had seen fill the hole with his finger; the bottle had come off with a *glug* when George had removed it. Calvin took a cursory glance at George. George had his arms folded across his chest, a podgy second chin where his head was sunken into his neck. He was glaring at Calvin with the same sulky expression as before.

'Go on then,' said George. 'I haven't got all day.'

Calvin twanged the wire with his free hand. Answering him came the same wonderful sound that George had made.

Now that he was closer it sounded even better. He could feel the bass vibrating through the wooden panel; the resonance poured out through the tin can; the shed had swallowed the sound and was chewing on it. Even the feel of the wire was new and exciting: it felt as fragile as a twig, but had a resistance similar to pulling a piece of fruit from a branch.

After twanging the wire a few times, pleased with each answering *tuh-dwwaaang*, Calvin could feel the bottle weighing heavily on his finger. He twanged the wire. When he put the bottle on the wire the sound muffled – the wood of the shed and the tin can were not even interested in swallowing much of it. He quickly slid the bottle along the wire. There was a slight change in tone, but that wasn't as exciting as the simple sound of the twang. As George had done, Calvin wiped the bottle on his pants.

'See?' said George. 'I told you it was broken, didn't I? Stupid thing that it is.'

Calvin twanged the wire. *Dwwaaang*. As the wire vibrated he gave the bottle another quick wipe, but this time held it away from the vibrating wire. As though by instinct, he twanged the wire and held the bottle against it as quickly as he could. Rather than pressing the bottle into the wire he barely touched it, just allowing it to rest against it.

When he heard the wire hum with joyous appreciation he could have flown with the birds and smiled like the summer sun. The sound of the bottle sliding on the wire travelled through his hand, up his arm, coursing all through his body and back down his arm into the wire.

Calvin kept trying; he kept playing. He found that he could even keep the sound coming by twanging as he slid the bottle, not having to wait turns. And rather than frantically waving the bottle up and down as he had at first, if he moved it slowly, imagining what sound would come next, the diddly-bow purred like a cat being tickled under the chin.

'Look, George!' he said. 'It ain't broke. It –'

George had gone.

6

When the front door began to open, Calvin was off Mammy's knee and halfway across the floor before it had opened an inch. 'Paw! Paw!' he yelled.

Stepping into the soft light of the sitting room, Cleveland Carthy peered around the door. 'My big Booya!' Cleveland scooped his boy up into his arms, his head nearly touching the ceiling of the little room. He kicked off his shoes and stretched his toes. 'You been waiting up for your old man?'

'Yeah, Paw, I have.' Calvin twiddled his fingers in the tight curls of Cleveland's hair. 'Got something good to tell you.'

'Must be important, keeping you from sleep.' Cleveland touched Calvin's nose with a finger.

'It is, Paw.'

Cleveland stooped and kissed Adeline hard on the lips. She resumed the knitting she had started earlier, before the bag of ants that was Calvin had climbed on to her knee.

Calvin's arm was around Paw's neck, to stop him from falling off his perch on Paw's arm. As Cleveland straightened to stand up, Calvin kept his arm around Paw's neck. Their eyes were level.

'What's this news you got for me, Boo?'

'You ever heared of a diddly-bow, Paw?'

Twisting his lips, Cleveland made a sucking noise, feigning thought. 'Diddly-bow? Now let me see.' He looked off across the room as if he could read the answer on the bare brick walls. 'Don't believe I do know what a diddly-bow is, Boo. You don't happen to know, do you?'

'Yes, Paw!' Calvin grinned. 'It's a instrument. I play on one today! Play it good.'

'You ain't pulling on your old Paw's leg now, is you, Boo?' Cleveland asked with a smile. Adeline was smiling at both of her boys, her hand skilfully and speedily knitting. Loosening the tie of his three-piece household suit, Cleveland winked at her.

Calvin put his other arm around Paw's neck, his face shining with excitement. 'See you smiling, but I serious, Paw,' he said. 'It's a instrument on Mister Henry's shed. Sounds like the music I heared in –'

He stopped.

'Well?' Paw smiled.

'Mister Henry . . . he play me some music,' Calvin continued. 'But he say I could. Play me Blind Lemon Jeff. You ever meet him?'

Cleveland shook his head. 'Don't think I made that man's acquaintance, no. Who he, Boo?'

'Umm . . .' Calvin strummed his bottom lip. 'Don't really know.' He looked to Mammy to see if she could help him out. She just smiled and knitted. 'He a man what makes country blues to come out the golden horn in Mister . . . Umm . . .?'

'Go on, Boo. I is listening.'

'I think Blind Lemon Jeff plays a diddly-bow,' said Calvin. 'Just like me.' He pointed at his chest.

'Sounds to me like this Blind Lemon fella got a rival.' Cleveland again winked at Adeline, counting stitches as she watched father and son. Love was as loud as opera, filling the room.

'Paw, we go down to the shed now, if you like? I can show you the biddly-dow,' his tongue tripping. 'The diddly-dow. Uh!' Calvin put his hands on his head. 'The diddly . . . bow,' he said, nodding with each word.

'Boo, think it's a bit dark to be going in Mister Henry's garden now,' said Cleveland. 'What if he thinks we is baddies and he turns one of his big guns on us?'

'He ain't gonna do that, Paw. Mister Henry knows who we is.'

'Not in the dark, he don't.'

'Aw, Paw.' Calvin stroked the light bristles on Cleveland's face, then played with one of his ears. 'He probably won't even know we there. We be *real quiet*.'

'Just don't think it's a good idea now, Boo,' said Cleveland, seeing the little face turn grumpy. 'You show your old man another time . . . what you calling it again?'

'Diddly-bow,' Calvin replied, lips downturned and chin wrinkling.

'That's it,' said Cleveland. 'Diddly-bow. By the time you show me you is gonna be even better at playing, too. I is sure you already better than any Blind Lemon fella.'

'Blind Lemon Jeff,' Calvin said, staring at the floor.

'Well he better watch out. They is a new diddly-bow man in town. Ain't that right, Mammy?'

'That's right,' Adeline answered. 'My sweet honey boy gonna be the best diddly-bow man they ever was.'

'Hear that, Boo?' said Cleveland. 'Who gonna be the best?'

Calvin smiled through his sulk, almost mischievous. 'Me, Paw.'

'That's right: Booya Carthy, the diddly-bow man. Ain't no one born gonna be able to touch you.' Paw touched his forehead on Calvin's. 'But even the best diddly-bow man gots to get his sleep, huh?'

'You tell me a story before bed, Paw? Ain't seen you in days. You ain't tole me a story in a long time.'

'Guess that couldn't hurt none. Sure I tell you a story. Come on, mister diddly-bow man, I know a story to tell.' Cleveland carried Calvin through to his bedroom, beginning his story about a little boy who one day found a piece of baling wire nailed to the outside wall of an old shed.

7

Calvin's feet were touching the floor almost before his eyes had opened. He wished that he could have slept in the shed, so that all he had to do was walk outside and there it would be: the diddly-bow.

Even so, he went via the orchard. He picked an apple – thinking it would be best not to eat up all of the pears – and stared a while at the empty cherry tree. He decided to take a peach to accompany the apple. Even without cherries, this could be the best morning of his life. Better than chasing butterflies. Better even than when he had trespassed into Mister Henry's room to find the glorious voice and had not been properly told off.

When he arrived at the shed, Calvin stopped with the half-eaten apple in his hand. Slowly chewing his mouthful, he didn't recognise the heavy feeling building inside him as anger, sorrow mingled with furious disappointment. He took two steps closer.

The baling wire was barely attached to the shed. The top nail was hanging. The weight of the bottom nail was trying to pull the wire free from the shed, a pair of slaves shackled to one another: one pulling, trying to run; the other sleeping, trapped, or dead. The piece of wood that the tin can was nailed to, which had pulled the wire taut, was nowhere to be seen, nail holes the only evidence of where it had once been.

It must have been some kind of animal that killed the diddly-bow, was all that Calvin could think. Only an animal could do something so bad. Even if the whole thing had just disappeared, that would be one thing. But to leave it looking so helpless, so pitiful, a last act of humiliation in death, it was this that was stirring the tumultuous feelings inside him.

He walked up to the shed. Nothing felt quite right. The sweet taste in his mouth was turning bitter. Something was glinting in the high grass; something green and shiny. Pieces of broken glass with sharp edges. The bottle. Broken, just like the diddly-bow.

Calvin couldn't reach the top nail to push it back in. He looked for something he could use to hammer the nail. The door of the shed was locked. There was a tall horse chestnut tree standing fifteen feet away. Sure enough, Calvin found a thick fallen branch and was able to use it to knock the top nail back into the wood. Finding the hole that the bottom nail had been pulled out of, he used the branch to nail that home too. The wire was still miserably slack.

Calvin remembered the piece of wood with the tin can, the missing piece. And then something occurred to him: if the diddly-bow had been attacked and pulled to pieces by an animal, wasn't it unlikely that it would have also pulled the piece of wood away from the wall of the shed? Even if it had, the missing piece would still be sitting, disregarded somewhere by the base. But it was nowhere to be seen. He snapped the branch in two over his knee and wedged a piece behind the wire. It didn't look as good as the tin can, and he didn't think that the vibrating sound of the wire would pour out of the branch, as it had poured so delightfully from the can. But the wire was taut, just the same.

Calvin ran his finger down the wire, just as George had before he had started playing the day before. He'd try it out, and then go and get a glass bottle and a tin can from somewhere. Mammy would know where. He smiled, pleased that he had re-built the diddly-bow. When he plucked the wire for the first time it fell slack; the piece of branch dropped away into the long grass. Both nails had again pulled away from the shed.

Kneeling in the grass, searching again for the fallen pieces, being careful not to cut himself on the pieces of broken glass, a voice bolder than the day startled Calvin. 'Young master! I have come to see . . . Oh,' said Mister Henry. 'Oh,' he repeated in a deeper tone. 'What has happened here? I'm sure that this doesn't look like it should.'

Calvin looked up from his kneeling position, holding both pieces of the broken branch in his hands. Mister Henry was wearing a blood-red jacket, a smoking pipe hanging from the corner of his mouth. He was holding George by the hand. Mister Henry looked down at George. He removed the pipe from his mouth and licked his lips. 'This wouldn't, by any chance, be why you were so reluctant to come down here with me to see how young master Calvin was getting on, would it, George?'

'No, father,' George spoke into his shirt.

Mister Henry pulled on George's arm. 'Eh? Speak up, boy.'

'No, sir.'

'No what, sir?'

'No I wasn't reluctant to come with you, sir.'

Mister Henry's voice in that half-shouting tone terrified Calvin. He was still frozen in the exact position he had been: kneeling and half-stooped, clutching the broken branch. He hadn't once blinked.

'Look at me boy!'

George looked up into his father's eyes. He looked a good deal more terrified than Calvin.

'I think that you are lying to me, boy.' Mister Henry waggled his pipe at George. 'In fact, I know that you are. It's written all over your face!' Mister Henry jerked George by his arm. 'What do you have to say for yourself? Eh? Speak up for yourself, boy.'

Despite what he had done, Calvin felt bad for George. It looked as though George might be losing that arm any second. There was no point in the diddly-bow being broken *and* George losing an arm. The words drumming around inside him were making him quiver. His tongue was beginning to hurt with numb pain from biting too hard.

'I will not tolerate this insubordination from you, George,' Mister Henry bellowed. 'Even if I have to beat it into you –'

'I pull it too hard,' Calvin spoke out, a canary tweet to Mister Henry's lion roar. Calvin was standing up now, still holding the useless pieces of branch in each hand. He was facing Mister Henry.

'I'm sorry, my dear boy?' Mister Henry said to Calvin, George still hanging by the arm.

'I . . . think I pull it too hard. The diddly . . .' Calvin answered, even more softly than before. '*Mister Henry, sir.*'

The shadow of a passing cloud blocked the light of the sun for a fleeting moment, before the light of the day returned. The bonnet of the willow tickled the roof of the shed, a few lime-green leaves fluttering down.

'Ah,' said Mister Henry. 'I see. Yes, well, we'll see if we can't do something about that for you. Is one to assume that you had some pleasure in playing the . . . instrument?'

Calvin quickly nodded, before his head sunk back down into his chest.

'Fine. That's interesting. Yes, very . . . interesting.' Mister Henry gave George's arm a yank. 'Isn't it, George?'

'Yes.'

'Has the cat got your tongue, boy? Eh? Yes, what?'

'Yes, sir.'

Mister Henry returned the pipe to his mouth, skilfully continuing as the pipe waggled with his words. 'Good. Now, young master Calvin, you must excuse me. I am incredibly busy at the moment with my work. I just thought that I would spare a minute to come down here to see how you were getting on with the dow-diddly. It has been a minute well spared, I feel.' Mister Henry laughed, his thin line of moustache defining the curve of his upper lip.

Calvin couldn't understand why Mister Henry was laughing; nothing seemed funny. Chin on his chest, he just looked up at Mister Henry, not even noticing that he was tapping the branch against his leg.

'You are coming back to the house with me, my boy,' Mister Henry said to George. 'The sun and the air are not for you this day!' he declared, and dragged George away through the long grass.

As George was pulled along, he kept looking back over his shoulder.

8

Calvin trudged back to the house. It was a miserable feeling. Every day before had been just fine without the diddly-bow, but now that it was lost to him he felt empty inside. When he looked at the trees they had baling wires nailed to their sides; when he thought of the horses their tails made a strumming sound as they trotted.

Nearly back at the house, a noise snapped Calvin away from his thoughts. Like sunlight through a cloud, the muffled sound of singing. It wasn't like the beautifully clear singing of the opera lady. It was more like the voice of Blind Lemon Jeff! Though deeper, perhaps even more sorrowful.

It was coming from beyond the woodland.

Calvin stood there, staring into the dark depths of the woodland. Mammy and Paw had both said that, when they were busy in the house, he could go where he liked on Mister Henry's land. "Long as you ain't troubling no one," Mammy often reminded him. "And don't be eating up all Mister Henry's fruit, neither. But you never go on your own in them woods, 'specially not when the dusk is coming. You ain't got no business going in there. All sorts of things going on in there that a young boy don't need to be seeing or hearing, hear me?"

Calvin knew that Paw sometimes went into the woods – Mammy told Paw off all the time for that, warning him of the trouble, too – and that was at night. He also knew that Paw always returned smelling of "the Moonshine" and talking a bit funny. Well, if Calvin saw some Moonshine he could just run back through the woods and hide in the house. Even though he wasn't quite sure what the Moonshine looked like – and he was almost certain that Moonshine only came at night – he guessed that he'd know it if he saw it. From late night angel's kisses he certainly knew its smell well enough.

He had decided: he would go quietly, and he would go carefully.

It was cool in the woods, hidden from the sun. There was a rich smell of earth and pine. As quietly as he could, Calvin breathed in the delicious natural smell. He watched a squirrel run across his path and speed up a tree. In a blink, the squirrel was on a branch high above him, holding a cone in its hand-like paws, staring defiantly at Calvin. Daring him to continue.

Even as Calvin warily approached, somehow the singing seemed a little further distant with each step, as if it were being caught by the woodland and flung around the perimeters. It seemed a friendly sound, but the darkness of the woodland dampened all but the sound of the bass, to die when it reached where Calvin was treading. It was summoning Calvin like the opera had. But where the opera had called him like a mother calls her son, this singing was warning of troubles. Deep down inside, Calvin had the same feeling that if he went to the sound he would be rewarded with some new discovery. Treading in Paw's footsteps, no matter for the warning signs, he had to find out what that prize would be.

Beneath his bare feet, the fallen pine needles on the soft carpet of rich, dark soil tickled and pricked. With each dozen steps he stopped to rub the soles of his feet on his calves to scrape away the sticking needles.

Calvin looked up through the canopy. The flaming sun and the pale brightness of the day could be seen through spiky silhouettes. It was still up there somewhere beyond the canopy, but the day could only wash through to the floor where the pines, branches and trunks allowed it. Florescent-yellow shapes a striking contrast against the dark ground. Like sticks of flaming fire.

Having adjusted to the gloom, Calvin's eyes were alive with dancing figures as he returned his interest to the direction of the singing voices. He looked back at the way he had come. The path he had walked through had closed to darkness behind him. The sound was louder here. It was coming from just up ahead, where the brightness of the day resumed its command.

9

Even before he was free of the forest, beyond an ancient-looking split-rail fence Calvin could see that the field ahead was shimmering with life. With nothing to repress it, the singing was alive here. In the field, bushy plants of fluffy white puffs and dark green leaves were swaying in time. It seemed that they had a voice, the bushes dancing in time to the song.

A huge man stepped up to a nearby bush. He was wearing blue denim dungarees, the shoulder straps fastened over his bare chest, the rounded muscles of his dark skin glistening with sweat. Slung over his broad shoulders was a bulging sack, so full that it trailed on the ground behind him. Singing as he worked, his massive hands swiftly routed through the bush, stripping handfuls of the white fluff, then stuffing it into the bulging sack. His was just one bold voice isolated from the grander sound that seemed to travel up to the roof of the sky with a thousand accompanists. And then another voice called out. The man sang the line over, nodding sincerely, his hands stopping for not one second as they tore at the bush.

Calvin couldn't make out most of the words being sung. Dearly he wanted to know what it was that they were singing about, what was entertaining this massive man one moment and then turning his expression to anger the next, his booming voice that could shred sticks to splinters.

Calvin heard the next nearby-worker's solo call. His voice was raspy, as if his yell was being dragged out of his throat.

From his vantage point behind the spindly shin of a pine, Calvin could see only a thin slice of the field. The view through the few trees that separated him from the field was not reward enough, not for the images playing through his imagination. He was shivering with nervous excitement.

Just as Calvin summoned courage to step around the tree, he saw another of the workers appear between two plants. This man's face was sickly-thin, skeletal. His brown skin was marked with scratches and scars, puffy pink lines against the taut skin of his face. His eyes bulged out of their sockets. His arms were merely bones with sagging skin hanging over them like dirty sheets on a washing line. When he sang, Calvin could see that the man was missing most of his teeth. This was definitely the man with the rasping voice. He was also a man whose attention Calvin most certainly did not want.

Calvin walked along the cool inside of the treeline, happily obscured by the gloom. Occasionally he would see another worker stripping a plant, again stuffing his pickings into a long sack trailing behind him. At one point Calvin could even see along a row of plants, where three more workers ripped at the fluffy cotton. Soon he had walked so far that the tempo of the song had changed. All of the workers here were singing in unison, filling the sacks on their shoulders in time with whatever song they were singing. And he could hear some more of their words, all of the men singing together.

'With my sweet Lord by my side, I will sink beneath the water
Down in the river in Galilee'

The further Calvin wandered, a vague memory of a field just like this one flashed as an image in his mind, how he had played the cotton through his baby fingers. There was something more than a bit familiar about this field and these songs. More than in Mammy's recitals. He could picture himself sitting on Paw's shoulders, his hands flat against the thick, dark, glistening curly hair, holding on for his life as Paw stooped and sang, even though he could feel that he was strapped on to Paw, jangling with his movements.

There was a break in the woodland coming up, the thick lines of pines dissected by a dusty, furrow-grooved road. Splitting the fence, there was a gateway into the field. The gate was open.

Calvin could have simply slipped between the split rails of the fence at any time; he could have been through in a second, into the field in another blink, but seeing the open gate was like being invited inside. He could quickly cross over the road and continue through the woodland on the other side of the road; or go back the way he had come without ever rediscovering the feel of the cotton in his hands.

The men in the field were just like him. They were bigger and stronger, but they were men like he would become. Men like Paw. Men like Mammy told him he was already becoming. He would keep out of their way, trying his best not to be seen. But either way he belonged here more than he did in Mister Henry's office.

The road through the gate ran directly through the field, splitting it like a hatchet through meat. Calvin had a much better view of the field from here. He could see how it rode up and rolled down, plants and men everywhere. In the distance he could just about distinguish the matchboxes that were barns and houses, where the road ran to an end. Beyond that was more dark woodland, as if this busy part of the world were intended to remain hidden. It was the great mystery that seemed to surround this place that stripped the last of his caution from Calvin. He withdraw from his cover of safety.

'Hey!' someone yelled. 'Lookout, Lenut!'

Startled back into the day, Calvin turned to face the drumming sound of hooves.

A chestnut stallion was heading straight at him. The white line between the horse's eyes, running along the snout, seemed to be sighting Calvin as if he were a target. The horse's head dropped, and in that brief second Calvin saw the man riding the horse. Then the horse's head lifted high up into the air and twisted to the side, baring its teeth, its eyes straining at the sockets, a wild and ugly expression on its face.

'Mollydodging nigger!' the rider shouted above the stamp of hooves on the hard, dry earth, above the painful-sounding whinny of the horse.

The horse's head was directly above Calvin, its flailing hooves pawing the air inches from his face. Spray from the horse's nostrils spattered on his forehead. Such was the size of the horse, he felt as if he were frozen beneath a falling tree. The sun was obscured. A hoof the size of his head stamped down a step away. Calvin could not move.

After what seemed like the sum of his entire life, the contorted face of the horse veered around Calvin. Still the hooves pounded the hard earth, the head whipping in a wild frenzy. He looked up to see the rider glaring down at him, scarlet redness high on his cheeks, a deeper red than on the rest of his sunburnt face. The shadow of the wide-brimmed hat he was wearing hid his eyes. Nevertheless, Calvin could feel the scorch that was radiating from them. The horse circled around Calvin.

The sun was hidden for a moment, then painfully glaring.

'Trying to get yourself killed, nigger?' the hidden face asked. The cruel mouth spat on the dry ground. The earth swallowed. The horse snorted once more, coming to a stop. Despite his cold fear, Calvin could not tear his eyes away from looking into the dark recess beneath the hat.

'Should've run you down,' the man snarled.

'Lenut,' said the voice that had warned the rider. 'Behave yourself.'

'That's right,' Lenut continued regardless, high up on his stallion. 'Should've pounded you back into the dirt.'

'*Lenut.*'

The rider looked towards the voice. Calvin followed his eyes.

A man wearing uniform – garments the same colour as the dusty road – was walking towards them. Just the other side of the open gate, he had been obscured when Calvin ventured from the woodland.

'Did you see that, Deputy Helland?' Lenut asked. 'See this little nigger trying to get hisself killed?'

Deputy Helland's face was as beige as his uniform. Deep pockmarks like the dry, cracked earth. He wore a horizontal scar diagonally across his forehead, just beneath his combed, side-parted hair. The scar didn't move when frown-lines appeared on his forehead. He put his hands lightly upon his hips and stared at the terrified little boy.

'What're you doing away from the field, boy?' Lenut asked, looking down at Calvin.

Calvin looked over his shoulder at the man on the horse.

'Huh? What, you too dumb to talk or something?'

As in Mister Henry's room, Calvin could not utter a word. He could barely move his head to look from one to the other man. Either way he looked he saw the unfriendly faces glaring back at him.

'Didn't you say you was aiming to get yourself a coonskin hat, Deputy?' Lenut asked.

'Sure did.'

'Well, would that be of the varmint variety or the shit-licking jungle bunny kind? Nearly saved you some lead.'

The horse whinnied and shifted its feet.

Deputy Helland grinned. His teeth were gleaming white. A toothpick appeared from behind his tongue. 'The man asked you what you're doing away from the field, son.'

Calvin's chin had found his chest. He continued to look up through his long lashes at each man in turn, biting his tongue between his teeth.

'Look at him,' said Lenut. 'Sweaty little nigger looks like he'd stick to anything.'

Deputy Helland laughed, his frown-lines rippling like a heat wave. 'Ain't got much to say for yourself, do you, boy?'

Calvin shook his head.

'He moves!' exclaimed Deputy Helland. 'Thought you might've just been frightened to death, standing there like a post.'

Again Calvin shook his head, a slight bit surer this time.

'Hah!' laughed Deputy Helland. He glanced up at Lenut on the horse and raised his eyebrows, wrinkling his forehead deeper still. The line of scar still defied the skin. Putting his hands on his thighs he crouched down to Calvin's height, as near as he could. 'What's your name, son?' he asked, squinting his eyes.

Calvin's lips trembled as he tried to open them. His chin wrinkled. His eyes scanned the harshly pitted skin.

The deputy tilted his head to one side, his eyes still narrowed, examining. 'Come on now, son. You can answer Deputy Helland. Just tell me, what's your name?'

'Boo,' Calvin whispered.

The deputy frowned, his lips drawing back into two thin, straight lines. 'Think I'm a goose, nigger?'

Calvin shook his head. Upon the horse, Lenut laughed. The stallion shifted its weight, again spraying Calvin through its nostrils.

'Trying to prove that you're brave then?' Deputy Helland raised one eyebrow. 'That it?'

Calvin shook his head. His lips were beginning to bulge; his cheeks were filling out. He could feel tears standing in his eyes.

'Well then, I'll arkse you again: what's your name? Don't be messing me now.'

'Booya Carthy,' Calvin answered. Even to his own ears, his voice sounded more high-pitched. 'Booya Carthy.'

'Now, I warned you, you ain't messing with me, are ya?' the deputy asked, his voice turning cold. "Cause I ain't got the time or the patience for being messed with, 'specially by a little nigger like you. Got enough *big* niggers I got to whip into line.'

Calvin shook his head.

'What kind of name is that, then? Boo-yar.'

'A nigger kind,' Lenut interjected. 'If they ain't calling their brats Stable and Cornsack, they're making up all kinds of names. Boo-yar. Sounds feral enough to me.'

Deputy Helland straightened himself up, returning his hands to his hips. 'Well now, Boo-yar, I suggest you get out of here. And don't be coming out of the field again. I ain't your overseer.'

'And the next time I *will* stomp you down,' added Lenut. 'Just give me another reason to do it.' As if agreeing, the horse jumped a little and clicked its hooves against the earth.

'He will do it, too,' said Deputy Helland. 'And there ain't nothing I can do next time, neither, *Boo-yar*. Damn, little nigger, you're lucky I was here *this* time.' He looked up at Lenut. 'You let them sing about whatever they like – what do they call that noise? Field hollers? Now you're letting their spawn ramble all over the place?'

'That's what I've been saying for years, Jacob,' Lenut answered. 'And my daddy before me, and my granddaddy before that. And they was doing, they was; more than just talking. Had to with that nigger-loving bluecoat bullshit. Why don't you let me stomp this little one into the dirt, huh, Jacob? Kill 'em before they get a chance to grow, that's what daddy used to say. Or my name ain't Lenut Colden.'

Entranced by the horror, Calvin watched Colden atop the stallion. He didn't understand much of what the man was saying, but his tone was definitely not friendly. And not in the way that George could be mean. Not even like Mister Henry's loud voice, telling off. Even now part of him expected Mister Henry to arrive and take control.

'I suggest that you get out of here, son,' said Deputy Helland. 'I ain't going to be able to hold Lenut here back for much longer.' He grinned, his white teeth like chrome. 'And we've got us business to talk over.'

Calvin stood staring at the deputy.

'Go on, git!' The deputy lunged towards Calvin. 'Get outta here,' he shouted. 'Back to work. Chop-chop.'

'Boo!' Lenut said.

The deputy laughed, his face turned to the sky. His white teeth glittered in the sun; the craters in his face became holes. Lenut was grinning down, the top half of his face disappearing deeper into the hat, the lower half glowing red.

Calvin took a few steps backwards. The stallion began to shift its feet. Calvin could feel the air from the swish of its tail.

'Boo!' the deputy said.

'Boo!' Lenut spat louder.

The horse stamped and whinnied.

'Git, nigger!'

'Not that way, ya dumb little nigger!'

Calvin turned and ran in to the field so fast that he could not feel the earth beneath the soles of his feet.

'Y'all right, boy?' a voice obscured by the bushes asked.

Calvin looked but could not see anyone.

'Was they talking bad to you, li'l 'un?' whispered another faceless voice.

A man stepped out of the plants. It wasn't a welcoming face that greeted Calvin. It was wrinkled, dark. Toothless. Saggy-skinned arms reached out to him. Skin-covered bones as fingers. He ran further into the plantation. He wanted to be hidden: from men on horses, from strange faces – scarred and taut, pockmarked, wrinkled or as red as hell.

He burst through a row of plants. The branches scratched at his skin. The white bolls of cotton tried to caress his ears.

A pair of legs the size of tree trunks were standing in front of him.

He changed direction, up and down rows of plants to get away from concerned-looking faces. Most of the faces seemed friendly. He thought of Paw.

He wanted to be in the orchard.

He wanted to be back home.

Mammy and Paw had warned him not to come here . . .

He was too frightened to cry. Too terrified to stop.

Mammy and Paw had been right: this was no place for a boy.

And now he would have to spend the rest of his life lost in a place where he had no business being. Like Blind Lemon Jeff in the golden horn.

Even the singing that had led him here was scaring him. It was in the air above him one moment, and then it was one voice just feet away from him. It was following him through the plantation.

When he had been carefully walking through the woods it had felt as though it were warning him. Now it sounded as though it were saying "Tole you so. Tole you not to come."

Where we tell you not to go?

Tole you so. Tole you so

Now never gonna make it home

Tole you so. Tole you so

He pushed through two plants and bumped off a bulging sack, falling down to the earth. A large man was leaning over him – the first man that Calvin had seen from his hiding place in the trees. The man reached down and picked Calvin up as if he were light as cotton.

'Is you all right, son?' he asked. His voice was deep, but kind. It was like Paw's voice. 'You lost your daddy?' the man asked.

Calvin nodded. And then he shook his head.

'Here. I help you look.'

Calvin ran from the huge arm reaching out to hold his hand. He looked left and right, sure that he would see the half-face man galloping around the field, trying to find him.

To stomp him back into the ground.

Darting to the fence, he ducked through it.

CHAPTER
TWO

1

Beneath his sheet Calvin couldn't stay still, the heavy air making him uncomfortable. Even under such a thin cover he was sweating. The bedcover was wet beneath him. No dry patch remained for him to roll onto. It was not just for the cloying air.

He'd dreamed bad dreams all night long: about snarling horses with faceless men astride their back; tall men with holes in their face, crouching on stick-like legs; plants with skeletal branches, beckoning him into their spiky embrace, until he was lost beneath the tall, rising spines, which were closing in, closer, closer, singing with rasping, leafy voices . . .

Breathing heavily, Calvin sat up. His skin was slippery, as if he had been soaked by pond water. He looked around the room, his breathing gradually slowing. There were no hideous half-hidden faces glaring down at him. There were no plants to grab at his ankles, dragging him over the floor. He wondered if it hadn't all been just a bad dream.

As he rubbed his feet together, Calvin could feel the dried earth flaking from them.

Something was different about his room this morning.

Calvin looked to his right. There it was, leaning against the wall. Maybe he was indeed still dreaming. There certainly hadn't been a brand new shining guitar leaning against the wall when he had crept into bed last night, he was sure about that. An unsure half-smile tried to climb onto his lips. He rubbed his eyes.

Keeping his eyes on the guitar, he peeled off the damp cover. Stepping over to the guitar, he reached out to touch it. The wooden neck was cold and smooth against his hand. He ran a finger over the smoky-brown lettering. *Marquette*. Picking it up, he carried the guitar out of his bedroom to look at in the sitting room, where the light was brighter.

As a fisherman holds a catch by the gills, he held the guitar away from his body as he inspected it. It had six wires! He'd never even dreamed of such things. In Mister Henry's office there had been instruments that looked something like this, but with the body covered in cloth, or made from animal shells. He put the guitar down next to the armchair. It clanged quietly, teasingly, as the body touched the floor.

Again he reached out, but withdrew his hand. He looked out of the windows at the dim day, blanketed by a cover of pale-grey cloud, compressing the stifling humidity. He looked over every corner of the little room, daring to look in the dark corners, the shadows of his nightmares. All was quiet; except for the mystery of the guitar, everything was as it should be.

His hand was hovering near to the strings. He touched one of them with a finger, ran the finger along the string. The pitches of sound became deeper with each string he touched.

The door crashed open, smashing into the wall.

Calvin jumped in the air. The guitar slipped from the armrest, falling to the ground with a clanging bang as he spun around.

'Booya! Well, by the sound you found your guitar!'

Filling the doorway, Paw was smiling as widely as Calvin had ever seen.

'What's wrong, Boo?' Paw asked, stepping to his son and crouching down onto a knee. 'Look like something's scared you. Was is it me busting through the door like a crazy hoss?'

Calvin nodded.

'Sorry, Boo. Just excited to see if you found your guitar.' Paw's keen smile slipped away as Calvin's terrified expression remained. 'Ain't broke, is it, Boo?' Calvin and Paw both looked down at the guitar. Paw picked it up and inspected it. 'Don't look broke.'

Carefully resting the guitar against the chair, Paw leaned an elbow on his knee. 'Hey, Boo, what's gotten at you, son?'

Calvin's bottom lip was rising up over the top lip. His chin was beginning to wrinkle. Paw picked Calvin up. 'Hey. Hey. Sorry I scared you, Boo, busting in that way.'

Calvin wrapped his arms around Paw's neck and squeezed. The fear of the night and waking was slipping to one side, away from the shield of Paw's embrace.

'That's my boy.'

'It's really mine?'

'The guitar? Uh-huh. Mister Henry give it you. Or ruther, he give it me last night and I leave it for you to find. Wanted it to be the first thing you see when you waked up. That's why I come busting in like I did: to come get you! We got to go thank Mister Henry for being so kind, yep?'

2

The smell of freshly cut grass was the only reminder that above the heavily shaded sheet of cloud something brighter existed. On a summer's day it was possible to shelter from the heat within the shade of a tree. But today there was nowhere to hide from the oppressive humidity.

'The change gonna come soon, Boo.'

'Like Mammy sings, Paw?'

Paw looked down at Calvin. 'I sure do hope that they right 'bout that; like Mammy sings, and they is all singing over in the picking fields.'

Paw's palm was sweaty, squirmy. It was as if they both had jelly smeared over their palms. Calvin gripped Paw's hand tighter. He looked around to see if any wildlife would leave their home on such a miserably grey morning.

Calvin couldn't ever remember walking in through the front door of Mister Henry's house before. Through the heavy front door was a tiled lobby, where double doors opened into a vast entrance hall. The wooden floor of the hallway was polished to a shine as reflective as water. A wooden staircase – so wide that a stallion could walk up without its swishing tail touching the sides – wound up to the balconied first-floor landing. There hung a glittering chandelier, made up of sparkling shapes of glass, bigger even than the one in Mister Henry's office, and much more magnificent in detail. And there were more paintings framed in gold and ancient wood, the oil so deep and rich they seemed like living landscapes. When their footfall suddenly stopped echoing through the chamber, Calvin looked down. They were walking on a rug, larger than Mammy's vegetable garden, which stretched nearly from one wall to the other, woven with exotic, oriental patterns.

Clothed by dark wood, it was cool in here and the light was dim. It felt inviting and homely in a way that he'd never imagined. But Calvin began to feel a terrible familiarity. Inside here was shadowed, hidden from the sun. One entrance in view, but the exit a distant, hazy light. It smelt of pine woodland.

As Calvin and Paw stepped through one of the doorways leading from the entrance hall, Calvin saw the open garden door that he had ventured through days before, framing the defiantly bright array of colours in the garden. Birdsong found its way along the corridor to reach their ears. A shouting voice shattered the sweet melody.

Calvin reached for Paw's hand, gripping it tightly. Paw drew Calvin close. They stopped where they were in the cool hallway, yards away from Mister Henry's office. There was no doubt that the shout had come from Mister Henry.

'I will not bow to any demands from the like of you,' Mister Henry's booming voice continued, the bass beating at the door as loudly as the opera had. 'You can threaten me until you run out of air, for all care. I was brought to this country because of my knowledge of routing railroads; highly trained in the greatest institution, by the most educated and cultured minds that can be found the world over! Can you make such a claim, eh? Can you? No!

'Never have I witnessed such an insufferable lack of dignity. And coming from a man of your position. You should be ashamed of yourself. Yes, deeply ashamed. I don't mince my words, sir. Never have; and I never shall!'

There were further words, but spoken, forever concealed by the thick door.

Whatever had been said caused Mister Henry to erupt once more.

'Well I've already told *you* that intimidation won't work on me, you fraudulent fool. I wonder if the sheriff would be interested to know of what you have said to me here today.'

There was a deep thud in the room – something being slammed down on a surface.

'It would be impossible to alter the plans now, even if I did care to. They are set in stone. This *issue* was settled with the necessary persons – those actually charged with making the decisions – over a year ago! The commencement of labour with go ahead on *my* say so. And with my conscience as clear as a glass jar. You mark my words, sir: work *will* go ahead.

'There is nothing more that I wish to say to such a . . . a negligible, menacing, nickel-and-dime subordinate such as you, sir. Now, good day to you!'

'Paw,' Calvin whispered.

'S'all right, Boo,' Paw whispered in reply. 'S'all right, son.'

There was a barely perceptible creak as the door of Mister Henry's room opened. With both hands, Calvin gripped Paw's thighs, pushing in closer to him.

'So,' came a drawling voice, 'I can confirm one final time that you ain't going to re-route the railroad, even since I arksed you so nice?'

'Get out of my house,' Mister Henry shouted.

The man stepped out into the hallway and began to walk towards Calvin and Paw. Paw stuck out his chest and gritted his teeth. Calvin tried to hide even deeper into Paw's leg. But he also wanted to see the face of a man who dared to make Mister Henry raise his voice. The gasp stuck at the top of his throat, a half-breath.

He could see the grinning, gleaming white teeth. A toothpick flicking from the tongue. There were deep pockmarks lining the man's cheeks. He was wearing the same beige shirt and trousers, the fabric tight against his long, thin legs. The man looked down to see Calvin looking up at him. Their eyes locked. The scar across the man's forehead didn't move amongst the wrinkles as he frowned. And then he grinned again, a hideous, gleaming grin.

Boo, Deputy Helland mouthed as he passed.

Calvin's legs felt as though they had turned to water. His nightmare had come to life and was following and tormenting him. And then the deputy was gone.

Calvin expected to see the man with the sunburnt face hidden beneath his hat following the deputy, maybe even riding his horse out of Mister Henry's office, the horse's hooves pounding, trying to stomp him into the ground.

'Come on, Boo,' Paw whispered. 'He's gone now.'

That was easy for Paw to say: he didn't have the man's face imprinted on the inside of his eyelids. Paw tapped on Mister Henry's partly-open door.

'*What?*' Mister Henry yelled.

Calvin flinched and clenched his arms around Paw's leg.

'Let loose, Boo.' Paw gently shook his leg and eased open the door. 'Mister Henry, sir? I, uh . . . I just got my boy here. He got something he wants to say to you . . . If now ain't a inconvenient time for you, sir?'

Mister Henry was staring into the fireplace, biting the side of a finger. Except for the soft red flush high on each cheek, his face was pale.

'Cleveland! My good man, I do apologise for bellowing. Please, do come in.' Except for his forced smile, none of the rest of Mister Henry's face moved. 'And, of course, young master. Good morning to *you*!'

Calvin's chin was on his chest.

'Come on, Boo. You got something to say to Mister Henry, don't you?' Paw squeezed the nape of Calvin's neck.

Calvin was looking up at Mister Henry.

Henry flicked a guilty glace toward Cleveland, obviously uncomfortable that his loss of decorum had been witnessed.

'I sorry, Mister Henry, sir. He . . . Boo just gone a bit shy, s'all.' Paw turned his attention to Calvin. 'Look, Booya, we come to say something to Mister Henry, ain't we? Ain't no point coming and disturbing and saying nothing now, is there?'

Calvin shook his head, looking at Mister Henry's shiny shoes, unable to settle on his face.

'Well?' Paw said, his palm resting on Calvin's lower back, easing him forward.

Calvin dared to look up at Mister Henry. His face had returned to its usual comfortable blend of austere and avuncular; his smile less strained.

'Thank you, Mister Henry,' Calvin said. 'Sir.'

'Thank you for what, Boo?' Paw encouraged, his hand still resting against Calvin's back.

'Thank you for my diddly . . . my, um, guitar.'

'*Mister* . . .' Paw reminded.

'Mister Henry, sir,' Calvin added.

'My young friend, you are most welcome. It was my pleasure. I would encourage anyone to pick up an instrument. Or sit down at one. One could not possibly pick up a piano, for example.' Mister Henry laughed at his joke. Paw laughed along.

Being before Mister Henry reminded Calvin that he had wanted him by his side in the field on the other side of the woodland. And Mister Henry had just proved that he wouldn't allow those bad men to speak that way.

'Maybe standing before me now is the next star of the country blues. Wouldn't you say so, Cleveland, my man?'

'Oh, yes, Mister Henry, sir. Sure do hope.'

Mister Henry clasped his hands behind his back and crouched down. 'Now, young master, there is *one* condition attached with my gift . . .' Mister Henry waited a moment. Calvin kept his hands by his side. 'One must practice an instrument for at least half-an-hour a day to attain any level of competence. This is the sole condition. That is all I ask of you.'

Calvin nodded. Mister Henry stood with his hands still behind his back, but occasionally gesticulating to draw his explanation.

'It is not much to ask. And I have already seen that I will not be disappointed. However!' Mister Henry stabbed a finger in the air. Calvin jumped. 'If one practices for an *hour* a day, I believe that individual will be soon be quite accomplished. *But*,' Mister Henry pointed a finger directly at Calvin, 'if one allows as much time as they can spare to play an instrument – if he works as hard as he can, whenever he can find even *one* extra minute – then anything can be achieved. The level of a virtuoso, even.'

Mister Henry crouched and picked up Calvin's hands, even as he held Calvin's eyes. 'Yes, yes, I can see it in you, young master. Truly.' He narrowed his eyes, nodding. 'You can be as accomplished as you wish to be.'

Calvin's head lifted from his chest a little, drawn up by Mister Henry's gaze. Mister Henry turned Calvin's palm upward. Calvin felt like it was no longer his hand Mister Henry was holding, a part of him.

'Don't you agree, Cleveland, my good man?' Still examining Calvin, Mister Henry hadn't turned to direct his question towards Paw.

'Yes, a'course, Mister Henry, sir.'

Mister Henry stood.

Paw glanced down at Calvin. 'Ain't you gonna promise Mister Henry you gonna practice, Booya?'

'I promise, Mister Henry, sir,' Calvin obeyed. 'To practice . . .'

'My young friend, I do not doubt that.'

Mister Henry walked to his desk and pulled from its drawers his pipe and a box of matches. He lifted a purple velvet smoking jacket from the back of his chair and, in one sweep, pulled it on. Puffing smoke from the corner of his mouth, he lit his pipe, shook out the flame, and sat in his chair, crossing his legs.

'Would it be terribly curt to enquire – I must admit that curiosity has rather got the better of me – but I am interested to know where that name comes from? *Booya*,' Mister Henry sounded out. 'Is it a sort of acquired pet name, or . . .?' He gestured with a circular motion of his pipe.

Calvin loved to hear Paw tell the story as much as he liked being called Booya. 'You tell Paw,' he said, surprised at the sound of his own voice speaking.

'Sure I will.' Paw coughed into his palm and straightened. 'You won't believe me when I say, Mister Henry, that this quiet young Boo what you see before you didn't come out crying . . . he come out *screaming*. You ain't heared nothing like it before, Mister Henry, if you don't mind me saying, I swear it.

'Me and his Mammy, we talking 'bout a name to call him by. Trying to decide on one, is more like I should say. But we couldn't hardly hear usselves think with our new little baby boy screaming like he was.'

Paw looked down at Calvin and smiled.

'So, your Mammy wanted to call you Calvin after her daddy's name; I was saying I want to call you Skip, just like my own Paw. Mammy didn't much like the name Skip, tell you the truth, Mister Henry. I think it was 'cause she didn't much like my Paw and his old ways. But it weren't his fault. He had to live through some awful times. But she weren't having no son of hers called after a man like my Paw. Nuh-uh. Not even if she had to run off in the nighttime with our boy and leave me to my own self.

'And then, just as I was coming round to her way of thinking, that Calvin ain't such a bad name – a'course, my thoughts couldn't be heared out loud 'cause of this boy screaming and screaming. But all of a sudden . . . he stop. Just like that. So I gets a chance to say that I don't mind the name Calvin none, and then this boy, not a two-hour old, just as I is settling to agree to Calvin, shouts out "*Booya*." Then he laughed! A newborn baby laughing! You ain't never heared such a thing, Mister Henry, sir, if you don't mind me saying.

'What I think really happen is he sneeze or something; got a little wind. But we, both of us, heared it loud and clear. Heh-heh. Booya. Well, I wanted that to be the baby boy's real name; I say then I think it's just fine and original. But Adeline weren't having none of it. Say that Booya ain't no name. So we named our boy Calvin. But for me it just kind of sticked – same as Boo calling me Paw instead of Pa since he was just little. Same as Adeline's family always calling their mama Mammy – and I call him Booya most of the time ever since that day. Ain't that right, Boo?'

Calvin nodded, Paw's hand coming to rest on his neck.

'Mister Booya Carthy,' Paw said.

'I agree with you, Cleveland, my good man.' Mister Henry puffed thoughtfully on his pipe. 'I think that it is a fine and original name. In this world of ours something that might seem insignificant – like a name – can actually make a man. Can make him stand out from a crowd of people with average names. Take the name of our George, for example. A name shared with the king of England!'

'Couldn't agree with you more, Mister Henry. I just wish that his Mammy come to agree the same!' Paw chuckled. It made Calvin chuckle, too – it often made him laugh when Paw spoke about Mammy when she wasn't there with them. He knew that Paw wouldn't dare say it if she were.

'I don't think that's any matter,' Mister Henry said. 'I believe a man has a right to be known by whatever name he wishes. Why should he not? Even a king often changes his regnal name!'

'And he likes it, too,' Paw said, his hands on Calvin's shoulders. 'Don't you, Boo?'

Calvin nodded.

'Then that is what I shall call you also, from this day forth,' said Mister Henry. 'If that is the name that you like to be known by, my young friend Booya.'

Calvin smiled at Mister Henry.

'Uh, anyways,' said Paw. 'I is sure that you is busy, Mister Henry, sir. Thank you again for your generous gift. I is sure Booya'll practice guitar just like you say.'

Calvin nodded. 'Thank you for my guitar, Mister Henry, sir,' he said.

'As I said, the pleasure is mine, Booya. I'm sure that you will endeavour to become quite the skilled virtuoso. Let's say, a year from now, you can give a recital to us all in the hallway, show us how you have come on.'

3

The swirling grey blanket of sky had turned to lowering black thunderclouds. Warning canons of thunderclaps rolled over the heavy clouds. Many menacing eyes glowered through the underbelly of the clouds, backlit by the full moon, seeking the next Godless place to torment. A storm to signal the end of summer had arrived.

Geoffrey –the Wilmington family's butler – knocked on the door to Henry's office. Beneath his greased black hair, sweat prickled on his high forehead, forming little streams to run the length of his aquiline nose. With his gloved hands he wiped away the drop forming at the tip of his nose; removed the handkerchief from the breast pocket of his jacket and patted it against his forehead. He adjusted his bowtie, and then readjusted it. In the heat of Mister Henry's office, his tightened lips appeared blue. He cleared his throat; looked down at the handkerchief returned to his pocket and neatened its corners.

'What is it, Geoffrey?' Henry asked. 'For goodness sake, what's come over you, man?'

'I am not quite sure how to address this to you, sir.' Through his gloves, Geoffrey pinched the webs of his fingers.

'Well? Come on, man. Spit it out.'

'There is . . . uh . . . a mob outside,' stuttered Geoffrey. 'Sir . . . they wish to speak with you.'

'A – what did you say? – A *mob*?' The word fell out of Henry's mouth. He put down the map he had been studying.

'Yes . . . yes, sir. A mob.'

'Well, what on earth do they think they will be able to achieve? What do they think this is, the crusades? Bloody fools. How many are we talking, Geoffrey? This *mob*. A dozen? Two dozen?'

Geoffrey moved the weight of his feet, stepping from side to side on the thick carpet. A shudder had invaded his being. Pushing his stomach out, he straightened his back.

'Come on, Geoffrey. Do pull yourself together. I'm sure it's nothing for you to be concerned about. I'll handle the bastardly miserable rabble. Come on: what would your closest guess be? *Three* dozen?'

'Many more, sir.' As was his body, Geoffrey's voice, usually so austere, perfect for announcing invited guests, was shaking. He cleared his throat. 'I think, sir . . . I think that there may be hundreds out there.'

'*Hundreds?*' Henry repeated. He sighed. 'I'm sick to the teeth with the audacity, the *effrontery* of these people. The . . .' Henry swatted at the air. 'The bloody-minded lunacy. We'll see to this.' Henry stood up and changed from his smoking jacket, buttoning his blazer. 'Geoffrey, be a good chap, go and fetch me a shotgun.'

Geoffrey turned to leave the room.

'Oh, and Geoffrey? Make sure you fetch me the Winchester.'

Geoffrey scuttled down the hallway, trying to keep the requisite sure-step of a butler, but at a greater pace.

'Yes,' Henry muttered to himself, brushing the lapels of his blazer, readying himself. 'The Winchester: best bloody weapon the Yanks ever made. Henry the Fifth might have had less firepower, and Lord Nelson a considerable amount more, but both advanced with doughty British spirit. If this were Isandlwana or France, our message stays the same: we shan't bow to your bloody brutish tribes. We shall defend the land upon which we stand. And we shall triumph, always.'

Henry smiled to himself. Entering the room, Geoffrey handed Henry the shotgun.

'Thank you very much, Geoffrey.' He raised an eyebrow. 'I'm sure you had the sagacity to ensure she's loaded?'

Geoffrey bowed.

'Good. Good man. Wouldn't want to go to battle with a blunt sabre, now, would we?' Henry pocketed the few spare rounds that Geoffrey handed to him. Geoffrey stood back to allow his master to pass.

'Be a good man, would you, Geoffrey? Go and see that Elizabeth and the children aren't frightened by this debacle. If they are, you assure them that their father is going to see to it right this moment.'

Henry strode along the hallway.

'Right . . .' he said, and stepped out of the huge front door, pulling it closed behind him.

Geoffrey had not been exaggerating at all, Henry realised, looking out at the many hundreds of faces. Despite the dozens of lanterns and burning flames held aloft, he could clearly see only the first few rows of faces. The rest were so shrouded by the dark, white or black, they might as well have been Zulus. But not with spear: they held shotguns, rifles and metal bars. Seeing pitchforks, Henry closed his eyes and shook his head. 'A hundred and fifty years of independence,' he muttered, observing the plain agricultural clothes of these simple folk.

The gathered horde were strangely quiet, as if waiting for Henry to preach to them, rather than they to make demands of him. Holding the shotgun tilted by his side, facing the thunderous sky, he placed a foot on a flowerpot.

'I want you to clear off my land,' he said. 'I want you to leave *immediately*.'

The crowd seemed not to know how to respond.

'Go on,' said Henry, gesturing with the barrel of the Winchester. 'Shift.'

Except for an occasional cough or whispered word, the scuffling of feet, there was no sound or movement from within the crowd. Mostly farmers and field workers looking back at him, clearly impoverished, rather than threatening, they presented themselves as if seeking employment.

'*I want you to get off my land this instant*,' Henry boomed. '*Do you* understand *me*?'

He fired the Winchester in the air. A few members of the crowd jumped. A murmur started throughout the gathered mass. The first drops of rain began to fall.

Henry pumped the fore-end, chambering the next round.

'I told ya to divert the railroad,' drawled a man at the front. 'Warned ya something like this'd happen.'

'Oh yes, *you*, I should have expected you to be here,' Mister Henry said to Deputy Helland. 'So the law takes the law into its own hands then, is that right?'

'Something like that.' Helland grinned. The toothpick clicked against his teeth. The deer rifle he was holding was facing the ground.

'I don't suppose that the sheriff is out there with you, is he?' asked Henry, surveying the faces, scanning the bleak expressions. He saw a man in coveralls with a child on his shoulders; a woman in a gingham dress bearing her few stained teeth like an Andean guinea pig; next to her a boy of no more than

42

sixteen holding a rifle as old as the war that they yet spoke of in this part of the country, his tanned face covered with sparse, wispy growth. Darker faces were staring from further back in the mass.

Deputy Helland played the toothpick with his tongue, his eyes slits, slowly shaking his head.

'We want *you* off this land,' said the man standing next to the Deputy, his sunburnt face half-hidden beneath his hat. This evening Lenut Colden was not upon his chestnut stallion. 'You tell us to leave ours; we tell you to leave yours.'

'Well, I'm afraid that it isn't as simple as that, my man.' Henry lowered his foot from the plant pot, taking position centrally at the top of the steps. He held the shotgun across his chest, his finger resting on the trigger guard.

'Now hear this,' he called out, 'I am under the employment of the Federal Government. They own and control all of this land, all of this country, not you. You say that you have come to run me from my land: someone else will move in. You think that coming mob-handed will terrorise me into changing the plans for the railroad: they will excuse me, only for the next man to plough the path. Mob rule can change nothing. However cruelly treated you feel, threats cannot change the minds of those who are in power.

'You must *believe* me when I say that I empathise with your plight. I do, truly. No man throughout the history of the civilised world has ever left his land without sadness in his heart. Without fight in his belly. It was the same for the natives of this very land. And later the same still for the Confederates: your people! I know how it must feel. I know how much it must hurt. But we have done all that we can to ensure your comfort throughout any disturbances caused, and to make this transition as easy as possible for all of you.'

'These is all lies,' the deputy called out, looking around behind him, addressing the crowd. 'Do not believe a word that this snake has to say. This English snake. He ain't even from this country he's putting to ruin. This is *our* land.'

Most cheered in response.

'No,' Henry called out. 'I speak the truth! I may be a foreigner to you, but I have always had your best interests in my heart. We are grafting to see that this project brings you all future prosperity. Yes, it will take time. Yes, it will not be easy to start with. But, in time, you will see for yourselves how you shall all profit. It will create employment; jobs for you and your people.'

'So you want us to help flatten our own homes?' the young boy at the front said. 'Prob'ly for no more'n a nickel a day? Us working to stuff the pockets of some governor who don't give two spits 'bout us country folk down here?'

'No, you understand wrong,' Henry answered the boy. 'You will be resettled. Your voices will be heard. This is the right action, and the right time for us to take action. With patience and forbearing, you will see.'

Henry Wilmington again surveyed the faces before him. He hadn't expected applause, but he had spoken from his heart. He wasn't sure if he had ever felt so proud, though his expression of stout determination would not defy him.

'You done?' the deputy drawled, eyebrows still raised, his line of scar caring not. 'Don't think that we're going to suffer here beneath your lies. We're a *proud* people. We've always been on our own together, however we've had to suffer. Well, we ain't going to suffer no more. This is our land, and we're going to do whatever it takes to keep it that way; do *you* understand? We decide what's going to happen to our land, not some fat-belly governor in a city we ain't never heard of, like the boy says. We ain't. And most definitely of all not to a English snake who ain't got no right to be here in the first place. That ain't right and it ain't fair. And we ain't gonna live like that no more.' Deputy Helland raised his rifle in the air, one-handed, and punched it upwards. '*No more!*'

The crowd cheered. Some joined in, chanting the Deputy's call. Some protesters, heads drawn upward by the increasing rainfall, the distant thunderclaps, could see the faces peeking from behind curtains, looking down from the illuminated upstairs windows.

'Then you will achieve nothing,' Henry said directly to the Deputy. 'Not like this. Not with gangs bearing arms. History has taught you what happens when you threaten violence to get your own way. For goodness sake, you have seen it for yourselves! Have you not yet learned? Take your arguments and your objections to those in charge. Take them well-written and clearly presented, and you will be heard.'

'We've done it that way,' said Colden, 'and it got us nowhere. It's time for us to take action.'

'I urge you to maintain your dignity. If you can't do that, then you really have nothing to stand for.' Henry took a step forward. 'But there is nothing that you can achieve here this night. Now, I ask you again, politely, please remove yourselves from my land.'

'Nuh-uh,' said the deputy. He spat out his toothpick. 'We ain't going nowhere. In fact, this is our land a hundred . . . no, a thousand times more than it's yours. You remove *yourself* from *our* land.'

The crowd cheered once more, now with more ferociousness. Thunder shook the clouds.

'I will not stand for this any longer,' Henry yelled above the noise of the jeering masses. 'Leave! Now! *Get off my land!*'

He aimed the Winchester high into the air above the crowd and fired.

4

The driver drew the reign. The carriage came to a clattering halt. He stepped down into a recently formed puddle. He opened the door, leaned into the carriage. Four of the five passengers jerked in fear. They were clutching each other. They pulled each other closer still.

'Won't be long,' said the driver. 'I promise.' He took a long look at them before closing the door. He could hear one of the passengers wailing, fear no longer able to contain their tears. The driver stopped in the pouring rain. Wondering whether to go back to the carriage. To reassure them. He looked at the sodden ground. Without panic, he quickly strode through the rain to the house, no time to care for his soaked clothes. He opened the door and stepped inside.

The sound of the rain was louder inside than out. The room was lit by candlelight. His wife was in the armchair. She looked half-asleep.

'Pack whatever you and the boy need,' he said. 'We got to leave. Don't know if we ever coming back. Looks like no.'

She began to sit up. 'I don't understand. Why right now? Why in the middle of the night?'

'Please,' he said, opening another door, dripping rainwater on the floor, 'just do what I say. And do it now.'

He walked into the room. The candlelight from the sitting room lit upon his son's sleeping face. He gently scooped up the boy, sheet and all. The boy stirred, reaching as he stretched.

'Don't worry, Boo,' Paw whispered. 'We just going away for a little time. Stay sleeping now.' Booya groaned and made a pillow with his hands, palms pressed together.

As gently as he could manage, Paw lifted Booya higher in to his arms. Booya nuzzled into the crook of his elbow. As Paw turned, he saw Mammy standing in the doorway. She had a shawl over her shoulders and was holding a garden bag, stuffed full of belongings.

'You think we will be coming back, Cleveland? 'Cause ain't got no clue what to bring. Please tell me wha –'

'Adeline,' Paw interrupted. 'Look at me.' She looked from Booya to Cleveland. 'Don't know the answer to any of it. Can't tell you 'cause I don't know. All I know is we got to get out of here. Now.'

'But what's happening?' she asked. 'Tell me. Why we gotta go in the middle –'

'Mister Henry's dead,' Cleveland spoke, his face running with water. 'They shot him over that railroad business he's involved in.'

Adeline gasped and put a hand to her mouth. 'You sure, Cle? I mean . . . I . . .' She gasped. 'You sure?'

Cleveland nodded. 'Was watching from a upper window. See it all. It was the deputy what fired first. And then . . .' He shook his head, scattering more drops on to the sheet. 'And then they was all firing on him. That's all I see.'

'That's what that noise was.'

He nodded.

'Thought that was something . . . thunder, or something . . . maybe the picking fields, but . . .'

'Please,' said Cleveland, shifting Booya's weight. 'You understand now we got to leave. They all gone crazy. Can't be sure they won't come down here and . . . I ain't willing taking chances, honey. We got to leave *now*.'

'Mister Henry's dead?' Adeline said beneath her hand. She looked down at Booya sleeping.

'You got everything we gonna need?'

She nodded.

'Might try come back in few days. Come on. They is a carriage outside. Got Mister Henry's family in. Can't leave them no longer. They scared as anything.'

'What is I gonna say to –?'

'Just don't say nothing,' Paw replied. 'They all ain't talking, nohow. Don't worry with that now. I'll come back and blow the candles in a minute. Let's get gone.'

Manoeuvring Booya carefully past the jamb, they left their house.

An escaped horse was stooped, drinking from a puddle at the side of the road, before suddenly galloping back towards the house. The sound of chickens in flustered uproar could be heard through the rain and the shocks of thunder. Skittish, the horses, seemingly all around, whinnied with each clap of thunder. Wet leaves were falling all around the carriage.

Paw hunched over Booya, trying to keep him dry. Beyond the hedge, the paddock, and the orchard was a roaring fire. It looked like the sun had crashed through the clouds and smashed into the earth. Maybe it would not rise tomorrow.

Adeline looked back at Paw, her hand on the carriage door-handle. With a nod, Paw encouraged her to open it. They could hear a chorus of rowdy voices. The pitch-dark world seemed to be closing in on the carriage.

As Adeline opened the carriage door, a flash of lightning struck somewhere beyond the trees, illuminating the shock on the wet, pale faces inside. Adeline looked at Missus Elizabeth. Her shawl-covered arms enshrouded George, Luke and Victoria. Even through her tears and her pain Missus Elizabeth managed a weak half-smile. The children's nanny, Nina, reached out a hand to Adeline. She accepted it. Nina helped to pull Adeline and her bag into the carriage.

Paw handed Booya up to Adeline. He looked down the track that led to the Wilmington House. He squinted, trying to discern if anything was skulking its way through the dark and the rain.

'We gotta go,' Adeline hissed. 'Cleveland, we gotta get outta here.'

Paw shut the door.

Thunder growled. The horses whinnied. Another of the escaped horses galloped back towards the Wilmington house. Towards the gold that was falling in flames.

As Paw ran back to the house, he could feel the rain splashing up the back of his pants. In the fireplace were three burning candles, blissfully unaware. Cleveland blew those out first. The bedrooms were already dark. He walked to close the doors to the bedrooms, blowing out two more candles on the kitchen table. He was out of time. Anything they might have needed to take with them would have to be left behind to chance. He would have to take that chance. It was their only chance. Just as he was turning to leave, lightning flashed outside, illuminating the room in stark bright light. Picking up the guitar up by the neck, Paw left the house.

CHAPTER THREE

1

'Mister Wilbur Harris?' Cleveland asked the man wearing a straw hat, looking down at him from the porch of the plantation house.

'Uh-huh,' the man on the porch replied. He looked down at the little boy with the big brown eyes and the large guitar – not the beaten-up kind of guitars the workers bashed about in the big barn away over the field at their nightly frolics. The guitar that the boy was stuck to looked fit for Carnegie Hall. His eyes lingered longer on the grand-looking carriage they'd clopped in on. After looking Cleveland's three-piece household suit up and down a second time, his eyes returned to the face of the black man standing before him. 'Who's arksing?'

'My name's Cleveland Carthy, Mister Wilbur, sir. We was told in the county store you might be looking for some help in the fields?'

Wilbur Harris looked once more at the carriage, assessing it might be worth as much as three hundred dollars for a piece like that. And they sure weren't mules who had dragged it on to his plantation.

'Well, you weren't told wrong, friend,' Harris said. 'Just so happens that I've got a house here recently vacated by some of my sharecroppers.' It was clear to him that this family had run from somewhere, from something. Unlike most who knocked upon his door to ask for work, they had certainly not come from nothing. 'That's a big guitar you got there, little man. Can you play that thing?'

Booya looked at his guitar, then up at the smiling man. His striped shirt was half-open, showing his tanned chest. His face was a field of blonde stubble over the weathered, lined skin, seasoned with grey, like the sun-bleached tangles of hair peeking out from under his hat. Arms crossed, leaning against a post on the porch, this man seemed kind enough; his bright blue eyes catching the light of the day. Booya shook his head.

Wilbur Harris laughed. 'Well, it sure is pretty looking. Let me go get my mule and I'll lead y'over to your new place myself.'

Sharecroppers watched in silent amazement as the carriage, behind Wilbur Harris on his mule, bumped along through the plantation.

As the man of the family, trying to keep a positive mask upon his face Cleveland managed to hide his disappointment as the new lodgings came into view. The wood was fiercely browned from age. Wilbur had informed them with much regret that the previous tenants had fled from his plantation without a parting word. Upon seeing the shack that was to become theirs, Cleveland wondered if the previous sharecroppers had not simply fled to avoid payment on such a ramshackle property. As they stepped onto the porch, the wood creaked and groaned, threatening to give way beneath them. The entire building was sagging from the small exertion of pressure on the porch. There were weeds growing up through the porch floorboards, and rusty tin cans piled to one side, skids of dried sauce still visible inside.

Booya noticed a wire hanging down from the porch bannister. He wondered if someone had once made a diddly-bow here. He was about to decide that he would ask Paw to help him make one when he remembered that he was carrying his guitar.

'Might want to patch it up here and there,' Mister Wilbur said, 'but it'll do you pretty good through winter. You've come just after the harvest, so there ain't gonna be much to do about the place 'til spring, but I'll make sure that you've got credit in the wood of the local store for food, clothes, fuel and such. You been sharecroppers 'fore now, Cleveland, my man?'

'Ah, yes, Mister Wilbur, sir. Not for a few years, but I was born to it.'

'So you know about the furnish: the seed and fertilizer you'll be needing to grow the cotton – that's your patch over here, by the way, just over an acre per 'cropper here.' They looked over at the patch of land Wilbur Harris indicated by way of his straw hat, showing the bald pate above the straggles of hair. 'Might be looking a little overgrown just now, but we're fallow now 'til spring, that'll give you time to tidy. I'll dig you out a few tools from the store.' Harris looked over at the horses. 'They might not be fit for ploughing, those nags. Maybe we could settle on a trade deal for a mule. I know a man in town looking for fine breeds like yours. And using these horses for ploughing would be like using a rusty spoon to eat a three-course supper in the Davis Hotel in Chicago!' Harris laughed alone.

'Anything you can do to help us, Mister Wilbur, sir,' Cleveland said, his stomach cramping, 'we sure appreciate.' He draped his suit jacket and waistcoat over the porch rail.

Wilbur Harris leaned his back against his mule, patting its hind, squinting in the midday sun. 'My wife Marjorie and me, we like to think that if we treat our 'croppers with kindness and humility then we'll be replied in kind, my man. It was the good Lord what told us, *led* us by His Holy Spirit, the way to help our fellow man in need was to set up here, open our land to families just like yours. That's why we charge just five per-cent interest on each plot. I'll see that you have some blankets and wood down here by nightfall. I do believe that Marjorie has made some homemade cornbread too! She sometimes does feel obliged by the Lord to distribute her food amongst our families.'

'Thank you, Mister Wilbur, sir.' Cleveland looked at Adeline. He noticed that her chest was barely rising and falling as she stared at the overgrown acre of land, her back to the house. 'Thank you on behalf of us all. Boo?'

'Thank you, Mister Wilbur, sir.' Booya was holding his guitar to his chest.

'That's my man,' Mister Wilbur said. 'And the pleasure is all mine. Say, I know what else I can do that'll help you settle in: how 'bout I offer you thirty-five dollars for that there carriage, right now? We can settle it against the furnish and rent on the land at the end of next season.'

2

The family walked through a door hanging precariously on rusty hinges. Booya bumped his guitar on the rotted jamb with a whining *tur-wang*. The guitar, too, seemed scared to enter. Booya was concerned that he might have done more damage to the house. He thought he would rather live in Mister Henry's shed than in this place. He was looking forward to going back home.

Adeline looked up to see sunlight coming through the roof, where parts of the boards had fallen away. Here the weeds were coming through the holes in the floorboards and, somehow, the ceiling. Their new house was only this one room: the door behind them, two decrepit sides, and another door on the far wall. It was a shotgun shack.

'Where Mister Henry, Paw?'

After glancing at Adeline, Cleveland crouched, looking Booya deep in the eyes. 'Mister Henry gone back to England, Boo. That's why we had to leave.'

'George go with him?'

Rubbing Booya's arms, Cleveland nodded.

Adeline clutched her hands to her heart. 'Cleveland,' she said, 'if we spend winter here, we'll die.'

Booya looked up at Mammy.

'Hush, woman,' Paw said. He looked down at Booya and smiled. The sunlight had found its way through one of the holes in the roof, directly on to his boy's face. At least God had travelled with them. 'Don't talk that way, Adie.' With his eyes, Paw indicated Booya.

Mammy put her arms around Booya's shoulders. 'Can't we just take a chance in going back?' she asked.

Cleveland shook his head. 'We can't go back. Not yet. We can't.'

'Oh, please, Cleveland. They must be something. We can't stay here. They ain't no way.'

'We got ten dollars. Try to add to that so we can leave here, find us a place of our own. But we got to stay 'til then. We just gots to put up here.'

She began to sob. 'Please, Cle, say we don't got to stay.'

Paw smiled at Booya. The wind whistled in through one of the holes in the wall. Upon seeing the terror on Booya's face, Paw knelt down and picked up one of Booya's hands. Looking from Booya to Mammy, fit to cry himself, Cleveland took one of Mammy's hands. 'Me and Boo, we gonna do repairs on the place, starting tomorrow. We'll get some wood. Use these ten bucks if I gots. I'll speak to Mister Wilbur, see what he can give us. And for what price. Maybe we'll get some chickens of our own. This is what we got for now, Adie.' Paw rubbed his thumb over the back of Adeline's hand. 'Ain't no use saying 'bout what we ain't got, huh? This what we got, and that's it all. We'll use what we got to grow, and get where we can doing it.'

Cleveland stood before his wife and child. He picked Booya up and pulled them close. 'We gonna make it, hear me?' he spoke. 'And we gonna have fun doing it, while we doing it! Yeah?'

Adeline sniffed.

'Yeah?' Cleveland asked again, forcing a smile.

'Uh, huh,' Adeline agreed. She wiped her cheeks on Cleveland's shoulders.

Paw looked at Booya, crossed his eyes and stuck out the tip of his tongue. Booya's face split into a sunshine smile. 'There my boy is.' Paw rubbed noses with Booya. 'Anything you wanna do here, Boo? Can do anything you want.'

'I like chickens, Paw.'

'Then we'll get some chickens.' Paw touched a finger to Booya's nose.

Adeline chuckled through her sobs.

'Anything else?'

'Umm . . .' Booya looked up through the roof to the sky. He shook his head. 'Already got my guitar what Mister Henry give me.'

'Yes, you do,' Paw answered.

'And I got you and Mammy, Paw! Ain't nothing else I need if I got both you and my guitar.'

'Right!' Paw chuckled, even as he swallowed down tears. 'Exactly right, Boo. And as long as we got you, too, Boo.'

They rubbed noses again.

Booya tightened his arm around Mammy's neck. 'Don't cry, Mammy. Heared what Paw say? We gonna get chickens!'

Paw wiped his eyes.

'You is the most precious little thing they ever was, sweet honey,' Mammy said, and kissed him.

With his free hand, Booya was gripping his guitar.

3

By foraging, frugality, and a lot of hard work, Cleveland patched up the shack that close season. He bought new hinges for the doors so that they would at least hang straight. He couldn't do much about the creaking and wheezing of the old shack, but at least it no longer felt as though it was going to fall around their ears as they slept. He even found an old and rusty stove, holes rusted right through, but still functioning enough to cook upon, offering a little heat throughout the winter months. Booya helped Paw as much as he could – more in the searching than the reparations.

Mammy said nothing. She just made sure that there was food to eat when her men came home to her.

As Cleveland walked through the plantation along a rutted track, the shirt purchased with some of his credit in the county store itched his neck. Walking past other sharecroppers, greeting them with a nod, he felt more comfortable than when he had wondered to Wilbur Harris' house wearing the tailored, lined suit. He found Harris sitting on a tree stump, chewing bacon.

'Hey, Cleveland, my man! What can I do you for?'

'Morning, Mister Wilbur, sir.' Cleveland readjusted the collar of his 'picker's shirt. 'Uh, Mister Wilbur, me and Adeline, we been wondering if you need any help in the house? Mostly for Adie. See, she knows more 'bout pressing clothes than digging furrows.'

'Now, Cleveland, my man, I have to say that my *curiosity* has been plaguing me a tad.' Harris narrowed his eyes, pulled a stick from behind his ear and used it to tip back his hat, and then discarded the stick on the ground. 'If'n you don't mind me arksing, where exactly did y'all come here from?'

Cleveland told Harris a little about the Wilmington house, explaining how they had been servants. They'd be happy to help pressing clothes, cleaning sheets, preparing food, even if just for a few rashers of bacon.

Harris sighed, stood up, and buried an axe into the stump, placing his foot on the protruding shaft. 'I got eighty families, Cle; just like your family. And all them is saying they ain't making enough bread. I got at least two mothers and their daughters – *at least*, I tell ya – coming to me each day arksing for work, where there just ain't none. Sure thing, they ain't all turning up here in a fancy carriage and proper stitched clothes, but, between you and me, they is slipping them out like rabbits on this here plantation. A whole bunch more little mouths to feed each season. Give them a crumb, they come back and arkse ya for a biscuit.'

Cleveland looked up at the house, then across at the fields, dotted with patched-up shacks. Into the far distance 'croppers were buzzing about their acreage; mothers with children on their knee; older children running around; husbands, sons and daughters preparing the earth for the close season. He nodded his head. 'Yes, Mister Wilbur, sir.'

Harris took a long look at Cleveland, ran his tongue over his teeth and spat in the dirt. 'We give out twenty logs a week to our families at winter, no extra charge. After that, I sell the leftovers in town, a little at a time.' Looking up into the treetops, nests of crow's feet deepening around his eyes, Harris drummed his fingers on his thighs. 'A smart man might be able to sell on his own firewood in town. He might even undercut me, if you hear what I'm saying, Carthy? So long as that wood ain't coming from my stack, I mightn't even see that happening. So long as . . . it ain't coming . . . from my stack,' Wilbur repeated, his blue eyes smiling.

On his way back to the shack, faces surveying the recent arrival, a sharecropper called Cleveland over. Soon continuing on his way, Cleveland was feeling a little lighter in his step.

*

'Gonna be out tonight, Adie,' he said later, lacing his boots. 'See 'bout making some extra bucks.'

Glancing at Booya out front with the chickens, Adeline folded her arms and nodded her head. 'You sniffed it out already, didn't you?' she said. Untying the perfect bow, Cleveland laced the boot again. 'Don't ignore me; you sniffed it out. We both knew it would be hidden away here somewhere, even as the wheels of the carriage first rolled on to the land. Plantations and bootleg liquor go together like clouds and rain.'

Cleveland straightened up and smoothed down his shirt, rolling his shoulders to ease the collar away from his skin. 'Don't you think we could use the extra cash? Wouldn't you like to eat meat sometime soon, ruther than all them vegetables?'

Adeline moved to the door and leaned against the jamb. The red evening sun was disappearing behind the trees. A shiver running through her, she pulled the fabric of her long-sleeved muslin dress tight against her back. 'It ain't gonna be like it was, Cle? You ain't?'

He stepped over to her and put his hands on her waist. 'All I gonna do, sweet pea, is what I gotta to make some dollars, ok?' They watched Booya chasing after a chicken through the dry, brown grass. 'He's getting bigger so quick, you know?'

She turned her head, looking at Cleveland from the corner of her eye. 'That's most of the reasons I don't want you slipping back in your old ways, Cle. Becoming like your old fool daddy again.'

4

Even if the sharecropper hadn't told Cleveland the way to the barn, hidden away beneath the tree cover, the noise alone would have led him. The sound of rowdy frolickers travelled through the woodland to meet him. The younger men standing outside the barn wore the glazed look in their eyes that Cleveland knew so well. Glaring at him, hands itching inside their pockets, they stepped aside.

Inside most people were dancing, white and black, spilling liquid from their cups, unshackled from their families and the fields. Through the moving crowd, Cleveland saw where the noise was coming from: a tiny man, wearing a derby, hollering at the top of his voice as he pounded a guitar; a big, round man, his head the shape of an overgrown cantaloupe, piping into a jug, bopping up and down; a man bent over, rapping spoons against his thigh, crazed as if trying to pull a parasite free. It was the little hollering man who kept claiming Cleveland's eye.

'So you finded us!' the 'cropper of that morning said, Ol' Bill, a tall man who stood below Cleveland's eyeline, his bonnet of thick hair closing the distance in height. He was broad-shouldered and muscular. This evening his eyes were excited, wild. 'A cup for you, man.'

'Ah yeah,' Cleveland said after sipping. 'Taste good!'

'Yep,' Ol' Bill said, 'always does after the sun gone down.'

Cleveland's gaze returned to the little man with the big voice. 'Who that, with the guitar?'

'Ah man, that's Roots – Rusty Broom.' Ol' Bill Laughed. 'Might look small as a chile, but he could drink the place dry by hisself. Man just don't never got to stop t'eat!'

'He sure can play,' Cleveland said.

'Sure don't never *stop* playing. Only way to shut him up is to dangle a cup in front of him.'

'He a . . . distributor?'

Ol' Bill's face split into a smile. 'No one in his right mind would trust Roots with nothing more than a patch a earth to keep warm at night.'

A frolicker bumped into Cleveland, spilling drink on his shirt. 'Better sup that out 'fore the old lady sees it,' he said, raising his eyebrows.

Ol' Bill laughed. 'Plenty more where come from, Cle. Say, man, you want in then?'

'Like nothing! How's it work out here?' Cleveland took another sip and exhaled with delight.

Ol' Bill looked around. Taking Cleveland's arm he led him to a corner of the barn, away from the dancers. 'We brew it just out behind the barn here. Most of the mens here help with the brewing, we all chip in what we can for the ingredients and such. But ain't gonna make no dollars just brewing for us all to have a time. Nuh.' Ol' Bill stole another glance at the nearby faces. 'To make dollars, they's a town full of thirsty folks just down the road. It's liquid gold. Few of us, we take turns bringing this Moonshine to Honahee. You know Honahee, town down the road?'

Cleveland shook his head.

'Few miles to walk; 'bout sevent'-five per-cent black. With that many thirsty brothers, a town like Honahee is gonna attract the revenue man like raptors to a carcass. So if we even sniff agents in the air, just tip and git, and the revenue man can't stick a pin through a dead fly. Don't matter for the loss, ruther than getting your black ass thrown in the cells.'

The fiery brew beginning to warm his belly, Cleveland watched the folks having a time; the tiny guitarist responding, singing even louder, furiously beating his guitar. By the look of his wild, rolling eyes, he was clearly fuelled by liquor. Cleveland took a larger sip, nearly emptying his cup. 'Many of y'all get catched 'fore now, Bill?'

'Well, this the thing: not many of us got the guts to walk that walk no more.' Bill's stare picked out a couple of faces. 'That's why we is needing more footmen, see? So if you is in . . .'

Shadows of figures moving around in the hay loft, high above the frolic, took Cleveland's attention. A woman was shimmying a few metres in front of Cleveland and Bill, lifting her worn and dirty skirts before the keen eyes of a crouched man, rapidly patting his hands on his thighs. Suddenly she whipped a cup out from beneath her skirts. The man cheered. And then she poured the contents over his head. Widening his eyes at her, he began to lick his face, jigging in time to the beat of an upturned pail, his feet skipping like a barking dog. She jumped on him, knocking him to the floor, proceeding to assist in cleaning his face of Moonshine.

Cleveland raised his eyebrows to Ol' Bill. Smiling, Bill shrugged.

'And Mister Wilbur?'

'Oh yeah,' Ol' Bill said, tilting his cup, 'a'course he's in. This being his land, he makes the most profit with the littlest risk. And he made us all agree that, if we is catched out here, if the warning word don't first come over the fields, he don't know nothing 'bout it. See, Harris, he a good man, fairer'n most of his skin. And he truly does believe that everything that he and Marge does is for the Lord, even as he skims of our asses. They ain't no man what counts every last penny like Wilbur Harris, nuh-uh. Once he sees we got the least we need to live, he keeps the rest – like when he selled your carriage and hosses, as if you don't know he made bucks. But he loves our families living on his land, we all think on the account of "the Good Lord" didn't see fit to give them one of they own.

'So if one of us all comes back here saying we had to tip and git, Harris would know if we is lying, keeping the profits usself. We all know he got informers in Honahee, making sure that his brew gets through. Funny thing is that it ain't never happened, thieving; it always does get through or is tipped in a ditch 'fore the revenue man sniffs it. Whether it's from knowing that he'd know, or just 'cause of the kind way he treats us all . . . guess I never will know. Still, if he's keeping us out here, all having a time with the Moonshine, I can drink to him for that.'

Cleveland turned his cup upside down and shook. 'I'll be happy to drink to Mister Wilbur, Bill. Just as soon as you show me where I can fill my cup.'

5

The sun finally awakened into spring. Families emerged from their shacks, blinking and stretching the winter hibernation from their bones. Father's had pink eyes. Mothers were showing the first signs of pregnancy. Children looked at the world from an inch or two higher than before the leaves had fallen.

The singing in Mister Wilbur's fields didn't impress Booya like it had done in the field beyond the woodland. Here the songs didn't seem to swim around the heads of the workers and ripple over the bounding fields. This was a flat land with fewer workers, segregated to private allotments. Their songs were just as private.

He, Mammy and Paw sang the hallies, the work songs, and the spirituals – that Booya had come to know so well from a winter cooped in the shack – sometimes accompanied by an unknown, faceless voice. But most times it was just Booya and Mammy, accompanied by Paw's hung-over groans.

One of those days when Booya and Mammy were singing, there was not a groan or grumble to hear from Paw. Just as Booya was going and seek him out, he heard Paw's voice coming from a few rows away.

'Where he at then, Cle? Dis boy a yourn.'

Booya stooped down and could see two pairs of booted-feet through the rows.

'Hey, Roots!' Booya heard Paw say. 'You come!'

'Uh-huh,' said the pair of boots, 'feel like I be wanderin' round lost fo' days.'

Booya heard Paw laugh, his new laugh that came with coughing.

'What time you start this morning, Roots?'

'Now . . . lemme see. Truth tole, don't think I stop since . . . I can't 'member when I start. Only solid thing pass my lips fo' days be titty.'

Paw laughed and coughed. Booya saw his boots moving with each retch. 'Hey, man! No talking like that in front of my boy, huh?'

'S'where he at, Cle? Leave him som'er you forget?'

'He here 'bout someplace,' Paw answered.

Crouched, his fingers clutching dirt, Booya was frozen. In the light breeze the shadows of the cotton plants pointed and teased. That morning he had seen a pair of white men on horses trotting around the perimeters of the Harris land. He had been here before, hiding in amongst the spindly, treacherous plants. Booya was certain that, upon the horse, half of the man's sunburned face would be hidden within the shade of his hat.

Turning on his stomach, the noise of the moving earth crashing in his ears, Booya slithered along. Stones prodded and poked at him. He could no longer see the boots, but now the noise of song was everywhere. He could hear Mammy's voice, humming softly beneath her breath; see her feet moving along in the next row. Booya pulled himself through the cotton plants and grabbed onto her leg.

'Hey, Cal!' she said. 'Easy on your Mammy. What you doing down there, huh? What bit you?'

Booya gripped her leg, trying to lift and hide in her skirts. She tried to untie his arms but he was holding on too tight.

'And here he is!' Paw said. 'Mister Booya Carthy. Hiding like a catfish in the rushes.'

Booya was snuffling into Mammy's thigh.

'What you gone done now, Cleveland?'

'Huh? Nothing! Got someone here come to see Boo.'

'Fine day, ma'am,' Roots said, lifting his beaten and dusty derby. 'All the finer fo' makin' yo' 'quanitance. Allow me ta innaduce myself: I is Russell Broom, or Rusty ta some. But most knows me as Roots Cryer. Or Rusty Roots.'

'So what is I to call you out of all them names?' Mammy asked.

'By the one you wanna. But Roots do just fine by me.'

'I guess you been helping keeping Cleveland wet at nights.'

Roots stole a glance at Paw, turned back round and swayed. 'Don't know nothing 'bout nothing, ma'am.'

Mammy puckered her lips and nodded.

'An' wha's yo' name, li'l man?'

'Hey, Boo, come out from under there! Come on. Roots here to see you,' said Paw. 'He's been waiting to meet you for time.'

Roots took off his hat and crouched down, a hand spread on the floor in front of him as an anchor. He swayed, and would have fallen over if he hadn't plunged the hand holding his hat to the ground, squashing the crown. 'Hi, boy,' he said. 'Yo' daddy tell me yo' quite a man on da geetar. That right?'

Booya slowly turned around, one hand still clutching Mammy's skirts.

The man that he saw crouching at his height, with both of his hands spread in the dirt like a toad, had a round, friendly face, neat curls of glistening hair on top of his head, a close, but none too neat, shave around the sides. Above his smiling crescent of grimy teeth was a wavy line of moustache. With his chin on his chest, Booya couldn't help but smile back at him.

'So, yo' da man I heared 'bout what play da geetar?'

Booya nodded. The smell pouring from the man was definitely the smell of angel's kisses, but it smelled dirty, rotten and old. The way that he spoke was how Paw sometimes sounded late at night, or early in the morning.

'And wha's yo' name, friend?'

'Booya,' he whispered.

'Booya? Well ain't dat a fine name fo' a blues boy. Good on yo' geetar, den, like daddy say?'

Booya looked to Paw for help.

'Go on, Boo. Roots' axing *you*.'

'Huh? Is ya, Boo?'

Booya nodded.

'He don't never *stop* playing on it,' Paw said. 'All winter long.'

'Dat what I be hearin.' Roots nodded. 'See, fact a da bidness is I rap an' frail on my geetar, too. Hokum, some folks is callin' my songs. But it ain't no hokum. It da blues.' The word 'blues' slid from Roots' mouth like a dribble. *Blooooz.* 'Yo' heared a da *blooooz*, Boo?'

Booya nodded.

'Uh-huh. I be playin' geetar since I's 'bout yo' age. Wha' yo' now, twelve?'

'Eight nearly nine,' Booya replied.

'Yo' a big boy fo' yo' height, ain't ya?'

Mammy and Paw looked at each other and smiled – Mammy with a frown. Fingering the dirt, Roots swayed on his crouching position. Loosening his grip on Mammy's skirts, Booya looked up at Paw.

'So . . . fact da bidness dis: how 'bout I come up yo' place some night an' show ya li'l a what I knows: how ta tune da beast proper, an' such. Yo' can show me whachu knows an' I show ya li'l of my rappin' an' frailin'. How 'bout dat?'

Booya looked up at Mammy and Paw.

'Go on now, Calvin,' Mammy said. 'What do you think of Mister Roots' offer?'

'You know Blind Lemon Jeff?' Booya asked.

Roots picked up his hat, pushed out the squashed bowl and ran his hand around the rim, dirt flaking to the ground. He stood, a little unsteady until he found his feet. 'Lemme see now. I knowed some dem blind hollerers, but damn if'n I knowed no Blind Lemon Jeff. Who he?'

'He play the country blues,' Booya said.

'Dat right now?'

Booya nodded.

'Well, I guess ol' Roots kin teach ya how ta play a li'l a da ol' country blues hisself, if dat whachu wanna learn ta play.'

'Yes, Mister Roots, sir. I do.'

Roots placed the hat on his head, pushed it down and swayed. 'Den dat what we gon' do, Boo.' He stood up.

Booya was surprised by how much shorter Roots was than Paw. He was closer, even, to Booya's height than Mammy's.

'Uh-huh, da country blues,' Roots said. 'Cut ma teeth on dat myseff, I did. Wanna shake on it, Boo?'

Booya looked up at Mammy. She smiled and nodded. He smiled and held out his hand straight.

'Dat a country blues geetar picker's hand if e'er I seed one,' Roots said, taking Booya's hand in his limp, bony grip.

6

Late May, 1933

Turning his straw hat in hands, Wilbur Harris looked out at the sea of faces standing before his porch. Running a hand over his bald head and through the tangles of long hair, he picked out each little face in the front rows, his cheeks twitching, reflecting the sombre faces looking back at him. Standing beside him, he looked at Marjorie, examining the floor beyond the porch. Making a fist, he chewed on his knuckles. He returned the hat to his head.

'Ain't no easy way for me to say this,' he said. He picked out a tree behind the crowd, addressing his words to it. 'In light of the Depression and the New Deal, we been forced by the Agricultural Adjustment Administration to lay the fields fallow until further notice.' Looking back at the crowd, no one had moved, no one murmured, not a soul responded to the words he had spoken. He looked again at Marjorie. She had been staring at the side of his face, but now looked away again to the dirt. He reached for her hand, found it, squeezed.

'I hoped this day would never come,' he said. 'I did. But come it has. We got no other choice than to close down the plantation. I'm sorry.' Now Marjorie squeezed his hand. '*We* is so sorry, but I can't employ you as sharecroppers no more.'

The crowd started to murmur. Mothers pulled their children close. Men looked at each other, unable to hold each other's blinking gaze. Wilbur Harris was unable to look any longer at the hands on mouths, the bulging eyes.

'I'm sorry,' he repeated, tucking a stray crop of hair behind his ear.

'But Wilbur,' a man said, 'what we supposed to do then? Where we supposed to go? Ain't got no other place we *can* go.'

Harris found the face in the crowd, a white man with sandy hair, one arm around his wife and the other on his daughter's shoulder. 'You are welcome to stay here and live off the land,' Harris said, trying to smile. Slipping a finger under his hat, he scratched his head. 'I can't pay you for work, but you can use the land you got to grow the food you need.' He breathed in, held his breath. 'All credit in the store is suspended 'til I know more. I'm sorry, there ain't much else . . . I can do.' He pulled down the rim of his hat, put his arm around Marjorie, and retreated into the house.

*

The redundant 'croppers suddenly found themselves with idle time on their hands, far too much time by the length of each day. The devil was quick to find work for them.

All over the Harris plantation drinking increased, by day and by night. Fights broke out regularly. With nothing to engage them, the same previously polite and friendly sharecroppers found themselves permanently drunk, insane and dangerous.

Within weeks, hell set up camp beneath the hot sun.

All of the families who managed to drag self-respect and dignity along behind them through the dusty, dry mud soon left the plantation; some families forced to leave the father or son behind so as they could make their escape, praying for the Lord to have mercy on their loved one. Like most of the families with no other place to go, scared to step outside their shotgun shacks – terrified to stay alone inside – the Carthy's stayed on in the plantation.

'You seen Paw lately?' Booya asked Mammy, stopping the song he was playing, slouched over his pallet on the floor. Her fingers were in a bowl of water, cleaning her spare dress, she shook her head. 'Think he's coming home soon?'

Mammy's hands stopped moving. Booya watched the slow rise and fall of her back, her breathing heavy. 'I is scared, Cally. Scared for his spirit and soul. He out there going buck-crazy with the rest of them, I know it. Ain't making dollars, like he say he is. I just can't make him see sense. It's like he ain't got no sense left.' She ran her hand around the bowl, then stopped, the water splashing against her wrists. 'It's like the freedmen I tole you 'bout all over again.' She continued scrubbing furiously.

A chicken hopped up and perched on the neck of Booya's guitar. He watched as it looked around, jerking its scrawny head, the feathers on the neck sticking up. Since a couple of the Carthy's chickens had been snatched away, the remaining chickens were now living inside. The unpleasant smell of guano filled the shack. Mammy feared it was like harbouring gold bullion with common thieves stalking outside their door.

'Please, Cally, carry on playing for me.'

Booya shook the chicken from the neck of his guitar, put the derby that Roots had given him on the night of his first lesson, nearly six years previous, on his head, and started picking out the melody of *Rock, Daniel.*

Mammy's hands had stopped once more. 'You such a good boy, sweetness. You know that hallie's my –'

The door burst open. Cleveland was standing there, steam rising from his body and head, swaying on his feet, as if a strong wind was blowing through his bones, his hands spread out by his sides. A silhouette in the dying red sun, he had a wild, native look in his eyes. 'Got me some pork?' he asked by way of greeting, his eyes rolling.

Mammy turned around, her wet hands dripping on the floor. Booya was surprised to see that her face was not wet. 'Cleveland, we ain't got nothing. Calvin and me got nothing. We is stranded here, Cle.'

'Well, where ya gon' fin' me some pork, woman?'

'Cleveland, listen to me: I can't *get* nothing. Can't you see? We ain't got *nothing.*'

'Ain't gon' get nothing if I ain't gots no pork.'

'Please stop, Cleveland. You scaring me.'

'Be plenty scairt yet.' Cleveland waved a finger in the vague direction of Adeline, as if trying to point out land from a ship in a squall. 'Get me . . . How' 'bout fixin' me one dem chicken?'

The chickens began to sound from the backs of their throats, gathering together.

'We got nothing but them chickens!' Adeline snapped angrily. 'And they ain't barely laying. Listen to me, you fool: We. Got. *Nothing!* Nuh-uh-thing. Not a thing. If we stay here we ain't gonna survive. Sooner than you know, Calvin will be big enough to be going out with you down to that stupid old barn. He's fifteen years old, Cleveland. You know how it goes. Want him to get stuck like Clara's Bill? Huh? Do you?'

'Boo ain't nothing like Ol' Bill. Bill dead, honey. Don't *you* unnerstan'?'

'Yes I understand!' Adeline yelled. 'Just ax yourself this: do you want Calvin to die like Bill?'

Booya placed his guitar on the floor as quietly as he could. Like the chicken, Paw's head jerked in his direction. Frowning, Cleveland saw two people where his son was sitting on the pallet.

'Hey, Paw. Where you been at?'

'Man jus' come 'ome ta get 'im some pork an' gets none. That too mush t'ax fo', Boo?'

'Paw, we ain't had nothing but eggs and yams for days.'

Paw scratched the back of his head as he looked around the rocking room. 'Tell it now: if I ain't gots pork sometime soon, I gon' be . . .' Paw breathed heavily and swayed. 'Tell ya I be . . . Jus' wan' me some pork, y'know?' Paw said, his voice becoming scratchy.

'Yeah, Paw. We all do. You on the sauce, huh?'

After glaring at the chickens and muttering to himself, Cleveland turned around slowly, staggered, leaned on the doorframe, and then took an unstable step into the red morning light.

Adeline began to cry lightly into her hands.

'Hey, Paw!' Booya called. 'Where you going?'

Cleveland hung his head, his body sagging. 'Gon' back'n da woods,' he mumbled. 'See if I kin gets me sumin'.' Without looking back, he took a weary step across the porch. His head wobbled as his foot came down. Slowly, he lifted his foot to take another step.

'Leave us here today like this, Cleveland Carthy, and ain't no need you ever coming back.' Mammy wiped her wet face with the back of her sleeves. 'You can get all the pork in the world you want, but we ain't gonna be here to share it. You can have it all to yourself. Have it with your boys in the woods, for all I care.'

Cleveland was standing and swaying, a soft breeze blowing his open shirt around him.

'So long as you understand me now, through your stupid thick skull. We getting out of here, Cle. Today. We is leaving. You can stay or you can come with, makes no difference to me. But if you stay, you ain't never gonna see me or Calvin again. Your Boo. Just understand that.'

'Mammy?'

Adeline turned her wet face to Booya. He could see from the stony of look of sorrow on her face that she meant it. He remembered the day when they had first arrived here.

The chickens began to strut around, desperate to be outside in the first of the violet sun.

'Sorry, Cally, but that's the truth of it. You hear that, Cleveland Carthy? I mean it this time. Walk away now and you walking away from us forever.'

Cleveland swayed. He steadied himself. His head was hanging between his sagging shoulders. Then he fell forward, his head in the dirt. Half-on and half-off the porch.

'Here,' Cleveland said. 'Let's stop . . . for the night . . . here. S'getting too dark to see.' Cleveland dropped the blankets he was carrying and put his hands on his hips. 'Ain't gon' be . . . no place better to . . . sleep tonight than . . . here.'

The last light of the day left the horizon as one long, jagged outline; the moon a ghost rising into the night sky behind them. A bird cried out in the darkness, fluttering its wings as it rose into the night.

'You sure it ain't just 'cause your head's hurting, you old fool?' Adeline said. 'And not just from the knock you give it when you hit the dirt?'

'Please, Adie.'

'You got a long way to go yet 'fore you can Adie me again.' Pinching her lips together, she turned to Booya. 'You okay, Cally?'

With a chicken under each arm, his guitar in one hand, Booya nodded. 'I think Paw's right, Mammy. I think that under that bridge is gonna be the best place we'll find this time of night.'

'What's my life come to,' Adeline asked the sky, 'when I have to sleep nights under an old bridge?'

'You think the other chickens will be all right?' Booya asked.

'We brung all we could, sweet honey.'

'Maybe I'll go back in a few days,' Cleveland said, nodding and stretching his arms above his head, 'see if – '

'Cleveland Carthy, you ain't never going anywhere near that Godforsaken place for the rest of your life, however long that might be, hear me?'

'You know where Roots' been Paw?' Booya readjusted his grip on the guitar, lifting the chickens. The sounds they had been gargling in their throats on the walk had been left further back down the road. 'Been months since he come over to play his *geetar.*'

'When he was wasn't so drunk that he couldn't,' Mammy said.

'When he was sober enough that he could,' Booya added.

Breathing heavily, Paw stared at the blankets on the floor at his feet. 'N'ain't seen Roots.' Picking up the blankets, Cleveland took a few steps before slipping to the bottom of the bank. They watched as he stumbled around, a silhouette in the shadow of the bridge. 'Hey, there's water running down here.'

'What else did you expect a bridge to be stretching over?' Mammy looked Booya up and down. 'I tell you, Calvin, don't become like him. You see what a fool can do to a old heart? Just stay sweet as you are. Ain't no friends to be found in the drink.' She sucked her lips. 'You still wearing that hat *he* give you, huh?'

'Look it, Mammy: that and Mister Henry's guitar is all I got.' One of the chickens began to cluck beneath Booya's armpit. 'Roots teached me everthing

I know 'bout playing the blues.'

Mammy wagged a finger. 'Calvin, your talent is a gift from God, not some frailin' drunk. Don't never forget that.' She looked at the old wooden bridge, her eyes travelling downward to the darkness beneath.

'What shall I do with Mister Henry and Lemon Jeff?' Booya looked at the two chickens under his arm. 'Think they all right down there with us?'

'They gonna have to be, Cal.'

'You any idea where we is out here?' Booya looked at what he could see up and down the road. Other than fields, undergrowth and a broken fence on one side of the road, and the trees lining the road further past the bridge, he could discern little in the dim light. The sun had taken most of the heat of the day with it.

Booya helped Mammy down the bank, where, at the bottom, they found Paw already asleep on the pile of blankets. Mammy woke him with a kick and dragged the blankets from beneath him, spinning him into the dirt. She moved further along, beneath the bridge, and began to set the blankets out in the darkness beneath the upright struts. Booya joined her.

'You know,' he said, 'I think this could be all right living here. I like it! I could live here.' Even through the gloom he could see Mammy's eyes piercing him – akin to look she had given the dancing silhouette of Paw when he had turned up steaming in the doorway. 'Seriously, what do you think we gonna do now? Where we gonna go?'

Mammy leaned against the bridge and closed her eyes. Booya could just see her lips moving. 'Prayer, honey. The Lord will show us where to go. Even if tonight we got to stay here, He'll show us the way.' By the soft light of the moon, Booya could see Mammy's cheeks glistening. 'You know, Cleveland Carthy,' she said, standing over Cleveland, 'the Lord giveth when he led us down to the Harris plantation, I see that now. And it was the devil brew nearly took it all away. *You* see that?'

Paw had fallen asleep again.

CHAPTER FOUR

1

July 4th, 1936

Independence Day was the day of the annual Honahee town picnic. It was a day that brought in folks from out of town, near and far; the day that locals looked forward to more than any other day in the calendar. It was a day of festivities, celebrated with musicians and dancers, singers, comedians and other assorted novelty acts, freaks, and poets.

All day happy noise encircled the town. Someone somewhere was constantly banging a drum, blowing a pipe, picking a string, or singing out their soul. The fruity smells emitted from the hot cornmeal-tamale stands danced in the sky with the joyous sounds. Peanut vendors moved their stalls around, trying to give the smell of the roasting nuts a chance against the powerful tamales. Watermelon juices ran from the chins of children as they slurped the tasty slices. A travelling medicine show had rocked into town, bearing tonics and elixirs of high alcoholic content, tempting those who need little temptation and the curious alike. In the centre of the madness, a bandstand had been erected days earlier, signalling the folks of the town to be ready. Let the excitement build, for the picnic is coming back to town.

On the stage, a white man with his face painted deepest black, wearing wide trousers and a white cotton shirt, was theatrically booming out a river song in a deep bass baritone. Some of the children chose to sit cross-legged in front of the stage, staring up at him with fascinated awe. Others made their own entertainment, holding hands and skipping in a circle around a selected friend, singing out their rhyme, giggling after they chose who would be the husband and wife of their game. More children ran around the crowds, through the adult's legs. Always ensuring they kept to the side of the bandstand permitted by segregation.

On the perimeters of the picnic were stationary wagons. Young adults gathered around as one of their number played guitar, creating their own little party. Sunny smiles frequently replaced by wary, guilt-ridden glances as they took turns to discreetly duck into the wagon, and then returned smiling.

Men who had momentarily split from the picnic casually sauntered over to the wagons, exchanged a few words, and then, after a furtive glance, slipped inside.

Cleveland looked towards the wagons before looking back to Adeline. He sighed. 'How 'bout one little tonic? Need me a little bit of medicine to relax. It was the good Lord what teached us to make the Moonshine, weren't it, Adie?'

'We here for the day, Cleveland,' Adeline huffed. 'You know if you have one now, you had ten by time the sun falls.'

'Gonna get me some chicken,' Cleveland said. He began to walk towards the wagons.

'Get me a wing while you there,' Adeline called after him. 'And don't go getting no fool ideas, Cleveland Carthy. Got my eyes on you.'

Hanging his head, Cleveland diverted towards the food stands.

Throughout the day Booya mostly watched the stage, enraptured by the entertainment. Occasionally, he glanced to the white's side, to see how they accepted the music – vaguely hoping that he might see Mister Henry or George. He was surprised that the whites wore exactly the same expressions as his kin. They laughed at the same things, applauded in the same places; frowned at the freaks, and nodded to the beats. They were just the same – even if they did own the land, the jobs and the motorcars.

As he surveyed the smiling white faces, Booya noticed that a girl was staring straight at him. When she saw him looking at her she didn't look away. She smiled; slowly blinked her thick black lashes, twice. Beneath a straw hat, wearing a white cotton dress dotted with big red circles, her waving black hair rested on her shoulders. She gracefully waved a fan beneath her delicately rounded chin. She looked like a child, and at the same time like a queen. Twice more, she slowly blinked, smiling again at Booya.

He looked around. Everyone else was watching the stage. He dared to smile at her. She tilted her head behind her fan, hiding all but her dark-lined eyes. She blinked once more: teasing and seductive. Helpless not to, a half-smile broke Booya's lips. And then Booya noticed that the man sitting next her was also staring straight at him – he needn't look around himself to recognise that. The hatred from the man's stare was travelling in waves as red as his sunburned face.

Booya returned his interest to the performance of the dance troupe on the stage. A few moments later, he dared to look from the corner of his eyes. There was something familiar about that man that Booya could not place. Familiar like a bad dream of his youth.

Booya watched the stage for another minute or two. And then he again dared to turn his head towards the man. But he was gone. And so was the girl. Sounds of the picnic returned to him. Again he could smell the sweet scents.

On the bandstand, the dance troupe were acting out a tribal-style West

Indian dance, accompanied only by percussion; provocative, sexual. Men were dancing with the men, the women with the women. From the audience, the women gazed lustfully at the shirtless men, their hands hovering over their bosoms as they began to ripple their body against their own man's side. The men were drawling into their laps as they watched the women drop onto their backs and begin to gyrate with a skill, a suppleness, and obvious experience that they could only crave. They were thankful for the men upon the stage, distracting their wives and girlfriends so that they could watch the writhing women without being clipped behind the ear.

And then everything went black for Booya.

A pair of hands had covered his eyes. It was her! He knew it. It was the girl in the white dress covered with the big red dots. The *white* girl in the white dress.

Around Honahee and on the plantation, Booya had heard talk of jealous men killing a rival: a story he'd heard as often as he'd eaten hot food. He'd even heard Roots sing about it in one of his story songs. Normally it was told that it had been a black man killed by a black man over a feud caused by a black girl. The body was burned or buried and the sun would rise again the next morning. But if a white man kills a black man over a white girl, even just for her showing interest . . . It would be as natural as fruit growing on a branch. They said that no white would even think twice, so long as they got to see the cheating nigger twitch and die.

The feel of the hands over his eyes was like the rope already tightening around his neck; his airways impulsively constricting at the thought, panic rising.

'Don't want my little Cal seeing any of this,' the voice behind him said.

'He gone all stiff, see?' said a male voice. 'His back, I mean. Sitting upright. Stiff like a tree.'

Booya heard Mammy and Paw laughing. Paw had a tickle of that old loose tongue. Somehow he must have gotten his own way, if even just for a day. Mammy released her hands from Booya's eyes and rubbed his cheeks. 'Bristly.'

On the stage the men and women had coupled off to dance, with as much sexual intimation as ever, restricted only by their clothes. Booya breathed as if he had found air after hiding underwater for five minutes.

'You okay, Calvin?' Mammy asked. 'Look like you just waked from a nightmare. You ain't had one them in years now.'

'I is all right, Mammy. Just been sitting down too long.' Booya climbed up and stretched his back, towering over Mammy. 'Might go for walk around the place.'

'Find yo'self some girl to *dance* with, you saying,' Paw slurred.

Mammy slapped his arm.

Booya laughed with them. 'Yeah, Paw. Maybe I do that. Make you a grandpaw 'fore the end of the night.'

'Calvin Carthy!' Mammy gasped, crossing her hands over her huge chest. She narrowed her eyes. 'Don't you go getting none of that red-eye whisky from in them wagons, neither.'

Booya glanced at Paw.

'They ain't no good,' Mammy continued, 'them boys what is only interested in them wagons. You ain't got no business with them. Ain't that right, Cle?'

'Oh that's right, big mama. Won't be catchin' me hangin' with them fools.'

'Right,' Mammy said, rolling her eyes.

'Not 'less I brung my own cup,' Paw replied, wheezing a laugh.

Mammy slapped his arm again.

'How 'bout we do little dance of our own?' Paw said, taking hold of Mammy's considerable waist.

Booya smiled. 'Just going for a look-see, Mammy. Sure don't need to be seeing Paw dancing.' Booya nodded in the direction of the stage. 'Know what I saying?'

Mammy nodded and puckered her lips, allowing Paw to take hold of her. Paw winked and dragged her away, swinging his hips.

'Just take care, Cal,' she called over her shoulder.

As he walked around, Booya tried to absorb as much of the picnic as he could. The dance, it seemed, had been an invitation for men and women all over the picnic to grab their partner, or to begin coupling up with any available stranger. Booya could see couples walking away into the rising darkness, holding hands or fiddling at buttons. Wherever there was no lamplight to harass the shadows, couples fled, young and old.

Booya watched them go, increasing the pace of his heartbeat. Some of the dancers up on the stage were so beautiful . . . sensual. It was almost a foreign feeling, similar to the feeling he sometimes had after waking, when a pleasant dream crept up on him and . . .

'*Oouf!* Sorry there, man. Shoulda watched where I was going.'

Booya's hands sprung out defensively. 'Sorry, sir,' he said. 'Was my fault. I wasn't watching . . .'

'Spare a bit of change for my tin cup, son?'

The man was holding out his cup. A few dimes that already littered the bottom jangled around as the man rattled the cup.

Booya looked up at the man's face. He had long hair, white and straight, and native Indian features – a thin, straight nose and a heavy jawline – but his skin was much darker. Any other features were just a distraction from the appearance of the stranger's eyes. The lids were tightly wrinkled and red-rimmed, skin like squashed origami, folded in strange lines, hanging uselessly above the irises; the irises so clear and pale that they were almost blended with the yellowed whites. There was no way that the man could have seen where was going: he was obviously completely blind.

Booya realised that the blind Indian was smiling.

Shoulda watched where I was going . . .

He pulled out his pockets, as if the blind man could witness the truth. 'Sorry, man. Ain't got nothing.'

The Indian grunted and shuffled on, asking other strangers for any spare change.

Booya watched him go a little way, bumping into anyone who didn't move out of his way. As he watched, he thought he saw an old familiar face slip out of view. He walked through the crowd, speed increasing as he went, easing people out of his way. He was sure that it had been who he thought, hoped, it was. Someone he had thought of often over the past few years.

Booya pushed his way through. Some folks stepped clear from the path of the big man clearly on a mission. He saw the face again. It appeared, and then it dropped away once more.

He walked towards the wagons. Faces scowled as he ploughed through, though they might as well have been invisible. Booya wasn't going to let him get away without talking to him. If he was in the state that Booya guessed he'd be in, there was little chance of his target getting anywhere quickly.

Booya found him on the floor with his feet in the air, flailing like an upturned beetle.

'Need a hand up there, Roots?' Booya held out his hand.

'Huh?' Roots Cryer squinted, waving a hand vaguely upwards. 'Nee's a han' up'n a new set a legs. 'Haps git us a new pair'f eyes widout ca'racts whils' yo' gettin'.' He tried to lift his head off the floor. '*Uhh!* Git me jus' everthin' yo' got goin', stranger. Can start by gittin' me off a ma ass.'

Ignoring Roots' hand, Booya lifted him like a child and leaned Roots against a wagon. Some of the mean faces he'd bumped past glared. Muttering amongst themselves, they turned away. From somewhere beyond a copse of trees, along with the rustling of leaves, Booya heard a woman moaning with pleasure, a man's voice speaking low words to her.

'Too drunken to stand, huh, Roots?'

'Wha'f I is?' Roots snarled. 'Wha'f a preacher touch a gal chile? Does he forgit how't preach? Nuh-uh. An' da flower . . .' Roots' eyes wandered, then his head rolled forward.

Booya tried to work out Roots' meaning. He could find none.

'Hey! Roots . . .' He lifted Roots' head by the chin.

Roots groaned. 'Guh? If'n I gon' die, don' e'en worry 'bout de hoss.' His head dropped down again.

'Roots. It's me, Booya.'

'*Gurr* . . . de stable door . . . !'

Roots stopped blathering and slurring. Slowly, and with some effort, he lifted his head, thudding it heavily back against the frame of the wagon. Someone inside knocked back on the wood. Again, a few faces turned to see what was occurring.

'If he finds a chewed piece of potato in Roots' pocket he can consider himseff lucky,' someone said. Booya heard laughter. 'Might as well rob a dead toad.'

Roots' head lolled to one side, but he was looking up at Booya. In the yellow-red eyes, Booya could see the pasty clouds of cataracts. This man looked like he could be Roots' elderly father. Roots hardly opened his mouth as the words he muttered dribbled out – Booya wasn't sure if Roots had any teeth left behind those wrinkled lips.

'You really you, Boo?' he managed.

'Yeah, Roots. Haven't seen you in . . . 'bout three years gone by now.'

Roots was looking up the full length of Booya's tall, powerful body at the big friendly face. Booya crouched down to stop Roots sliding to the side. 'Three year s'it? I bin dead twice'n 'at time. An' look . . . now yo' grow up big'n. An' I shrunk down small'n e'er was.'

'Might be bigger these days, Roots, but I is still wearing the hat you give me. See?'

Roots grinned. He closed his eyes for a while, groaning with apparent ecstasy, and then opened them again. 'I 'member, yeah: *unner dis hat'n dis'n dat'n da shack,*' he sang. 'I 'member. We 'ad some times dere, sho. Don't got no hat fo' my ol' bowl'a bones no mo'. Cain't keep'un atop a my head fo' fallin' 'bout.'

Booya realised that he was almost pinning Roots to the wagon. He loosened his grip on Roots' shoulders. Roots began to slump down to one side. Booya resumed holding him. He took a quick look at the men Mammy had warned him about. They were still scowling and frowning at him in turns. A couple of them simply stared, not quite as impassive as the expressions they were wearing. Booya refocused on Roots.

'Where you been, Roots?'

Roots laughed. 'Ain't Roots no mo', big Boo. I jus' plain ol' Rusty dese day.'

'But where you been at all these years?'

'Um . . . I bin down a da . . . a da place, y'know? S'up runnin' 'gain.'

Roots was leaning his head back against the wagon. His eyes were closed. Booya could see the big, spiky Adam's apple moving as Roots spoke. It looked painful against the thin skin.

'I on'y ever did git lost in'n 'mong dat cotton. But it ain't like it was befo'. Ain't ne'er bin like it was befo'. All de nigger wid an' sense runned off from dat place. "Hellsfire" wha' we was callin' it. But we didn' none a us mind. We *loved* livin' in hell.' Roots opened his eyes. Suddenly he seemed to have perfect clarity. 'Don' never git wid da devil brew, Boo. He drug yo' down to da waste, like he done drug me. An' he lef' me nothin' but wasted. Don't let yo' beau'ful hand git idle by drinkin' like ol' Roots done, hear me say? Yo' da bes' li'l blueser I ever hear.'

The smell from Roots was like a pond of whisky had stagnated inside him, worse even than the first time he had met him on the Harris plantation. It was as rank as the smell of rotting death.

'You wanna come back and play sometime?' Booya asked. 'Come and see where we living. You can stay!'

Roots eyes were closed again. 'Yo' mean Rusty can come'n stay wid yo'n Cle? Cle still live?'

'He doing good, Roots. And he'd love to spend some time with you.'

Booya could still remember the different person that Paw had become when he had witnessed his drunken dance on their last day on the plantation. He tried not to remember. If Paw had chosen to stay that day – or maybe if he had been able to walk away that morning, rather than fall face-first into the dirt – Booya had no doubt that Paw would too have become the dribbling mess that Roots had.

The crowd began to cheer. Everyone began to shift towards the bandstand, crying out.

'Hear that, Roots? The band is starting up. The country blues band! Come with me. Paw's 'bout someplace. Come and have a time with us.'

Roots laughed in his throat. 'De coun'ry blues. Devil brew kilt ol' Roots fingers so 'e couldn e'en play his evil music no mo'.'

'Come on, man. I'll *carry* you if you want me to! Come with me and see Paw.'

Again, Roots growled a laugh. 'Uh-uh . . . cain't. Lay Rusty down 'ere a'whiles, Boo,' he mumbled, a blissful smile creating new creases in his wizened face. 'Gots ta res' ma head a whiles now. Come find ol' Rusty after an' he come wid ya den.'

Booya relaxed his grip on Roots' shoulders and gently lowered him to rest against the tall wagon wheel. He looked pitiful. 'You gonna be okay here, Roots?' he asked.

But Roots was already snoring, a guttural growl grinding through his chest, whistling through the gaps between his few remaining teeth.

2

Distracted by the blues band, the interest in and around the wagons had waned, visited only by folks refilling their cups. In the audience, the sexually suggestive dances and grinds had grown. No longer acting surreptitiously, it seemed now that almost everyone was holding a cup.

Over the heads of the crowd, seeing the stage clearly, Booya smiled. He could see a big, fat blues boy sitting on a chair. The guitar perched upon his stomach looked like a toy. The man standing next to him was blowing a harmonica, bowed one moment and then jumping in the air, thumping his foot wildly, as though a poison fever was driving him crazy. Almost hidden from Booya by the chubby guitarist, a drummer was pushed into one corner of the stage, paying out a vendetta on the drums, shouting as he abused them, a devilish and maniacal grin on his face. Towards the back a tall, skinny man was pounding a double bass, sucking his cheeks, thoughtfully watching something invisible move through the night air as he pummelled the strings. If a guitar were a child, Booya thought, then this instrument was the uncle. Watching the meditative pace of the double bass man one moment, and then the long and chunky fingers of the chubby blues boy's hands the next, one pair of eyes was barely enough.

'Y'all having a good time?' the blues boy asked after they finished the song, nodding and smiling and sweating as the crowd hollered their approval. 'Good to be back in Honahee, y'know. Been a while, yep. But like with my baby doll, no matter how long you been away for, whatever you been doing, you *always* gots to go back, right?'

The crowd cheered, clapped and heckled.

'My name is Levee Banks,' he said. 'And this here's the Ol' Creek Stompers.'

Someone at the front yelled something that Booya couldn't hear.

'Not quite that way, lady. But ax them yourself. Mostly they stomp anything they get they paws on, right fellas?' Levee exchanged words with the band. They were all grinning and nodding. 'This next song is dedicated to any Yankees might be here today. This number called *Take Yo' Hands Off My Begging Bowl.*'

White and black, the crowd applauded frantically, whistling and crying their appreciation. The band started the song to the pace of sprinting down a steep hill.

Booya was looking everywhere he possibly could at once. Everywhere he looked, people were lost to everything but the music and the person they were holding in their arms. It felt indecent to watch what some couples were doing – writhing and crawling all over each other – but he was helpless to look away. The whites who had stayed to watch the blues band from their side of the bandstand were smiling, even laughing as they swayed with their partner. Booya didn't realise that he too was wearing the biggest smile across his face. And then something grabbed his hand. So small was the hand, so light the touch; it was gently tugging.

She looked like a daisy growing through blacktop. His thoughts were as drunk as the folks swinging all around him. At first he could barely wonder why a white girl was this side of the bandstand.

'Quick,' she said. 'Come.' She tugged on his hand once more.

He looked down at her, looking up at him, only halfway up his chest. The cold look on her face reminded him of the expression George often used to wear. He wondered if he knew this girl from somewhere – you don't forget a face so pretty – but he couldn't place it. To be tugging at him that way with her little bit of strength, it was obvious that she recognised him. With terror constricting his heart, Booya realised who she was. Even before the wild, native dancing had begun, it was when stumbling upon her stare earlier that day that the pilot light of impossible passion had first lit inside him.

She was wearing a black woollen cardigan above her dress. But in the shadow at the knees, he could see the big red polka dots on the white cotton. Now that the sun had gone down she was no longer wearing her straw hat, her black hair full and bouncy. She was wearing lipstick as bright as the red polka dots, such a startling contrast to the white skin and dark hair.

'Will you please come?' she whispered, pouting like a scorned child. 'Are you *trying* to make trouble for yourself?'

A smiling man of about Paw's age looked them both up and down. 'Think you better be doing what the lady says, don't you, buddy?'

With leaden feet, Booya began trudging in whatever direction she wanted to pull him. A suffocating lump in his throat, his earlier fears again began to tighten around his neck.

She didn't speak another word as they moved away from the crowd and towards the waiting darkness. She led Booya quickly towards the wagons, tugging harder. She pulled back the canvas cover of one of the wagons and leaned inside. Within seconds, she slipped backwards with a full cup of Moonshine in each hand. The group of black faces around the wagon stared with open mouths. A bodiless head peered out around the canvas with a quizzical look on his face. As Booya was led towards the shadows he prayed that Mammy and Paw were dancing by the stage.

'Can I ax your name?' Booya managed to ask.

'You can ask,' she said, glaring through her thickly made-up eyes. 'But that don't mean that I'm going to tell you.'

'Do I . . . know you from someplace?'

She laughed and turned her eyes to Booya, amusement clear on her face. She was immaculately beautiful. With her haughtiness wiped from her face, looking into her eyes was like looking up at a perfect starry sky on a clear night.

'I *don't* think so.' She continued to smile. 'Come on, big man. Don't be so slow. We ain't got long.'

Her hand was so small and delicate in his, but her control was complete. He remembered when he used to try and catch butterflies in Mister Henry's orchard. They were hard to catch, but when you did you had to treat them so gently. That's what it felt like, his big rough hand encircling hers.

'You ain't got any venereal diseases, do you?' she asked. 'And don't lie to me. I shall know if you're lying.'

'Uh . . . ? No,' he answered. 'I is fine.'

She laughed. 'Good. Come. In here.' She pulled Booya into a space between the low hanging branches of a cluster of winged elms.

He could barely see her in the dark. He could make out only the dress and the occasional patch of white skin, so white it could have been the dress. In the dim light he watched her lifting her knees as she carefully removed her tiny panties. He watched as she hung them with precision upon a bough. Struck dumb, he hadn't allowed himself to think fully of what the white girl's intentions were. But it was happening right before his eyes.

'You just going to stand and watch, big boy?' She stood with a hand on her hip. 'I already told you we ain't got long.'

Booya didn't know if he should allow that deep, wonderful feeling inside him to rise, embrace it, or pray to the Lord for forgiveness before he joined Him – as he surely would in the very near future. White girls and black men just weren't supposed to be, that he knew. The girl picked up her cup from the ground and daintily sipped the fiery brew. Booya poured the entire contents of the other cup down his throat. It made his eyes water. It made his stomach shudder in complaint, rising into his throat until it warmed and relented. It steadied and controlled his energy. If she tried to get away from him now, she wouldn't get far.

'Need me to give you a hand there?' She rolled her eyes. 'Jesus! Come here.' She undid the buttons on his pants and helped him out. 'Oh *my*! What a good pick I am.'

Booya allowed the tiny hands to push his chest towards the floor.

'Get on the ground. I don't want to get any filthy dirt on me.'

She pushed him to the ground and straddled him. Inexperience lent him no problems – and she was certainly not. Booya was perfectly ready for her by the time she guided him, lowering herself down with a moan and a gasp. He could hear that she was doing just fine by him – he had never heard such low language coming from any lady.

She pushed down on his stomach as he lifted her up. She was helpless in attempting to stifle her satisfied, deeply pleasured squeals and groans. Lost in the moment. The fear of being caught forgotten. Booya wanted more of her.

'Don't touch my skin,' she breathed.

Though his head was swirling, Booya could hear people all around them, passing them by or hidden further along in the trees. No one paid any interest to any other couples, so long as they were going to have their own way.

Her warmth so soft, a rose petal moistened by dew. Her gently muscular strength like her language, keen to overpower his strength as near as she could.

'My . . . *Gawd*,' she huffed. 'You work like a mule, don't ya?'

'I guess,' Booya grinned, holding her by the waist, gently lifting and using her.

'You guess, huh?' Gripping a branch above her, she paused for a moment . . . then pushed both hands on his chest, emitted a low puff of air on a soft moan, and patted his chest. Her hand lingered for a moment. She picked up the cup from behind her and took another ladylike sip.

'You want some?' she asked raising her long, thin eyebrows.

'Uh-huh.'

'Finish it if ya like,' she said, watching him curiously.

In one massive mouthful, Booya finished the whisky. It shot through him, shaking his body. It felt as though in the last five minutes he'd fallen some way into the earth. The girl eased herself off him and carefully stepped into her underwear. With the afterglow of passion cooling in the air, Booya just lay there. He eased himself onto an elbow. 'When can I see you again?' he asked.

'Aren't you gonna, uh, do yourself up there?' she asked, indicating. 'I helped him out, but I ain't putting him back, partner.'

He did as she said and sat up.

'Axed when I can see you again.'

Having finished brushing herself down, she turned sharply on Booya, hissing as she spoke. 'Don't be so stupid and immature. We both know what this was: I wanted something; turned out you had it.'

'Didn't you like it, though?'

'Well . . . yes, of course I *liked* it, but . . . Just stop asking me questions. If I want to see you again then maybe I will.' She scoffed. 'But that is highly unlikely. So don't go thinking any stupid thoughts in that big head of yours.'

Booya thought of all the other serpentine bodies moving together at the picnic. There were plenty of other women about who could tease this new sensation from him. And if they felt anywhere near as comfortable as this girl had . . .

'Sure is.' He jumped up.

She took a step back and stared up at him. From what Booya could read in the darkness, the girl looked both scared and arch. And then she smiled.

'I had a good time here,' she said, fluttering her eyelashes – just as she had earlier that day, the first of her feminine snares.

As they stood there, standing and staring at each other, a voice began calling from beyond the trees. '*Maisy!*'

'Oh shit!' she spat.

'That you?' Booya whispered. 'Maisy?'

'Uh-huh,' she replied. 'And *that's* my old man calling me. Look, I'm sure I don't need to tell you, but if you ever say anything about this and it gets out it will cause more trouble for you than it could ever cause me, you know what I'm saying? They'll hang you if this ever comes out. My husband happens to be friendly with the law.'

'Take care of yourself, Maisy,' Booya said, holding out a hand to her.

'You big dope.' She pulled his head down and kissed him on the lips. 'Ain't never kissed a black man before,' she said. A strange smile began to bloom on one side of her bright red lips. Leaving him with a soft chuckle, she was away, brushing through the trees.

Ain't never kissed *a black man before*, Booya thought, smiling.

He waited a couple of minutes before leaving the trees through a different cluster of branches. As he wandered towards the site of the picnic he felt like a new man; maybe felt like a man for the first time. He was warm inside. And in his trousers was a strangely comfortable reminder. And then he remembered Roots.

'Oh shit!'

The crowd had thinned out. Couples were creeping out of the shadows, to slow dance to the new pace of the band, or to seek out a new partner for the night. There was life in the picnic yet. For some there was no point having a night without seeing the sun rise.

When Booya arrived by the wagon that he was sure he'd left Roots slumped beside, Roots was nowhere to be seen. Further along, men were still standing around the wagon. Booya recognised them as those he'd seen earlier, joined by a few new faces. One of them caught the direction of his stare.

'Hey, man,' Booya said.

'S'up?' the man replied. The entire group, maybe twelve of them, turned to face Booya.

His confidence slipping for a second, he looked around at the unfriendly faces. Most of these men wore scars on their faces and murderous looks in their eyes. They were almost certainly the "crazy niggers with the sun-fried minds" that he had heard about, those who lived on the old plantation. Roots' home.

'I, uh . . . Any of you know Roots Cryer? Left him lying down here by the wagon 'bout a hour ago.'

'Yeah, I know Roots,' replied the man who had been staring. He addressed the gang. 'Hey, anybody seen Rusty?'

'I seed him lying they.' The man indicated the spot by the wheel where Booya had left him. 'Man, he was passed out in a bad way.'

'Some ol' dude come an' take him off, think,' someone else said.

'Thanks,' Booya said, trying his hardest to smile. 'Promised to come back. Then when I come back . . . Well. He ain't here!'

A couple of the gang laughed.

'Dat ol' Rusty. Reliable as a bucket wid holes in.'

Twisting his lips, smiling and nodding, Booya began to walk away.

'Hey!' someone called after him. 'Big man!'

Booya turned to them.

'Wanna join us for a little . . . drink?'

Booya stopped. He looked at the men for a moment and then glanced back over his shoulder, away from the wagons into the darkness of the night. He looked towards the stage; most of the people he saw were young couples.

'Err . . . yeah, why not?' he said, accepting the cup. And it tasted good. He had finally found the nasty smell he loved. Angel's kisses.

'Say, friend,' said the man who had passed him the cup. 'Wha's yo' name?'

'Booya Carthy.'

'Booya, huh? Good name, man.'

'You play da easy rider, Booya Carthy?' one of the gang asked, holding up a guitar by the neck.

'Guitar? Sure, I play,' Booya answered.

'Well . . . play den.'

Booya set down the cup and took the guitar. He strummed it a few times. It was way out of tune. He quickly tuned it up, just the way that Roots had shown him.

'Hey, someone fill the man's cup.'

'He drunked dat a'ready? Jesus!'

As Booya began to play, the members of the gang looked at one another with eyebrows raised.

'Dis better dan anythin' been on da stage today,' whispered one of the gang, his friend nodding agreement.

Booya started singing and the friend stopped mid-nod.

3

The first thing Booya saw when he opened his eyes was a dirty ceiling above him. The ground was hard. His neck and back ached; it hurt to straighten both out. His eyelids were stuck together. He wiped a hand down his face; crusted dirt crumbled from his fingers. It was his head that hurt most of all, painful pressure with each pulse of his heart. The touch of his fingers felt foreign, senseless, as if they belonged to someone else. His throat was raw as grit. His stomach was empty and tight, churning like a cotton gin. But there was no mistaking the sound of splashing water.

When he sat up, Booya's stomach lifted all the way to his throat. He leaned forward and vomited between his legs, too weak to move his legs out of the way. He groaned and curled up his knees, trying to remember a single thing about himself.

Mister Booya Carthy.

They had been at the picnic, he, Mammy and Paw. There had been sweet-smelling food and music and dancers . . .

He rubbed the back of his head where it was throbbing. It was beating at his temples, too.

His stomach lurched.

The sound of splashing in the water was ducks. Through his crusted eyes, he could see them now, swimming from beneath the shadow of the old wooden bridge and into the fine day. Though the sound of water was quite refreshing, compared to the writhing snake pit inside his head, the world wasn't suffering with him. If he didn't feel so very weak perhaps he would have joined the ducks in the water. Pure liquid.

And then the memory of the girl came back to him. The *white* girl.

What had he done?

Booya ran a hand around his neck. He couldn't feel any rope burns or ligatures.

He'd left her – or, she'd left him – and he'd joined up with the men from the Harris plantation, the men that Mammy said were "crazy and wild" but had been perfectly friendly to him. He'd played their guitar, their *easy rider*. How long he'd played for he could in no way remember, but his fingers were thrumming as if they had their own battered brains.

There had been more girls. He couldn't remember their faces so much as he remembered that delicious feeling, wanting more and more of it, giving more and more, feeding that feeling more fiery fuel. Soon there had been crowds of girls gathered alongside the crazy men, listening to him playing guitar and singing. And then he'd become like the white girl. He could remember now. He'd put down the guitar and pick whatever girl he wanted, the crazy men encouraging him, cheering him on.

What had been going through his head?

He'd thought that ache in his groin was another side effect of drinking.

So, he'd left the white girl – she'd left him – and there were the crazy men and the easy rider, the drinking and the girls . . .

What had led him to hook up with that questionable crowd?

Roots!

Hadn't that one guy with the mean, scarred face said that a man had taken Roots off? That man must surely have been Paw.

Booya eased himself up, bitterly thinking that a lesser man wouldn't have so much trouble lifting their more meagre frame. He took a moment to stand, watching the river flow. At least the world seemed to be moving at a slow enough pace today.

It was only then that he'd realised where he'd chosen to sleep. This was the bridge that he and Mammy and Paw had slept beneath on the night that they had left the Harris plantation, on the day that they left the world-gone-insane behind them. Booya couldn't remember making the decision to sleep here last night, nor whether it had been a decision made by night or if the sun had already been rising to shine.

Stumbling as he went, he pulled himself up the steep riverbank, tenderly patted down his hat and trudged slowly on down the road towards home.

*

The work that he and Paw had done over the years on their claimed patched of land had created quite a homestead for them. They had rendered and extended their original cabin, built using materials reclaimed from derelict barns and buildings, to create separate bedrooms, a parlour, even a storeroom for surplus vegetables and the preserves that Mammy like to make and store away. Outside, they had a vegetable patch as big as they'd ever had, as plentiful as they'd wished to make it. Along a path cleared behind the house, in a clearing where previously only wild berries had grown, a few fruit trees, grown from seed, had begun to bear fruit. The chickens – Mister Henry and Lemon Jeff – had died from age, plaintively spared the pot, and buried. They had been replaced by a new batch of a dozen bantam hens, keeping the shelves in the storeroom loaded with eggs. Paw had even acquired a mule – named Mister Wilbur by Booya. Mister Wilbur was allowed to wander free in the land beyond the house, choosing to spend most of his time in the clearing. The truth was that they had little use for Mister Wilbur, except for at winter when they gathered masses of wood for the stove.

Paw worked the land and Mammy had got a job at Huck's Place, one of the county stores in Honahee. Every morning Paw walked with Mammy to her job in town. And then he'd walk back to fetch her in the evening, patiently waiting on the stoop outside Huck's until Mammy finished work for the day. Booya would stay back at the homestead, playing guitar in the clearing, entertaining Mister Wilbur, the birds and the open sky. Mammy's job enabled them to buy the little that they needed: warm clothes for winter, fresh meat, seeds and guitar strings. Paw had *acquired* some pieces of furniture, including the wooden chairs that he and Mammy were sitting on when Booya trudged off the road and onto the homestead, hidden from the road and the world by bushes and trees.

Paw chuckled when he saw him. 'Find much out 'bout the world last night, Boo?'

Booya smiled at him. He had expected trouble and was not disappointed: it was writ large all over Mammy's face. He tried to stand as erect as possible but couldn't stop his tired and aching shoulders from slumping.

Rather than sit and stare at him that way, Booya wished that Mammy would just say something. At least she'd call Paw names out loud when she was telling him off. The years had been kind to her. She had not a single line or wrinkle on her round face, her skin as plump and vibrant as a teenager's. Aging had only taken a toll on her withering hands. After years spent living from the land, when they had first left the Harris plantation, famine had slimmed her stout body. But now she was more generously covered than she had ever been, the flesh of her chubby thighs and backside spilling over the edges of the chair.

'I know that look,' she said eventually. 'Calvin Carthy, I know that look. Don't think you can hide it from me. Ain't got nothing to say, huh? Just look at your boots?'

Booya looked up to Paw for help. Paw shrugged.

'I had a time, Mammy.'

'You had a time,' she repeated, nodding her large head.

'Go easy on him, Adie,' Paw said.

'Oh yes, the great Cleveland Carthy,' Mammy said, turning on Paw. 'A'course you know all 'bout *having a time* your bad self, don't you? See what your influence has had on our son?'

'C'mon, mama. He ain't a chile no more. And you yourself was . . .'

Mammy's glare left Paw as trapped as a fish on land. He held her stare, but was gutless to challenge it.

With Paw defeated, sighing heavily Mammy turned again on Booya. 'Listen, Cal, I understand that you got to go your own way. I do. Ain't no one else what can make your decisions for you, good and bad. But you don't got to end up like this old fool. Just understand that they is some dangerous rivers to ride in this life. And they dangerous enough without riding on the river of Moonshine. Men what ride them rivers ain't no good. They ain't no good, and they headed downstream, caught in the flow, and ain't never coming back. This old fool here,' she cocked her head toward Paw, 'he lucky enough to have a woman like me to throw a rope round his scrawny old neck, pull him back to the bank when he be in trouble.'

Biting his bottom lip, Paw just stared at the vegetable patch.

'But the rest them fools is all headed over the edge, where they ain't no one to save them. Just think, and think hard 'fore you step on that river. Understand what I is saying, Calvin?'

Too tired to understand much, the nod that Booya tried to summon would not come. As best he could, he meagerly indicated that he understood what she had said.

'Good. Just understand that.' She placed her hands on her thighs and leaned forward. 'Now, you hungry?'

Booya's stomach jumped with keen vigour, and then as quickly cowered deep into his guts, whimpering. 'I, uh, wouldn't mind setting my head down a while first, Mammy.'

'Hmm . . . Well, all right. Fix y'up something later.' She managed a half-smile. 'Say, Cal, you see that Levee Banks and them Battered Stompers – whatever they called – last night?'

'Yeah, Mammy. He can play like anything. Him and his band.' And then he remembered. 'Hey, Paw!'

Vanishing into Mammy's life lesson, Paw jumped in his chair, startling himself.

'Where's Roots at?' Booya asked.

'Old boy Roots Cryer? Rusty? Hee-hee, ain't thought 'bout him in time. What you mean?'

Booya couldn't stop the beat of his sore heart from slowing, suddenly scared for Roots and the state he'd left him in. 'You mean, you didn't find him at the picnic, help him back here?'

'Nuh-uh. Didn't even see him.'

'But . . .' With his glands struggling to life on the walk home, Booya's mouth had regained some semblance of lubrication. Now it was as dry as when he had awoken beneath the bridge. He tried to swallow the foul taste. 'See him there at the picnic, Paw. He was, uh, in, uh . . . a bad way.' Both men flickered a glance at Mammy. 'Say to him he could come back and stay. You know, to help him up on his feet a bit. But I leave him a while . . .' Calvin felt his skin heating up at the thought of being lured away by the white girl. His words stuck in his throat and his groin squirmed. 'When I come back to find him Roots weren't there no more. Some fella say Roots'd been helped off. Guessed it was you what helped him.'

Paw shook his head. 'Like I say, didn't even catch a sniff of him. Man, if I knowed he was there . . .'

Mammy beat Paw back with a glowering scowl.

'Like to say Howdy to old Rusty, s'all I was aiming to say, woman,' Paw replied. 'But I didn't even see him, Boo. Old Roots Cryer. How long's it been since we tipped a cup?'

Mammy glowered at Booya. 'Was it Roots get you in this state?' she asked, her voice a tone deeper.

'No, Mammy . . .' Booya stopped his hand from reaching his aching crotch. 'No, it weren't. Roots was already on the floor when I see him.'

Paw chuckled, saw Mammy's expression, and frowned.

'Wonder what happened to him then, if it weren't Paw.'

'You best not ever knowing is my guess,' Mammy said. 'He sailed a long way down that Fool's River.'

'Poor ol' Rusty,' Paw added. 'Ol' Roots Cryer. He sure always did have a weakness.'

In the clearing, Mister Wilbur was snuffling through the long grass. Flies were buzzing around him, landing on his face and eyelashes. With the patience of spring, Mister Wilbur paid them no mind. A selection of maples, cypresses, chinquapins and ashes hugged the clearing. Unlike woodlands of pines, the neon-glow green leaves lit up the clearing with an almost preternatural light. It was chorusing with song and chatter. The scent of the trees mingled with the wild forest flowers and swirled peacefully on a gentle breeze.

As he munched on a juicy pear, Booya thought that waking under the bridge had been as fine and peaceful a place as the clearing – all of the tumultuous noise had been trapped inside his head. Today he felt as refreshed as the air after rainfall. Mammy's well-practiced hangover feed of bread and meat, coupled with a long night's sleep, had worked its black magic.

Booya recalled how, when they had first arrived, he had wandered far and near to find fruit he could steal. On one of his scrumping missions he had climbed over a split-rail fence and crept into a well-kept garden – though nothing like as exotic and plentiful as Mister Henry's. Again he had been led, but this time it was the fruit that had been calling to him.

The orchard he found was the property of a Yankee sawmill owner. He had come down south to cash in on the continuous growth of the southern towns and cities, settling into the rubble; there for the money, and nothing else. Unlike many of the immigrant "carpetbagger" Yankees before him, he both feared and hated the blacks. He was a so-called Copperhead: named after a venomous snake, a nickname given to Democratic sympathisers. Many times he had said to his friends and workers, to any white who had an ear within his radar, or any black worker who he wished deliberately to demean: "The only time I'd ever talk to a nigger is to tell him which direction he can find a plague. I've never spoken to one, and I never will. Don't know how my foremen do it without ripping their heads off, spending whole days under the same roof as them animals. Don't even like sharing the same sky. But I'll use them to make me money. Yes, sir. They work for nothing, and mostly they know their place. Yep, just waiting for any excuse to blow the head off one of 'em. Just imagine! No matter how many deer and rabbits I ever shot, I can't wait to bag me a nigger. Day can't come soon enough. Season's always open on a nigger, far as I'm concerned."

Booya was fortunate that the day he was caught in the sawmill owner's orchard it was by his wife. No less racist than her husband, but at least she didn't tote a shotgun, willing a black man into her sights, as she walked around her husband's land. She had shot unmentionable abuse at Booya that day, but no lead.

So it had been years since Booya had eaten fruit picked fresh from the branch. It tasted as good as it ever had. He flicked the stem away into the grass, picked up his guitar and started to gently pick the strings. It came effortlessly to him these days, even with his fingers tender and viciously calloused after the night of the picnic.

The world beyond the road on the other side of their homestead had never held much interest to Booya – especially since he'd been chased away from the orchard by that crazy-eyed white woman, yelling nigger-this and nigger-that. Now the world was wide and full of new wonders, even if they didn't all shine like gold.

He walked through the avenue of trees that lead back to the homestead to find Paw stooped over, planting seeds in a neat line in the vegetable garden.

'Hey, Paw.'

Paw fell to his knees and clutched his chest. 'Shit, Boo! Damn! Scare the life outta me. You trying to kill yo' ol' man, or something?'

Paw put a hand on the base of his spine, straightening his stiff back, and groaned. The chickens were gathered around his feet, trying to get at the seeds he had sown. He stamped in the middle of them. 'Go on now, git!' The chickens fluttered away from his foot, pretending for a moment or two to have no interest, before cautiously edging closer to the seed once more. 'Come to give your ol' man a helping hand, Boo?'

'Mammy down at the Huck's Place today, Paw?' Booya kicked at the dirt.

'Uh-huh,' Paw nodded, rotating his shoulders to stretch his aches. 'Walk her down to Hon'ee myself this morning,' he said. 'Want to do all this as a surprise for her 'fore I go fetch her back.'

'It's just . . . I was thinking, Paw,' Booya said, swinging his guitar, avoiding eye contact with Paw, 'I might go down to Honahee and see her at Huck's.'

Sticking the tip of his tongue out his mouth, Paw eyed Booya. 'Sure you ain't aiming to go and *bump* into some girl or other?'

Still swinging his guitar, Booya smirked. 'Not one girl, Paw, *all* them girls.'

'Heh-heh-heh. You go get 'em all, Boo. And tell yo' mama that I is coming to get *her* later.'

'Sure, Paw.' Booya read behind Paw's smiling eyes. '*Aw*, Paw!'

'Heh-heh-heh. Git outta here, you mangy chickens,' Paw shouted, stamping his foot. 'I tole ya'll ready: git! Ain't telling y'gain. Or I is making soup.'

*

This was the first time that Booya had ever walked to town alone. The world looked different. It was as bright and dry as it ever was, but a new tone was in everything that he could see and hear. It was like a thousand field hands were all humming a cheery melody at the peak of summer, the clomp of his boot steps keeping a perfect time. He saw an eagle glide silently overhead, its head tilted at a slight angle, scouring the fields for prey.

When Booya came to the bridge he felt compelled to stop and look. It was a wooden-slatted bridge, the colour grey by decay. It looked as though it would struggle to bear the weight of a mule and cart. In the field on the far side, rutted tracks made by cartwheels had worn a deep groove through the dirt leading to the bridge. Booya was standing on the two-year old blacktop that ran all the way into town. It was as though on one side of the river was the old country that Mammy and Paw had told him about over the years, the fields that held secrets of death and destruction, secrets it would mercifully never yield, lifetimes hidden beneath corn and cotton. But on this side of the river was a world eager to move on. A world where honey-coloured voices poured from golden horns. Booya wondered who might have walked over that bridge throughout its lifetime, stepping out of the old world and into the new. And he was still wondering as he continued along the new road that led to Honahee.

5

The streets of Honahee were paved with shambling, uneven granite setts – another time-weary contrast to the finish of the blacktop at the town's perimeter – but when Booya saw the new gas station he raised his eyebrows, wondering how employed it could ever be. Of all the things that surprised him, nothing surprised Booya more than the motorcars bumping along the streets. The cars were mostly black, but there were a few that were as green as figs, and some as purple as ripening blueberries, all of them gleaming and new. The weathered town around them reflected in the highly polished panels. All around him, everything seemed to have matured and grown almost beyond recognition, exacerbated by the aging facades.

During previous excursions into the town his surroundings had proved of little interest. But now Booya was looking at the world through new eyes, where every sight to behold held a newly imagined story. It was curious that the whisky had made Booya's eyes clearer when it had drawn red lines all over the yellowed whites of Paw's eyes, and turned Roots' cloudy and half-blind. In the town, the same people were plying the same trades, but now they mostly had proper stores to sell them from, rather than the rickety stalls of old. And it was apparent that the gradual makeover had served Honahee well. The stores and the streets were packed with people.

It seemed to have all grown from around the General Store, which still looked as decrepit as Booya remembered it. As he passed, Booya looked in through the tall glass window of the barbershop. There were men standing along the back wall, more men sitting in the line of barber's chairs. Including the barber, they were all laughing. One of the men inside was picking at a guitar as he laughed along. It struck Booya as strange that the man in the chair in front of the barber was wearing a hat. The barber said something to the gathered men and, out in the street, Booya could hear more responses of laughter. The barber continued to snip away beneath the rim of the hat. Booya tipped the derby forward on his head.

Further along, every other building seemed to be a barrelhouse or juke joint. They mostly looked no more glorified than a badly painted barn. If the building had ground-level windows they were likely to be painted over. The signs hanging outside were of piano keys, guitars, trumpets or jukes with the name of the bar painted over them, the music blaring out of each door competing with the next. Some played country-style music, bluegrass, typically melodic and upbeat. The most popular sound from the joints was the brassy, jumping sound of jazz, blasting out louder than the others could compete with. Through one door the music must have been coming from a live band – Booya could hear the cheering; a bandleader or singer encouraging the unseen crowd to cheer even louder. But lilting through the air to Booya, like the smell of meat to a hungry man, came the sound of the blues. *'I belie-eve, I believe my time ain't long,'* came the voice. The tenor of the voice sounded almost white, but Booya knew that there's no white man who sings that way unless he's trying to sound black. There was no doubting that the singing man knew the blues.

On the black wooden guitar hanging from the front of the shabby building was a name painted in white. The name of the joint – Booya assumed it was the name, not just a statement blaring as loud as a jazz trumpet – was *Blacks*.

A few paces on there was another new building. A long, thin building, stretching far back from the street. It stood out for two reasons: it was built out of bricks and, as well as on a swinging sign, the name was printed on the inside of the window. *Stanza Studios*. It was at least as popular as the barbershop. Through this window, everyone that Booya could see was clutching an instrument. Just as he was about to look away, a small white man in a suit, holding a piece of paper, walked through an interior door and began to address the sitting and standing men. Unlike in the barbershop, there didn't seem to be much joy inside that building.

Booya walked past some new clothes stores. They didn't just display the clothes for workers and country folk – you could buy all those things at stores like Huck's Place, where Mammy worked – there were smartly stitched suits like the white man in Stanza Studios had been wearing, and jackets similar to the ones Mister Henry had worn. With those items on display, Booya thought that the owner was fortunate that his window was still in one piece, gleaming where it should be, and not in pieces all over the floor of his empty store. But then the brick buildings at the end of this street would surely act as a deterrent to anyone thinking of thieving clothes.

The courthouse was as much a showpiece of the town as was the town hall. They stood opposite each other, glaring imperiously over the town square. It was a sober reminder to all who walked into the courthouse what that square piece of land signified.

In the gardens of the square, the decision to leave the hanging tree standing as the centrepiece had not been as contentious a subject as perhaps it should have been for the town planners. Once could say that the hanging tree was the true centrepiece for the town to grow around. It was estimated that more than a thousand men had choked their last breath from those iconic branches. The square and gardens were officially called Redemption Square, but were quietly better known as Justice Square by the whites, and Persecution Square by the blacks. It had been nearly fifteen years since the last pair of swaying feet had blown in the breeze. It was simply known by most as Death Square. Whatever was the chosen name, the tree had remained redundant since the erection of the gallows behind the closed doors of the jailhouse.

The other buildings around the square housed the jailhouse and a bank, the house of the town mayor and houses of affluent whites – solicitors, doctors, business owners, judges – their servant quarters standing in the walled land behind. Redemption Square and the houses surrounding it were so different in grandeur to the rest of the town it might as well have been its own tiny county. Beyond the square the street continued as a symmetrical reflection of the road that Booya had walked through. The brick buildings quickly became wooden trade-stores – the few surviving stores that were as old as Honahee – one of which was Huck's Place.

Huck's was an old wood-built house that, over the years, had been converted into a store. There was a time when it would have been one of the grandest sites to see if one had travelled the local area for a week. It no longer had the picket fence that walked around its grounds, but the stoop that ran the length of the building remained, welcoming customers like it was still the warm house it had once been. Lovingly restored and preserved over the years, Huck's was as much a part of Honahee as the town name.

The General Store on the other side of town was Huck's main rival, undercutting Huck's on products that it had no demand to keep, just to draw people through its doors. But Huck's Place had a loyal clientele, even if the General Store drew more custom.

This side of town was considered to be the more genteel side. The barrelhouses and juke joints on the other side of town attracted folk that this side of the town declared it didn't really wish to trade with anyway, thank-you-very-much. Huck's Place and the General Store were standing apart like a pair of old spinsters, one refined and one frivolous, both scornful and disdainful of the other's attributes. Unlike the two spinsterish stores, Honahee was a town that couldn't decide what it wanted to be. And the cultural divide had forced it to remain that way.

Sound of fife and drum snaked down the street. More of a battle song to march to than it was a dancing song, it sounded like it required a crowd of people to make the amount of noise that Booya was approaching. Coming to stand in front of Huck's, when Booya saw who was creating all the noise at first he was shocked. And then he couldn't help but smile.

A girl of no more than thirteen, with long dark hair riding down past the waist of her dirty red dress, her skin the unwashed colour of pine wood, was rapping at a drum hanging on a strap around her neck, simultaneously kicking the skin of a big bass drum on the floor in front of her with her bare feet. The sticks were moving in a blur; each kick of her foot in perfect time.

In front of the bass drum, swooning and swaying back and forth as he blew on his fife, was a tiny little boy, only a little taller than the drum beside him. There was clearly something not quite right about him: his legs were stumpy, his fingers were round, his neck was non-existent, and he looked as though he was wearing a melted rubber mask. He seemed as though he'd been squashed down rather than grown that way, marching with his feet and legs apart as if he was wearing an intrusive diaper. It was funny that, in spite of his appearance, he held himself with a certain self-importance, with his nose pointed in the air as he waddled along in his tiny red-checked suit. His face could either have been that of a wise eight-year-old or an immature eighteen-year-old, but was as pleasing as it was captivating to look upon. He certainly knew how to blow that fife.

Folks sitting and watching from the stoop of Huck's Place shared both humour and frustration. The immense noise that these two little individuals were making, albeit entertaining, was most definitely obtrusive.

The girl bashed away with determination. The boy glided like a swan through the street, lost in sincerity. With a final glance, Booya walked up the steps, over the stoop and into Huck's.

Huck's Place acted as grocer, butcher and bakery – the warm smell of bread the most prevalent smell in the store. Huck's sold vegetables, fruit and seeds, tinned and packet food, plates, bowls, cutlery and crockery, cleaning soaps and toiletries, animal feed, equestrian tack, labouring clothes and boots, garden tools, ropes, logs and coal, rugs and blankets. Huck's Place hadn't fled at the first site of the General Store coming over the horizon like, folks still joked about with bitter drollery, the Confederate Generals Lee and Hood had when they saw the Union Army approaching. Huck's had embraced the battle with a doughty chest.

Booya strolled around the aisles with his hands in his pockets. Even inside, the sound of fife and drum livened the packed shelves. Without noticing, a hand wandered free of his pocket to play with the buttons on his shirt. A kneeling lady, loading tins on to a shelf, stopped what she was doing and stared at Booya. She began to stand as he ambled along the aisle towards her. Sensing her glare, Booya turned his gaze. He recognised her defensive poise, ceased fiddling with his buttons and stopped in his step, facing each other like duellists. He wasn't sure why he began to feel guilty.

'Can I help you?' she asked.

Noticing that her hands were clenched to fists, Booya didn't really know what to say.

'If they ain't nothing you is aiming to *buy* you can just go on and leave.'

'I, uh . . . I was looking for Mammy.' Lips curling, her face began to soften. 'I mean, Adeline. Adeline Carthy?'

'Adeline?' The woman's stony face cracked almost instantly. She transformed completely, becoming girlish all of a sudden, playing with the hem of her apron. 'Say, you ain't her Calvin, is you? Her boy with stardust in his fingers?'

'Yes, ma'am.' Booya felt his cheeks warming.

'Well, I heared so much 'bout you. Adie talk 'bout you all day, ever day. Say you is as good a gee-tar man as they is. I sure would love to hear you play sometime. All the girls here'd say the same. You could bring down your gee-tar and sit out on the stoop with the other boys what gather there to play. That's if ever anyone hushes that girl and her boy crashing 'bout out there. It's like she shows off that boy like he's a trophy and ain't got no shame.'

Booya turned to look where the lady was looking, as if they could see the creators of the noise. Then they were again facing each other wordlessly.

'Oh, sorry, hun,' she said. 'You ain't here for me; you is looking for your ma. Last time I see her she was arranging the flowers. Right over there.' The lady pointed.

'Thank you, ma'am.' Booya lifted the hat Roots had given to him years before.

'Been my pleasure meeting you, Calvin,' she gushed. 'I is Betsie, by the way.'

Booya smiled. 'Good to meet you, Betsie.'

He walked on, rolling his eyes and puffing out his cheeks. He found Mammy with her nose buried deep in a display of flowers. When she looked up, she glared at Booya.

'Hey, Mammy. It's me!'

'Well, yes, Calvin; I can see that. Took me by a world of surprise, s'all. What you doing down here?'

'Just come down to see where you spend all your days,' Booya replied. 'Ain't been in time! Ain't you glad to see me?'

'A'course I am,' she replied. Mammy hugged and kissed him. A smile blooming, she held on to his thick arms. 'You really come down just to see your old Mammy?'

'Uh-huh. Sure did.'

'Then this is the finest surprise I had in all my days. You just have to meet all the girls, Cally. Tole them all so much 'bout you.'

'Already met a lady called Betsie.'

'Betsie!' Mammy shrilled. 'Well, I is surprised that loose old girl kept her hands off you.'

Booya hadn't ever heard Mammy speak that way about anyone before. Bringing a warm feeling to his belly, he thought of the girls at the picnic – they sure hadn't been able to keep their hands off him. Thankfully Mammy didn't seem to guess that his satisfied grin was raised by those memories.

He toured around the store with Mammy, the ladies clucking to Mammy as if she were the alpha-hen in the henhouse, swooning at Adeline's big and talented boy. Booya managed to hide his disappointment well that the only woman he was introduced to who was young enough to claim the same generation as him looked like she'd been grown in a soil drained of nutrients. After nearly an hour he was able to make his escape, crunching on a rock of homemade honeycomb that one of the women had insisted he try. She had made it herself that morning.

When he'd been in the store, Booya hadn't noticed when the sound of fife and drum had ceased. Outside, the comparative silence was deafening. Standing on the stoop, looking around for the pair of little entertainers, he saw them standing on the cobbles at the corner of the building. The tiny boy was sitting on the bass drum, the girl feeding him pieces of watermelon. As Booya turned back round, from the corner of his eyes he saw a group of three boys in shabby suits, two wearing beaten hats, sharing a bench on the stoop. Two of them were eyeing him curiously, each of them with an armed draped over a guitar. Before Booya could react in any way, someone bumped into him. He heard the rattle of change in a tin cup.

'Spare any change?'

It was the blind Indian from the picnic. For a moment Booya was hypnotised by the aimless swirling of the sunken eyes.

'Ain't got no money, sir.'

'Got an'thing t'eat?'

Booya was holding the last bite of honeycomb in his hand. 'Can have this if you want. It's honeycomb. Tastes sweet. Tastes pretty good!'

The blind Indian was already holding out his hand. 'Don't put it in the begging bowl, naw. Give it me here.'

Booya placed the honeycomb in the centre of the man's palm. The Indian sniffed it, dropped it on the ground, and continued on his way, shaking his tin cup and bumping into people.

As he wandered homeward past Redemption Square, Stanza Studios was possibly even more packed than earlier. The music was still battering at the insides of the barn-like buildings, spilling out of the doors, each sound-style competing for his ears.

Strolling within the radius of Blacks, the black guitar sign painted with white words swinging with a barely perceptible creaking noise, Booya stopped mid-step. Even after all the years since Mister Henry had first played it to him, there was no mistaking the voice and guitar of Blind Lemon Jeff.

6

The building and windows were painted black. The black guitar, gently swaying above Booya, screeched. If ever the good Lord had forsaken a mosquito bite upon the earth Blacks was it. Booya opened the door and stepped inside.

After the atom-clogging heat, the second sense that struck Booya was the putrid mixture of sour smells. It smelled as though the wooden floor had been soaked in stagnant vinegar, like milk curdling to dirty cheese, sweaty and sick. Perhaps it had only been cats and dogs that had pissed up the walls; perhaps they had a liberal urination policy for all who stepped inside Blacks. In the heat, swathes of rotten smells wafted around Booya. Hidden somewhere in amongst those smells, Booya could sense Paw's Angel kisses.

The melismatic sound of Blind Lemon Jeff was walking on that pungent air.

With all natural light barred from Blacks, saucers of light hanging from the ceiling by heavy chains weren't sufficient to greatly illuminate the room. It was as if the triumphant combination of smells had thickened the air, too thick to see through. Looking around, Booya saw candles dripping from holders along the walls above tables and booths, more candles dotted on the tables, adding a dim glow to the blind light. In the middle of the room was a large fire pit raised above the floor, covered by a domed spark guard, the fire glowing inside only adding to the stuffy heat. Through the fog, Booya noticed that there was a stubby cylinder attached to the ceiling, like he'd seen on the scaffolding above the stage at the picnic. He looked to where the unlit cylinder was pointed: a stage against the far end of the room, beyond chairs, tables and pillars. The stage was empty. At least, it was empty of performers.

Across the gloomy room a girl was sitting on the stage, her legs hanging over the edge. A man was standing with his waist between her knees, his back to Booya, his hands on her bare legs. Further along, three young men were sitting with an even younger girl. Each of them was wearing a bored, grim expression on their face as they watched a man dancing jerkily on the open floor in front of the stage. One of the boys turned smiling to his friends and muttered something behind his hand. A few other couples were dancing on the sticky floorboards. A scattering of men and women were sitting at the tables around the room, or skulking in the booths around the edges.

Blind Lemon Jeff was still singing and strumming, giving life to the dancers.

Booya inhaled deeply of the foul air. They must have a golden horn in here . . . whatever Mister Henry had called it. Captured in some kind of trance, Booya had walked some way into the room, standing just short of the tables. It was quickly obvious that there was no golden horn. He had only ever seen one for those few moments on that magical morning, but he longed to look upon one again.

A few of his senses, mostly asleep since the picnic, were reawakening. They were crawling up inside Booya, growling greedily, caged inside the perimeter fence of his ribcage. Their teasing tails tickled tantalisingly as they swished along his ribcage; ducking away, only to come again with an even fiercer force.

Booya squinted, adjusting to the dim light. Even though the sound was bouncing off the ceiling and walls, Booya guessed that it was originating from the furthest corner, just beyond the long wooden bar counter. Though the music was unmistakably the sound of Blind Lemon Jeff, it wasn't the same as hearing him pouring his plight from inside Mister Henry's golden horn, where the sound was sticky sweet. In here Blind Lemon Jeff sang powerfully and might have been playing a guitar the size of a tree, circling in amongst the rafters.

Behind the wooden counter, wiping a rag inside a glass, a big black man wearing a bandana cut from a white sheet was staring at Booya. Beneath the bandana, his face was tough, sharp and mean. He cocked his head back, either inviting Booya to come forward, if he dare, or warning him to not even attempt to. Booya noticed that his ears were pierced with bone. He was wearing a white string vest. Although the man was not nearly as tall as him, Booya was quite sure that the vest wouldn't be quite so tight around his own shoulders. The man's head wasn't small but it looked like a berry on a brick pillar. Without disrupting his glare, the man put down the glass and picked up another, proceeding to wipe the rag around the inside of the next glass. He jerked his head back once more, clearly asking of Booya. The fearsome, lustful animals inside Booya slunk deeper into the darkness.

Something bounded up to Booya and grabbed his arm, attempting to swing him round.

'Tell me it's you, yeah?' the pretty girl squealed. 'She – that one there – say it ain't, but I knowed it was you from the second you walked in. It is you! I know it!

'*It is him!*' she shouted across the room. '*Tole you it was!*'

Booya didn't say a word. But the animals inside his guts were suddenly becoming vocal.

'Tell me you remember me too,' she squealed.

He was certain that he'd never met her in his life. 'Yep,' he said, looking from her top to her bottom.

'Oh, you just saying that, ain't you. You don't remember. Knowed at the time you was way gone down the road. And well, you know . . .' She played a finger in her hair. 'I was probably just another girl to you, weren't I? But I just know it's you.' She removed her finger from the tight curls of her long hair, disappointment beginning to creep over her face. 'Never forget someone as big as –'

'*Well? Is it or ain't it him?*' one of her friends yelled from within the fog, a deep-toned but feminine voice.

The way the girl was looking up at him – so seductive, yet betrayed by a slight innocence – another animal began to stir, battering to be released. 'I's jus' kiddin' wid yo',' Booya said, raising himself to his full height. 'Course I dat same man.'

She squealed and tugged on his arm. 'I just knowed you was.' She thumped him gently on the chest. 'You big kidder. Say, you gonna come over and sit with us a while?'

'Sho,' Booya answered. 'I come sit wit'chu a while.'

'Don't suppose you got your guitar with you today?' she asked, looking at his hands.

'Nah, I ain't,' Booya replied, helpless not to talk in a different manner than he had talked to Mammy's worker-friends in Huck's Place. This girl was quite a little piece in that tight-fitting, yellow cotton dress. At least, in the haze, he thought it was yellow.

'That don't matter,' she said, licking her tongue along her teeth and then rolling it around inside her cheek. 'I be happy to give you some more of what I give you the other night. Been aiming to bump into you, you know?'

Picking up his hand, the girl led Booya over to the booth that her friends were sitting in, observing the thick stalactite of wax stuck to the wall.

'You remember this man from the picnic?' she asked her friends, raising an eyebrow.

'Yes!' he said. 'The picnic!'

'What's your name again, honey?' her friend was saying – by her deep-toned voice, obviously the friend who had called across the room. 'Sorry to ax, but at the picnic everone was calling you Big Boo.'

'Well, dat's close,' he replied. 'Name's Booya.'

'I gonna call you Big Boo,' laughed the girl in the yellow dress, a mischievous grin on her face.

Booya was looking down at her. Her eyes were huge, as playful as her smile. She had a tiny frame, accentuated by the pressure her generous bosom was applying to the front of her dress. From his height, he tried to look her in the eyes.

'Rosie!' the friend squealed. 'You *must* excuse her *behaviour*,' she said to Booya. 'Not all us is so *loose*.'

This girl was half-hiding behind her long skinny fingers that led to her big hands, adjoined to her long slim arms. Her eyelashes, as ridiculously long as her fingernails, were fluttering at Booya. Her broad shoulders were bony, though it was clear that she was making some effort in holding herself to appear prim. She could hide behind as much facepaint as she wished, but she spoke with such a ludicrously affected voice. Despite her floral dress, with her unfeminine extended features and the exaggerated effort to compensate, in the poor light Booya could not decide if she was an unfortunate woman or an unsightly man.

Booya sneaked another look at Rosie and her inviting figure. There was another girl, too, gazing at Booya as if she were a peasant beholding Jesus.

'So I knows Rosie,' Booya said, putting an arm around her, to touch her bare skin. 'Wha's yo' name beautiful?'

The long-limbed girl's eyelids fluttered more rapidly than a hummingbird's wings. 'My friends know me as Petal,' she said in her sultry, whistling voice, '*handsome . . .*' she added with a titter and blush.

'How 'bout yo'self, sugar?' Booya asked the other girl, moving in closer to Rosie.

The third girl had a round and rather plain face, her small eyes too close together to be considered alluring. But her unsure smile revealed a perfect row of teeth. For some reason, she felt the need to act with the same ridiculously fake and timid coquettishness as Petal.

'Mah name's Virginia,' she slathered, startled from her trace. She didn't seem to know whether to add anything else. Booya could almost see her mentally kick herself for being so transparent when she added, '*Handsome . . .*'

'I ain't never seed such a attractive group a ladies,' Booya said, feeling his lips stretch into a grin.

Petal and Virginia fanned themselves with their fingers: one hand long and masculine, the other stubby and plump.

Rosie squeezed Booya's side. The touch of her small hands tingled through him, finding a place to shock with volts, and then quickly shooting elsewhere. He felt like the jerking dancer. Looking up at him with that same lascivious look, Booya realised that she must have sensed it. Petal and Virginia obviously sensed it, too – they didn't know where to look to hide their comical disappointment.

'Mind if I join yo' fo' awhiles?' Booya asked the two seated girls.

'Slide in next to me,' Rosie cooed, pulling him into the booth.

With Petal managing to find confidence through her disappointment, and Virginia echoing most things that Petal said, Booya mostly listened. Under the table Rosie's hands were moving all over him. Petal and Virginia tried not to stare; Booya tried to conceal his pleasure.

In the background the music continued. Other "rappers and frailers", as Roots used to say, had long since replaced Blind Lemon Jeff. Booya again became aware of the music.

'Y'all git live musicians like Levee Banks up in here?' he asked.

'Yeah,' said Rosie. 'Levee's been here. Quite a lot of them come through. But most nights just anyone can take up on the stage, unless they got a special visitor from outta town to play. Some say that even Bobby Johnson come through from Hazelhurst and sat on that very stage one night, God keep his soul.'

'Did he?' Booya asked with measured coolness.

'Uh-huh,' Virginia joined in, 'that's the truth. My mama was here that night. She see him play. Spoke with him afterward, too. Say he was making eyes all over this room.' Virginia looked at Petal. Petal's arched eyebrows and puckered expression indicated that she didn't approve. Virginia frantically fluttered and flitted and batted and tittered to make up for her unapproved outburst.

'Say,' said Rosie, digging her nails into Booya's leg. Petal and Virginia quickly glanced towards the movement, and then sucked their cheeks and jerked their heads as if they were trying to suck a stone from a wooden olive, looking anywhere else. 'You gotta come meet Cole. He runs this place. Soon as he hears how good you is, he's sure to let you play some night. Stay here, girls,' Rosie said, picking up Booya's hand and pouting at her friends, deliberately sticking out her backside as she stood. 'That's Cole.' Rosie pointed out the mean-looking man, still staring at Booya from behind the bar counter. They walked over the sticky floor.

'Hey, Cole, this here's *Booya*,' Rosie said, springing up and down, simultaneously rubbing Booya's arm. 'You just gotta hear Boo play, Cole.'

Cole narrowed his eyes to dark slits, staring Booya long in the eyes. 'Yeah?'

Booya nodded. 'Pleased to meet you.'

'Yeah?'

'Hey, come on now, Cole,' Rosie said, slamming her hands on the bar. 'You ain't gotta be the tough man with ever new person you meet. Not ever person what come in here is the sneaking spy of the revenue man.'

Slow as the sun rises in the fall, Cole's lips began to upturn as he stared at Rosie. 'Just like *you* ain't gotta go jumping on ever new person what come in Blacks 'fore they gets a chance to know what they 'bout.'

'Now that ain't fair.' Sticking her bottom lip out, Rosie folded her hands beneath her bosom.

'It's a game for two, Miss Rosie.' Cole held out his hand to Booya. 'Was just playing. Booya is it? That's what me and this little chicken does, seeing as she *lives* in this place.'

'Yeah,' Rosie said. 'Never mind his *rough* exterior, Big Boo, Cole's a pussycat really.'

Cole eyed Rosie once more. 'A tiger's a pussycat too, you know,' Cole said. Rosie growled at him. 'It's like holding a tiger by the tail with this one, man,' he said to Booya. 'Name's Cole Kitchens,' he continued. 'This here's my joint. None of that screeching jazz; nothin' but the blues. You a blues man, Boo?'

'Uh-huh.'

'Well Blacks' the place for you. Two ways we play it here: you can bring your guitar down here a night and wait in turn 'til the stage is empty, wait 'til ever other chancer's either been applauded off or dragged off; or if you pass a audition with me first I'll see that the stage is cleared for your own set.'

'Boo the greatest, Cole!' Rosie said. 'He gotta play.'

Cole laughed. 'Yeah? Come down anytime you like then, Booya,' he said, smiling. He turned to face Rosie. 'Otherwise I won't ever let you and your little friends in here ever again.'

Rosie put a hand to her bosom and gasped. 'Well, Mister Cole!' And then her smile brought light to the room, making Booya grin.

'*Booya.*' Cole stroked his chin. 'It ain't Booya Carthy is it?'

Booya nodded.

'Thought I heard that name someplace. Some fella ax me if ever I seen you play. Say he see you play at the picnic.' Cole picked a glass out of a pile, wiping the rag inside. 'With the endorsement your girl just give, 'long with that other fella, I is looking forward to hearing you. Still gotta audition though, man; soon's you like. Just make sure no fool talks you into that thieving dipsie-doodle 'cross the street 'fore I gets to hear you.'

Booya smiled at Rosie. Those bright eyes were again gazing up at him, crying indecent proposal.

7

Two cars passed each other by on the new blacktop. One signalled a greeting to the other by a honk of the horn, answered by a quick hoot in return. They trundled on down the road, one moving away from town and the other headed towards it.

The noise made Booya spring to life, sitting upright the moment he awoke, mumbling, 'What is I gonna tell Mammy? What's I gonna say?'

The river was passing slowly by. The underside of the bridge was as dirty as ever. The ducks were elsewhere today. There was no violent battle raging inside Booya's head. He felt hungry, but not sick. Booya grinned, put his hands behind his head and laid back on the riverbank.

The memories weaved back through his mind. The two of them had gone back to Rosie's place for a little while. When they returned, he could remember Rosie speaking to Cole and, even though he had stared at Booya in that threatening way again, from beneath the bar Cole had produced two cups of White Lightning.

In the foggy stink, Petal and Virginia had still been sitting there, as straight as sawn wood, theatrically displaying their displeasure at being walked out on with no departing word; still looking as though they were sucking on something bitter when Booya and Rosie returned. They said that a mean man had come by and asked them, "What's two ladies doing in a place such as dis?" and that they didn't have anyone there to protect them from him!

"We is still quite shook from the ordeal," Virginia spoke.

"He was acting like he'd been *drinking*!" Petal exclaimed, shuddering, wearing an expression one might wear upon being pulled from a river just before breathing their last breath.

"And we gonna have a few drinks now, too." Rosie put her cup on the table and her hands on her hips.

"Oh yes, let's," Petal said, clapping her hands, skilfully shaking the terrifying ordeal from her broad shoulders.

Soon enough, the whole building was full to the webbed rafters of rowdy drinkers. Although mostly populated by coloured men and women, there were a few poor whites, mostly workers at nearby plantations and sawmills. A pair of boots or shoes filled every square foot of floor space, dancing to the music or yelling above it.

Another memory arrived . . .

He had been dancing to music from the juke when the crowd began to cheer. Rosie pointed to the stage. The three black boys in suits that Booya had seen earlier that day outside Huck's Place were walking across the stage, shaking their guitars above their heads. For the first minute or so, Booya couldn't hear a note they played or a word they sang. Blacks had become even crazier and louder, people bumping each other, grabbing one another. Men lifted girls up so that they could see. Girls wriggled to the stage through the packed bodies.

Able to see over all the bobbing heads, Booya had grabbed on so tight to Rosie that she'd had to pry open his grip. She pulled him away from the middle of the crowd. It hadn't been so hard for her to move through the crowd, but Booya had trodden on men and women, eased people apart with his big arms, causing many a head to turn with fuelled glares.

She told him that the boys on the stage had recently become quite a regular sight in Blacks. "Mostly they play them funny hokum songs," she said. "The girls think they cute. And they make the men laugh. That's why they is so popular right now."

Letting out a sigh beneath the bridge, Booya couldn't remember when or why he had left Rosie and girls. He could vaguely remember downing a few cups and then wading back into the crowd to hear the players better as insobriety took control of him. A girl – not as pretty as Rosie, but at least as well blessed – had shouted in Booya's ear that some crazy fool was aiming to stick him with his crab-apple switch, by business of having his toes trampled on. Booya never saw the whites of the man's eyes. The last part he could remember for sure was, minutes later, sneaking out through Blacks' backdoor with the girl.

He couldn't remember if he'd gone back inside at any point later, though he could vaguely remember staring blindly at a jazz band in some other joint, drumming on the rim of his hat and stamping a foot in time to the swinging beat. He couldn't recall if he'd returned to Rosie and the girls, though somehow he thought not.

And he couldn't remember at all why sleeping under the bridge had, again, seemed so appealing to him.

*

Paw was in the same place Booya had last left him: digging and sowing in the vegetable plot. When he heard footsteps approaching, Paw turned. 'So,' he said, looking over his shoulder at Booya, continuing to turn the soil, 'hear you find your mama at the store yesterday.'

'Yeah, Paw. She . . . at the store today?' he asked, looking around.

'Uh-huh.' Paw ceased digging and lowered himself to sit in the dirt and weeds beside the vegetable patch. He picked at the dirt beneath his nails then looked up at Booya, haloed by the midday sun. 'Take you a awful long time getting home, Boo. You have a time?'

'Could say that, Paw, yeah.' Booya grinned, but this time he felt guilty even talking to his seasoned Paw about his travails. 'Had no idea all the places they got down there now, Paw. Was just looking round, seeing where it's at. After seeing Mammy, I was out in the street and I heared this music coming out the door of one them juke places. Knowed straight off that it was Blind Lemon Jeff, Paw; you know the one Mister Henry played me?'

'I know,' Paw responded, still unsmiling. 'You liked him so much you named a chicken after him.'

'Yeah, Paw.'

'Ain't no greater accolade for a man than to have a chicken named after him.' Paw laughed with Booya, even though something was obviously itching him.

'Maybe you'll have a chicken named after you yet, Paw.'

'Be disappointed if I don't.' Paw wiped a rag around his neck and down his back and rested his arms on his knees. 'But, Boo, that don't account for a entire day and night spent in 'Hee without no word.'

'Was getting to that, Paw. So, I heared Blind Lemon Jeff singing the country blues and, thinking it were the real man hisself, went inside Blacks to see –'

'What'd you say?' Paw snapped, his expression suddenly intense.

'Say I think the real Blind Lemon Jeff was playing,' Booya laughed. His smile vanished upon seeing the dangerous expression on Paw's face.

'The next bit. You went in Blacks?'

'Yeah, Paw,' Booya whispered.

Paw shook his head. 'Son, I know you finding out 'bout the world. And that's fine by me. But they is a bad crowd hanging round in Blacks. They all cutthroats and villains, all them, ever one. Ain't no good can come from hanging in a place such as that. Believe me, son, I is a man what knows. Spent my worst years in that place.'

Pins pricked at Booya's skin as he stood watching Paw rub his hands on his thighs.

'Yep, bad things go down in Blacks since the day it first open its doors,' Paw said.

'Was just there for the music, Paw. See, I meet the guy what runs the place, Cole, and –'

'You meet Cole? He still there? Man, he a good man, Cole. Might look like he eats chilun for fun, but he a good man.'

'Uh-huh. And he say I can go down there with my guitar sometime, play my own songs on the stage. You gotta do some of the popular songs, Cole say to me, but I get to play my own, too.'

'Well . . . if you got Cole Kitchens looking out for you . . .' Paw rubbed his chin, lingering a look at Booya. 'Playing your guitar down there, that keeps folks on your side mostly – looking out for you so you still alive to play for them again. They is jealous men, them villains. See it myself. But it's they womens trying to get your attention, that's where the trouble's at, see? Let people know that Cole's got your back. Them outlaw womens – that's what we call 'em: "outlaw womens" – they get they kicks having men fighting over them. Might be you ain't never even looked in her direction. But them outlaw womens being interested in *you*, making they eyes and such, ain't no different to her man than if you is rummaging in her drawers.

'Might not seem it, Boo, but singing them blues is a dangerous game. Gotta play it wise, son. Gotta play that business wise. You gotta make all them like you, so they smile ruther than stick you when they womens wanna play.

'And you, mister, make sure you keep your dirty snout outta my growing vegetables,' Paw pointed and warned Mister Wilbur the mule, who had wondered through from the clearing. 'You is fed well enough.' Paw stretched his back and sucked his teeth. 'Be back in a moment, Boo,' he said. 'Just stay here, now.'

Paw returned with two dirty tin cups in his hands.

'Now, you tell your Mammy 'bout this then I might as well be sleeping on the riverbed or 'neath the sweet potatoes, hear me? This be our little secret, Boo. I say it don't hurt none, just a cup now and 'gain. It's the truth what Mammy say that if I'd stayed with them fools then I woulda ended up like old Rusty. But the occasional cup, that ain't gonna kill no one. You hear me now, Boo: play your guitar 'til the sun comes up, but always sip around the edge, like this . . .'

Booya laughed at Paw, daintily slurping from the cup.

'I serious, Boo! You go swimming in Moonshine and you sink. I sunk 'fore now. I is a man what knows. You go in like this . . .'

Booya laughed hard and kicked his feet. 'Sorry, Paw.'

Paw laughed along. 'You do it now, with your own. I sip along, too. Like this, see?'

Avoiding Paw's eye contact, Booya swirled the last of the homemade corn whisky in the bottom of his cup. 'When you go collect Mammy, Paw, I is coming with you.'

'Yeah? Gonna take a walk with your old man?'

'Yeah, Paw. Gonna take my guitar and go in Blacks, see if Cole will let me play tonight.'

Paw sighed. 'If that's what you feel like you gotta do, son, then you do it. Guess they ain't no use having a beautiful garden but never telling no one how nice it grows. Just make sure that any womens what feel like freeing they drawers for you ain't already got a man. Or ain't got one he's already thinking in his head is his. But most, don't forget to sip around the edges, like this.'

8

With his hand beneath the slim rim of his derby, Booya shielded his eyes. In the white glare of the spotlight he couldn't see much except ghostly outlines of circles from the afterimage of the light, shapes of arms waving like corn. It looked as though Blacks stretched back infinitely. He wished that Paw could see him now, up on the stage, each smiling face he could see smiling back at him. He wished that Mister Henry could see how he'd kept his promise. More than ten years since he had seen him, he wondered what George would say.

"So your old man is the great Cleveland Carthy," Cole had said after Booya's audition. "Man, in days gone by he's supplied me with enough Moonshine to float a Mississippi steamer. If you is Cleveland's son then I definitely got your back, man."

"You like my playing?" Booya asked, sitting on a chair in front of Cole, his face feeling warm from having sung sober. He had played only two songs before Cole had stopped him.

"Boo," Cole said, leaning against the bar, "I don't give out no praise for nothing. I got a business to run." He inhaled, smiled. "What you played for me here today is better than most anything I ever heared played in here 'fore. Better even than most of the hoboing musicians we had come through Honahee. Hell, better than most of what I play on the juke! They really original songs what you make up yourself?"

Looking down at his guitar, Booya shrugged. "Just sang and played what I thought you'd want to hear." Tapping his feet together, he pinched the tip of his nose and looked up at Cole. Just as Booya had first seen him, Cole was glaring at him.

"So you make them up on the spot? On that they chair? Just now?" He tightened his bandana and puffed out his cheeks. "Man, you sure you ain't heared them played someplace else?"

Again Booya shrugged. He wiped a speck dust from the neck of his guitar. "It's just how I do," he said to the filthy floorboards. "How I was teached. What I always done."

Cole slapped his hands together. "All right, here's how we do in Blacks. First: you playing; tonight. If the crowd likes you I'll give you a dollar a song. See, if they don't they is just as likely to stumble a few doors down to listen to some dude with neat hair, wearing a chalk-stripe suit and white brogues tootling on his trumpet. If you can just," Cole held out his palms, facing the rafters, "do what you done here today, however it is you do it, making it up as you go, whatever, the stage is yours to kill. Five, six, songs. Boo, I got a feeling you gonna do OK."

Beneath his hand, Booya could just make out Cole behind the bar. He was nodding and smiling. Booya was grateful for the whiskies Cole had given him. Even after playing five songs he could feel his heart beating boldly and steadily as the whisky mixed with his blood, driving his fear away. The crowd was yelling for more.

Booya smiled for the first time since he had been upon the stage. He showed his smile to Cole, then raised a hand in the air and the crowd began to quiet.

'This the last song I is gonna play.'

The crowd booed.

'It's called Whisky Whisky,' Booya said, and then launched into an inspired, upbeat tribute to the illegal sauce.

The crowd cheered and bumped, jostled and jumped, spilling their cups.

'*Whisky whisky*,' Booya sang.

I'd even take rum
I'd drink anything what makes my head numb
Drink thinner and turpentine

Anything bitter and sour
Drink it in the tub
Take it any hour
But mister if you got some whisky
I'll pay you with my guitar . . .'

Booya's hands were skipping all over his guitar, filling the space before his next words. Some other force was showing him what to sing and play next to entertain his crowd, already in wild raptures.

As he played, he dared to sneak a glance at Cole. He was laughing at every line Booya sang. Booya even saw a few of the faces in the front row of people pushed up against the stage. They were sweating and laughing and dancing, lost in the noise at Booya's fingers as they beat on the strings. He'd heard that mostly folks just sat at the tables, waiting to be entertained. Tonight the tables and chairs were lost in amongst the crowd, if they weren't being danced upon.

A girl was beaming up at him, her body wriggling in ecstasy. Next to her, the big man's face stood out from the crowd. It was the only one scowling at Booya. Booya forgot about him in a second, carried upon the force of the waving hands and cheering voices.

' . . . *Baby I'll give you everthing I own,'* spilled from Booya's mouth.
'Just give me one more shot
'Fore you taking me home
Whisky whisky
Man, give me a drink
A drop, a dribble
A tear or a wink
So long as I gets enough
Can't remember to think
Bourbon or vodka
White wine or red
As long's I well watered
Don't care if I been fed
So mister if you got some whisky
I'll pay you with my guitar . . .'

Looking up into the thick, ancient webs in the dim light of the rafters, Booya closed his eyes and listened to the crowd calling for more. It was deafening. Opening them again felt like waking from an afternoon dream. This could not be the same building that he had stepped into late that afternoon. This many people could not fit inside that place. From the candles glimmering on the walls above the booths on one side, to Cole standing behind the bar on the other, shaking his head, Booya could see bodies packed in shoulder to shoulder.

Someone tapped him on the back. Turning round, Booya saw one of the boys from outside Huck's, the ones that he had drunkenly danced to, before continuing his dance outside with Rosie, on his first night in Blacks. As Booya stood from the chair, the boy slapped his shoulder, his eyes continuing upwards as Booya rose to his full height.

'Nice show, man,' he said. 'Good skills.'

'Thanks,' Booya replied.

The boy lifted his eyebrows. 'Our turn?'

'Oh, yeah. Sorry, I . . .' Booya picked up the chair, moved it to the back of the stage, and began to walk off. Another of the boys slapped him on the back. The third boy was waving his guitar above his head, working their crowd, ignoring Booya completely.

Of all the people who clamoured to be near him, to touch him, as he stepped from the stage, one familiar face bounced over to him.

'I should be angry with you, *Big Boo*,' Rosie slurred. She was wearing an even lower-cut dress than the yellow one she had been wearing the last time. 'Maybe you'd like to make it up to me some way?'

Booya grinned. 'Ain't gonna find me saying No to a offer like that?' He bent to her ear, she raised onto tiptoe, and whispered, 'Got quite a lot of energy I need to get rid of, as it happens. Not sure if a little doll like you's gonna be able to take it.'

Rosie bit her lower lip. 'If you able to stand when I is finished with you,' she replied, 'I ain't never gonna come bothering you again.'

'Challenge accepted. First I gotta ax Cole to keep a eye on my *geetar*.'

'Maybe get us a little *whisky whisky*,' Rosie smiled.

Moving through the electrified crowd was not easy, and would have been less so if Rosie had not been leading him. Frolickers moved aside, shouting Whisky Whisky directly into Booya's face. Girls wanted to touch him, kiss him; men smiled and slapped him hard on the back.

As soon as they arrived at the bar Cole went to Booya and Rosie. As he exhaled, Booya whistled. 'That was −'

'That was *incredible*, Boo!' Cole said. 'Great work, man. Hey!' Cole yelled to a youthful-looking man trying to get his attention. 'Just wait your turn, fool.'

Smiling, Booya shook his head. 'I enjoyed it. Thanks, man. Say can you look after my guitar? It means a lot to me; can't be replaced.'

'You could give me all the gold in the Federal Reserve and they ain't no fool crazy enough to try take it from me. Give it here.'

'And, uh, Cole, maybe a little . . .'

'*Whisky whisky*?' Cole asked.

'You ain't mad none?'

'Get outta here,' Cole said, handing over two cups. 'Figure even a revenue man hisself find his toe tapping to that.' He turned his fearsome countenance on the young man. 'What?'

As Booya and Rosie were stepping into the darkness behind Blacks, a deep voice called from behind them. They both turned to see the scowling man from the crowd.

'You give my girl the idea you wanna make something with her,' he growled.

'Leave your troubled mind alone,' Rosie spat. 'Can't you see he got a girl right here with him?'

'If you don't keep that mouth shut, bitch, then I is gonna cut you right after I cut him.' The man pulled out a crab-apple switch from his pocket, the blade glinting in the disc of light above the back door.

'Look, buddy,' said Booya. 'I never even set a eye on your girl, let alone made them. Everone in there was looking at me. And I looked right back at them. Saw you too, didn't I? And like she say, this my only girl right here. Think we got some kinda mistake, is all.'

'Oh, they ain't no mistake in my mind, *nigger*.' The man took a step closer. 'Only thing I is still deciding on is whether to make you dead or just bleeding.'

Booya lifted Rosie's hand from his waist, easing her behind him.

She stepped in front of him. 'Uh-uh. If this mollydodging fool gets anywhere near you, I is gonna pick his eyes out.'

'You think you might be able to try, bitch,' the man said, assuming an attack pose: his legs apart, the knife held out in front of him. 'Think I decided myself that one less musicianer in the world to keep away from my girl the better.'

'And I is telling you,' Rosie spat at the man, hands on her hips, 'your loose girl ain't never even got a chance with a man like my Big Boo.'

'Rosie –' Booya tried to interrupt.

'She probably inside right now going with some toothless cracker.'

'Oh you gonna get it, bitch.' He came forward at Rosie.

Booya pulled her out of the way, dumping her to the side.

There were only five big paces separating Booya and the man. And he was quickly filling them. At the same time as an echoing blast, half of the man's side exploded. The knife disappeared, the arm holding it ripping to shreds. Holding a sawn-off shotgun at his waist, Cole was standing in the disc of light.

'Evertime anyone steps on that stage to sing or play, this damn fool gets thinking that someone's aiming for his girl. Evertime. Truth is that she's making it with half the town. Even tasted her myself! Goddamn crazy motherfucker had that coming to him, anyways. Don't know why he ain't just done hisself a favour and keep his girl home. I done *her* a favour, ain't no doubting that.'

On the floor, the man began to moan.

'Oh, Jesus the Son . . .' Cole rolled his eyes. 'Go now, Booya. Get outta here. Gonna make sure that this fool don't crawl his bloody ass back in my joint.'

Nodding to Cole, Booya and Rosie walked past Blacks' backdoor.

'Oh, Boo,' Cole called, the shotgun trained on the dying man. 'How 'bout you play again tomorrow night?'

'Yeah, Cole. Maybe.'

The man groaned another dying moan.

'Aw, man,' said Cole. 'Still dying?'

Booya walked into the darkness with Rosie. They each felt the other shudder when they heard the second blast.

CHAPTER FIVE

1

No cars hooting. No ducks splashing. No solid dirt as his bed. Booya awoke the next morning with soft breaths moistening his ear. Rosie was lying over his arm, her head on his shoulder. He could feel the rise of her chest before each sighing breath. Their legs were entwined. She felt so warm – warm enough to make his skin slick against hers. Except for the draft on his feet, which were sticking out and over the end of the bed, Booya was warm all over.

He looked around the room. There were a few picture frames on top of the dresser. Hanging on the wall was a bigger picture of Rosie. She was standing with her back against a motorcar, one knee bent, looking sassy. One of her fingers was prodding a white man in the chest between his open shirt, digging a nail into his tanned, toned skin. She was holding a smoking cigarette in her other hand. The man had his hands out to his side, palms open, as if saying: "What you gonna do, li'l gal?" It looked as though she was prepared to do plenty. Booya was sure that she was wearing the same yellow dress in the black and white print that she had been wearing when they first met.

The soft morning light seeped in through the flimsy white drapes, rising up the walls, giving new life to the fading yellow paint – he could vaguely remember Rosie telling him that it was her favourite colour. A breath of air from the open window brushed the drapes, rippling them like willow fronds. From their clothes on the floor, his eyes wandered back to the picture, thinking of how she had stood in front of him last night when the man had threatened them. She'd said that she would pick his eyes out. Seeing that man shot five steps from him had been his first waking thought. He pulled his feet in under the sheets. As he looked around the room, he noticed that they were not alone. His body jerked, banging his head against the wall.

Rosie stirred.

'Look,' Boo said. He was staring at a spider hanging from its web, two feet above his chest. 'A big little thing, ain't he?'

Rosie climbed on to Booya, looking into the distance of his eyes. 'You scared of spiders? Even a man big as you?' She rested her head on her hands and wriggled her hips. 'You heared the story 'bout the mouse and the elephant? One where the big elephant is scared of the tiny little mouse and tiptoes around? You is like the elephant. Here . . .'

Grinning the smile that had first enticed him, Rosie climbed out of the bed and grabbed a gown. She carefully cupped the spider, took it to the window and dropped it out.

'You sure it's gone?' Booya asked. 'It ain't climbed up on your arm or nothing?'

'The big, bad spider ain't coming back, li'l boy Boo,' she teased. 'You safe for now.'

She jumped on the bed and he pulled her close. She eased an arm under his head, draped the other over his chest. As she played her fingers over his skin, she closed her eyes and moaned. 'I got the morning blues,' she whispered into his neck.

'How many men you seen killed, Rosie?' he asked after a time, still staring at the picture.

'Huh?'

'You see men killed 'fore last night? See men killed in Blacks?'

'They is fights in there all the time,' she mumbled. 'Some get cut; some don't.'

'Ever see a man shot?'

'Twice. One time when a drifter come through town, got all crazy over another man's girl. To be fair to him, he twice warned the drifter. Dumb drifter went a third time, got hisself shot.'

'The other time?'

'Other time was when a fight didn't break itself up. Everone seemed to be swinging a knife and threatening everone else. Normally they don't care none, but The Law come up inside Blacks. Sheriff shouts out, "Who started this?" Everone started ringing around him, like they wanna get involved. So the sheriff fired his gun in the air. "Who started this, I axed?" he shouted again. "I'll build a new jailhouse, lock y'all inside and throw away the key if I don't find out right this second." And then some damn crazy fool shouts, "I did," and run at The Law. Sheriff unloaded everthing he got, gunned him down. Fool skidded to sheriff's feet, dead 'fore he stop sliding. "Break it up, now," says The Law. And then he just leaves the building, cool as a cougar, happy at having killed hisself a "nigger".' Rosie laughed. 'And he'd just tell you he was doing his job, all for the good of the town.'

Booya watched the rippling drapes. 'You see Cole handle it like that?' On the floor, Booya had six dollars in the pocket of his pants. 'Is Cole gonna have to save my life ever time I play, Rosie?'

'Oh, Big Boo, it just ain't worth thinking 'bout him no more, not one more thought. Cole handled it, and that's what's important. Right?'

Leaning on his chest, Rosie was looking at him. Booya couldn't return her gaze.

'Look at me.' She tried to turn his head. 'Boo. Look at me.'

He flickered his eyes at hers, and then settled on her chest.

'You can't let one man like that stop you showing the town what God's given you. That man only come at you 'cause he was drunk and jealous. He come at you 'cause you is the best thing he ever seen! They ain't gonna be one person what was in Blacks that don't know what happened. Everone knows Cole's got your back. It makes *you* look like the outlaw to fear, don't it? Huh? You walking and that fool dead?'

Rosie rolled off Booya and, from the side of the bed, picked up his hat and placed it on his head at an angle.

'See it. Ain't no man gonna mess with Booya Carthy now.' Sticking out her bottom lip, she rubbed his cheeks. 'Such a *sad face*. Seriously, Boo: what if Jesus stopped spreading His word 'cause of a few evil men and bad priests? What if He decided one day to just go back to cutting up wood? See how the world would change? Sure, you might have a few more tables and chairs to sit and eat at, but ain't no one gonna go to church and sing and pray 'bout that.' She kissed him. 'You is meant to do this, Boo; born to do it. If Cole's gotta shoot a Roman down ever now and 'gain that's just the way things gotta be. Huh?'

Looking Rosie in the eyes, Booya swallowed.

'There's that smile!' she said. 'Now, 'fore we get something t'eat, I know a way of cheering y'up a little.'

2

'Your guitar get you many womens, Boo?' Paw was wearing a wickedly knowing grin. His eyes were twinkling. He pulled out the cup hidden behind his foot and took a sip, from around the edge.

'Paw!'

'Thing is, see, they's but three reasons for a man to stay out all night long. First is drinking – we both know 'bout that one now, don't we?' Paw tilted his cup and sipped. 'Like that remember, son. Sipping. Around the edges. Second is gambling. That a worser addiction than the brew. If a gambling man only got his soul left to talk of, he gives that away to stay in the game, yep. Third reason you come home after the sun's already up is womens. Now, you don't look like you drunk more'n a fish. Pray you ain't *never* that gambling way, like them fools up all night in the back of the General Store after it closes its doors. So then . . . it's womens.'

Booya sat down in Mammy's chair. 'Pretty clever ain't you, Paw?'

Paw leaned back and crossed his stretched-out legs. 'Ain't nothing 'bout being clever, son. I been there, remember? I watch 'em come and see 'em go. Just remember that some them womens is as dangerous as a man with a knife.' Paw turned to Booya and wagged a finger. 'Don't never be forgetting that. And don't forget to sip. See?'

'No, Paw.' Booya noticed a knife lying on the floor beside the vegetable patch. He massaged his fingers as he stared at it. 'Like you say yourself, ain't got no drinking look 'bout me today!'

'Yup. So I repeat my question: how many womens did the guitar playing get you?'

'You know, Paw, I ain't bragging or nothing, and I ain't aiming to make a old timer like you jealous,' Booya chuckled, wagging his finger at Paw, 'but I coulda had any of them in that place. They went wild soon's they see me. Truth is last night I got me just one.'

'She got a place of her own?'

Booya frowned. 'Huh?'

'See that you ain't got no grass or mud on the seat of your plants. After you come home day after the picnic, look like you'd been ploughing on your ass.'

Looking Paw up and down, Booya grinned and shook his head. 'Why you axing, Paw, if you already know so much?'

'Living so long with your Mammy and her all-knowing ways learned me something after all these years, Boo.' Paw tilted his head and tipped his cup. 'Ahh. Maybe I just ain't so good at it; prob'ly ain't no person alive who is. So fill in the spaces for y'old man, huh?'

Booya sighed. 'If you wanna know –'

'Yep, I do.'

'– she lives some place outside town; somewhere up behind the General Store. Nothing special, I guess. Just shares a house with one of her friends.'

'You got any particular designs on her, Boo?'

'What you really axing, Paw? No more riddles. Come on out an ax.'

'Well, say it like this: fact is, when a man and a women . . . when they *spending time* together, the longer they spend, and the more they *together*, the more likely they gonna add another pair of eyes to they party. Sometimes it happens real soon. Don't need but *one* time, Boo. I see it happen time and again my own self. Ain't nothing wrong with that; it's a blessing direct from the Lord. We as fertile as this here earth, us people. White folks would love to be able to cultivate our seed, telling you. Heh-heh-heh. I is always guessing that's why they employ us to dig they soil, hoping our blood and sweat gets down in that earth, or something.' As he laughed, Paw clapped his hands and rocked back and forth on his chair.

Booya could see that the whisky had impressed its effects on Paw already today – he had a tendency to laugh at his own rambling when drunk.

'Back to the real business though, Boo: you gotta make a decision then, if that happens. Ain't the right thing to do to leave womens in that situation. See it happen many times in all my years. Believe me: it happens! Some womens think they can use a little baby chile to keep a man. But if the man got shoes on his feet – damn! even if he don't – if he wanna go walking they ain't nothing she can do and stop him, let me tell ya.' Paw sighed.

'Yep, the right thing's to stay. It don't do no good for no chile to be growing up with no Paw, nuh-uh. They the chilun what grow up to kill for nothing and do no good in they life. A chile needs a Mammy to feed 'em and a Paw to teach them. That's the thing right there: circumstances. You know 'bout them, Boo? Circumstances they change. Understand?'

'Yeah, Paw. I –'

'Nuh. They change. So . . . Ah *shee-it.*' Attempting to point his cup at Booya, Paw spilled whisky over his leg. He wiped at it absently. 'That dry 'fore I go get yo' mama. Huh! Just 'bout distracted my flow. What's I 'bout to preach?' Watching a passing cloud, he slapped his hip. 'Oh yuh . . . you love her, Boo? Enough to stay with her for the harvest, if the ploughing go real good?'

'I don't know, Paw. I know to do the right thing if I was in that situation. But right now I ain't got no plan to get in the family way.'

'Uh-huh. And I see many men say the exact same thing.' Paw nodded. 'They go on thinking with they . . . you know, they *thing.* Then *consequences* is what follow them circumstances: that's the word. Always come in a pair: consequences and circumstances.'

'She a good lady, Paw. And real pretty. But I only just meet her. Right now we just –'

'– having a time,' Paw finished. 'Heh-heh.'

'Yeah, Paw. Exactly that. We having a time. Consequences. Circumstances. They can wait. If they do come along . . . I don't know. Guess I shake them by they hand and let them show me the way, if I meet them.'

They sat silent for a while, listening to the breeze through the trees. Booya stared up at the moving leaves. Paw sat nodding to himself, a dreamy grin slathered across his lips.

'You a good boy, Boo,' Paw said after a time. 'Always knowed you was. Now you a good man. I trust you to do the right thing by this girl. By me and yo' Mammy. By everone! And I don't tell you is the best guitar man just 'cause you my boy. I seed fine players in my years and know you is one even better. Yo' skill's y'own. But just don't let no womens use you if they ain't the one you wants for good. That's all I been trying to say, I guess.'

'You probably see that happen quite a few times in all your years, huh, Paw?'

'Oh, yep, I see that kind of thing 'fore now. You better believe I see it . . . Hey, what you chuckling to yo'self 'bout? You poking some fun at me, boy?

Ah shee-*it*! That dry 'fore I go get yo' big mama.'

'I is gonna head down to Huck's, Paw, after a clean. Ain't seen Mammy in a pair of days, now.' Taking the hat from his head, Booya inspected the thin rim. 'Thinking of just staying back here on the homeplace for a whiles after.'

Looking at the side of his face, Paw watched Booya's hands turning the hat. 'Something go down at Cole's place, son? That why you is so sad-looking today?'

Booya's eyes shifted to the knife lying on the floor. 'Just been a fast couple a days.'

'All right, son. You know what you 'bout. Just change your face 'fore yo' Mammy see it – you know she'll know what you don't want her to know.' Gripping his thighs, Paw leaned forward. 'How 'bout I go get us a pair a cups? I gone dry. Wearing most of it.'

3

Standing outside Blacks hours later, a howl of music coming through the door, Booya was paralysed with apprehension. He needed to retrieve his guitar from Cole. He scratched an itch in his eyebrow, where it had begun to tingle. *Ain't no problem*, he thought. *Just walk inside* – thanks for keeping a eye on my guitar, Cole – *and walk back out again.*

But if there was no problem, why had he begun to sweat? Why did he fear that he might not see the sun for days after? And why couldn't he stop scratching the itch bugging his brow?

'Only picking up my guitar,' he mumbled as he pushed open the door.

At night, with all the sweating bodies writhing around the place, it was easy not to notice the smell. In the daytime with the sun beating on the roof even an undignified pig would think twice about staying. Before the door closed behind him Booya even noticed a couple in the street gasping as the evil smell wafted over them. Only the hanging domes and the firepit were alight; the candles dormant. The fire was open, the guard leaning to one side. Blacks was empty.

Booya could hear a sloshing sound coming from behind the bar counter. 'Cole?' he called out. The sloshing sound continued. Booya stepped slowly towards it. Above the music and the strange sloshing sound he could hear his steps. He looked around to make sure that there was no one else in there, lurking behind him in the darkened corners, hidden by the painted windows.

'*Sail on, pretty girl, sail on,*' crooned the deep, avuncular voice from the Seeburg juke behind the far end of the bar. The guitar was chirpy, rolling and teasing, perfect to dance to. The fact that there was no one in here to dance added to the eeriness of Blacks.

'Cole?' Booya called again. He wished that he could listen to this music without feeling as though his heart might burst out of his mouth. The voice, so rich and clear, added to his wary fear. His hands were above the bar counter, about to land on it.

The firepit spat out a blackened piece of wood, skittering over the floor. Booya turned in time to see the glowing ember vanish.

He began to think that maybe he should just come back later, maybe when there was a bit life in the place. But then he saw his guitar behind the bar, leaned up against the wall. He tapped on the bar and began to walk to the far end.

'When you get back there, you may not have a place to stay,' sang the voice, the pace of the guitar changing.

The sloshing sound suddenly stopped.

Booya continued running his hand along the counter, gently tapping.

The song came to end.

Blacks was silent.

Booya slid his hand over the surface of the bar. Just as he turned his head to face where the sloshing sound had been, Cole jumped up from behind the counter, brandishing his shotgun.

'Jesus!' Cole shouted, pointing the shotgun to the ceiling, tearing it away as if swinging a gator by the tail. 'Boo! Man, I loosed the trigger on this thing. Don't be creeping up when I got it in my hand. Hey sorry, Boo. You all right, man? Look like I half near killed you anyway.'

'Uh-huh,' Booya managed, his jaw locked.

'I got some motherfuckers saying they gonna kill me,' Cole said. 'Say I done something to they cousin. Ain't no way they is gonna take me down without dying.'

'Uh-huh.'

'Hey, man, relax.' Cole hid the shotgun under the bar. ''I's just a bit on the edge, y'know?'

'Uh-huh.'

'Hey, overhear people saying some good things 'bout your set last night. Everone in the place loved it.' Cole's face darkened. 'And don't even be thinking 'bout that gone fool. Tole you last night, man: he got what was coming to him. Know that Cole's got your back. Here, was just preparing a batch. You wanna cup?'

Senses whooshed back into Booya. Tongue tingling, he could taste the whisky in the rough air. The itch in his eyebrow had returned. He raised a finger and slowly scratched it. It felt beautiful.

'Just come in for my guitar, Cole,' he said. 'It's . . . there. Leaning over . . .' Booya coughed and itched his eyebrow. 'Over there.'

'Sure you don't wanna cup? On the house?'

Saliva was streaming down Booya's throat.

'Gotta go down to Huck's,' Booya answered. He wondered if Paw had ever stood in that same place and said No. 'Really, I just need my guitar.'

'Sure,' Cole said, eyeing Booya. He walked over to the guitar, picked it up, brought it over and gently placed it on the bar.

On the juke, the singer crooned, *'Easy rider, where you been so long?'*

Booya barely noticed that the blaring music had resumed.

'Listen, man, wanna apologise for startling you. Can see it on your face. Was only offering you a cup to settle down your jumping nerves. Damn! I is having one. Feel as jumpy as you look right now.'

*

Booya walked out of Blacks with his guitar over his shoulder, holding it by the neck. He felt much more settled. And he was delighted with his discipline: he had only had two cups. And he hadn't asked for either of them. It was like Cole had said, his nerves were jumping.

Cole had told him a little bit about the singer on the juke. He said that he'd twice been released from prison on account of his playing. In the prison, a white man and his son who were touring around, trying to capture the sounds of the south, had visited and recorded some of the man's songs. Apparently the governor had so loved his music that he felt it was a crime in itself to keep such a beautiful sound locked away. After he was released he'd his throat slit in a barroom brawl. Surviving the attack, he had worn the scar like a medallion around his throat.

"However popular, a blueser's gotta keep his eyes open," Cole said. "Or have someone keeping they eyes open for you."

Feeling light and content, Booya strolled down to Huck's place.

He was delighted to see that the midget – or child, or whatever he was – and the young girl were outside Huck's. She was helping the boy up on to an overturned fruit carton. A crowd had gathered on and around the stoop. The girl smiled at the midget-boy; he smiled back at her. After brushing a hand over his jacket, she stepped back. The boy put a small fist to his mouth, cleared his throat, and began to call out the local and national news in a high-pitched, reedy voice, like talking through a kazoo.

Some of the crowd whispered and tittered amongst themselves at the display.

The girl obviously doted on the boy. She was staring at him with a heartening, loving look on her face. Booya was fascinated to watch the little fellow: his professionalism, his delivery. And, like Booya, he could recite from memory: information on the growth of Roosevelt's New Deal and on the economy, how the recent climate had encouraged a burgeoning harvest . . . But Booya was shocked to hear a story towards the end of the speech.

'Last night,' called out the little, bold voice, 'a local man named Clayton Hunter, known around as Clay, was shot to death somewhere behind the strip of jukes on the far side of Redemption Square. His body was found this morning, crudely covered by undergrowth in the cypresses. It is believed by The Law to have been a vendetta over unpaid illegal gambling debts. A source says that The Law, I quote: "got no leads or witnesses and is unlikely to exhaust resources to solve a crime committed by a vigilante over debts related to illegal activity."'

'So the usual excuses as a reason,' someone from the crowd cried out.

'I is merely the bearer of the news,' the boy said, and bowed.

Some in the crowd applauded him as the girl with the long dark hair helped him down from the fruit crate.

Together they walked around the crowd, shaking an upturned hat at the locals. Some were happy to drop in the odd piece of change or food – nuts, bread or fruit. Booya watched them both as they approached him. They were holding hands, the girl holding out the hat.

Booya took a dollar – earned last night – from his pocket. When they were in front of him, he dropped it in to the hat. The girl looked up and smiled. The boy – who barely reached past Booya's knees – also looked up.

'Thank you, sir,' the boy rasped. 'Generous of you. We'll be here next week, bringing you the news.'

'Then I'll be here,' Booya said. 'Say, what's your names?'

'I is Frankie,' said the boy. 'And this is Maribelle, my mother. Thank you again, sir.'

Maribelle looked up, still smiling. And they continued on their way through the crowd. Shocked, Booya could only stand there, unsure what he'd heard. The boy, the midget who looked like he was aged somewhere between eight and eighteen, had a mother who looked like she was no older than thirteen. As he digested the equation, trying to make sense of it, Booya saw Mammy leaning on the doorframe with her arms crossed over her ample chest. She had a grin at the side of her mouth. She obviously hadn't yet seen him. With her arms still folded, she walked back inside Huck's.

Booya eased his way through the departing crowd, through their amused or concerned mutterings, and found Mammy walking along an aisle, away to the storeroom.

'Hey!' he called. 'Mammy.'

She turned. 'Oh, you *hey*ing your Mammy now, is you? Ain't that nice.'

'I come down 'specially to see you.' He held out his arms.

'Like you come down 'specially to see me the other day?' Standing with her hands on her hips, her expression was stern and she was – to no great effect – sucking in her cheeks.

Holding his guitar by the neck, spinning it around on the floor, Booya's head was on his chin.

'Where you been, Calvin?' When he had no explanation to immediately offer, waving a chubby palm, she helped him. 'Don't be telling me nothing I don't wanna know. I can imagine where you was, not that I wanna be imagining such things for my boy. Unless you joined in with a travelling preacher, I don't want to know.'

'I joined in with a travelling preacher,' he answered with a smile. When he offered his open arms to her a second time she walked to him and nestled.

'Least you don't smell like that devil brew,' she said. 'Least you don't smell like that old fool Paw of yours always did. And still do. He don't fool me; I know what he's up to all day.'

Booya could feel Mammy gently laughing into his chest. He didn't know how she had escaped the smell of whisky, even as it warmed his belly. Mammy stepped out of his embrace and looked up at him. She hadn't been laughing.

'You gonna stay mine, ain't you, Cal?'

'Oh, Mammy.' He pulled her back to his chest. 'Ain't never been nothing but yours. All I been doing is playing my guitar to some folks. Made some dollars! And I was gonna give it all to you. I did come here today to see you, honest. That's why I got my guitar with me. I is ready to be a performer, is what I been thinking. Paid and all. Just been getting used to playing to folks, is all.'

'Really? Oh, Calvin.' She wiped her eyes. 'The whole world's gonna wanna listen to you. Don't forget your old Mammy when you is grown too big for this town. I know you gotta go your own way, Cal, just like I always say you got to. But don't forget me. I always will be your Mammy.'

'Who's being a fool now, huh? How you don't remember that if it weren't for you I wouldn't be doing this at all. Remember how we used to sing in the shack, how it all started, my playing and singing? This is all for you. And because of you. With Roots, you showed me how music is.'

Sorrow dropped from her face like a weight, becoming stern in an instant. 'Well make sure that you do it for yourself then. Don't want no guilt on me when get yourself killed over some loose girl.' She fell into his arms and sobbed.

'Hey, Adeline?' came a voice from behind them. 'I really need them bags of sweet potatoes. We getting . . . Oh!'

Booya looked over his shoulder.

'*Oh!*' said Mattie, a sour-faced old maid that he had met once before. 'Calvin,' she cooed, her tone softening. 'Didn't see you arrive. Didn't mean to . . .'

Mammy stepped away from Booya and peered around him.

'Say, is everthing . . . everthing all right?' Mattie asked, seeing Mammy's tear-streaked face.

'The old man ain't dead, if that's what you is really axing, Matts.'

'Well, I . . . *No*. A'course I ain't. I was only trying to see 'bout some sweet potatoes.'

'Have them in a minute. If you can wait a minute that is,' Mammy replied, narrowing her eyes.

'Adeline, my sweet, you take all the time you need.' Mattie smiled. 'Nice to see you again, Calvin.' And she waltzed away.

'I swear she's a witch sent by the devil,' Mammy spewed, the corner of her lip curling.

'Mammy!' Booya couldn't help but laugh.

'Telling you real now, Cal,' said Mammy. 'Don't never spend no single minute with her alone, hear me? I mean it. And take nothing from her. Just stay away from her, Calvin.'

Booya chuckled, delighted to hear that Mammy hadn't stayed sad for long. 'Let me help with them sweet potatoes,' he said.

'Uh-huh,' Mammy said, hands on hips, staring after Mattie. 'And make sure you let the witch see you helping.'

4

Mammy and Booya continued their conversation by the front door of Huck's Place in relative privacy. Mammy smiled to Mattie, who kept looking over at them, before shooting arrows in her back as soon as she looked away. Any other colleague of Mammy's who saw him sang Hi to Booya girlishly, Mammy sticking her chest out further each time, standing closer to him, reminding the other women to whom her coveted son belonged.

Frankie, the midget broadcaster, was skipping in front of Maribelle, his mother, clicking his fingers above his head. She was laughing, clapping, and stamping her feet, not caring that her dress was dusted with dirt.

'What you know 'bout them?' Booya asked.

'I know the rumpus they make. Always laughing, banging 'bout outside here. Annoys the hell out of Huck – not that he's ever here. But I think they pretty harmless.'

In his waddling manner, Frankie was imitating the gait of passers-by. When they noticed the crowd's laughter, he turned away and whistled to the air. Despite the huge and beautiful smile on her childlike face – childlike because she was surely just a child – Maribelle seemed to be telling him not to do that.

'She really his mammy?'

'So they say.' Mammy bit her lips together. 'Story what goes round is that she was got in the family way by her daddy. Can you believe that? Truth tole, don't even like it to pass my lips. The little fella definitely belongs to her, whoever the daddy be. She had him when she was just twelve-years-old, though she don't look a day older even now. The little fella must be, I don't know, maybe eight? Nine? Don't think she even knows for sure. Don't know if she can count that high. Even more than that, I'll never understand how something so small, bred in the way he's tole to be, can be such a clever thing. And how he knows the things he speaks 'bout. 'Specially as folks around say that she been mostly mute for all her life. That ain't the truth, though; you can hear her whispering in his little ear. Even him looking like he does, they love each other like I ain't never seen. And I see the kind of money they making out here, too.'

They watched as little Frankie waddled over to Maribelle, put his hands on her knees and used them to jump up and down, higher and higher. Clapping her hands, Maribelle just chuckled at him.

'They sure is a sight,' Mammy said. 'Yep. But it's just a wonder to think that two such little people can make such *noise*.'

Frankie was spinning around with his arms straight out, with no care for the passers-by, except for their eye. The little guy who had appeared so austere when delivering his broadcast was squealing in a high, flat pitch, *wheeeee*. Maribelle had her arms spread out to her side, her feet tapping simultaneously – running on the spot sitting down.

Mammy sighed. 'I gotta get back to work. Could watch them for hours. He never, never stops causing entertainment. See you tonight then, Cal. Provided you ain't . . . you know . . . following the preacher elsewhere,' Mammy said.

'See you tonight, Mammy.' Booya hugged her and Mammy walked into Huck's.

The guitar was conducting electricity into his hand, telling him what needed to be done. He looked around at who had taken a perch on the stoop. It didn't look as though there were any potential murderers out here.

To his left an elderly lady was knitting, her husband beside her on the bench, smoking his pipe, watching Frankie with a quizzical expression on his bushy brow. On the corner of the stoop four children were running up and down the steps, slapping palms as they passed one another. On another bench a man lay asleep, his hat covering his face despite the shade. To his right, two couples occupied one bench, also watching the manically entertaining Frankie, whispering amongst themselves. Further along, a mother was sitting with children gathered around her. Booya could see nine, maybe ten of them, waiting like hungry ducks. She was trying to keep some order about them as she handed out hickory nuts. They were bouncing up and down, the bigger children pulling the smaller ones in front out of their way to reach their reward first. A little girl with pigtails was standing at the back of the bustling group; her hands crossed in front, patiently waiting for her treat.

The mother was only paying attention to the loudest, those fighting forward. Booya had a mind to go over and pick the little girl up and stand her on the bench next to the mother. But he could see a stout determination behind the little girl's sequential blinking as she shuffled her feet forward, pigtails gently swaying. Booya smiled; she'd get her reward.

And then he caught a cursory glance from one of the three boys in suits. Then another one looked, but he didn't look away.

'Hey man,' he said, beckoning to Booya with a nod of the head.

The boy who beckoned him was the one who had patted his shoulder on the stage. The boy who last night just raised his eyebrows at Booya was the one who had just now glanced and then looked away. He was looking again now that his friend had spoken to Booya. The third boy was playing with the tuning keys on his guitar, paying Booya the same absence of attention that he had last night.

With his guitar on his shoulder, Booya walked down the steps, along the dirt, and stood in front of the three boys in suits. Now the third boy looked up at him, his eyes squinting in the sun.

'Hey,' Booya said. The boy who had called him over offered his hand. As Booya went to shake it, the boy slapped Booya's palm away.

'Personal belief of mine, friend,' he said. 'I makes my living outta these here fingers. Anything what's a threat to them – and I believe that shaking hands is one – I ain't getting involved in. Just a personal belief. I is known 'bout as Black Jack, by the way. Man just to my left here, this is Steal Throat Sam . . .'

'Hey,' said the youngest looking of the three – the one who had glanced.

'And to my right be Rocky Rivers.' The most dapper of the boys slowly looked up from his tuning keys and nodded, almost only with his eyes.

'What's your name, friend?' Black Jack asked.

'Sorry. I is Booya Carthy.'

'Oh yeah, they was saying last night. *Booya*. Nice.'

'Nice,' Steel Throat Sam agreed.

Rocky Rivers maintained his interest in his guitar.

'Was a killer set you performed at Blacks,' Black Jack continued.

Steel Throat Sam sniggered. 'Yeah. Killer . . .'

Booya even saw Rocky Rivers nearly betrayed by a smile.

'We all heared 'bout what happened, Booya,' Black Jack continued. 'That fool give us enough grief ever time we play Blacks, too. Ain't no loss to the world.'

'Yeah, lucky Cole was there,' Booya said, looking around to make sure no one was listening to their conversation.

'Man, Cole looks after all his performers that way. He ain't gonna take no shit. He don't want it so when some player from Chi, or wherever, wants to visit they is fearing for they life.'

'How many times you played Blacks?' Booya asked.

'Well now . . .' Black Jack tipped back his hat. Seeing his full face, the fine hairs of his moustache, looking past the suit and the confidence Booya could see that Black Jack was just a boy, maybe fifteen. Black Jack ran a finger over the soft skin of his chin.

Steel Throat was watching the side of Black Jack's face. 'Gotta be ever night for a week now, ain't it, Black Jack?'

'Say it's gotta be 'bout that, sure,' Black Jack agreed. ''Fore that we was going in there and climbing the stage whenever we gets a chance. Weren't it someone recommended us to Cole?'

'Yeah, your ma's sweet on him,' said Steel Throat. 'She axed him when they was in the sack, after they business was done.'

The treacherous smirk stayed longest on Rocky Rivers' lips.

'Yeah,' Steel Throat continued. 'Your ma was cleaning the floor in Blacks with her skirt, rolling around on it as much as she does.'

'Eight nights now,' Rocky said, licking his lips as he softly thumbed the strings.

'Say what, Rock man?'

'Play there ever night for eight nights now.'

'If you say. Really we is three solo players,' Black Jack addressed to Booya. 'We doing this little gig out here and at Blacks for a while to shine us up 'fore we go to Chi. That's what we is heading toward. Within a week or two we saying, ain't we boys?'

Steel Throat gulped. 'Uh, yeah . . .'

Black Jack turned to Steel Throat. 'Still scared your ma ain't gonna let you go, Sam?'

'Nah man, ain't 'bout ma. I just . . . We gotta be real ready for it to be worth going.'

'Could go tomorrow,' Rocky said.

'I think,' agreed Black Jack. 'Someday soon, anyways. 'Til then, like I say, we spending our days here – like we always done – and our night in Blacks. Say, Booya man,' Black Jack whispered with a wink, 'you'll find, as a blueser, you can get some fine womens in Blacks. And they all up for *whatever* you want.'

'You think Rosie weren't there last night?' Steel Throat asked Black Jack.

'Don't know, man. Didn't see her.'

'She was there,' Rocky Rivers said. Something akin to friendly understanding lurked within his glance at Booya.

'They gonna stay in tune this time, Rock?' Steel Throat asked.

Sliding his middle finger along the strings down the neck towards Steel Throat, he answered him with a glare. Steel Throat coughed.

'So this how it works, man,' Black Jack said to Booya. 'We set off playing a rhythm. If one of us wants to break into a solo, he just fits this kind of a lick

. . .' Black Jack walked his fingers skilfully along the strings. 'Then we keep a rhythm going; whatever we is feeling. But whoever do *this* kinda lick . . .' Black Jack showed Booya again, a slight variation. 'He owns the next piece. Then when he's done leading, nods to us and does a shuffle like this . . . Got that?'

'Yeah,' said Booya. 'I like that way that works.'

'So . . . ?' Steel Throat said, holding out both palms. 'You gonna play standing up?'

'Oh right. Didn't know you was axing me to join with you.'

They all three laughed.

'What you think I tole y'all that for?' Black Jack smiled. ''Cause I like bragging 'bout how clever we is? See you got your easy rider with you. Having one and not using it is like standing up for a girl and her closing the bathroom door, know what I saying?'

'Nah,' said Booya, grinning. 'Know what you saying from the start, Black Jack. I was messing with *you*.'

'Black Jack's used to mens messing with him, ain't you, Black Man Jack?'

'And Sam can only ever tell you what a women looks like from behind, as he watches her walk away. Ain't *that* true, Steel Throat *Jam*?'

Steel Throat pretended to beat on Black Jack, taking soft digs into his side.

'Hey! Hey! Watch the hand, Sam.'

'They is a joke in there,' chuckled Steel Throat. 'I just know they is.'

'Keep it clean, boys,' Black Jack said, patting down his hat. 'Keep it clean. This here's a family establishment, don't you forget it. Oh yeah, Booya. Out on these streets, might not wanna be singing none them songs 'bout drinking whisky. The Law don't bother us none if we sing mostly hokum songs, but they come outta nowhere the second you mention whitey or Jim Crow, things like that.'

'Keep it in order now, boys,' Steel Throat mocked, sharpening up his southern drawl, 'or y'all be cooling down in the jailhouse tonight.'

Grinning, Rocky looked across at Steel Throat. Booya couldn't decide if Rocky was acting diffident or was just plain shy.

'Justice Square ain't seen no action for a while,' Steel Throat continued in his authoritative voice. 'And frankly, boys, I think this town needs itself a good lynching.'

'Yeah, long as you ain't saying things like *that*,' Black Jack said, 'then we ain't gonna have no trouble. Hey!' he yelled. 'Frankie! Over here, man.'

Not leaving her seat, Maribelle watched with a half-smile as Frankie waddled over to the boys.

Standing next to Booya, Frankie held out his little hand, skipped forwards like an excited puppy, then skipped back, kicking up dirt. 'Hey, man,' he said. 'Got a buck for me, huh? Gonna gimme a buck?' Frankie reached up and slapped him on the thigh. 'Messing with you, man,' he rasped. He put his hands in his pockets and shrugged. 'What up, Black Sack?'

'You gonna announce us, li'l man?'

'I guess I shall, if that's what ye require.' Frankie saluted Jack.

'But today you can announce The *Four* Free Riders.'

'Don't wish be acting like the big man in charge or nothing,' said Frankie. 'But I gotta add that this giant here ain't wearing a suit. Might look a bit like a shepherd went and get hisself lost and arrived late with the three wise men.'

Black Jack laughed. 'I don't think the good folk of Honahee gonna be judging too much by our outfits, Frank. He got a hat and buttons on his shirt, don't he?'

'You gonna play standing up, Mister Giant?' Frankie asked Booya.

'Oh.' Booya sat down next to Steel Throat. 'Here?'

'Just follow our lead,' Steel Throat whispered. 'We seen you play.'

'My fair ladies and fine gentlemen,' Frankie screeched, slapping his tiny, round hands together. 'I ask you to gather to witness a special moment in the history of the stoop outside Huck's Place. You seen play The Three Free Riders . . .' he gestured. 'Now, this day, it is my delight to present to you . . . The Three Magi and the Herder!'

The crowd, and The Three Free Riders, laughed. Maribelle covered her face with her hands.

Booya grinned and rubbed the strings of his guitar. Like in the spotlight at Blacks, there was nowhere to hide. His stomach cramped, empty of fuel. What he would give for just one drop of whisky, even a sip of Paw's homemade mud . . .

'Two, three, four . . .' Black Jack said.

Booya had no trouble joining in with The Three Free Riders. Hiding in the background of the song, he picked on his strings whilst the other three strummed rhythms. After a while, he began to feel at ease within the quartet as he improvised to their tight renditions. At intervals they paused to discuss what they were going to do next, and to quietly praise each other for a clever lick or word.

'Gonna do a quick run of See-See Rider,' said Black Jack in the fourth interval. 'That's been sure popular recently. And then, Booya – doing good, man – you gotta do a piece of your own, right? Either one of your own, or play one we all know. You can draw a bigger crowd to us, for sure. You one of The Free Riders now.'

The crowd had certainly thickened. Frankie was dancing on the cobbles in front of the stoop. Unlike last night, Booya could clearly see the faces all around, in the street and along the stoop. After the initial nerves had worn away, hiding within the quartet, Booya was now feeling a touch rubbery again. That was when he looked up and saw Paw standing in the crowd, red-eyed and grinning from ear-to-ear.

'Why don't you come see me play?' Booya asked at supper a few evenings later. He turned to Mammy. 'Both of you?'

'We see you playing outside Huck's Place, Boo,' Paw answered. 'See you play here all the time, too! A private session for the elderly folk.'

Mammy sneered at him.

'Not at Huck's, Paw. And not here. At Blacks. The sound don't get lost like it does in the outside air. Sounds different with a atmosphere feeding it. Blacks' a real blues joint!'

'Well, I –' Paw began.

'No!' Mammy snapped. 'Won't see me stepping a toe in any them places. And that old fool ain't going nowhere near without me. Real blues joint; listen to yourself. A church for the devil is all it is. Drunken men and loose girls slithering all over them like snakes. It ain't right, Calvin; it's *sinful*. Now, I don't mind you going – that ain't to say I like it. And I have to snap tongues to stop the girls talking 'bout it – but you is going there for a different reason, God keep you safe. I don't doubt that they was some rogues in the crowd what Jesus teached to: that's how I tell myself it ain't no harm for my boy to be in there. Tell them gossiping witches that, too. 'Cause even Jesus Hisself run His hands over lepers. Even let a prostitute cry on His feet, then in His way allow her to dry them after with her hair. I ax you . . . He spent time with people less than He was, and that's right, in His way. That's what good and great people do for the lesser. But I ain't never going in there, no, no, no; uh, uh, uh.'

'Only to see me play, Mammy. If you like, Cole will let you stand way over in the side away from –'

'I said No, Calvin,' Mammy interrupted. 'Pass me them chitlins, Cleveland. If I wanna see you play, Cal, then you can go and perform in that yard for me, like when you was little – sweet little boy, you used to be – but I ain't going in there.

'And Cleveland Carthy, you can get that hurt puppy dog look from your dumb old face and sit on it. Ain't gonna turn me into a loose woman, like ever one of them girls what lets theyself be seen in them places. Nuh, I like it just fine watching you outside Huck's. You should hear what the girls say 'bout you, Cal. Makes me so proud. You gonna come down and play tomorrow? And Cleveland, I axed you to pass me the chitlins. And then you can get that clucking chicken outta the house 'fore the whole place turns into a menagerie.'

*

Mammy and Paw had left before Booya awoke the next morning. Walking to town alone with his guitar, Booya spent his time imagining stories to make into songs to play outside the store, picking the strings as he walked. He was distracted, thinking endlessly about Rosie and what The Free Riders had said about her.

Outside Huck's, Booya crunched on a piece of honeycomb – Frankie sitting next to him, clipping bits from his own piece of honeycomb with his big front teeth – by the time The Three Free Riders came into view. By the look of them, they'd had a time the night before.

Frankie jumped up and bowed. 'Have ye a pleasant time in the clutches of inebriation?'

Steel Throat Sam coughed and spat in the dust.

'Haven't slept since I don't know when,' Black Jack answered. 'Sleeping is for the dead and the dying.'

'Would ye agree with that, Mister Rocky Rivers?' Frankie asked, skipping around Rocky's feet.

Curling his lips, Rocky sat down and picked at something in his ear.

Holding a tall paper bag that nearly hid her face, one of Mammy's colleagues glaring after her, wondering what she might have stolen, Maribelle came to collect Frankie. With a dull look of recognition on his waxen face, Frankie's narrow shoulders slumped forward.

'Can't stay 'n' play,' he said. 'Gotta go see my daddy today.'

Queer looks were discreetly shared amongst The Three Free Riders. Sam almost blurted, "See your granddaddy at the same time, huh, Frank?" But he managed to quickly slam closed the door in his steel throat. Instead he coughed.

Maribelle smiled and handed Frankie some pecans. Spilling them to the floor, he scrambled to pick them up. The five nuts he held filled his little palms. Still smiling, Maribelle jerked her head towards the street and nodded once.

'Yes, mom. I gotta go, boys,' he said. 'Don't do anything Tony Camonte wouldn't do.' Without looking back, Frankie waddled beside Maribelle as fast as his legs would allow.

'You got any idea what he was talking 'bout?' Steel Throat asked Black Jack.

'Not a clue,' Black Jack replied.

'Scarface,' Rocky mumbled, picking at a button on his suit.

'What's that Rock?' Black Jack asked.

'Nutin.'

Except for Rocky, they watched as Frankie skipped ahead of Maribelle, the arms of his little suit waving in the dust he was kicking up.

'You ever wear anything 'cept for them suits?' Booya asked, wearing the same brown pants as ever but a different white shirt, acquired by Mammy from Huck's.

'Steel Throat got a spare shirt. But Rocky and me only ever wear what you see us in now.'

'Ever day for eleven days,' Steel Throat said.

'Twelve,' Rocky corrected, not looking up.

'You got a suit, Booya Carthy?'

'No, Steel Throat, I ain't,' Booya answered. 'Have to think 'bout getting me one.'

'If they even make 'em in your size!' Steel Throat Sam replied.

'Ain't no good wearing your hat with them picker's clothes,' said Black Jack. 'That's a blues boy's hat, but clothes only fit for fieldwork. Looks like you sleep wearing that old derby. If you is coming to Chicago you gonna need you a suit, Booya. Won't be no good dressing like a picker in them city joints.'

'Ah, man. I ain't coming with you to the city.' Booya ran a hand down the front of his shirt. 'I . . . I is a country boy with the country blues. Maybe one day, but not now. Sure ain't ready yet for none of that. Only been playing for folks for a handful of days.'

Rocky was smirking.

'Mean to say you ain't interested in the bright lights of the big city?' Black Jack asked, his eyes wide. 'Everone who's anyone – or ever gonna *be* anyone – has made they way up there. That's where the dudes is cutting discs of they own songs. And making real money doing it – not like down at Stanza where you pay! They even getting they discs played on the wire in New York. Someone you ain't never gonna meet, playing your song!'

'You ever heared of Blind Lemon Jeff?' Booya asked.

Black Jack's mouth was open, frozen words sticking in his throat. Steel Throat Sam was waiting to see if he should break into laughter. Rocky sniggered.

'Heared of Blind Lemon *Jefferson*,' Black Jack answered. 'My guess would be that they ain't no one ever heared the blues that ain't heared of Blind Lemon. You heared Charlie Patton? Papa Charlie? Leroy Carr? Huddie Ledbetter? Tommy Johnson? *Robert* Johnson?'

'Uh, yeah,' Booya answered. 'Robert Johnson played Blacks one time.'

'You is big, but you sure is dumb.' Black Jack sucked his lips, inhaled, and then snorted out the air. 'Most they all play Blacks some time or other, man. Get real. And most them bluesers ended up in Chicago, opening the way for new bluesers to follow in they footsteps. *Us.*'

'Chicago gotta be the most talked 'bout city in the whole country,' Steel Throat joined in. 'They got more motorcars there than nearly everwhere in the world added up! They got theatres with them moving pictures showing all day long. Even the hotel signs is made of lights. They is so many whorehouses that you can pick any kind of women you want, and won't even be strung up.' Steel Throat whispered that last part. In his excitement, he was spraying a fountain of spittle as he talked. 'You ever heared little Frank talk 'bout Al Capone? And John Dillinger after him? They is notorious gangsters, that's who they is. And they owned the city. The Law couldn't touch them. They had it all: money, girls, motorcars, guns. And it was only one place they choose to be. Name of that place is Chicago.'

'Uh-huh. And that's where we going,' added Black Jack. 'Ain't it, boys?'

'Damn right,' said Steel Throat.

'You watch your language, Samuel Covern,' said a woman passing into Huck's. 'Or I tell your mama.'

'Uh, yes . . . yes, Miss Patricks. Sorry.'

The other Free Riders rolled on to the floor. Black Jack imitated him, bringing more laughter, and a glare from Steel Throat.

'Ha-ha. You better go home and make sure yo' mama ain't warming no milk for you, *Samuel.*'

'When I get to Chi . . .' Steel Throat looked carefully all around. 'I ain't gonna listen to no warning words from no old maids.'

'But I thought yo' mama was coming with,' Rocky spoke, grinning – Booya noticed for the first time that Rocky's teeth were stained all tones of yellow.

'I say that when we gets to Chi we have us a competition: see who can score the most womens,' said Steel Throat. 'Then we see who talks 'bout who's ma.'

'Yeah,' said Black Jack, 'you gonna be talking 'bout going back home to yours.'

They all laughed, Booya included.

'You gonna see, man. I'll show ya,' Steel Throat said. He began to tune his guitar with such fury that he broke a string. 'Shit!' he spat.

'Oh, that's done it now, Samuel Covern,' said Miss Patricks, just as she was starting down the steps. 'I is going right over to see your mama now. See if I don't. I don't know, in front of women and chiles.' She was still shaking her head as she hovered away.

The three boys were apoplectic with laughter. Heads turned from all around to see them rolling from the stoop and into the street, Steel Throat sitting grumpily between them.

'Gonna play me some of that five-string blues, Sammy?' Black Jack laughed.

Eventually Sam smiled along.

'So, you coming, Booya?'

'Man . . .' Booya didn't know what to say. 'Like I say, might come meet you after y'all settle. After I got a bit of money stashed. You know – ha! – buy me a suit!'

'Gotta live life like a leaf on the wind, Booya Carthy,' Black Jack said, gesticulating. 'Go with the breeze or you get left behind on the ground.'

'Yeah. Well I got time to think first, I guess,' he answered, drawing in the dirt with the toe of his shoe.

'We is going any day now,' Rocky said to the ground. 'I ain't waiting much longer for Sam's ma to dry his cotton diapers. Go to the city without y'all.'

'And me with him,' said Black Jack.

'You ain't leaving me behind, no matter what you say 'bout my mama,' Steel Throat Sam said. 'We The Three Free Riders. But, Jack, you really think that nighttime is the best time to be going? I mean, what if we can't see the train coming?'

'Listen, man, one minute you say you is keen for the coming, then the next you is acting scared as a girl chile.'

'All I is saying is that leaving at night is way more dangerous than going in the daytime. Wanna get there alive, don't we? And jumping the train . . .' Steel Throat picked slinters of wood out the painted porch step. 'I mean, we can afford to pay the fare, and that way we get to sit down all the way!'

Black Jack bowed his head, chuckling lightly to himself, as if he and Steel Throat were sitting in armchairs, alone, beneath lamplight. 'We The Three Free Riders, Sam, not The Three Riders What Pays For They Ticket And Boards The Train At The Station. Look: if you don't wanna come, you don't wanna come. Stay home safe with your ma. But that's how The Three Free Riders do. They going to Chicago even if they only two.'

6

Inside Blacks, people slapped him on the back and called out to him as Booya pushed through the crowd. *Hey man, where you been? You playing tonight, man? Ain't see you play in weeks!* A couple of frolickers yelled *Whisky! Whisky!* into his face, spraying the contents of their words on his chin. A woman who seemed familiar, maybe a colleague of Mammy's in Huck's, wearing a dress that barely concealed the skin of her worn-out chest, tried to grab his face, to pull him into a kiss. Pulling his head from her grasp, Booya smiled and eased her aside. Moving further through the crowd more faces turned to him, distracted from their interest in the man on the stage playing spoons and a harmonica at the same time.

'Hey! Hey, Boo!' A strong hand turned Booya's shoulder. He staggered, treading on people's toes. They glared at him, then smiled, reached up and patted the big man on the back. The man facing Booya had a scar running from the corner of one eye down to the top of his moustache – one scar amongst others on his gnarled face. 'You gon' play tonight, man? See y'got yo' geetar.'

Booya stared down at the man, drawn to the mean-looking scar. You couldn't forget an acquaintance with such a face. He lifted his guitar. 'Guess I will.'

'Tole Cole after I see you play at da picnic he gotta get yo' to play,' the man said, gripping Booya's arm in a tight lock. Booya moved his guitar between his legs, to protect it. 'Y'know, I know den I knowed yo' fum someplace. We both growed up at the Harris Plantation. My daddy knowed yo' daddy. My daddy is – was – Ol' Bill. I still livin' dey –'

Another man had replaced the spoon player on the stage. He was trying to bash his guitar above the noise of the rowdy crowd. When the crowd moved as one, the grip on Booya's arm fell loose. Ol' Bill's son started yelling at the stage. 'Y'in't shit nix'ta Booya Carthy, son. Hear me, shit!'

Booya allowed the crowd to ease him away, towards the bar counter.

Seeing Booya, Cole stopped midway through serving. The man waiting started to yell at Cole, then saw Booya and pumped a fist in the air.

'*Yeah*!' he yelled. '*Booya*! *You playing, man? Hey! Booya's got his guitar. Booya Carthy's here!*'

'See how you been missed?' Cole said, showing his palm to those waiting.

'Yeah, I see,' Booya replied, unable to look Cole in the eyes. 'Cole, I didn't want to seem ungrateful for what you did. I know it was way more than a week ago now, and I ain't been back in, but not many men would –'

'Hey! Boo!' Cole slammed a hand on top of Booya's. 'Stop. Just . . . stop, man. It's done. Forgotten. You ain't got no debt to pay. And I'll do the same again if I gotta.'

'Just been taking some time out, y'know?'

'I get it, man,' Cole replied, nodding. 'I get it. And tell you the truth, it kinda worked out for me, too. People been axing when you'll be back. Trying to find out what town you is travelling through next.' Cole laughed. 'Couple womens even ax me where you live at!'

Booya's eyes lit up. 'Yeah?'

'Yeah!'

'You didn't say I live out with Mammy and Paw, did you, Cole?'

'Nah, man. Say: "Booya Carthy? Well, he a travelling man if I ever see one. Lucky to ever see him down this way again. Though I did hear he might be in the area still, looking to sneak back into town."'

'You say that?'

'Uh-huh. And I got you to thank, Boo. Got in her drawers 'cause of you.'

'Happy to help,' Booya replied, grinning.

Another man was yelling at Cole for service. With one stare, Cole crammed the words back down the man's throat, much further than they had travelled to reach him.

'You playing tonight, then, Boo? I need you, man.'

'It's crazy up in here.' The force of the crowd squashed Booya against the bar, nudging him further over the counter. 'Guess I will if the place is still standing.'

'Couple of cups help you make up your mind?'

Booya got his cups and carried them in one hand, his guitar in the other.

The guitarist on the stage was having a hard time. People were yelling at him. *This Blacks, this ain't Cathy's! You is hurting my ears! You the reason they invent Seabirds! Sing another word and I gonna pound yo' mouth!* Cups were bouncing off him; the crowd louder than the music he was struggling to play. Wet to the soles of his worn-out shoes, he relented.

'You ain't gonna drink both them cups yourself, is you, Big Boo?'

'I got two: one for me; one for you.'

Rosie wrapped her arms around Booya and kissed him, long and hard. 'Missed you, Big Boo. And I mean, I *really* missed you.'

'Yeah?' he answered, holding the second cup away from her.

'Is that all you got to say: yeah?' Rosie said, pulling a sulky face.

Sucking his lips, Booya looked up into the shadowed rafters. 'Guess it is. Yeah.'

Rosie thumped him. He handed her the cup.

'Hear you been playing down at Huck's.'

'Man, news *travels* in this town. But whoever tole you that ain't no liar. Ever day I been there, trying out some daytime bluesing.'

'Was gonna come down and see you play. I mean to, but . . . you know.' She twirled a finger in her hair. 'I been kinda busy.'

'Yeah? What you been doing?' he asked. Booya took a sip and sucked his teeth.

'Oh, this and that.' She was swirling her dress from side-to-side in time with the music – a blues band who had just started up on the stage – and continued playing with her hair. She was half-smiling at Booya, a challenging, devious smile. As he stared down at her, biting his tongue, the guitar filled the space between them.

Petal and Virginia sauntered through the crowd. Both of the girls gazed at Booya.

'Haaiii,' they drawled – husky voice trying to be girly and squeaky voice trying to be sexy.

'Big Boo,' Petal added, the words running off her lips like hot butter.

'Big Boo,' Virginia added a moment later with a confused sideways glance.

'Where you been for all my life, *big boy*?' Petal cooed, running a finger over her curiously absent cleavage.

'Been waiting all my life for you, that's where I been.' Booya leant forward and left a long kiss on Petal's lips, then stooped and did the same for startled Virginia.

With another quick glance, Virginia acted how she had seen Petal respond: forcing her breaths to come in little staggered gasps, hand to breast, fluttering as if she could leave the ground. Then she breathed, '*My!*,' and pouted outrageously, as if she were trying to kiss around a corner. 'I never . . .' she echoed – but Petal had not finished her proclamation, so neither did Virginia. Booya's attention had already returned to Rosie. Someone bounced off him. He didn't notice. With a finger, Rosie beckoned him to her height.

'Wanna see what I got outside?' she whispered in his ear, running her tongue over the curve of the lobe.

'Wanna see what I been trying to keep inside?' he whispered in reply. The words felt cold as they left his tongue.

Taking control of his hands, Rosie led Booya away through the backdoor, leaving Petal and Virginia to relax their stiffened faces.

7

The disc of light above the back door of Blacks was suffocated by the depth of the night. A cool wind blew over the tops of trees, whistling up into the clear sky. A whippoorwill sang out from the depth of cypresses, calling its name. Nocturnal mammals stirred the silence of the undergrowth. Music and mania beat at the back walls of the juke joints and barrelhouses, disturbing the exquisite silence beside the two cups of whisky waiting upon Booya's guitar.

Rosie was sitting in between Booya's legs, her back to him. His arms were around her, holding her to him; her hands resting on his thick forearms. He could feel every rise of her chest. He sipped at his whisky, just as Paw had shown him. Neither of them had spoken a single word since they finished making love on the grass and twigs.

'You ever see your Mammy and Paw?' Booya asked.

'Never knowed my pa,' she replied. 'Ma say that she hardly knowed him, neither. Say that he was a travelling preacher what come knocking one day. She was living in the hillies – Senatobia. That place was dull, man. Empty houses and soil too plain and dry to even grow weeds. I definitely understand the situation my ma was in: that any young-enough man coming through with any kind of offer would attract a young girl, like my ma was at that time. That preacher come, done his thing with my ma, and then moved on to the next lonely young thing. So I never did have a pa, 'cept for the one night he was needed.

'And then ma died. Just all of a sudden, like that. No one ever knowed for sure what happened. She just collapsed by side of the path when she was walking back up the hill from getting groceries. Me, I never really knowed her, neither. Not properly, me just being little when she died. So I went to go live with my aunt, just a few houses down.

'It was the kind of place no one ever leaves; you grow up only ever knowing the folks you always knowed. Someone like me was never gonna be able to stay somewhere dead like that. So, soon as I was old enough, I run away. Felt bad for my aunt, but if I axed her first she never would a let me leave. Probably have chained me to a tree 'til I was old enough for a travelling preacher of my own. I went town-to-town, meeting people and staying with them.

'When I come here Petal was one of the first people I meet. She was so kind to me. Petal, she don't got a lot of confidence. I think she wanted female company around so as she could start feeling a bit more womanly herself. Was dangerous for her, you know. Always has been, looking as poor Petal does, with folks always making up they own mind 'bout her. It ain't fair on her, bless her soul. I think she's beautiful, in her way. Soon enough, she say that I can stay with her. And I stayed ever since. She likes it, and I like it. So we is both happy enough.'

Rosie sniffed. When she tried to chuckle it caught up with a sob in her throat. 'Damn! Was only gonna tell you where I was from, not how I never had nothing 'til Petal.' Rosie wiped tears away from her cheeks.

'Hey.' Booya leaned round her. 'You crying?'

'Nuh-uh. Well . . .' Rosie looked up at the night sky, her breath making a deep cluck in her throat. 'Don't know what I is doing! Ever time I think of how Petal just take me in without no question it makes me wanna laugh out with joy. I love her so much, Boo. She'd do anything for anyone, yet it always seems like people in this town would stand on a flower if she was trying to pick it.'

In the silence, Booya could feel the rising Goosebumps on Rosie's skin. He pulled her closer. And then he began to sing to her.

'*Ain't no angel in the world come down from the sun*
Some folks walk on forever without never finding none
Ain't no love gonna fall from out the sky
Some, they is just happy to let it all pass by
Sweetest honey comes from the bee
And you is the sweetest piece of fruit in the tree . . .'

Rosie giggled and snuggled in tighter to Booya. 'You make that up for me?'

'Sure did.'

'My own private song,' she said, kissing his forearms. 'You and The Free Riders, you the best things what ever happen to this town.'

Clenching his teeth, resting his head on hers, Booya breathed into her hair. 'You think that you can stay with me, Rosie? Just you and me? You be my girl and I be your man only?'

Turning her head to the cypresses, Rosie folded her hands over her chest. 'Keep singing for me, Big Boo.'

'*Ain't no diamond what can buy —*'

Blacks' backdoor slammed open. The shadow of a big man filled the meagre light thrown from the disc above the door. Above the beat of the music they could hear heavy breathing. The head was turning, scouring the darkness. 'Boo?' the figure hissed. 'You out here? Where the hell you at, man? Boo!'

'Hey,' Booya called. 'Cole. Over here.'

'You there! Jeez. You gonna come and play some time, or not? Man, I ain't gonna pay you for just sitting out here getting the end of your thing wet.'

8

Word travelled through Honahee as quick as fire through scrubland. Everyone in Blacks knew that it was the last time they would be seeing The Three Free Riders for a while, maybe ever, before they jumped the night train to Chicago. Blacks hadn't seen such a night since Bessie Smith had rolled into town in her finery and jewellery.

'Next time y'all is seeing us will be in the city!' Black Jack told the baying crowd.

Guitar across his chest like a sword, Rocky Rivers was striking a pose, nothing moving except for his eyes.

'Only catch us in *Sweet Home Chicago* from now on,' Black Jack continued. 'Wanna take a second to thank Mister Cole Kitchens for supporting us . . .'

From behind his bar, Cole surveyed the crowd, nodding his acknowledgement.

'And before we finish tonight, The Free Riders wanna thank y'all, Blacks.'

The crowd went wild. Their uninhibited response lifted the ceiling and scuttled the floor. After pushing the letter from his ma deeper down into his back pocket, pointing his guitar like a rifle Steel Throat picked out girls in the crowd, clamouring for the attention of any of The Free Riders.

Rolling his shoulders, Black Jack pulled the lapels of his suit, brushed them down, and put a hand to his hat with a nod and smile. 'Y'all is too kind. 'Fore we hand y'all over to the new resident performer *extraordinaire*, Mister Booya Carthy! — y'all heared of him?' Leaning towards the crowd, Black Jack cupped a hand around his ear. He looked to where he had earlier seen Booya standing over at the bar with Cole. But Booya was no longer there. 'Axed if y'all heared of Mister Booya Carthy, Blacks!' The other Free Riders smiled with Black Jack, moving towards the back of the stage as they were engulfed by the rapturous applause, the noise like a thunderstorm in a silo. 'Ha! Okay, that's more like it. Now Blacks, this is The Three Free Riders special *au revoir* to you, never heared in public 'fore now. This called *The Womens In Black Done Everthing To Me* . . .'

Starting into a slow-paced song in the country blues style, Black Jack turned to Steel Throat. 'Man, you seen Boo?'

Chewing his bottom lip as he swayed, his eyes for a girl in the front of the crowd, Steel Throat shook his head. 'Nuh.'

Each of The Free Riders had two verses to fill with a solo piece, before joining in as a trio for the finale:

'The womens in Blacks done everthing to me
Don't tell my ma they even done my daddy
They do anything you want them to
And other things beside
The biggest man don't have a clue
When we wriggling between they woman's thighs
'Womens in Blacks this a special song for you
When we gone we gonna miss them things you do
There's still time tonight to show your love
And I'll be keepin' it in my heart
Thank the bad Lord down below
Thinkin' of you with your legs apart'

*

Half-hidden beneath a floppy-brimmed hat, a lot of heads had turned when she slipped in through the door. They didn't often receive well-dressed, pale-skinned beauties walking into Blacks off the street. In fact, they never came in Blacks at all. They didn't even peek through the door. And they definitely didn't walk in like they owned the joint. Above their sinister lust, the men were sure that the classy lady would quickly realise her mistake and stride back the way she had come.

She didn't.

The door closed behind her and she began to look around with the haughty aloofness that prosperity, and skin-colour, granted. The further she advanced, more hesitant grins had appeared on puzzled faces. Intense smirks followed her as she strutted confidently over to Booya.

Upon seeing her, Booya's initial reaction was as shocked as everyone else – the lady had obviously made a dangerous mistake. Using his popularity, he would see that she at least made it back out to the street with her slip in the same place it had been when she had walked in. And then he recognised her. Could even remember her name from when her sunburned old man had called it out.

Maisy.

'Come with me,' she demanded, before Booya could offer to be her chaperone to the safety of the street outside.

'But, miss, uh –' Booya began.

Maisy picked up Booya's whisky and drank from it. 'Come, I said.'

Even the girl on the stage trying to take off her clothes, simultaneously beating her man away from her with a shoe, couldn't distract the attention of the frolickers near the bar.

'Come wh . . . I can't!' he said. 'I is waiting on my girl.'

'Are you trying to say No to me?' Maisy asked, raising her long, thin eyebrows. She brushed her hair back over her ear. 'Well?'

'I got a girl now,' Booya replied.

'And that makes a difference to me how?' Maisy asked, lips tight. 'You don't say No to me.'

Booya looked around at the many faces still interested in the prim little lady he was towering over. Most of the faces fell away as Booya's look of helpless terror met their gaze. He looked for Cole, but could not see him. He put a hand to his neck and pulled the skin. On the stage, The Three Free Riders were approaching the end of their set.

'My old man's next door,' Maisy continued, 'watching some of that dreadful, blaring jazz noise. I'm sure that he would be very interested if I were to go and tell him how you dragged me off at the picnic. Now come. It won't be long before he notices that I'm gone.'

Booya saw her dark eyes twinkling in the shaded darkness beneath the brow of her hat. Picking up his guitar, he led her around the far side of the crowd and out through the back door.

'Here,' she said. 'Down on the ground.' Pulling up her dress, Booya noticed that she was wearing no underwear. 'Quick, quick, quick.'

As soon as Booya pulled the top of his trousers down she was upon him, pounding him into the dirt with animal ferocity. He tried to grip her thighs but she batted his hands out of the ways with her elbows, breathing heavy as a horse through her nostrils, her hair falling over her face, her hat to the ground, growling with each crazed lunge. Riding with her, Booya gripped her ankles, glaring back at her, upping her pace to a gallop. The plod of The Free Riders' country blues, slipping like jellified liquid from Blacks' backdoor, was left far behind.

If he was forced to cheat on Rosie – if cheating was what this was; their lovers pact of this exact site still just days old – this white lady was a pretty warm and sweet place to cheat, even for the danger she brought to his life. It was more like enforced labour as punishment for a crime than it was cheating.

Still on top of him, with not a speck of dirt on either her sequined dress or her white feather boa, she picked up the cup of whisky, took a sip, and handed the cup to Booya. She pushed her hair back from her face, her pale childlike beauty startling, and smiled. 'Did you like that, mister?' she asked him in a soft voice, carefully placing her hat on her rearranged hair.

Fire behind his eyes, Booya nodded as he sipped. With her on top of him he felt a strange protection. His life was in her hands – or between her thighs. Lifting his hips, he raised her up, to feel her, closer.

'Well, there can't be a problem now, can there?' Smiling, she pushed her weight down on his hips, until he could feel her hairs roughening against his skin.

'Guess not,' he said, hating the satisfied grin that spread across his face like hot oil.

'So . . . how do I compare with your girl?' she asked.

'Ain't no comparison, miss,' he answered.

'Well,' Maisy said, drumming her fingers on Booya's chest, 'you won't mind if I come calling again then, will you?'

Booya rubbed his hand over his eyes, and then scratched the itch that had begun to pulse within his eyebrow. 'Can't say No, miss.'

'Right!' She laughed. 'And it's Missus, actually,' Maisy said as she eased herself off Booya. 'Missus Lenut Colden, for your information, as you don't seem capable of remembering that I *do* have a husband. And seeing as we're intimate now . . .' She laughed an execrable laugh, like a witch's curse – a sound that Booya didn't like at all. 'I imagine that it will serve you well to remember that.'

As his fear rose within him, Booya's heart was already pounding.

He didn't know if it was the hat half-shading her face that reminded him, or whether that name had been forever etched on his fears, lying dormant. But he associated the name immediately . . .

'Will you come?' Maisy Colden demanded. 'I ain't hardly going to walk back through that place on my own.'

Clutching his pants, Booya stumbled to his feet. Maisy Colden laughed at him, that same nefarious laugh. He was trembling all over, a shiver hard enough to visibly shake him.

'Are you going to leave that out here?' Maisy asked, shaking her head and smiling.

'Hu . . . huh?'

She chuckled and clapped her hands together. 'I do rather like you. Not a brain cell to boast of, but rather sweet. And most definitely entertaining. Your *instrument*, darling. Lying down there on the floor.'

'Oh . . . uh . . . tha . . . thank you.'

'Do pull yourself together. What's happened to you? It is most unbecoming of such a . . . man of your size.' She fluttered her eyelashes – an affectation that from Petal and Virginia was sweet and childlike, on this woman became callous, sinister, threatening, vulgar.

'Kiss me out here, you big fool. And when we are inside you walk behind me all the way to the door without a word. You look at no one until after I'm gone. When I am, you can do as you wish. But you should be reminded that if word gets around . . . Ha! Well, I'll just say that my husband has a bit of a temper on him. And it would be such a waste if you were to hang.'

With blood turned to swamp mud, Booya walked in through the backdoor, holding it open for Maisy. Men scowled and grinned, leered and frowned. Maisy hid beneath the sanctuary of her hat. Booya had nowhere to hide. He patted down his derby. Daring to glance up, Booya saw Rosie almost immediately, sitting alone in one of the booths and playing with her fingers. At least she was until she saw him and clenched her fists.

Marching behind Maisy, their path led directly past Rosie. He managed to hold her gaze – her glare – for a moment. It seemed that Rosie magically lifted his chin to pierce his eyes with angry questions.

Booya walked Maisy to the door. The door closed and Maisy Colden was gone. Staring at the closed door, he breathed in . . . and then breathed out the weight of his world.

'You in a whole world of trouble, man!' some helpful, smiley fellow pointed out to Booya exactly what was trying to kill him from within.

Cole caught Booya's eye. He went to the bar and held up two fingers: two cups. Another finger appeared – another one of his fingers, presumably with a better idea. Cole brought three cups to him.

'I understand, man. Whatever you think you was doing with that white lady, I got you. Do what you gotta do with Rosie, but you is going on stage straight after. I ain't putting up for no more of this drunken song and dance, not when they is paying people in here waiting for they own song and dance.'

'The Free Riders left yet?'

'Yeah, Boo. 'Bout ten minutes ago.' Teeth clenched, Cole wiped a rag over the bar counter.

The guitar a weight in his hand, Booya sighed.

'Black Jack say for you to look 'em up if you ever make it to Chi, if they ain't too big to be associating with you then, he say.' Cole huffed a laugh. 'Go,' he said. 'But be back.'

Booya set down a cup in front of Rosie. She just sat and stared at him. Booya had only brought two of the three cups with him. The other was sitting empty on the bar. He sipped at his second cup. 'I had no choice, Rosie,' he said. 'Can explain it all to you. Ain't gonna lie to you. But I had no choice.'

'Oh, you ain't gonna lie,' Rosie replied. 'You can explain and you ain't gonna lie. Tell me what makes it all right for a man to do what he wants? But what, you think I should just stay home so I can't have my fun? I thought you mean what you say 'bout me being your only girl, Booya. But obviously that means shit so long as you is getting yours, *wherever* you gotta get it.' Rosie crossed her arms and sat back, hard.

'Rosie . . . See . . . at the picnic, the day I first meet you, they was this –'

Almost sensing it, Booya looked up in time to see the doors of Blacks burst open. With his hat low over his sunburnt face, Lenut Colden was brandishing a long-barrelled six-shooter. Even though he looked like an image from a child's nightmare, this bad dream had become dangerously real. Colden looked ready to empty his lead into the first person who filled his sights. Booya couldn't see Colden's eyes, but he could imagine them: cold and dark as flint, ready to burst into flame.

The sheriff and two deputies filed alongside Colden, their firearms readied by their sides. A few women screamed. A couple of men screamed, too. The wizened national steel player on the stage fell from his stool and slithered across the boards. Some of the hardened regulars of Blacks dreamed of moments like this. They slowly slid switchblades and assorted knives from their pockets, intent flickering in their eyes. Others hid their cups behind their backs.

Cole Kitchens was already around his bar and approaching Colden.

'Where's the nigger what done my wife?' Colden yelled, breaking the silence.

He raised his gun, levelling it around the crowd. 'All y'other niggers can go 'bout your business as soon as I get the nigger what done my wife. Tell you now: fuck the jailhouse; you'll be hanging in Justice Square tonight, even if you're already dead by the time you're strung up. So tell me, niggers: which one of you motherfuckers done my wife?'

The sheriff put a hand on Colden's gun arm and whispered something into the darkness beneath the hat.

'Get the hell offa me,' Colden shouted. 'I ain't doing nothing 'til I get that nigger.'

The click of blades opening accompanied the crowd advancing upon Colden, beginning to encircle him and The Law. Breathing steady and low; solid shoulder pressing into solid shoulder, moving as a wall. Muscles flexing as fists clenched; chins jutting forward and brows lowering. The rest of the crowd began to edge slowly away from the aggressor as the emboldened inched forward.

A shotgun concealed down the back of his pants, Cole continued to approach Colden.

'Rosie,' Booya whispered. 'Come with me.' Booya reached across the table to her.

She was still too angry to pay much mind to the dangerous ruckus. As Colden's gun pointed at the crowd, her glare was trained on him.

'I gotta get outta here *now*,' Booya hissed. 'Please, Rosie.'

'How 'bout I just stand up and tell him that cheating nigger's right over here with me instead?' she growled through her bared teeth. 'How 'bout I do that instead?'

'Rosie, please. I gotta leave now! I can tell you it all, but I gotta go. You gonna come?'

'Are you gonna hand him over to me?' Colden yelled. 'Or am I gonna have to start shooting me some niggers 'til I get the right one? Believe me, I don't care if I do.'

Booya noticed that a few treacherous looks were being arrowed in his direction.

'If I stay in here another minute I is gonna *die*, Rosie,' Booya whispered, his teeth rattling as his jaw trembled.

'Why don't you leave my joint 'fore anything gets ugly?' Cole said.

The only sounds that could be heard were breathing, the creeping of shoes and the occasional metallic click of another opening switchblade. Colden swung his gun on Cole, standing ten feet from the end of his barrel.

'Got something you want to say to me, nigger?'

'Yeah . . .' Cole stared deep into muzzle, and then held Colden's eyes. 'I can't guarantee that you'll leave here with your life if one nigger falls in here. Just so you know. If that's what you want.'

'You threatening me?' Colden hissed.

'If anything, I is protecting you. All you.' Cole indicated the sheriff and his deputies.

'That right?' Colden replied.

'Yep,' said Cole. 'See, I would guess that if anything *did* happen with your wife, it weren't the fault of no nigger in here. Ain't trying to imply nothing, but you might just yourself killed over that. Gotta ax, *is* it worth getting yourself killed over?'

'Stay back, Cole,' warned the sheriff. 'Just shut up and watch yourself, nigger. Easy, Lenut.'

Lenut Colden's jawbone was pulsing with fury. Coiled around the trigger, his finger had begun to moisten. 'You trying to antagonise me, motherfucker?'

'Sheriff, you know what I is saying. Ain't no way all these here men is gonna stay standing back and watch this man shoot at us.'

'Lenut,' the sheriff began after a vicious glare at Cole. 'We'll get the nigger. But I think that we should take some time to consider –'

'I'll give a hundred dollars to the nigger what gives up that bastard nigger to me,' Colden called out to the room.

Those were the last words that Booya heard Lenut Colden yell, as the backdoor to Blacks closed quietly behind him. He grabbed Rosie by the arms and pulled her into the darkness.

'Listen, Rosie, all I can say now is that if hadn't done that with her she would see me hanged.'

'But you did it anyway. And now all you gonna get is shot. Good choice, Booya.'

'It ain't . . .' He lingered a look at the backdoor, quiet beneath the dull saucer of light, and calmed his voice. 'It ain't like that, Rosie. Explain it to you another time. But I gotta leave this place. Now. Tonight. Can't go back to Mammy and Paw – I ain't gonna bring no trouble home to them. You hear him saying just now that he's gonna give a hundred dollars for my name? Some fool will act the snake for sure and tell that crazy fool where I can be found if I ain't gone from here, you know that. I can't bring that on them. Maybe if I ain't there though . . .'

'So where you gonna go then, Booya? Gonna bring your trouble to mine instead, that what you saying?'

Glancing up again at the backdoor, Booya gripped Rosie tighter. 'Gonna see if I can catch up to the others. The Free Riders. They going to Chicago right now. Rosie, come with me.'

'And have you cheating on me again, but hundreds of miles from home? Nu-huh. Thanks, but no way, Booya.'

'I can promise –'

'Yeah. Promise . . .' Rosie pulled her arms from his grip and crossed them over her chest, transferring the weight on her feet.

'I *can* promise . . . Look, Rosie, I love you. But I gotta go *now*. Can't *stay* no more. Just say you gonna come.'

Gripping the neck of his guitar, Booya gritted his teeth and stole a final look at the door. The image of Rosie was becoming kaleidoscopic through his moistening eyes.

'Just want me to leave everthing behind and come with you, even though it's clear I barely know you, you doing what you just done?'

'Please, I –'

'I ain't going with you, Booya,' Rosie said, shaking her head. 'If you stay around I might give you a chance. But I ain't leaving here, no way. I can't just leave Petal and everthing I got here.'

'If I stay I is dead.'

'That's your choice.'

'They *ain't* no choice!' Booya growled in a harsh whisper. He pinched the bridge of his nose hard, to feel the pain. Spittle sprayed from his lips. 'I don't wanna go, Rosie. But I don't wanna die, neither.'

He tried to touch her arm but she pulled away from him. The sound of music pounding from the inside of the jazz joint mingled with the sound of insects in the undergrowth. Looking at Blacks' silent backdoor, Booya felt a tear fall from his cheek.

'Please go to Huck's Place and tell Mammy that I had to go. Tell her whatever you have to. Please do that for me, Rosie. Adeline Carthy's her name. Tell her that I is gonna write her soon as I can. Please. Just do that one thing.'

Staring away from him, over her shoulder into the darkness of the

145

cypresses, Rosie didn't say a word.

'I love you,' he said.

Clutching his guitar, he walked backwards until he could no longer see Rosie, as the night-shadows enshrouded her.

CHAPTER
SIX

1

From the roof of the stoop, the smell of blossoming honeysuckle filled the air. Everything appeared the same, but different, older, as if it had slipped even further back through time as the world revolved forwards. It was mostly old folks gathered on the stoop outside Huck's Place, gossiping, eating, or sitting side-by-side in silence, shaded from the sun. A young boy was inexpertly but patiently picking at the strings on a guitar many times too big for his knee. A girl, a younger sister perhaps, was sitting cross-legged on the cobbles in front of the boy, watching him. The blind Indian was shuffling his feet, bumping into people. Children were imitating him: hands spread out before them, repeatedly bumping off each other, apologising, asking for change. A pair of dogs began to growl, bark, and then scrap, a blur of bared teeth and raised hackles. It was the only sign of tension in an otherwise blissful and contented town.

The boy noticed that a large shadow had crossed over him. He stopped playing and looked up, running his eyes over the hard guitar case, up the suited chest. High above him, silhouetted by the sun, he could just see the eyes of the big man under the brief rim of his hat. The little girl was also looking, peering under the shield of her hand, sheltering her eyes from the blazes of 'Old Hannah'.

'Gonna be a blues man?' the man asked the boy.

The boy shrugged. That posture of chin on chest, looking through the tops of the eyes, was familiar to the man. He too had once seen through those eyes.

'Keep on practicing, man. That's a country blues guitar picker's hand if I ever see one.'

The man walked away, leaving the boy and girl inspecting his hand as if it were something they had dug up.

The flowers and grasses in the gardens of Redemption Square were in full bloom; the hanging tree only conspicuous by the lime-green leaves growing upon it, rather than the gnarled black trunk and infamous limbs. This was the prosperous third of the town, attractive and unpretentious. But everything around was bland and dust-covered compared to the bright lights of the city. They were linked only by railroads, like an unpolished gem hanging on a trinket bracelet next to a shiny bullet.

This third of the town looked just as run-down and wheezing as when he had left. The barrelhouses and juke joints seemed even more tired than he remembered. Back when he had nothing to compare it with. The nervous-looking hopefuls behind the window of Stanza Studios looked younger, less distinguished, like tiny fish in a small pond. In the barbershop the men were still gathered round, still laughing and slapping thighs. But they too appeared older, balder, less rambunctious.

Just when he was thinking that at least there would still be one place left to raise sand around here, he saw the facade of Blacks. At first he thought he must have remembered it to be in the wrong place. There was no black guitar sign creaking in the breeze; no raging music blasting the door ajar; no red-eyed drunkards hanging half-in and half-out the door. There was just a dull-grey wooden barn with the windows painted out. It might house storage crates or pigs, there was no way to tell. The only noise in the street was the happy tinkling of piano keys coming from behind another door.

The man gripped the wrist of a passer-by. The stranger responded by looking at him as though he was trying to spread rabies.

'Hey man, sorry. Didn't mean to grab you like that. You know what happen to Blacks?'

'City types,' the man said to no one as he walked away with his nose pointed to the sky.

The big man watched him go. He was obviously travelling back to Huck's side of town.

'They was a brawl,' said a voice from behind him.

The man spun round. The perfectly round face with the high hairline looked vaguely familiar; as did the jaundiced eyes. This man had definitely been a frequenter of Blacks. Upon seeing the stranger's face, the man narrowed his eyes.

'You Booya Carthy, ain'cha?'

Booya removed his derby. The difference between the stifling heat of the city and the breeze-washed warmth of Honahee was total. But it was a hot day beneath that same sun they shared. Today the sun was a guiding star, pulsing directly above the country town.

'Yes, sir,' he replied.

'Been you to Chi?' said the man, looking the suit and boots up and down.

'Yep.'

The man's line of questioning exhausted, he began to walk away.

'Hey, wait! You know what happen to Blacks, man?'

The man pulled a rag from his pants pocket and rubbed his chest inside his shirt, his armpits. 'They was a brawl,' he repeated. He wiped his forehead and face and put the rag back in his pocket.

'What happen? Why's it closed?'

'"Member Cole?'

'Yeah, sure,' Booya replied.

'A'course you would. Well Cole, some fellas was saying that he raped they cousin. Y'know, take her without –'

'I know what you saying.'

The man looked the sorry barn up and down. A bead of sweat swung from the tip of his nose. 'So these fellas come here one evening. Didn't even do it when Blacks was empty. They done it when the place was near rammed to the rafters.'

'Done what, friend?'

Booya put his hand in his pocket and pulled out a dollar. He had only a few. With it he had inadvertently also pulled out a train ticket. He gave the dollar to the man.

'What's this for?' asked the man, staring at it as if he wasn't sure what the strange piece of green paper could do.

'Your story,' Booya answered. In the city if you needed directions to the street around the corner you had to pay for the privilege. 'I wanna hear it.'

'Was getting to it.'

Booya nodded.

'So, these fellas, they come drugging they girl cousin in with 'em. They ax, pointing at Cole, "He the one what done you up?" And she's screaming, this cousin. She scream, "Yeah was him. But I wannid him to." Saying she loved him and such. She was screaming, "Don't hurt him. I love him." Seem like these fellas ain't liking her screaming that. One of 'em, he put the back a his hand 'cross her mouth, send her to the floor! I mean, you 'member that floor, don't you, Mister Booya? Weren't fit for rats to shit. But that stop her screaming. For 'bout minute at least.'

The man pulled out his rag and continued his ritual wiping, chest first . . .

'Sure is a hot day today in Hon'ee,' he said. 'Was the city real hot, Mister Booya?'

Booya nodded, fingering the few remaining dollars he had in his pocket. 'What happen next, friend? What did Cole do?'

'Well, them mens, they was saying, "See how you make our poor cousin crazy?" and such. "See how you done warp her mind?" Now Cole, he wasn't saying nothing, but you could see his hands moving under the bar for his shooter. I knowed then – we all us in they knowed – that they weren't gonna be settling this over a drink.

'"Was her choice to do what she done," Cole say after a time, something like that. "She knowed what it was she was doing." Maybe Cole shouldn't have sayed what he did with a smile, 'cause that gets the mens all up in a bigger rage. "She carrying, you mollydodger, you know that? She carrying your chile and saying she loves you and you won't even speak with her. You done ruint her life, nigger" – s'cuse me, Mister Booya – "You done ruint her life, and now we is here to ruin you."

'The look on Mister Cole's face told me that he didn't know then that girl was carrying his chile. He look at that girl like maybe he wannid to kill *her* first! Then he was screaming back at them that she done it to try and get him, to keep him. That she put a hexing voodoo curse on him. Cole say she be rubbing her piece on gravestones at midnight and all such things. That she deserve to die with the unborn bastard still inside a her. He just go crazy. And that was when all hell braked loose.' Holding the damp rag in both hands, the man hung his head.

'Don't know if that girl ever did die with that baby a Cole's inside her, but she gotted away that night. She the only one of them what did. Mister Cole take both them fools down with him when he went. They was both already done and dead and he was standing over them, bleeding like you won't believe, Mister Booya. Look like he was shot in half!

'Was a Saturday night crowd inside Blacks the night it happen. Everone was just standing and watching, not believing what they just seed. Y'understand, the whole damn thing didn't take but more than a couple fingers of minutes. Just when it look as though Cole was gonna try and make sure that bubba weren't never born, he falled down. And he never did get up.'

Booya lifted his head, put his hat back on. 'Anyone else die that night?'

'No. No one else die. But Law say they wannid a piece of cooling off time. See, The Law see the sum of cash Cole had stashed by running the bootleg liquor. A'course, no one was gonna tell the law the source of all that sauce, heh-heh. Law say that 'til someone telled where it was coming from this place can gather dust. And that's all it's been doing ever since, Mister Booya. Must be near on a year 'go now, soon after you jump town. Yep, sure looks a sad and sorry old story now, Blacks.'

Booya pulled out another dollar and stuffed it in the man's hand. Then he continued on his way, leaving the man to wipe sweat from his body.

2

Having journeyed so far to return to this place, standing on the skirt of blacktop Booya wasn't sure if he could take the final step. This was not returning after a night or two beneath the bridge. Everything looked and sounded just as it should, but happy memories could not come. Through the trees and bushes, Booya could see the modest wooden house that he'd helped to build. But it didn't feel right. How could he travel back to his own past and be a stranger?

The suit on his body felt tight, becoming tighter. He stepped off the blacktop and onto the tired earth. He expected crazy, viperous niggers to come running, waving their hundred dollar reward in the air. He expected that half-hidden face to come stepping through the doorway, noose hanging over his shoulder. *I've been waiting for you . . . Boo*

But it remained as peaceful as ever. As peaceful as dying alone.

Booya opened the front door. It was new; it had a window and tied-back curtains. The room was exactly the same; mostly the same things on the tables and shelves. But it smelt damp and cold, not as he remembered it at all. He could remember it smelling of the fruity aromas from Mammy's boiled preserves, of burned wood and roasted meat. Homely. This smell was bitter, unwashed, rotting and lifeless. Even though he'd stopped by the river to drink, his throat was dry. The water that had dribbled down his front had dried in minutes.

Throughout the house it remained the same, seeing it bringing instant recall. But both beds were unmade; dirty dishes in muddy dishwater in the messy kitchen. The clothes that littered the floor definitely belonged to Mammy and Paw. There were even a few of his own. But everywhere was untidy, as if a bear had ripped through the little place. From the armrest of one of the chairs, a chicken watched him as he walked outside.

Vegetables were growing in the patch. A few had been lifted and strewn. *Mister Wilbur used to do that,* Booya thought, hand on his heart, *if he didn't munch them first.* He remembered now that, when he had been curled up in the city smoke, the noise of life and motorcars passing by outside, it was the perfect serenity of the clearing, Mister Wilbur snuffling nearby, that he had tried imagine to carry him from his stupor. But he could never quite hear the birds in the background; could never quite smell the rich country soil. Drinking in the city could never be the same as sitting out here sharing a cup with Paw. But he had drunk.

He looked over his shoulder. The chairs that his folks used to sit on out front weren't there. At least he finally knew what had tortured him on his journey home, tormented him for a year; what he didn't want to know: they had left, or . . .

He had done this. He had brought this ending to their lives here. Hard as it was to admit it, he'd had a choice: the city or the noose. He had chosen himself over Mammy and Paw. Though baked as dry as the earth, a tear found its way from his eyes. He slumped to the ground. His derby fell from his head and rolled away. Barely noticing that he was hugging his guitar – scratched, battered but in one piece – he stayed on the ground for what seemed like a long time. A city minute. Over the last year he had passed many hours that way.

When he had the courage, no matter for the consequences, he would return to the town and try to discover what had happened to Mammy and Paw. As no one was any longer living in the house, his heart overflowing with sorrow, Booya decided that he would reclaim it. But not now.

Mister Wilbur might have somehow survived to live in the clearing, if he hadn't wandered off or been led away by some chancing soul. Summoning the last from his empty barrel of strength, Booya stood up. To get away from the house, he decided he would take the guitar out to the clearing, play only the songs and hallies that he and Mammy used to sing until the sun fell from the sky. If he didn't sleep out there, he would come back, light a fire, plan how he might set up his new life. Deep inside him he felt hope bobbing about like a pear on acid. Maybe he could find Rosie and she could come and live out here with him. Might Mammy and Paw have returned to work for Mister Henry?

A flight of butterflies came at him through the sunlight as he trudged down the woodland path. As they clouded around him, invading his route, Booya stood there in miserable wonderment. He felt brushed by angels, just like when Paw used to . . .

Booya had barely given notice to the standing tears crystallizing his view. He blinked, his eyes clearing enough to see Mister Wilbur, thin and frail, rooting in the grass. Mister Wilbur appeared shorter than he could ever remember him being. With the same big white patch on his side, there was no doubting that it was him.

Booya rubbed Mister Wilbur's course-haired back as he tore up browned grass and ground it in his teeth. With his mouth full, Mister Wilbur looked up at Booya through one big oily eye, seeming to accuse him.

'I is sorry, Wilbur,' Booya said aloud, stroking the mule's mane. 'Real sorry, boy. But I gonna make it up to you. Gonna plant you some of your own –'

'Calvin?' The voice was soft and croaky. '*Calvin?*' Then it was shrill, shouting: 'Is that you? Is that really my boy?'

As he spun round, Booya stumbled back onto Mister Wilbur, nearly knocking the old mule over. Though not quite as round as he remembered her, Mammy was easing herself up out of her chair. She put a hand to her mouth and gasped loud enough to shake birds from the branches.

'It is you! It's my Calvin!' Mammy lifted her hands, showed her face to the sky and dropped to her knees. 'Oh Lord. Oh, thank you, Lord. Thank you, Lord. Oh, thank you.'

Springing up, she turned and slapped Paw hard on the shoulder. 'Wake up, you old fool.' Falling from his chair, Paw managed to catch himself halfway to the ground. 'The good Lord has returned our *son!*'

'Booya?' Paw looked frail, skin-covered bones. Still, he leapt from his chair and skipped across the clearing, free as a child, chuckling as he went.

His sallow face made the shine of his smile appear even brighter, a smiling face that could make the moon glow. 'Hey, Boo,' he said, nearly managing to pick Booya up. 'You been having a time?'

Mammy thumped Paw out of the way and merged to her son.

'Being honest, Paw,' Booya sobbed, 'I ain't had much of a time, no. Not without y'all.'

'You telling me!' Paw hugged his long, bony arms around Mammy and Booya.

They stood that way for a time: Mammy sobbing, Booya sobbing, and Paw chuckling like a chicken. Booya noticed that the smell of Angel's kisses was coming not only from Paw; he'd had a companion to sail on down Fool's River with him. And then Mammy said the same thing that Booya had been thinking, strange wonder of sight after a year.

'Tell me it really is you. Say you really is my boy, my Calvin, and not some evil trick of the devil.'

Except for Booya had been thinking a gift of God.

'It's me, Mammy; I swear it.' Booya began to sing *Rock, Daniel* – the song that he and Mammy used to sing in the dilapidated shack. One of the first songs that he had ever learned to play. The first song that he had pledged to himself he would play this day in the clearing.

'Let's have us a fire,' Paw said, relaxing his embrace, 'out here in the clearing. Celebrate you coming home. You gonna fill us all a cup, woman?'

'Ain't no way you gonna catch me drinking the devil's brew, Cleveland Carthy,' yet wetting the shoulder of Booya's suit. She sighed. 'Wait, Cle, seeing as it's a celebration . . .'

*

The light turned to night, the chickens returning to roost in the trees, or the house. Paw had fashioned a rudimentary spit from branches. Having turned the chunk of pig roasting above the embers, he dropped unsteadily onto his chair.

'You hear 'bout Cole, Paw?' Booya asked.

Clasping his hands together, Paw watched the devils dancing over the branches in the fire. Mammy pulled a blanket tight around her shoulders. 'I heared, Boo.'

'I still don't understand why you run to the city, Calvin,' Mammy said, reaching out to touch Booya. 'Why you just run without a word.'

Looking up at Mammy, his eyes settling on the ground halfway, he moved his guitar behind him. 'They was word around that some men, some crazy jealous fools, was planning to rid the town of musicianers. And that me and The Free Riders was top of the list – that's why we leave together. Turned out it weren't true, it was Cole they want all along.' Booya glanced up at Paw – he was still staring deep into the fire.

Mammy nodded. 'Please say you ain't gonna play in they no more, Cal.'

'Blacks' closed, Mammy.' Booya laughed through his nose. 'Truth tole, the whole thing makes me wonder 'bout if ever I want to play *anywhere*. Hey, Mammy, why you crying again?'

'Oh, Calvin.' Using the blanket to wipe her face, Mammy enshrouded herself. 'You can't know how ever time that little Frankie stepped up on that fruit crate, all I . . . all I ever thought he was gonna say . . .' The blanket heaved up and down. 'I can't. I can't even say it.'

Paw laughed so hard that, this time, he did fall off his chair. 'Pull yourself together, woman,' he said, in turn pulling himself up off the earth. 'Boo's back with us now, ain't he?'

'How can you say such a thing, Cleveland Carthy?' Mammy spat. She threw her cup at Paw; he watched it pass his head approximately five seconds after it had. 'You know how hard it's been hurting. Even though you got the hard, stupid head of a fool, been hurting you too.'

'What I is saying is we should be joyful, woman! Not live sad, but with love and cheer. Maybe a little drink to add a dribble more cheer. It don't hurt none.'

'Don't think I don't know that, foolio? These is mostly tears of *joy*. Now, can I please explain to my son just why I feared for him so bad without getting interrupted ever five seconds by a hen-head like you?'

'You always have done what you done if that's what you want done.' Paw frowned, walking himself back through his words.

In the quarter-turn of her head, Mammy changed from austere and returned to sorrowful, sniffing and wiping her eyes. Staring into the bottom of his empty cup, Paw sighed.

'Folks was saying, see, that you was dragged out behind that devil's place and killed, like happens from time to time. I know they is lies, Cal, but they was mostly saying that you was caught with a white man's wife, and that he was aiming to kill you. That the sheriff, even, was gonna help him string . . .' Once more Mammy began to sob. A shiver ran through Booya as he looked in to the darkness beyond the fire. 'Why couldn't you just tell us you was going?'

'I tried, Mammy,' he said, attempting to see her through the blanket. 'I mailed letters to Huck's, with a return address on the back. When I never heared back . . . I was scared as you was!'

Slowly peeling back the blanket, Mammy glared at Booya. 'You wrote me at the store?'

Booya nodded. 'Uh . . . huh. What?'

Shaking her head, Mammy gripped the blanket, stirring the fire with her eyes. 'If I leave a grocery list on the counter one of them dragons would stash it in they pinafore to dissect later. One of them *knew*. Standing next to me, watching little Frankie with your letters in they pinafore, they *knew*.' Mammy narrowed her eyes to slits. 'And I got a good idea just who it might be, evil witch.' Opening the blanket, she looked up at the pale moon. 'My Calvin. My boy. Oh, the Lord must have heared my prayers, even with so much evil going on in this world. A miracle, ain't nothing short.' With furrows appearing on her forehead and her lips twisting in all directions, she turned to face Booya. 'I never give up on you, Cally. Not once. No matter what them dragons and fools was saying 'bout you. And that little Frankie up on his crate . . . The Lord is a good Lord. Had my doubts in my darkest moments. Even Jesus Hisself be tested by the devil at times, you know, Cal. But the good Lord didn't never give up on you 'cause I was axing Him to keep you safe for ever second you was away. My Boy. My Cal . . .'

'See, there you go again, woman,' Paw said, pointing his cup. 'I remind you, that's the same kind and omnipotent Lord what give Moonshine as a gift to His people on earth.'

'You lucky I ain't got nothing more to throw at you, you old fool. But don't think I won't come over there and whup yo' ass.'

Paw cackled. Mister Wilbur joined them in the clearing. 'Hey!' Paw yelled. 'Hey! That damn mule's been at my vegetables again.'

With his heel, Booya kicked his hat behind him. 'Mammy, in the days after I leave Honahee, did no one come to you in the store and say how I had to get away? Girl called Rosie.'

'Nuh, never got no message from no one,' Mammy replied. She narrowed her eyes. 'Even if those witches would hide a letter, they would a passed a face-to-face message along, for sure.'

3

Comfortable in his itchy picker's clothes, Booya grabbed his boots and spilled out of the front door. 'Hey, Mammy! Paw! Wait a minute; I gonna walk to Huck's with you.' Hand-in-hand, Mammy and Paw exchanged glances. 'What? You don't want me to come?

Magnolias in full blossom, like blooms of scented cotton, surrounded the house. The sun was yet to breach the thick canopy, teasing the tops of the pines to red. Around the vegetable patch, the chickens pecked the ground for discarded seeds. Paw glared at them.

'Sorry, Boo,' he said, walking towards Booya, Mammy following. 'Just that, you know, the last time, when you never come home . . . Gonna take us some time to get over. All us.'

'You can trust me. Look at me!' Booya held out his arms. 'I is a big boy these days.'

'A big boy with a gentle heart,' Mammy added with a weak smile, stroking Booya's arm. 'It ain't 'bout us trusting you, Calvin; we always have done. It's that you is so free to trust everone else.'

Booya looked up at the tops of the pines, knitting his eyebrows. 'I did learn some things in the city, you know. "We live and we learn by our mistakes," ain't that what you always like to say, Mammy?'

'So long as them mistakes don't kill you first, Cally. So you can learn to live by them again.'

Widening his eyes, Booya looked at his hands. 'I is here now, ain't I?'

'Caring Calvin Carthy, that's what I'd like your singer's name to be,' Mammy said. 'Ain't all gotta be Evil Snake this and Devil Head that. You can show all them others the way.'

Booya shook his head. 'I is out the business now. Ain't barely played Mister Henry's guitar since I come back. Don't care if I do. I is more like Cultivating Calvin Carthy now.'

Paw laughed and slapped his hands together. 'Yep. Helping out your ol' man on the homeplace, that's what you for now.'

'Cally, you ain't gotta waste your talent just 'cause you was offering it up in the wrong place,' Mammy said, waggling a chubby finger, glancing at Paw. 'They's a place for you in the church, with your gift being God-given and all.'

'Maybe one day, Mammy.' Booya fanned his fingers. 'For now these is just farmer's fingers.'

'For the land and for the Lord,' Paw said.

Mammy glared at him. Then she softened and agreed. 'That's right. You might yet find yourself wanting to play again for them crazy fools,' she said. 'And that's just fine too.'

Smiling, Booya rolled his eyes and shook his head. 'But you don't want me to come with you today?'

'We'd love for you to walk with us,' Mammy said. 'It's just . . .' Looking around, she sucked the tip of her tongue.

'It's just been a while since you left the homeplace, Boo,' Paw continued. 'Was beginning to think you never would again!'

*

When they arrived in the centre of town, the sheriff and his deputies were standing on the courthouse steps, adjacent to Redemption Square. A civilian white man was standing with them. He was wearing no hat. The chin did not appear to be as angular as Booya remembered that of the Colden's; his cheeks not as reddened by the sun.

Booya lifted his hand to adjust his hat. But he had left it back at the homeplace.

One of the deputies was saying something; the sheriff and the co-deputies were laughing. Their laughter travelled to Booya like voices muffled through a coffin lid. As he passed, their laughter faded. It seemed that each man was looking at him in turn, watching him pass. Even though he was more than a head taller, he made sure that he was walking between Mammy and Paw.

Tempting a last glance over his shoulder, Booya finally relaxed when they were free of the square.

'What's it 'bout The Law what makes them so hated, Paw?'

Mammy looked at Booya skeptically.

'Don't know if hated is the word so much as feared, Boo. Yep, give them a badge and they just become vigilantes; do whatever they feel like doing 'fore axing any questions, whether it's within the legal law or not. When I was young we used to be able to laugh with them. And they call us fellas, not niggers. They just become bolder and bolder the longer they is in uniform. I always thought it was just us black men what feared The Law. Me myself, I never was afraid of them none. Until I see with my own eyes kind Mister Henry murdered by that deputy in cold blood. And he –'

'Cleveland!' Mammy snapped. Heads turned. 'We agreed that we weren't never speaking of that in front of Calvin,' she hissed. 'Now look what you gone done with your whipping tongue, just like as is in this town. Old fool.'

'Is that the truth though? That The Law . . . ? Mister Henry's dead?'

'It happen all them years ago, Calvin,' Mammy said. 'When you was little.'

'But it was really The Law what done it?'

Mammy sighed.

'Uh-huh.' Paw nodded. "Fraid that's the truth of it, Boo. See it with my own eyes, like I say. It's the sad truth, but the truth it is.'

'But why did they wanna kill Mister Henry?'

'Was political. They didn't get they own way with words, so they done it with a gun. That's the way our country seems to work, ain't it? And rather than locking them up they give them a shield.'

'But . . . Mister Henry?'

The grinning, pock-marked face of the deputy in the hallway. Booya could clearly picture the face that had looked down at him.

Like a burn scar

Boo

Booya's body had ceased shaking, but he shivered.

'You ain't got nothing to be afraid for, Calvin,' said Mammy, eyeing him. 'Don't listen to the old fool. It's the sad truth of the business, like *he* say. But it was a long time ago, far away from Honahee.'

'But don't never trust The Law, Booya,' Paw added. 'That's all my advice is: don't trust them.'

Keeping step in time with Mammy and Paw, Booya hunched his shoulders, looking at the ground. Mammy kept looking at Paw, then at Booya, narrowing her eyes at both of them. A man up a ladder, painting the front of new store, called out to Paw, who nodded. A window sliding upward with a screech made Booya flinch. A black lady wearing a pinafore, her hair tied up with a headwrap, leaned out of the window and began to beat a rug.

'Anything particular you wanna eat tonight, Cal?' Mammy asked, breaking their silence as Huck's came into view.

'Um . . . that cream chicken you do?' Booya asked. 'With okra?'

After a kiss from each of her men, Mammy walked into Huck's.

'Anything you need, son?' Paw asked. 'Need to get me some wood oil. Gonna fix up the place a bit.' Booya saw a sad and guilty expression pass over Paw's face.

'Nah, Paw. Don't think. Just gonna wander.'

'That oil's cheaper in the General Store other side of town,' Paw said behind his hand, beneath his bad breath. 'But if I buy it from them and your Mammy finds out then my life ain't worth living.'

'And she's got her ways of finding out,' Booya added.

'Ain't that the bitter truth?'

Scuffing his feet along the floor, head down to avoid Mammy's colleagues and any others who might recognise him, Booya turned into an aisle. And that was when he saw her. It was as if some indefinable sense made her look up at him at the same moment, distracting her from loading a shelf with soaps. Her bow of lips were slightly parted. Booya's head felt as though it was swelling. He couldn't have spoken if any words had made themselves available to him. She was wearing her hair tied back in a bun. Her skin was toffee. Her eyes were huge and sparkling, the irises a whirl of coffee, aside her tiny, straight nose. Her cheeks were full, but her cheekbones sharp and straight, leading to a dimpled chin. And above that, her parted silken lips; should they ever open to smile or, pray, to kiss.

Booya could not blink should he miss a moment of her beauty – a city minute of a different kind. And then she was gone.

4

The morning sun warmed Booya's back as he stood in front of Huck's Place the next morning. Hot beneath his suit – complete with tie and hat – he looked at Mister Henry's guitar in his hands, wondering what it would be able to tell him of their time in the city, what was written in its scars. His eyebrow began to itch. Lowering the guitar to his side, he looked around at the few folks sitting on the stoop. No one was looking back at him. He tipped his hat slightly further forward. Breathing in, holding it, he exhaled as he climbed the steps.

Even with the windows open, the air inside Huck's Place was stifling and close. He glanced around as if he had never been there before, trying to peer around corners. With measured steps, undoing a button on his suit and then doing it back up, Booya began to walk through the store.

A couple of the female faces looked familiar to him, women he had met when being shown off by Mammy. There was Betsie – he was sure that was her name – the first woman he had ever met in Huck's, the woman who had assumed that he had been preparing to thieve.

She saw him, glared, softened and smiled. 'Aw, hey. That you Calvin? Thought it was you.'

Booya removed his hat, holding it by the rim, playing it through his fingers.

'I *heared* you was back from . . .' She hesitated. 'I guess that's just what a boy's gotta do if he feels the need, leaving like that. Got a son myself. So I knowed all along just how it must feel for your mama. See, Calvin, my Isaac, he leave years ago to seek his fortune in the city. Always dreamed of being a mechanic, working on them motorcars, you know? Still get the occasional letter from him, but . . .'

Although Booya was watching Betsie's mouth moving, he was not really absorbing a word she spoke, his mind wandering elsewhere. He couldn't keep his eyes from wandering too. His heart fluttered at the thought of the girl; that she could step around the corner at any second. She could be just the other side of this aisle right now!

He scratched his eyebrow.

'Uh, Betsie, will you excuse me?'

'Oh sure . . . sorry, Calvin. You ain't come here to share hot air with silly old me. But it sure is a fine thing seeing you, looking so well and all.' She looked his suit up and down.

Booya returned the hat to his head and patted it down. 'And sure is nice seeing you, too, ma'am.'

'Such a nice young man,' he heard Betsie gushing as he walked away.

At the end of the aisle, after looking both ways, seeing no one, his heart running ahead of him, he turned left. Two aisles along, Booya saw another familiar face. She wasn't as made up today as he remembered her – usually she would be plastered with face paint and cheap jewellery. Furthermore, there was something even more tragic about her appearance now. He smiled, even as his heart sank a little. Tilting his hat forward, he walked to her. She was holding a pink-blossom candle in her left hand and a daffodil-coloured candle in her right, seemingly staring at neither.

'Hey, Petal,' said Booya. 'Gotta say you is looking sure fine as ever, like the first morning they ever was.'

She looked up and began to flutter her eyelashes, a weary reflex that looked like crying without tears. And then, gasping, Petal recognised him, showing off her mouthful of teeth.

'Handsome! My, my, my, my, *my!* Ain't you got even more handsomer on your travels.' She pulled the candles to her chest and gasped again. '*Yaayis.* Oh my. Oh my, my, my. Look at you, suit and all. Check out them fancy clothes. You is a sight for this girl's eyes, that's for sure'.

'How you been, Petal?'

Shocked by the difference, it was clear that she hadn't spent any time looking after her appearance at all. Her hair was matted and as tired-looking as her eyes. Booya couldn't remember ever noticing the lines of wrinkles beneath her eyes before. Even her pout was more forced than he remembered, a sorry attempt at coquettishness. She was wearing a long, dowdy dress that was so unlike such a glamorous girl as Petal – leaving her natural features aside. When he had last seen her she could have passed as a person in their early twenties, more feminine than masculine. It seemed that a year was a long time indeed.

She fluttered her eyelashes as if they generated all of her power. 'Oh, I never guessed that I would be crossing the path of a handsome stranger today, or I sure wouldn't have dared dream of leaving the house looking like I do, like something the cat sicked up.'

'Nah,' Booya said. 'I think you is looking quite the lady 'bout town.'

'Stop it, you villain,' Petal replied, feigning to punch him. 'But when did you get back is the question? I heared that you gone running with some married girl all the way to Washington and ended up on some warship.' Clutching both candles in one large hand, Petal fanned her face. 'I nearly did *die* when I heared.'

Cocking his head, Booya frowned. 'Was only in Chicago,' he replied, lifting his guitar from his shoulder. 'Just playing blues with The Free Riders. But it weren't for me, the city. Or I weren't for it, could say.'

'Even dressing so fine, you is just a big old country boy, ain't you?' Petal said, waving a hand halfway to Booya, too feminine-bred to actually touch him.

'I guess,' he agreed. 'That's what I was always telling folks.'

'Well, we sure is pleased and grateful to have you back again, safe and handsome.'

'You still, uh . . . living in the same place, Petal?'

'You can just out and ax me, you know?' Petal replied, her eyes regaining a touch of their former sparkle. 'You ain't gotta dress a sheep in wool to call it a sheep. Rosie's still here and living with me, yes – seeing as that's what you axing. Didn't talk to no one for days after you go chasing off to Washington.'

'Chicago. The city.'

'But don't you worry yourself, handsome; she was over herself quick enough. Between you and me, normally she's the one being chased by all the men. Having one running off on her, her pride just weren't prepared for. I know how much she liked you, handsome. And do any of us girls blame her? Nuh-uh. And *sure* not this one. She was back to her usual self within a few days, once she had a new line of them trailing her skirts.'

Staring at the floor, Booya bit his tongue and tightened his grip on the guitar.

'Say, we is hosting a frolic tonight at our place. Why don't you come along? And bring that . . . old piece a wood with you,' said Petal, curling her lips as she looked at the guitar. 'You still something of a local star, and I know for a fact that everone would just love to hear you play again. Everone talk 'bout you for a long time after you disappear. Never stop talking, come to think it. And now that you ain't gotta worry 'bout Rosie no more, handsome, you got me all to yourself!'

Booya grinned. 'Tempting a offer as ever they was. Wear something pretty. Most likely be seeing you there.'

Petal pulled the candles to her chest. 'So you gonna bring that easy rider of yours, so's I can tell some friends you is?'

'If that's what you want, honey lips.'

'Oh, mister, stop!' Petal flailed a fist towards Booya.

'Got some things to do first,' he said. 'But I guess I'll be seeing you later.'

'Baaai, Big Boo,' Petal drawled, waving just her fingers. 'Oh, handsome?' she called when Booya was halfway down the aisle. 'Pink-blossom or daffodil?' she asked, weighing the candles.

'Pink-blossom,' Booya called back. 'Matches your sweet tongue.'

'*Waaayel.*' Petal used the candles to fan her forced blush.

When he left the aisle, Booya saw Mammy with her head in the flowers – her speciality section.

'Hey, Mammy,' he said.

She turned and placed a hand on her hip. 'Still *heying* me, then, huh?'

Booya shrugged and grinned.

'You becoming more like your old fool Paw ever day.'

'Where's the old fool, Mammy?'

'Hmm, you sure did rise late today. If he weren't back at the homeplace, he probably dipped into some drinking shack on the way back, like he don't know I know what he does. At least no other woman would have him; I is safe in that, at least. Anyhow, what you doing down here, sleepyhead? And what you all dressed up for?'

Booya spun his guitar. 'I was gonna play out on the stoop a while. Maybe see if little Frankie wants to pipe along.'

'Uh-huh,' Mammy said, and stuck her tongue in her cheek. 'And what's your other reason, the real reason? You can lie to me if you want, but you might as well try and catch a cloud.'

'Wha . . .? What do you mean?'

'I see it writ all over your face, Calvin. Don't ever be forgetting I is your Mammy, no matter how grown you is. You might get one over on that old drunk fool, but you ain't never gonna be able to fool me. So, now . . . who is she, the girl you gonna go visiting on?'

'Say . . . now you mention it,' said Booya, licking his lips and looking out of a dusty window. 'They was this girl working in here yesterday . . .'

'Oh, here it comes. And the bush bursts into flame.' Mammy was grinning. 'You couldn't hide a single leaf in a pile of them from your Mammy. But ain't nothing to be found in here but us old gals, Calvin. I think you can do some better!'

'No, Mammy. She was working here yesterday, for sure; she was in the same pinafore. Wears her hair tied back. And she got as pretty a face as ever I see, I swear.'

Mammy gasped. 'Labella? She help out in here yesterday, for just one day. She don't really work here. But I tell you one thing: you wanna know what she'll grow up into, just look over there.' Mammy indicated a woman who Booya had met. Mattie, the sour-faced woman who had bothered Mammy about the sweet potatoes when Mammy had been crying into Booya's chest – the "witch sent by the devil".

Mattie was staring at them now, her face as fierce-looking as an eagle and as dour as a gargoyle. She noticed them looking, smiled and waved. Mammy smiled and waved back.

'That's Labella's mammy right there.'

'Not ever girl grows like her mammy,' Booya replied with hope.

'You think?' It was funny how beneath this roof Mammy became a clucky gossip-girl, when at home she was just all-knowing Mammy. Again standing with her hand on her hip, she pushed her backend to one side. 'You wanna take a chance eating a kicked apple? I'd stay away from anything to do with *that* woman, if I was you. She's like demon in a hag costume. And that definitely ain't the best chose disguise.'

5

The door to Petal's place was standing open. Guitar in hand, Booya stood outside, staring at the little wooden house. Through the windows he could see a crowd of people dancing, surely drinking and having a time. Though he couldn't discern individuals, he was desperate to see the girl whom his heart had been itching for this last year, even as his mind begged him to run away, reminding him of the uncompleted task that he had entrusted to Rosie.

Most of the furniture had been relocated outside to clear space for a dance floor. Booya slumped into an armchair, guitar across his knees. It was funny that Petal had asked him to bring his guitar – the music pouring from the open door was the new craze of jazz that he didn't care for. The only music that he had ever liked that wasn't the blues was the opera that Mister Henry had blasted from his window, entrancing the little boy that he had once been.

With the last of the sun disappearing in a red haze beyond the town, the noise of the jazz washing over him, Booya rubbed a finger over the scratches on the face of his guitar.

Someone staggered from the house, over the porch, and leant on the supporting column.

With his back to the door, Booya's finger stopped tracing over the guitar. He held his breath.

'Oh, *man*. Whoo!' A girl's voice. She was breathing heavily, chuckling to herself. 'Hey? Who that there?'

It might have been a year but Booya instantly knew that the voice was Rosie's. And, as he was the only one out there, she must be talking to him. Cursing his size, he quietly exhaled as he heard her approaching.

'What you hiding from, stranger . . . making use of my furniture?'

With a hand on the backrest, Rosie slithered around the chair and looked down at Booya. Her broad smile slipped away with the cresting realisation; a frown clouding her brow.

Trying to act cool and calm despite the frantic workers in his warehouse of emotions, trapped, Booya tipped back his hat. She jumped on him and kissed him hard on the lips.

'Big Boo, you come!' She wrapped her arms around his neck and looked long in to his eyes. 'Man, have I missed you?' Booya pulled his guitar out from underneath her. It wasn't only Rosie stirring in his lap.

'Hey, Rosie.'

'Heared you was back from the city. Been kind of nervous 'bout meeting with you, gotta say,' she said with arch shyness.

Booya looked at the quiet light behind windows across the street. 'Listen, Rosie, you and I, we gotta –'

She pressed her a finger hard across his lips. 'Ain't never gon' speak a word 'bout it,' she slurred. 'Big Boo! You back! That's all what matters. Hey, check you out, all suit and boots. What the hell you doing sitting all alone out here, anyways?'

She sprang from his knee and was pulling him up from the chair.

He picked up his guitar. 'Got anywhere I can leave this?'

'Glad to see that old thing. We all missed him nearly as much as we missed you, him being your . . . thing. Sling him in my room, if you like. But you is playing later; don't think that you ain't. Been too long, Boo.' Rosie left the words to linger, and then dragged Booya inside.

Petal was dominating the hallway. She was dancing her tall, styled hair from side to side whilst listening to some weasely-looking man. Her eyes set upon Booya as soon as he was through the door.

'Oh, handsome, you come!' She put her hands on his jaw and kissed the side of his lips. He could taste the whisky.

'You axed; I come, sweet honey.'

Petal fanned herself and fluttered ridiculously.

Beside her, Virginia was already fluttering. 'Hi there, handsome. Got one for me, too?'

Even though she had spoken so timidly and softly, as soon as Booya's head was within her range she grabbed him around the neck, pulled his lips towards her, and shot a victorious look at Petal and Rosie. 'Oh . . . *my!*' she squealed, wiping the back of her hand across her lips, her eyes rolling.

Booya wondered who had brewed their Moonshine.

'Didn't take long for you to find him, miss!' Petal said to Rosie.

Witnessing Petal's disdain, Virginia copied her dress-up scowl.

Rosie grabbed Booya's arm. 'Finder keeps and loser weeps.'

'Even though you already got your own man here?' Petal continued. 'Well he sure ain't gonna be happy.'

'Petal!' Rosie shrieked.

'What, you aiming to have them both? Can't have them all, Rosie,' Petal said.

'Well . . . I . . .' Rosie was lost for excuse or reason.

Booya looked down at Rosie. He felt her grip on his hand tighten. 'That the truth?'

'Him? He don't really mean nothing to me, or nothing,' Rosie said, shaking her head frantically. 'He ain't no true beau.'

'Oh! Sure he don't know that, even over the fact that you been going together since before Thanksgiving?'

'Petal!' Rosie shrieked again, stamping her foot.

'Only the truth, ain't it?' Petal smiled at Booya – as did Virginia a moment later. 'I ain't got no agenda.'

'The hell you ain't,' Rosie said, folding her arms, pushing up her breasts. 'If you really wanna know, I ain't really sure we a item no more. Weren't never gonna last.'

'I ain't stepping on no man's toes, Rosie,' Booya said, pulling his arm free of hers. 'Ain't no way. Just make sure he knows that.' He looked down at her pretty cotton dress, then tore his eyes away.

'Really, Big Boo,' Rosie pleaded. 'It ain't no thing.'

'That ain't no concern of mine now, Rosie,' Booya told her. He knew only too well how, in a town as small as Honahee, a piece of tumbling weed would likely be the size of a bale by the time it reached the town border.

Rosie murdered Petal with a glare. Virginia looked confused, left out;

unsure whether to glower at Petal or look hurt.

'I don't mean to hurt you, darling,' Petal said to Rosie. 'You know I love you. Just don't want no trouble up in here tonight. You know what Morgan's like over you. If he see you acting around . . . I just don't want that.'

'Yeah,' Rosie spat. 'Sure.'

'I should go,' Booya said, back-stepping towards the door. 'Was a bad idea, my coming here.'

'Don't be stupid, Boo,' Rosie said. 'I'll show you where you can lay your easy down.'

Without any kind of witness, Booya was sure to go no further than the doorway of Rosie's room as she stashed his guitar. He was thankful that he hadn't had more cups with Paw; a part of him, even now, wanted to follow her in. He could see the picture of her on the wall, pressing her finger into the white man's bare chest.

'Call yourself a man,' she said as she barged past him out of the room.

Petal linked her arm in his. 'Don't you mind her, handsome,' she said, running a finger down his chest. 'She gotta understand that one man has to be enough for a woman.'

'Sure,' he said. 'Say, you got something to drink round here?'

*

'That's him,' Petal whispered a few cups later.

'What?' Booya answered. 'Who?'

'That one with the guitar. Morgan. Rosie's beau.'

Across the roomful of bodies, Booya had been watching Rosie watching him as Morgan beat out some blues. He wasn't a small man.

'Don't know if you ever noticed, handsome, but Rosie gets a thing for most men what ever climbed up on a stage. That's how she caught Morgan, at Blacks, 'fore The Law close it down. Yep, she always in the front of the queue. 'Til the next one come along, at least.'

'Yeah?' Booya smiled.

'Oh, you know you is the special one, handsome. You just know you is. Uh-huh. Most men it's only they mama's tell them that. But with you it's ever girl in town.'

'Yeah,' Virginia drawled, eyes still rolling. 'You know you a special one, *handsome*.' She hiccupped and put a hand to her mouth, looking around to see if anyone had noticed.

'I mean, Morgan,' Petal continued, 'he's a all right player; all right singer; quite handsome; shitty songs. But you got it all, man. You know that folks was always requesting a Booya Carthy song ever night at Blacks after you leave?'

Booya continued to stare at Rosie through the crowd, she back at him. As she moved her hips, her eyes were as steady as a leopard stalking prey. He looked at Morgan, still playing and singing in front of the window, agreeing with Petal that he was not at all bad. But he definitely didn't look like a man to mess with. He had muscles and he had scars. Booya could have guessed the place that Morgan would call home.

He turned to Petal to whisper as much to her.

'Oh, sorry,' came a soft little voice below him.

Booya looked down and the world rushed through him. He had no past. No Rosie. No care for the mystery of his reputation.

Looking up at Booya was Mattie's daughter – the girl from the store who he had seen and sought.

Just as before, they could only stand and stare, hypnotised by each other. The rest of the world was spinning – Booya could vaguely hear Petal talking and Morgan playing – but for Booya and the girl the world was a unique and frozen sphere. A hurricane could have ripped away everything around them and they would have been left alone in the eye, standing there and staring at each other.

Mammy had told him her name. He had to say it.

'Labella.'

Her perfect lips formed a smile. 'You know my name.'

His eyes were whirling in circles, to look at her lips, eyes, skin, chin, lips, eyes . . .

He reflected her smile. 'Think you gotta be the most beautiful thing on this earth,' he whispered. 'Ain't no doubting God made you.'

Whisky-tongue had its benefits, too.

Her smile grew and Booya finally saw the row of perfectly straight white teeth. Sweeping her long straight hair back over one ear, she looked downward.

'And you is the nicest looking man I ever looked upon,' she said.

'You wanna get outta here?' he asked.

Her smiled disappeared. 'I ain't going outside with you, if that's what you thinking.'

'No. I mean . . . No! Wanna to talk with you, is all.' Booya sucked his tongue, trying to find saliva. 'Spend some time, y'know . . . Not . . .'

Booya felt her lift his hand, the feel of her touch upon his skin as soft and delicate as a butterfly.

She smiled and he breathed again. 'Sure.'

They went through and sat down at a table in the kitchen. There were people around – couples and inebriates – but no one was paying any interest to anyone else. In the relative solitude, Booya was grateful that he no longer had Petal hovering on his ear and Rosie pining from across the room.

'I heared 'bout you,' she said, unable to hold his gaze.

Unless to look at those soft, golden lips, he was unable to take his eyes from hers.

'Where you hear 'bout me from?' he asked, masking his concern.

Labella smiled, again showing her teeth. Booya's heart leapt.

'From my mama,' she answered, looking into Booya's eyes, then settling on his hands. 'She say that ever time you sing and play outside the store, all the women stop working and gather round, just to hear you.' She chuckled, her toffee skin turning to bronze with her blush. 'Mama say that all the women think you is the nicest thing they ever did hear; that you is the best musicianer that ever play in this town. And she ain't the only one I heared saying that.'

Now Booya felt the heat rising in his cheeks. Beneath his hat, his brow began to sweat. For the first time, he looked away from her face.

'Didn't know they speak 'bout me that way,' he replied. 'I just like sitting out there and playing.'

They settled on an awkward moment; neither of them knowing what to say to break it. Summoning all of his whisky-drenched courage, Booya slid his hand across to hers and cupped it. He felt her shudder and begin to pull away. Then she let him cover her hand.

'What else you hear?' he asked.

When she looked up her eyes were wide, startled with concern. She pulled her hand from his.

'Not that they *is* anything else,' he added. 'I was just . . . just curious, is all. You know how they like to talk in Huck's.'

Labella chuckled and raised an eyebrow. 'Thought you was gonna say you is married or a criminal or something. You know this town.'

'Sorry to disappoint you,' Booya replied, regaining some cool. 'But I ain't none of them things.

'Well that *is* a relief.' Her skin again glowed bronze.

This time she didn't pull her hand away.

'How'd you find yourself here tonight?' he asked.

'Oh! I got a friend here some place. She's a friend of Virginia. It's the first time I ever drink any of that *stuff* before.' She laughed, pulling a face as if sucking something sour, indicating Booya's cup. 'I don't much like it.'

'Yeah, kind of rough-tasting, ain't it?' Booya's free hand had been around his cup. He loosened his grip on it. 'But it's, uh, good for loosening my voice.'

'Really?'

Booya smiled and nodded. 'Yeah. It gives a blues man the blues, you know?'

'You playing here tonight?' she asked, leaning forward in her chair, putting her other hand on top of Booya's.

His body reacted all over. He cleared his throat. 'Sure. Petal – you know Petal? – she axed me to.'

'You friends with *Petal?*' A comically bemused expression crossed her face.

'Sure,' Booya said, his hand instinctively moving to the cup. Noticing Labella watching, he stopped halfway. 'She a sweetheart.'

When Labella giggled Booya drowned in the sweetness. He could see the innocent bright-pink of her tongue. He could smell the sweet perfume of soap from her lily-green dress, dotted with tiny flowers. The scent of her, in this place, was as juxtaposed as finding a meadow in the centre of a city.

He tasted the roof of his mouth. It was like licking a swine.

'You sure you ain't gonna drink some of that then, if it's so good for your voice?'

'I've had enough,' Booya answered. 'It's only so good for a while.'

Frowning with distaste, Labella nodded in agreement.

From behind Booya, Petal sauntered into the kitchen.

'*There* you is, handsome.' Petal smiled towards Labella. '*Haii*,' she cooed briefly, before redirecting her attention on Booya. 'They is calling for you to start playing. Some fella's saying he wants to hear you sing that *Drunk Smile Blues* the folks at Blacks used to like. And me personally? I *need* to hear *Got Caught Cheating Again*, whatever you call it.' Petal looked down at Labella. 'Catch myself singing that one over and again walking down the street. Telling you, folks look at me some funny. Guess they never heared no harp sing 'fore now.'

Sighing through his nose, dropping his elbows on the table, Booya glared at Petal. A few minutes later, at the head of the dance floor, he played both songs anyway. After discreetly downing the rest of his cup.

Though a fiftieth of the size, it was like Blacks all over again. Frolickers were dancing in the hallway and even out in front of the house. Even after all that time, most sang along to every word. Some folks, whom Booya didn't recognise, called out requests. Most were for his own songs, but he could play all the other songs requested from hearing them in Blacks or in the city, or dredged up from who knew where. *Crazy Blues; Black Snake Moan; Just A Dream; I Be's Troubled; See See Rider*, the verses that he could recall of *Roguish Man*, inventing others to fill the empty spaces. His fingers and bones came to life.

As the frolickers danced around him, Booya watched Labella. She smiled every time he caught her eye through the squirming bodies.

Soon he announced to the room, 'This next song is inspired by someone I only just meet the first time tonight. Calling it *She's A Sunflower*.'

Booya's fingers found the instrumental melody that he had been picking that morning. But now he effortlessly found the words that he had so struggled to conjure. They radiated across the room towards him.

'*She's a sunflower and she smiled up at me*
She's a sunflower, most beautiful I ever see
If the sun fall down out the sky

My sunflower keep the light a-shining
If my sunflower say —'

'That ain't the blues, man!' someone yelled out. 'That's Nat Cole. Play some blues!'

Some booed jokingly, but most cheered. Booya didn't mind: he had seen Labella's reaction.

'Play some blues! This ain't the Dipsie Doodle!'

As the crowd laughed, as Booya and Labella connected, Rosie ran up to Booya and dropped to the floor, clawing at his knees. At some point the top buttons of her dress must have loosened, her breasts almost spilling out onto his knees. The crowd's joviality grew in witness of the familiar sight of a love-struck girl pawing a musician. Only some were surprised that it was Rosie.

'Play that love song you make up just for me, Big Boo,' she wailed.

A few continued laughing and heckling, but now most of the crowd had stopped to watch where the undignified show might lead.

Forming a pillow of her hands, Rosie dropped her head onto Booya's lap.

'What you doing, Rosie?' Booya whispered. He looked up, shrugged and grimaced – intending to show the crowd his apathy towards Rosie's sudden madness – only to see Morgan take a step towards him, his eyes aflame.

'Sing me the song what tole me you love me, Big Boo. *The Sweetest Piece Of Fruit In The Tree*. Please play it. *Please*. You got to. For me.' Rosie was now wetting Booya's knees with her tears.

'Rosie!' Petal boomed, barging through the crowd.

'Some shit's brewing in Honahee, right now,' a frolicker called out, laughing.

'My money's on Boo.'

'I say the blues man dies this time,' someone shouted. 'His luck run out at Blacks over that white bitch.'

Morgan stepped up in front of Booya. By the hair, he pulled Rosie's head away from Booya's knee. She screamed and slumped to the floor, sobbing, before trying to scrabble over the floor to Booya again.

'What say you and me step outside and sort this right now?' Morgan growled, fists clenched.

Petal pushed him in the chest. 'Stay away from my Boo, Morgan,' she warned.

Morgan staggered, obviously way beyond drunk.

Petal dropped down to see to Rosie – starting with buttoning her up, to cover her normally unshakable dignity.

'Listen, man' said Booya, palms showing in truce. 'I ain't got nothing to do with none of this.'

'Nothing to do with it, huh?' Morgan snarled. 'Is that why my girl is crying on the floor at your feet?'

'Rosie,' Booya appealed to the heap at his feet. 'Sort out your man, yeah?'

Rosie lifted the mess of her head. 'I love *you*,' she shouted through her tears. '*You* my man. You tole me you love me,' she cried into her arms.

'Rosie, calm yourself down now, honey,' Petal hushed, smothering Rosie and shooting a glare at Morgan.

'Telling me that's *my* problem?' Morgan growled, uncurling his fists, then clenching them again.

Booya could no longer see Labella through the crowd. Putting down his guitar, he started to get to his feet, to go and find her.

Morgan smashed his fist into the side of Booya's face, knocking him back over the chair. Howling, Rosie crawled over the floor to Booya. Petal jumped up and wrestled Morgan manfully to the floor.

'You ripped my dress, you motherfucker,' she growled into his ear. 'You gonna pay for that. Or I'll kill you.'

6

It felt strangely comforting to wake up beneath the bridge. Booya sat up, rubbed his stiff, filthy neck and dusted down his suit. It had certainly seen better days, and now was looking a bit worn and beaten. After a while watching the river slowly rolling by, holding his sore jaw in one hand, he looked right; he looked left. He didn't have his guitar.

'Aw, man!' He pounded a fist on the ground.

Rolling over, he looked up the bank. When they slid down together, there had been times when the guitar had slipped past him, stopping perilously close to the river. It was nowhere to be seen.

Booya checked his head. Somehow he was still wearing Roots' hat. They were the only possessions in the world that he cared anything for. He would walk naked for the rest of his days, so long as he had Mister Henry's guitar and Roots' hat.

The only likely place the guitar could be, if it wasn't lying by the side of the road, or stuck in the reeds further down the river, was Petal and Rosie's place.

*

Most of the furniture was still out front. Booya gently tapped the glass panel on the front door, hoping that it would be Petal who greeted him.

From the corner of his eye, Booya saw the front room curtain twitch. It pulled back to reveal Petal's smiling face, showing every one of her big teeth in her long, unmade-up face. Booya put a finger to his hat and mouthed Hi.

Petal lifted up the guitar and waved it like a pendulum. Placing a hand on his heart, Booya sighed and pointed towards the front door. As the curtain caught a breeze, Booya realised that, in the unlit room, Petal wasn't wearing a top. He found that he was mildly curious about that.

The front door opened.

'Hey, Rosie,' Booya said, unable to decide if she looked upset or guilty, or just plain hung-over. He doubted that Rosie could still count on Morgan as her man, even if she wanted to, ditching him as she had. But then again, this was Rosie. There was probably another man waiting just around the side of the house.

With her hair standing up on one side, she didn't look as pretty as she ever had. Last night's makeup was scrawled over face, silted streaks where tears had carried traces over her cheeks. She was still wearing last night's pretty dress too, only it didn't look so pretty now that it was rumpled, with black smears on the breast and dusty dirt on the seat. Rosie didn't reply, simply looked down.

Now wearing a gown, Petal appeared behind Rosie.

'Hi, handsome.' It had never sounded such a ridiculous greeting as it did then.

'Hi, handsome,' Booya heard Virginia squeak, unseen, somewhere behind Petal.

'Hey, girls,' he said.

Petal looked at the top of Rosie's head, then up at Booya, wearing a dramatic expression of expectation. Virginia squeezed in next to Petal's shoulder, peering around to see what was happening.

'Can I talk with you?' Rosie asked, looking up at Booya.

'Don't think they's much for neither of us to say.'

'Can we talk anyway, Booya?'

'Come on, little pretty. We ain't needed,' Petal said, turning in her gown, sweeping Virginia from view.

'Baai, handsome,' Booya heard Virginia's little, disappearing voice call.

'Come in please, Boo,' Rosie said. 'I don't need folks seeing me this way. You know how they is.'

'Just understand that I've only come for my guitar, Rosie,' Booya replied. 'Wouldn't be here if it weren't for that.'

'Boo, can you just come in and hear me out?'

On the wooden hallway floor were drink spills and tobacco, nuts and smoked ends. There was a slip and a man's shirt, various other clothes, cups, and a worn-out shoe. Hanging from a small sideboard was a dirty, damp rag – presumably at some point someone had started to clean up some of the spills, before giving up. Around the few bits of furniture that had been moved back in to the front room were more innumerable spills, smoked ends and clothes. Near the window was a pair of chairs passable enough to sit on.

Rosie looked into a corner where a skinny man – whom Booya recognised as the man Petal had last night been talking to in the hallway when he arrived – was slumped against the junction where two walls met. He seemed to be breathing – no doubt Petal would already have discovered that, in here all alone, Booya thought. Removing a sagging bunch of flowers, Rosie pulled the chairs to face each other. Before sitting down, Booya grabbed his guitar.

Rosie was just sitting, staring at her knees. She checked the buttons holding the front of her dress together.

'What do you want to say, Rosie?'

'Please, Boo, don't make this hard on me.'

'But I don't understand! Thought we was clear: I went away and you got a man. Seems as plain as day, to me.'

Ruffling her messy hair, Rosie smiled. 'I missed you, Big Boo.'

He exhaled, hard. 'And when I was away, I missed you too, Rosie. Truly, I did.'

'We had something, didn't we?' Rosie asked. 'You and me?'

'Well . . . yeah. But they is a lot of water passed under the bridge since then. We changed. Whatever they was between us . . .' Booya left the words to pass into the dank-smelling room.

'We can get it back, Boo. Sure we can. We just gotta give it a try to see, don't we? We was good together. You remember that, at least.' She smiled one of the smiles that once would have robbed Booya of all conscious thought.

He rested his chin on his hand and looked up at her. 'I just don't see any way ahead for us, Rosie. I just don't.'

Rosie's lips began to quiver and turn down. A tear climbed the levee of her makeup and found a route through her silted cheeks.

'But you say you missed me when you was away, Boo. What's so different now you back?'

'Rosie, I was missing you for all the wrong reasons,' Booya said. 'I know that now. Only telling you straight 'cause that's the only way what's fair.'

'How can you tell me that's fair?' Rosie's mouth bubbled as she spoke. The tears were running freely now, cleaning some of the detritus from her face.

Seeing her that way made it easier for Booya. He found the spot by the wall where Labella had been standing.

'Huh? Tell me, Boo, how's that fair?' Rosie blubbered. 'You just took what you wanted and now you don't need nothing else.'

'It ain't like that –'

'It's exactly like that,' Rosie interrupted. 'How else is it?'

'This time yesterday you was with a different man.' Booya managed to keep his voice calm, his emotions in check. 'You weren't missing me, Rosie, no matter what you say. You done all right with me gone.'

''Cause I thought you weren't never coming back!' she cried, lowering her head into her hands. 'You don't know how I cried ever night 'til I meet that fool Morgan. You can never know how much I hate myself for not leaving with you when I had the chance. For days all I thought 'bout was following you. So no, Boo, I wasn't doing *all right*; not for one second. I didn't forget 'bout you, I just had to get on with my life.'

Through a gap in the curtains, Booya looked at the white silk clouds in the bright blue sky. He saw two birds fly slowly past, wing-to-wing. His eyes followed them as far as they could until they were gone. Rosie sniffed and lifted her head. Her face was a blurred mess.

'Please, Boo. I love you. Love you more than I ever loved anything. Please say you'll give us a chance. Or at least say you'll think on it, huh? You breaking my heart all over again.'

Booya wrapped an arm around his guitar, pulled it to his chest and steeled his heart.

'Rosie . . .' She looked up, her hands open, holding the invisible mask of her face. 'In more than a way, you saved me, you know?' Booya said, taking a moment to bite his tongue between his teeth before he continued. 'I won't never forget you for that. And I know I hurt you; I know I did. Won't even try'n explain how I was caught in a trap, 'cause that don't make no difference now, and you didn't want to hear it at the time. I just want you to know that I had no choice then, and that's the truth. I spent whole days thinking 'bout how much I hurt you; picturing how you was when I leave.

'But when I went to the city I needed you. Don't think I ever needed anyone more than I needed you then. Not just that I needed you with me, Rosie . . .' Booya inhaled through his nose. 'I axed you to tell Mammy that I weren't killed. I don't blame you for not coming with me, Rosie. But I needed you to do that one simple thing. Knowing how much I hurt you, I can't really blame you for not delivering my message to Mammy; not now I is home safe. But that's all gone now.'

Booya looked through the gap in the curtains and sighed. Rosie lowered her head and began to cry again.

'We weren't made for each other. I used to think different, but we weren't. The whole sorry business has at least showed me that. I love you for you, Rosie; always will. We had some times, sure we did. But I ain't gonna do you like that no more. Myself neither. We just ain't the ones to make two.' Booya lifted the guitar halfway to his lap, then tucked it under his arm. 'I is going now.'

Rosie lifted her head and nodded her wet face. When Booya opened the door, Petal and Virginia nearly spilled through the gap.

'Wuh! Oh . . . *handsome*,' Petal gasped, wiping a finger beneath her eyes. 'We, uh, uh, we . . . My! We was cleaning!'

'Oh, *handsome*, we was cleaning!' Virginia gushed, waving the damp rag.

Booya nodded, smiling. 'I got my guitar, girls. Hope that helps some. Even though y'all got some fella to clean round in there.'

Petal blushed. 'Us three little girls left all alone with a fella? My!'

'My!' Virginia added.

'See you, girls,' Booya said, walking towards the door.

'Baai, handsome,' they chorused, affecting their usual coquettish poses, tittering and fluttering.

'Bye, Big Boo,' Rosie said, walking to the door behind him. Arms across her chest, she followed him outside, lifted a hand and wiped her face. 'You ever wanna come see me, just to talk, whatever, don't you stop yourself. It don't mean we can't be friends, right? And I always we will be your biggest fan.'

'Thanks, Rosie,' Booya said. 'Take care of yourself.'

Rosie smiled, maybe a more natural smile than he had ever seen cross her lips. 'And I always will be open for anything else, mind,' she chuckled with a sob. With a single nod, Booya smiled.

'Oh!' Rosie called, the moment he had turned. 'Big Boo.'

Petal and Virginia were gawking over and beside Rosie's shoulder.

'Blacks is reopening,' she said. 'Not as Blacks but as a juke, just the same. Thought you might wanna know.'

'Yeah? Thanks. And thanks for last night, girls,' he called across the furniture-strewn yard. 'I had a time.'

The girl's faces suddenly all turned queer, guilty-looking. They seemed to be looking past him. Frowning, Booya turned. Behind him, standing there across the street, holding a basket and looking as pretty as summer with a bow and flower in her hair, was Labella.

'Ain't that 'bout right,' she said, turned with her nose in the air and began to walk away, her long hair bobbing along behind her.

The poplar trees and picket fences lining the street stood puddled in their shadows, the sun high above. Booya stomped on his as he ran after Labella, catching his hat as it fell. Her skirts were swinging as she increased her pace; her basket swinging in time with her step. A few faces in front yards watched as the big man in the grubby suit lumbered up the street after Mattie's pretty girl, looking dressed for church.

'Labella, can I talk with you for a second? Please?'

The collar of her plain white dress flapping against her hair, Booya inhaled the soapy scent following Labella. She didn't turn, just spoke to the empty air that she continued to walk into. 'Oh, you done with them girls for the day now? The night *and* day?'

'Labella, please, it ain't like that. Really, I can explain.'

On one toe, now she did turn. 'Oh ain't that nice. I really would like to hear all 'bout it. Like I want to hear 'bout why that girl was pawing you all over last night. Then another man wanting to fight you for her, right after you sing nasty songs 'bout drinking whisky and cheating on your woman. And folks saying your luck run out over a white woman? Think you already explained quite a basketful last night.' To illustrate her point, Labella lifted her basket.

'All that, that's just –'

'That's why you want what ever man wants,' Labella interrupted. 'From what I heared 'bout you, I thought you was different. Well, I ain't that kind of girl; not the kind of girl you want.'

'You is exactly the kind of girl I want, Labella. You the most beautiful I ever see. And sweet, and –'

'But one clearly ain't enough for a man like you, is it?'

'I mean it, Labella. Ain't never met no one like you.'

'Huh!' She turned on her toe and continued down the road.

Booya was stunned. His guitar clanged as it fell from his hand to the ground.

'You is a sunflower!' he called. He felt pathetic. It had sounded pathetic.

She stopped. He saw the slight turn of her head; could hear the light brush of her hair against her dress as she shook her head. When she continued on her way, his shoulders slumped.

'He ain't lying to you, girl.' Rosie breezed past Booya, strutting above her shadow. In the broad light of day, Booya saw just how filthy her dress was: about five shades of dirt contrasting against the yellow cotton. He closed his eyes, pinched the bridge of his nose and then stroked his hand over his cheek, watching Rosie close in on Labella. 'Last night Booya did leave right after you.'

Labella stopped again, her basket swaying. Booya could see half of her perfect profile; her soft, clean hair breezing away from her face; the sunlight making her golden skin radiate.

'I know 'cause I was watching, waiting for you to go,' Rosie continued. 'I was a fool last night. Drunk too much and make myself look a *darn fool*. Ain't gonna lie: I did love him and want him, was all over him . . . but he say No to me. He leave 'cause you did. Leave to try go find you.' Jutting her weight to one side, Rosie put her hands on her hips. 'I let this man go one time. Let him go and it was the worst thing I ever done. Only telling you this now 'cause otherwise I know how you'll feel when you is thinking over him in months to come from now. It ain't a pretty feeling, girl, telling you. I ain't ashamed to say that I known some men. Telling you now they ain't many like him, if they is any left at all. He a good man, and tole you ever word of the truth. You be a fool to walk away from him, girl, I know that. And that's it all . . .'

Rosie turned and walked back past Booya, winking at him on her way. Sitting on the steps of the house, dressed in only a gown, Petal was sobbing. Virginia was wiping her eyes, forcing a sob.

Watching the rise and fall of Labella's shoulders, Booya was lost for any words. Everything he processed through his head sounded weak and pleading. He could vaguely feel the girls watching him; could hear Petal sob and Virginia weep. He could still see just a small part of the perfect toffee-skin of Labella's cheek. She turned round; her cheeks were lined with a perfectly curved wet trail where one tear had fallen from each eye.

'Is this the biggest mistake of my life?' she asked him, her lips just downturned of straight. So innocent and vulnerable; so beautiful. 'If I trust you, would you end up hurting me?'

'Don't think I could hurt you if it saves the world from drowning,' Booya replied.

One more tear fell as Labella chuckled. 'You got a way with your words, mister.'

'What do you say?' He could hear his voice croaking, sure that he would soon join those weeping. Booya felt that he had said enough – now that Rosie had done his talking for him. He knew, now, how she must have felt.

Dropping her basket, Labella ran to him, fell into his chest, her white dress becoming dusted by dirt, and he wrapped his arms around her.

7

'Word has reached this news-teller that bodies have been found on the site of the former Harris Plantation, on the skirts of Honahee.' Frankie was standing on his upturned crate, one palm held out. He made eye contact with Booya but did not acknowledge him – delivering the important local news, Frankie was as sightless as a radio broadcast. Folks preferred him to the wireless; he was accurate and eloquent in his high-pitched voice. And a sight more entertaining. Also, this wasn't the kind of news that the wireless broadcasters would bother ears with.

'New owners of the plantation,' Frankie continued, 'were filling over a stockless pond to increase the acreage when a skeleton was found. After informing the local authorities, the pond was found to contain more than thirty skeletons and decomposing cadavers. It is believed that the murderers were amongst the number of former workers who had been living on the plantation in its fallow years. The authorities are not optimistic about apprehending any suspects since the former workers had already been chased from the site, scattered into the surrounding area. To date, unconfirmed reports have indicated that Mister Wilbur Harris – former plantation owner; claimed to have left his land to his workers – and his lady wife Marjorie were amongst the bodies recovered.'

'That's horrid,' Labella said, linking her arm through Booya's. 'Makes me feel sick to my stomach. I think that maybe the little man should save some of his news from the everday folk. Hey, you okay, Calvin?'

Booya's knees had gone weak and his head was spinning. If Labella hadn't joined her arm to his when she did, he felt that he would have collapsed. Those "crazy niggers" that they had lived amongst, whom Paw had one time counted as his friends, were responsible for the murders of two of the kindest white folk that could be found – their miserly foibles forgiven. The Harris's had done everything within their means for their workers, finally giving their lives as well as their land. Booya hoped that their Lord had recognised their charity.

'Just feel sick, is all,' Booya replied, swallowing. 'I knowed Mister Wilbur – the man they say was found – when I was a boy. He helped my Paw; me and my family.'

'You want to sit down, Calvin?' Labella asked, a hand on his chest to steady him. 'Looks as though the sun might have burned through to your head. Let me take that.' She reached around him for his guitar. He pulled it away from her.

'No! No, I got it. Sorry, I . . . Let's sit for a while, like you say.'

Sitting on the benches, watching the world pass them by, Frankie suddenly appeared before Booya – feeling much better, though his stomach was empty.

'Give me a dollar, mister,' Frankie said, holding out his tiny hand and grinning. He slapped Booya's knee. 'The Flee Riders back with you?' he asked.

'They still in the city,' Booya said, smiling, fighting an urge to pick the little man up. 'Think they there to stay.'

'Hey, you gonna play, Mister Rider Rider?' Skipping from foot to foot, Frankie pointed at Booya's guitar.

'Wasn't thinking of playing, man.'

'You thinking of taking a chance thinking again?' Frankie asked.

'Oh, Calvin, why don't you play?' Labella said. 'Just for a while.'

Frankie tipped his hat. 'Ma'am, you a fine looking lady, if you don't mind a handsome fool telling ya.' Frankie turned to face Booya. 'You gonna disappoint a fine looking lady and a handsome fool, Mister Rider Rider?'

Booya didn't know where Frankie had got that new nickname – Mister Rider Rider. He didn't know where Frankie found half of his quirky talk. 'Got your whistle on you, little Frank?'

'Me foife, me foine fellow. Ain't no hu-whistle; it's a foife.'

'Got your fife, then?'

'Oi must say that oi don't. All down to you, it is.'

Booya pulled his guitar up on his knee. 'Got a dollar, mister?' he asked Frankie, smiling.

'No, oi don't. But oi have me foife,' Frankie replied, pulling his fife from a jacket pocket.

Eavesdroppers laughed at the exchange. Labella squealed and laid a hand on Booya's thigh. There was nothing sexual in her expression of excitement, but of all the things that Booya had done, with all shapes and perfections of different women, just that small gesture felt like the most erotic advance of his life. If they weren't on the stoop outside the store that Mammy worked in, he would quite enjoy for her to keep her hand there. As if sensing his thoughts, she removed her hand and clapped a couple of times, rapidly tapping her toes.

'Oi'll tell ye what we'll do.' Frankie pulled himself up on to the bench and cupped a tiny hand around Booya's ear. 'Thought you might wanna know: Colden leave town soon after you. Ain't gonna bother you no more,' he whispered through hot air. 'And believe me when I say, you ain't never gonna see his wife again no place. Never.' Frankie hopped down off the bench. 'Ye get that, Mister Rider Rider?'

Booya looked in the direction of Redemption Square. Relaxing his shoulders as he exhaled, he blinked several times and wiped a finger around his tear ducts. Smiling, he nodded to Frankie. 'Yeah, man. I got it.'

'Ye lead, und oi'll follow,' Frankie said, skilfully spinning the fife over his stubby palm.

The instrumental version of *She's A Sunflower* seemed the most obvious choice of song. It also meant that Booya didn't have to sing in front of the gathering crowd of strangers. At least the big man had little Frankie to hide behind. Frankie leant an entirely new melody to the piece, somehow both chirpy and mournful at the same time, like a New Orleans funeral dance. He sawn-necked up and down the steps, weaving through the gathering crowd in the street, marching back-and-forth on the stoop in front of Booya.

Booya was looking along the stoop to see what size of audience wee little Frankie had drawn, and there was Mammy, looking proudly at her boy, though cautiously at Labella. Beside Mammy, Mattie was looking lovingly both at Labella and her daughter's esteemed companion, all the while prodding victorious glances at Mammy, trying to announce: "I won your son!"

As he played, Booya aimed a wink at Mammy; she smiled. Mattie blushed and pouted, stealing the gesture as her own. Labella – who had been gazing from the magic of Booya's fingers to the side of his face – followed his look. She saw her ma pouting, and then she noticed Adeline's frosty stare trained on her.

After bringing the piece to an end, with an intricate and emotional finale from Frankie, Booya said, 'Come meet Mammy,' forgetting that Labella and Mammy had already met on the day Labella had worked in Huck's. Labella followed him along the stoop.

'Oh, you really is the most wonderful musicianer I ever did hear,' Mattie cooed.

'Calvin, you make me so proud to be your Mammy ever time you is out here,' Mammy said, her eyes moistening. 'And looking so much like a man in that suit.'

'Wasn't here to play today,' Booya replied, rolling his eyes. 'Just come to say Hi to you, Mammy. You must have . . . left this morning 'fore I waked up.'

Mammy lifted her hands to her chest and her eyes to the sky. 'Such a son, thinking 'bout his Mammy first thing each morning.'

'You was just wonderful, Calvin!' Mattie lavished. She hovered a gaze over her pretty daughter.

Labella was looking from Adeline to Booya.

'You sure is looking fine and pretty today, Labella,' Mammy said. 'I just love the way you wear that bow and flower in your hair.'

Mattie wrapped an arm around Labella, smothering her, and kissed her cheek. 'She just gets more beautiful with ever day.'

A gentle smile rising on the bow of her lips, Labella blushed.

'What you chiles doing today?' Mattie asked, her wing still clasping her daughter.

''Cept for coming to us old gals?' Mammy added. With her smile hidden behind her eyes, Mammy lingered a look on Mattie.

'Well, had nothing further planned than coming down here, really,' Booya replied.

'It's as fine a day as God ever willed,' Mammy said. 'If I didn't have my duties, I think sitting by the river would be what I'd like to do.'

'Oh, Adeline,' Mattie gasped, a hand to her chest. 'That's a perfect idea. Oh! What a beautiful way to spend a fine day.' She lifted her chin, raising her eyebrows in Mammy's direction.

Booya looked down at Labella; she had been gazing up at him.

'What do you say?' he asked.

Labella nodded. 'That'd be fine.' She smiled.

*

Butterflies flitted and dragonflies droned over the reeds. A weeping willow tickled the water. Fish jumped to catch flies, making the water chuckle. Birds sang along to the soft harmony of Booya's guitar playing. They had the bank and river to themselves, alone together for the first time.

'She's a sunflower and she's smiling back at me,' Booya sang, strumming his guitar. He could hear the nervousness in his voice, hoping that it didn't transmit. It was a strange feeling for him: he hadn't felt this shy performing for an audience of one since the first days in the shack with Roots. He looked

181

for Labella again and she was still there beside him. It was still her. 'She's a sunflower . . . most beautiful I ever see.' The shakiness remained in his voice. He continued by humming and the birds sang the words.

When he felt Labella's lips touch gently upon his cheek, he couldn't be sure that he wasn't dreaming the day. The birds continued *a cappella*. Labella was looking at him through the top of her eyes, her head lowered. A smile flickered upon her lips.

'Sorry,' she whispered. 'It was just so beautiful to hear you . . . And I . . .' She was blushing so deeply, molten gold.

Over his guitar, Booya leaned towards her and picked up her chin. Her eyes were closed. All he could do at first was look upon the perfection of her face, the blend of toffee-skin to the silken rose-colour of her lips. He leaned forward and kissed her.

CHAPTER
SEVEN

1

The newly painted sign hanging outside Blacks stole Booya's attention: a bowl with the word JUJU floating in red liquid. Perhaps it wasn't going to be a barrelhouse after all; maybe one of those fancy diners that he had known in the city had found its way down to the country town.

JUJU
SPECIAL OPENING NIGHT
THIS SATURDAY
LIVE PERFORMANCES!
FREE CUP OF FRUIT PUNCH!

Putting the guitar to his shoulder, Booya tried the door. In the old days of Blacks it would have opened, locked or not. This door remained firmly closed. Stepping back, he looked at the front of the building. But for the new swinging sign, it looked just the same as it ever had. The piece of paper plastered to the door said Saturday night. He could wait twenty-four hours.

*

Those waiting outside Juju were all wearing their best clothes as they queued. Booya looked at the faces; he didn't recognise a single person as being a frequenter of Blacks. The door was open, a red rope all that barred the entrance, a weak red light spilling into the street outside. Booya slid down the side of the General Store and up the street.

The effects of the cup that he had drunk had nearly worn off. Walking up the poplar-lined street, folks on their stoops watched him go, leaning forward from their chairs to see where he would stop. Booya glanced at Petal and Rosie's place. Like Blacks, he had changed now for good. He'd love the three girls forever, but those old days could stay old. He continued up the road to the modest little house, quiet and further from the town.

Carefully latching the gate behind him, Booya stepped up to the door. Out here all eyes were focused on their own business, enjoying their own front yards. He checked his hat; it was not there, just the ghost of a feeling where it spent most of its days. He twice cleared his throat. Brushing his hands down the front of his clean white shirt, Booya lifted his hand to knock. The door began to open before he could tap on the glass panel. And the frantic beat of his heart stopped.

Smiling up at Booya with her chin halfway to her chest, Labella was wearing a sleek white dress with small black dots, a black shawl draped over her arms and a matching hat pinned at an angle. He had not previously been as far as her front gate. Glancing inside he saw a table with a thick candlestick throwing dim shades of light into the room; two comfy chairs with blankets draped over their backs; a tall cross on the mantel beneath a painted picture of Jesus. Labella held out an arm for him to lead her from the door. Booya patted down where his hat would be.

'Ma'am.' He offered his arm. Labella giggled and accepted.

The sun was yet to go down. Some of the heat of the day had blown away down the road, but there was still damp warmth in the air as they joined the queue outside Juju. Down the street music blared from the barrelhouses; the General Store had finished its licensed trade and was opening its back rooms to the gamblers. A low hum generated from the inside of Juju, travelling on the reddish light.

'Thanks for axing me to come down here for the opening with you,' Labella said, playing with her shawl.

'You ever come in here when it was Blacks?' Booya asked.

'Nu-uh. No way. Was invited, but I was scared to. Friend of mine come one time and she say that just walking through a crowd of them men . . .' Labella blushed. 'Well, I don't like to say what she say.'

'Sounds like Blacks,' Booya replied, smiling.

'You used to go?' Labella asked, eyes widening.

'I used to play!'

'Oh yes, they was saying at the frolic.' Labella looked at the ground.

'They say a lot of things,' Booya replied. 'And ain't none of it true. Those folks, besides everthing else, they couldn't help themselves but whip up the water whenever it begins to still, just so they could sail out all kinds of crazy, made-up stories. It might be hard to understand, but it's just how that place worked. It was always alive under this roof with clouds of lies, where you couldn't tell what the truth was most times. Creating a mystery created a kinda legend. And that's what folks felt like they had the right to do; to make it seem like a story from the Bible was being acted out in there. 'Specially if you was someone that they all knowed.' Booya saw the adorable frown upon Labella's soft brow. 'That make any kind of sense? It's kind of hard to explain if you was never there.'

Labella looked up at the gently creaking sign and pulled the shawl up around her neck. 'You don't think this place is going to be anything like that nasty place, do you, Calvin?'

Booya couldn't help but grin.

'No one what come to that old place has never even heared of fruit punch! Doubt they could even taste the fruit no more if they tried! Here . . .' Booya pulled Labella close to him; she buried in even closer. 'If you ain't feeling comfortable, we ain't gotta stay a second longer than you want.'

She felt warm and smelled amazing: of lavender-scented soap, which wouldn't have smelled this fine on anyone else. Even the soft feel of the simple woollen shawl, draped about Labella it might have been made from heavenly fleece. She looked up at him and smiled, pushing against him and putting her arm around his waist.

Handing out pieces of card on the door was a tall and broad man, his shaved head painted white, a bone through his nose, wearing a multi-coloured poncho and a feather around his neck. His muscular skin was as dark as Booya had ever seen in Mississippi, as black as the gnarled trunk of the hanging tree in Redemption Square.

'Da mysteries of Juju, sir, ma'am. Immerse yo'selves in de spirit of da islands wid a sip of snake blood.' The man handed Booya two pieces of card. Written on them was: ENTITLES BEARER TO ONE CUP OF SNAKE BLOOD. 'Please mind de step. An' enjoy yo' stay in Juju.'

They stepped through the door.

'Da mysteries of Juju, young sir, ma'am . . .' they heard the man say to the next folks behind them.

It hadn't been painted and the lighting was the same – even if the saucer lights had been cleaned of decade's worth of dead flies – but inside it was much brighter than Blacks had been. In the old days, Booya had never noticed that some of the saucers must not have been working. Along the walls were tall, thick-leaved exotic plants, lit red from beneath to create a shadow of leaves on the wall. Excepting the exotic additions, essentially it was still Blacks: the long bar counter was the same; the spider webs had not been cleaned from the rafters and crossbeams, capturing the red, white and green light, adding to the jungle feel. The same booths lined the far wall, above which dripping candles – red, where they had previously been mostly white, when there had been any at all – created little globes of light. There was a whiff of tobacco in the air, a sweet smell of an incense that Booya couldn't place, but the smell of sick and urine, bedded deeply in musk, was absent. There was a slight wash of polish mingling with the incense and tobacco, but otherwise it just smelt plain and clean. Because it didn't stink at all.

There stage was still there, but unoccupied. There was music playing, but it wasn't shaking the walls and rattling the ceiling as it had done in the days of Blacks. The music sounded to Booya like a forest would if it formed an orchestra of its flora. It was languid and tranquil, hypnotic, almost spooky. He liked it; it made him feel welcome and at ease. It felt as though he could easily fall into a daze – like being gassed to unconsciousness by sound.

Though it was nothing like as full as it had been inside Blacks on a Saturday night, some of the other good folks of Honahee had come to pry on Juju. And people were sitting at the tables and booths in a civilized manner! There were a few dressed in the same strange fancy dress as the man on the door, mingling through the mostly seated crowd. Otherwise, everyone looked as plain and out of place as Booya, dressed in his simple picker's clothes.

'Kind of eerie, ain't it,' said Labella, echoing Booya's thoughts. But he noticed how she was marvelling with wonder.

'You like it?' he asked.

She nodded. 'Ain't as I imagined it. Is this what it was always like?'

He laughed. 'It used to feel like the hogs had left through the backdoor just 'fore you come in through the front.' Labella grinned and dropped her shawl to her elbows; shivered, and then pulled it back up again.

'I like it,' she said.

'Could I interest you in some snake blood, pretty lady?' Booya asked.

'Thought you would never ax!' she replied, her beautiful smile shining, filling her round cheeks.

With a talent for keeping people waiting patiently and in order – whatever order he chose – Cole used to need little help behind the bar. It was always obvious what most of the waiting people wanted anyway: whisky. Cups were either lined up ready, or would take no longer than dipping his hand in a barrel to fill. In the daytime Cole had always acted surreptitiously, but the revenue men would never have dared entered a premises like Blacks at night.

Behind the bar counter of Juju, however, were two men and three girls, all with dark eye-paint and white markings on their faces. The men were topless, wearing feather collars and baggy trousers; the women wearing tasselled dresses and flower necklaces. Stark and ominous beneath their dressed-up countenance, it was only when they smiled that they looked completely human. With a smile on his face, it was one of the men who came to serve Booya and Labella.

'Hey, man,' he said to Booya. 'Snake blood, by chance?'

Booya handed over the cards. 'Make that two snake bloods, friend.'

'Right up.' Reaching under the counter, the man produced two cups.

'How many snakes had to die?' Booya asked.

By the malevolence his painted face added to his frown, Booya thought that maybe the man was summoning a curse. Then all in the space of a second, he broke into a smile.

'Oh! Yeah, man, forest is empty of 'em. All extincted in a day so that the folks of Hon'hee gets theyselves a drink! Let you in on a secret, man,' the man whispered. 'Snake blood tastes a lot like orange and mango.' Both Booya and Labella laughed.

'You know if they have plans to start up the blues again in this place?'

Booya asked.

'You a blues man? Me too! Man, I gonna *insist* they do. Ain't gonna work here long if I gotta wear this paint ever night.' With his mouth hidden by his hand, he returned to the same whispering posture. 'Telling the truth, I think that this is all just to show folks how different it is to Blacks. Tonight we got all sorts of different sounds to pound our ears. But after this scene for opening night, the blues'll be back, for sure.'

'Who I got to speak with to find out?' Booya asked.

'You'll be wanting Maluch; the man what's on the door. He the new owner. Ain't gonna be able to get through to him tonight, but come down tomorrow. We gonna be open all day, ever day. If I don't get to put some Blind Lemon Jefferson on the juke then I's gonna put a real hoodoo curse on this place.'

2

Quiet and soothing jazz was playing in the background, a rasping trumpet accompanied by jangling piano keys. Booya had forgotten to look last night, but there it was in the corner, the same old splintered upright piano from Blacks, half of the keys with the life beaten out of them. In Blacks, Cole would never have permitted more than two minutes of jazz a month, but unlike some of the music last night, at least this music was indigenous to America.

'Kind of lost a piece of its soul, ain't it?' Paw said, sniffing the air as he looked around at the floral additions and dimly coloured lighting. 'More like a whorehouse than barrelhouse.'

At the central tables old boys were playing games of craps. When one of the old boys lifted his hat, Paw flicked a thumb to him.

'Yah, you be best playing to the lazy and crazy wasters hanging out at the General Store,' Paw said through the side of his mouth. 'Least they know they is alive. Well, mostly.'

'Paw, I ain't gonna play at the store.' Booya laughed. 'How many times do I gotta tell you? Rather play in a graveyard.'

'Well, maybe that's the best place left, then.' Sometimes it was impossible to tell when Paw was being serious. He certainly didn't look like he was joking. 'What we doing here, anyplace?'

'It was you say you wanna come in and see!' Booya replied. 'But I was gonna come in anyways.' Booya's smile slipped from his face. Turning his head, he looked towards Paw. 'To see if they'll let me play.'

'You ain't joking with your old man, is you, Boo? Ain't no blues *here* no more. All the ghosts of the great men have gone found somewhere else to spend they nights, chased outta the place. Can tell it just by looking.' Paw wasn't directing a word to Booya, he was talking to the building. 'They might only be spirits, but they still got they class. They still got *soul*. Heh-heh, won't even be catched *dead* in this empty barn. Who's gonna want to come through here now and –'

'Paw, I is gonna see if I can find the owner, ax him 'bout playing.'

'Huh? Sure, son.' Ambling behind, still looking around and muttering like a blind man lost, Paw followed Booya to the bar counter.

The man behind the counter was massive – nearly the same height as Booya but as broad as an ancient tree. His face was as big and round as a boulder, covered in the blackest of skin; his lips were huge, as if he was sucking on two skinned pigs. Deep laughter-lines cut into his cheeks. Just as Cole would have been doing, he was wiping a cup with a rag and glaring.

Booya watched the man's glare pass over his shoulder to where he could hear Paw muttering behind him.

'Hey, man,' Booya said. 'Maluch here today?'

The man frowned. 'Who lookin' for 'im is de question?' The man's accent was part African and part American, lost somewhere in between; his voice as deep as Booya had ever heard, even deeper than the river singers.

'Erm . . . me.'

'But I don't know you. 'Less you is called Me.'

'No, erm . . . My name's Booya Carthy.'

The exotic beast of a man began to grin over Booya's shoulder, with his teeth like whittled bones showing. His smile was met by Paw's laughter.

Booya hadn't even noticed that he was being played with. Not much slipped past Paw though, laughing along.

'He's Booya,' Paw wheezed with laughter. 'I is Me.'

Laughing so hard, Booya was concerned that Paw might collapse.

The terrifyingly loud laughter of the man behind the bar matched his appearance. It sounded like an avalanche. The sound of him and Paw combined could drive a man to craziness.

'Me too,' said the man.

'Ay-yuh. Same name my cousin's got!' Paw cackled.

When the man slammed his pan-sized palm on the bar, Booya was surprised that the wood didn't split and splinter. When he had finished laughing – even though Paw still had more to go – he eyeballed Booya.

'What yo' lookin' fo' me fo', man?'

Not sure if he was still joking with him – helped none by Paw's constant heaves of laughter – Booya just stared at the man, standing, smiling and wiping the cup. Cries of anguish came from one of the tables. The man glared at them, before turning again upon Booya. Something like impatience crossed over his face.

'I is Maluch,' he said, his facing returning to passive imperiousness. 'What yo' want me fo'?'

Without his face paint, Booya hadn't recognised that this was the same man who had greeted them at the door last night, handing out the snake blood cards.

'My name's Booya Carthy. I play the blues.'

'You must be da fella dat ax Tiger last night 'bout playin' down 'ere at Juju. 'E tole me someone was axin'.'

'Hey, man,' Paw interrupted, leaning on the bar, 'you gonna fill that cup full of Moonshine for me?'

Maluch glared at Paw, snapped, 'What yo' say?'

'I is gasping for a cup! You got one for a thirsty old man?'

Ignoring Paw, Maluch addressed Booya: 'I see you ain't got no guitar on you now. What experience you got of playin'?'

'Used to play here when it was Blacks. Played up in Chi at clubs and jukes for 'bout a year, too. Played for all my life.'

'When you wasn't chasing womens . . .' Paw added.

Booya breathed in deeply, wishing that Paw would just go and join his friends at the tables and leave him alone to talk with Maluch.

'How often you wantin' to play?'

'Play ever night, if you want me to play ever night.'

'I like de blues. I feel dat if you is a black man dat you got music inside you, wherever yo's from. Where I come from, de music is make up from de African music of our fathers. I believe it come over da seas on da boat centuries even befo' our ancestors, when brothers was stole from da motherlan'. I first heared da blues when I come to America and I felt it in my soul, in my blood, like we feel dem shackles of our brothers dat first land 'ere.'

Booya wasn't sure if Maluch was waiting for him to respond. Better him than Paw. 'You know Blind Lemon Jeff . . . ? Jefferson?'

'You play like Blind Lemon Jefferson? Must say, haven't heared much. Tiger dat you meet, he crazy for dat sound.'

'Country blues is what I learned to play first.'

'What other blues you play?'

'Outlaw blues,' Booya answered before thinking.

Lying in her bed a lifetime before, the morning after Cole had killed for him, the outlaw blues was how Rosie had said that Booya should sell himself. That he would be known around town from then on as dangerous. And that was how he had been introduced to audiences in Chicago.

'You runnin' from de law?' Maluch asked. It was impossible to tell if his full lips were attempting to smile.

'You on the run from The Law, Boo?' Paw echoed. 'Them stories I heared 'bout you and your reputation true?'

'Nah, Paw. It's just called the outlaw blues.' Licking his lips, Booya glanced at Juju's front door.

'I like it,' Maluch said, setting down the cup, now definitely grinning, 'even if you ain't appearin' much like a outlaw in dem picker's clothes. You wanna play tonight?'

*

Following the same jug band who had played on Juju's opening night, that night Booya played both the country and outlaw blues. Using an amplified sound that stripped Blacks old system apart, he debuted a song that he had last played sitting by the tracks with The Three Free Riders as they waited for the city train to come rolling in. A song called *Travelling*. A dark song full of despair. He also improvised a new song, *Days Of The Outlaw Blues*, designed to demonstrate to Paw that it was a song-style, not a lifestyle. For Mammy and Paw were two amongst his crowd.

They'd had to reassure Mammy that, besides sharing the same rafters and floorboards, Juju had nothing to do with Blacks. That she would remain an unloose woman. For the first time, Booya's parents witnessed the reception that their son's outlaw blues received – Paw reciting to Mammy over the ruckus that Booya wasn't a real outlaw, just a name that he went by when singing the blues.

It was the closest thing to a Blacks response that greeted the performance.

They went wild. Tables and chairs were danced upon and spilled, just like back in the day.

Cheering as loudly as anyone in the crowd, Mammy had found herself dancing wildly, commanding the space that her generous size required. And all with her wings wrapped protectively around Labella – when she wasn't bumping off Mammy's heaving bulk.

When Booya finished playing, Mammy managed to clear a group of young men from a booth. Booya thought that there was no other person in the place who could have encouraged those men to desert their seats. It was amazing how, even on her first visit, Mammy could act like the most seasoned person in the place.

'Booya Carthy ma wants my seat?' one of the boys said. He looked up at Booya and tipped his unblemished Derby to him. 'S'honour to share the same town. You the reason I bought me a geetar.'

Booya had recognised some of the faces; Paw too. It was clear that, like rats to a new corn silo, some of the old Blacks clientele had found their way back to Juju. Booya also noticed that many of them had smuggled in their own homemade bootleg liquor.

He huddled next to Labella, noticing Mammy watching her whilst also watching him, all the while strictly ensuring that Paw was behaving. Booya noticed too that Mammy was studying Labella with a loving twinkle in her eyes. Freeing his arm from Labella, he slid from the booth.

'Just gotta go speak with Maluch a while,' he said, seeing both Mammy and Labella telling him with their wide eyes not to leave them for a second. It made him smile.

As he moved into the crowd it made way; many nodded to him, smiling eyes twinkling with recognition. No back-slapping; no toothless old crows grabbing his face; no acquaintances from the Harris plantation yelling in his ears. 'Good playing, man,' he heard more than once, before they stepped aside to allow the big man through. 'Sounded great!' Not needing to shout to be heard above the mellow drum of noise. Booya saw Rosie's recently-despatched beau Morgan. With no signal of threat, Morgan's cheek twitched in a kind of resigned defeat before he vanished into a crowd that was hustling for Booya's attention. They began to call his name as he passed, grinning and wanting to shake his hand, even just to touch him.

Booya accepted the appreciation of the crowd as inconspicuously as he could – even as he struggled to keep his hat on his head – smiling at folks and thanking them as he went. He stepped on not one toe.

When Booya finally found a path to the bar, the singer of the electric blues band upon the stage – a second Juju performance from The Soul Stealers – announced to the audience: 'If y'all be so kind, treat us just as if we is following anyone else. We ain't never had to follow no Booya Carthy before.'

The crowd applauded, stamping their feet as if it was still Blacks' roof they were shaking.

'Tole you I ain't never wearing that paint *an' dat Wes' Injun* shit again!' Tiger said – the man who had served Booya and Labella snake blood – laughing and brushing his shirt and waistcoat proudly. 'That's some of the best blues I ever heared, man! If ever you is planning to go to Stanza's, I'd get me a record of that to play back at my digs. We definitely gotta get together and play sometime.'

Booya just smiled, nodded. 'Say, man, you got any of last night's fruit punch?' Bouldering over, Maluch told Booya that he could play Juju any time he wanted, night or day.

''Ere,' he said, glaring at any eavesdroppers through his thickly-lined eyes, 'come wid me.'

Booya followed Maluch to a room at the end of the bar, a room he had never been in before. It was a storeroom of sorts, stacked with empty cups and bottles, unlabelled barrels and crates of fruit. The smell of the fruit filled the room with a deliciously sweet aroma. The room clearly doubled as an office: there was a desk and chairs – some of them broken. Candles in a candleholder on the desk offered a damp light to the dark room. Vaguely illuminated, Booya saw that there were more boxes of candles and an array of musical instruments – as far as he could see, like the chairs, they were mostly broken. There was a banjo hanging on the wall, sorry remnants of strings hanging down like torn vines.

Hanging next to the banjo was a framed black and white picture of a skinny young black man wearing a suit. Beneath cracks in the glass, the picture was torn and water-stained in the corner. The man was grinning broadly beneath his fedora – the hat that everybody in Chicago had been wearing, black with a white band – and resting his easy rider on his knee; his long bony fingers standing on the strings, ready to pick. Above an illegible scrawl was scribbled: *Blacks da bes playce I play at in al my hoboin life.* There was something alluring in those eyes, innocent, yet dangerous. Mixed in with the scent of fruit, Booya could smell wet corn and yeast fermenting.

Maluch removed a stack of crates, revealing a hidden plastic barrel. "Ere, man.' He handed Booya a cup. 'Ain't on de menu, but it yo's if yo want it.'

With the cup in his hand, saliva was gathering on Booya's tongue. A minute ago all he had been craving for was a cup of lumpy fruit punch.

Maluch stepped away from the barrel with a cup of his own. 'Dis ain't in da house. If anyone ax, yo brung you own wid yo', hear? Ain't *in* de house, but it *on* de house.' After a booming laugh, Maluch tipped back his massive head and drank heavily, emptying the cup, then licked his bulbous lips. 'Ahhh.'

Booya sipped at the whisky. Damn! It tasted fine.

A voice came suddenly from behind him. 'I can keep me a secret, too. Got a spare one for a old man, huh?'

'Paw!'

'What? Ain't gonna leave me out now, is you? Your own old man? I been keeping secrets from your Mammy for my whole life – for all yours, at least. I is come quite good at it!'

'Yeah,' Booya said, lifting the cup towards Paw's hand and stupid grin.

"Old up, Booya,' Maluch said. "E is da pap of de new star attraction. I tink we can find 'im a cup of 'is own. But make sure dat de door closed.'

Paw did. Then he whooped and licked his lips.

*

As soon as they were within sight of their booth, Mammy knew exactly what had been going on. With the ridiculous expression across Paw's face, along with his arm-flailing, knee-shaking dance to the electric blues, it was more than a little giveaway. With wide-eyed, innocent wonder, Labella marvelled at Paw's craziness. But Mammy was grinning.

'You is just a old fool, ain't you?' she said, looking her jerking, dancing husband up and down and pouting.

'Uh-huh,' Paw agreed. 'A old fool with the rhythm! You ever feel a rhythm like this, Boo? Feel it, huh?'

Legs apart, Paw frantically tapped his feet; his arms moving as if they were clearing spider webs from his path. Mammy was laughing out loud. Labella, too, but behind her hand, helpless not to blush.

Booya felt a tap on his shoulder. Rosie smiled up at him in the devil-could-care fashion that she had worn of late. Wearing a plain cotton dress, she looked beautiful, just as he remembered her from the first day that he had met her. She smiled at Mammy and said Hi to Labella. Labella smiled and blushed golden.

'We watched you play,' Rosie said. 'Just wanted to come tell you how amazing we think you was. Best ever, Boo!'

'Thanks,' Booya replied.

Petal and Virginia were standing next to Rosie, fluttering and blushing like crazy.

'Haai, handsome,' they choroused.

Having briefly stopped jerking around, Paw joined the new arrivals. He was staring at Rosie.

'What's your name, girl? Damn!'

'Rosie,' she replied, with the look that she knew worked so well on any man. 'And you must be Big Boo's Paw. I heared all 'bout *you*. Now I can see how Boo growed up so big and handsome.'

'You know, girl, if my old woman weren't here, you know what I'd do? I'd –'

'Cleveland!' Mammy yelled. 'You trying to fetch yourself a whupping?'

'Yah.' Paw waved a hand at Mammy. And then his eyes fell on Petal. 'Damn! What the hell –?'

'Paw,' Booya shouted, realising what Paw was too tactless not to say, seeing it coming before he'd said a word. 'This is Petal. And that pretty little thing with her's Virginia.'

'Haai, handsome,' Petal cooed, sticking her hip out to one side.

Virginia was too busy fluttering, smiling shyly and blushing to utter a word to Booya's Paw. Paw wouldn't have heard anyway. Aimed over about fifty bobbing heads, he was shouting something at the band.

3

There was nothing different about that day. It was midday; they had chosen to sit in the shade to shelter from the glorious heat. Booya was leaning back against a tree, his hat tilted at an angle. Labella was sitting between his legs, leaning her head on his chest; her skirt tucked primly beneath her legs.

'All of Honahee loves you, you know,' Labella said. 'You should hear what they say when you is on the stage. Say that you is unrivalled; destined for bigger things than this town. You know that?'

Booya rolled his head to stretch his neck. He resettled his hat. 'Don't matter none to me, sunflower. Our days down here means more than any of that.'

Horses were grazing in the pasture beyond the river. The fish were jumping, snatching insects from the surface of the water. Hummingbirds darted through the tall flowers, scattering seeds to the ground as they disturbed the leaves. The buzz of life was fragrant in the still air.

'Your Mammy and Paw go see you play Juju much lately, Calvin? All them nights you play?'

Booya smiled. 'Paw come one time without her. Ain't never gonna happen again.' He laughed. '"Down there's a young folks' scene, you old fool," she say to him. "Time for you to act your age, 'bout hundred and fifty by the look of you. You starting to look shrivelled as a date!"' Labella giggled. 'So no, not much. Paw, he's more popular 'bout town than I'll ever be, from his . . . older days. It's like his life's catched a second wind.'

'Rosie come much?' Labella asked. ''Cept for when I ain't there with Virginia and Petal?'

His heart leaping to his throat, Booya opened his eyes. Red and yellow dots danced in the brightness of the day. Sticking out his bottom lip, shrugging, he moved his head from side to side, blinking the sun dots clear.

'Can't say,' he said. He affected a radio reader's voice: 'After the show, *everone* wants the *attention* of the blues man *destined* for *bigger things* than this *one horse town*.' He shook Labella's shoulders. 'Huh?'

She answered him with a '*Hmm*.'

Lingering a look at the side of Labella's face, her eyes remaining closed, Booya leaned back against the tree. He breathed in the day, filling his lungs.

'How many women have you been with, Calvin?' Labella asked before he could exhale.

His eyes were open. 'Huh?'

'How many women you spent the night with?' she repeated. 'I don't mind, just want to know more 'bout your past.' She was holding her straw hat to her chest. Booya could feel that her breaths were slightly closer together – not an indication that she didn't mind at all. 'Everone else in Honahee seems to know, and I want to know, too.'

'How many grains of dust ever fell on a uncovered dresser?' Booya answered.

Labella slapped his leg. He couldn't see that she was smiling.

'Be serious, Calvin. I want to know the truth.' Labella twisted around and looked up at him through the corner of one eye. 'Calvin, it's a simple question. And I already say that I don't mind, didn't I? If we is going to be together, I just need to know a few things.' Facing the river, she resettled against his chest.

'But we is together already, ain't we, honey? If I knowed you was coming my way, I'd a waited my whole life! Why you need to know now?'

'I just do, okay?' She sighed. 'How many?'

'A few,' he answered, pouting.

'How many's a few? Three? Five?'

'Yeah, 'bout that.'

'What, five!'

'Say 'bout five, yeah.'

Pulling her hat closer, she squirmed. 'You mean . . . you don't even *know*?'

'Yes, I know. You axed, Bella, and I say five.' She allowed him to wrap his arms around her. Lenut Colden's wife, pretty in polka dots, flickered through the afterimage of the sun daze. Opening one eye, he scanned the pasture beyond the river. 'Come on, sweet sugar. Say just now you weren't gonna get mad.'

Picking at the hem of her dress, Labella leaned her head against his arm. 'I know you and Rosie used to go together.'

Booya gripped Labella's arms. 'What she say to you?'

'Nothing, Calvin. It's just plain obvious. Don't need to be a judge to see that it's written all over both of you.'

Booya sighed. 'It was a long time ago, Bella. We was best friends at the time. It was . . . different then. And now you and Rosie is friends too.' He pinched the bridge of his nose, hard; purple joining the red and yellow sun dancers.

'It's still in ever look she gives you, Calvin. Can't you see that? She clearly don't see it the same as you do. Thought of axing her, but –'

'But I love *you*,' Booya interrupted. 'She knows that, just like *everone* does. She *knows* that we is just friends, me and her. You can trust her, Bella.'

Again Labella was silent for a while as Booya stood on the edge of a place unknown to him; again glad that she was not looking upon his face. Her warmth was radiating into him. He could smell the perfume that couldn't be so sweet coming from anyone else. To break the tense silence, he was about to change the subject – say what a fine day it was, or some other triviality – but Labella had not yet finished.

'You been with any women since we been together, Calvin?'

Having dropped Labella home, most nights temptation deviated Booya's path. Knowing she was warm in bed, it couldn't hurt Labella if he had a little nightcap before he wondered on, probably to sleep beneath the bridge. So, as the popular performer about town, with a free license to visit Maluch's storeroom, Booya regularly slipped back into Juju. Leaning against the bar one time, his eyes rolling, Rosie bounded over to him – she wasn't a girl who needed her bed early.

"How 'bout it, Big Boo?" she said, rubbing herself against his side. "Won't mean nothing, just like it *never* did. Ain't no one gotta ever know but us . . ."

"You gotta stop doing this, Rosie," Booya slurred, swaying. "Labella's yo' *friend!* And *we's* just friends."

"It's our unfinished business, Boo. S'all I is saying." Rosie pulled the cup out of Booya's hand. Holding it in both hands, she tipped it back and drank. Pushing her body ever closer against his, she continued to grind against him, raising one eyebrow as he rolled his head to look down at her . . .

'Course I ain't, Bella.'

'You telling the truth, Calvin?'

'I love you, Bella, okay? Ain't no room in my heart for no one else for me to love 'cause you is taking up all the space, pretty lady. *Okay?* Don't know how many other ways I can say.'

Forgetting to hate himself for a moment, he kissed her forehead, lingering to show how much he meant it. Leaning back against the tree, he wrapped his arms around her, surprised by the inconvenient stirring in his pants as she shuffled to get comfortable.

'Can I ax you a few more things?'

'Why you trying to hurt yourself this way, Bella?' Booya replied, sighing. 'Tole you it can't do no good.'

'Please, Calvin; I don't want to explain yet. I just need to know.' She kissed his forearm. 'Please? I won't be mad, I swear. I believe ever word you say. I trust you. And you'll realise why I want to know soon enough. Yes?'

'Ax me whatever you like,' he replied. 'We got all day!'

'You ever been in one of them whorehouses?'

'Only when they mail come through my door and I had to take it to them, do the postman's job.'

She slapped his arm again and giggled. 'The truth, please, Calvin.'

'How do you know that ain't the truth?'

'You saying it is?' Labella asked, smiling and wide-eyed. 'You took they mail to them?'

'No,' Booya laughed, pulling a face. 'Nope: never been in one. Seen them from the outside,' he added. 'But that's as close as I ever been.'

'Truth?'

'Uh-huh.' He bit his tongue.

'Have you ever killed a man?'

'Bella, you really think I the kind to kill? Ain't never even been in a real fight!'

'You ever seen anyone killed?'

'Just one time.' Readjusting his backside, Booya moved his guitar slightly further away from the tree. Looking up into the branches above, he scratched his head; itched his eyebrow. 'But I was on stage and it was across the whole other side of the barrelhouse, so I couldn't really see nothing. Didn't even know what it was 'bout 'til later. Didn't wanna know. In the city I see a hundred nights of fights. But only ever fists.'

Labella was giggling, her elbows digging into Booya's thighs. 'Ever go with Petal?'

'Sure,' he replied. 'She was my first love. You ain't never gonna be able to replace a girl like Petal. Or, no, wait . . . Petal ain't never gonna be able to replace –'

Labella grabbed his hand and squeezed. 'Calvin, don't!'

Now that he was able to laugh with her, it felt as though all of his sins had been washed away. Cleansed, he felt that he had just about passed whatever test it was that Labella had planned for him. Stroking his lips, he watched the ripples of the river reflecting the sunlight, and the horses twitching their tails in the pasture beyond.

'Calvin, is it true what they was saying that night at Rosie's 'bout the white woman? That a man wanted to kill you over his wife?'

Booya swallowed dryly. 'That is true,' he said. 'Don't know why she choose me of all people, but she did. Say that . . .' He squinted his eyes, moistening in the bright light. 'Say if I didn't do what she wanted me to she'd tell her old man and the sheriff, any white folks who wanted to listen, that I tried to . . . take her by my own force and will. Say that she'd have me hanged if I didn't. It's the truth; I didn't have a choice, you gotta believe that's the way it was. So I did as she say . . . just to stay alive. And then she was gone.

'Only her husband, he find out somehow. And that's when I went running to the city. Who wants to go running from they folks if they got a choice?' He sighed. 'Was gonna be killed either way that night if I didn't run. So I went to the city 'til I couldn't stay no more. Wanted to come back home to my life ever day I was there. Them the worse days I ever had, the way I leave and not knowing what was happening back home.'

'That's horrible,' Labella said. 'Surprising that you don't hate all white people.'

'Well, you can't blame many for the works of few – that's what Mammy always say 'bout such things.'

'She's a wise lady, your Mammy.'

'You have no idea,' said Booya, feeling Labella's soft laughter breeze onto his arms. It felt amazing. 'Also, she don't know 'bout all that. Not many people know that real truth, and that's just fine by me. They happy to make up they own tales. Can you keep all that to yourself?'

'Uh,' she agreed. 'You can trust me too, Calvin.'

'Okay. I got just one question for you,' Booya said, sliding her up his chest, onto his lap. 'It's the only question I is gonna ax. Like you, I'll accept whatever the answer is. Yeah?'

'Sounds fair to me,' Labella agreed. 'What do you want to ax? Ax anything.'

'How many men *you* been with?'

'None,' she answered.

'There must be *one*,' he said, frowning, half-hoping.

'No,' Labella replied, readjusting the folds of her dress beneath her. 'It ain't right to me, Calvin. I ain't going to judge you over your past, 'cause we could really have something if we is honest 'bout everthing, always, now that we know everthing 'bout each other.'

His frown remained. Two horses nuzzling in the pasture made him smile. A craving for fruit tickled at his taste buds. 'You know we got something good, don't you, Bella?'

'That's why I had to know them things, Cal. Ain't saying one's better than the other, but I is a church girl, you know? Some of them other girls at church don't even believe it's proper for a girl to go round with a man without them being tied. You know: married.'

Even though the day was still near its hottest, Booya could feel that Labella had begun to shiver a little. He pulled her closer. She seemed warm, perfectly so.

'You cold?' he asked.

'Nuh . . . Nuh-uh.' Still she shivered. 'I do want to . . . be with you, Calvin. To, uh . . . to *make love with you*,' she whispered.

Booya's head began to swim in the other direction. If he felt any more emotions wade in on him so quickly he was sure that he would either melt away or explode! Could she possibly know what she was doing to him? Did she know what she was putting him through? He could feel the blood pulsing in his ears. He had been waiting for this moment since the very first time he had seen her crouching in the aisle. He had never had to wait for a girl before – except maybe the year in Chicago waiting to see Rosie again, only for his lust for her to become stupid "unfinished business".

'That's why I wanted to know everthing 'bout you first,' Labella continued. 'That's why I axed them questions of you.' Turning, she saw the frown on his face. Labella's tone changed and she leaned forward, away from his chest, to pick up her woollen shawl. 'I just knowed that it would make me end up looking like all them other girls. Just forget that I say anything. It's too soon, ain't it, to be talking that way? I just knowed that –'

'Bella, no. No!' He laughed. 'It's 'cause . . . I love you *so much*. I want it to be right for you. Just want you to be sure. That's all I ever . . . *You* is all I ever wanted. You ain't like no one else I ever meet. Here. Come here.'

He pulled her towards him and began to lift her onto his lap. Pulling her knees together, becoming as stiff as a pole, she rested her head on his shoulder.

'I don't mean here and now, Calvin. I don't just want to roll around on the floor or in the bushes with you,' she whispered into his ear. 'You making money from your playing now, Calvin, and even though I know you love living out there with your Mammy and Paw, if you get a place of your own with all the money you making . . . I'll *make love to you there*. And I don't mean I'll just accept the first shack or dirty closet you find. I ain't moving out from mama's to live in a outhouse.'

'You mean . . .' Words escaped Booya. He looked at the soft bronze skin, which had turned paler in the golden sunlight.

'Calvin, if we is . . . *making love* . . . don't you think that . . .' Labella shuddered in Booya's arms, her nerves and body jumping. ' . . . That it would make sense for you to take me as your wife?'

4

The crowd were frenzied before Booya had spoken a word, or even played a note. From a booth with Rosie and the girls, Labella was watching Booya up on the stage. Guitar across his knee, Booya sat smiling at the crowd. When the crowd hushed, sensing his intention, Booya leaned forward to the microphone.

'You is all beautiful.' The crowd whooped with pleasure, arms in the air, cheering. The discs of light shook within the rafters. 'But I want everone in this room to know that the most beautiful girl in the world is here with us tonight.'

Petal fanned her face. Rosie put an arm around Labella and squeezed. Some folks in the crowd looked towards where she was sitting; only few with a sneer. Labella pulled her hair forward to hide her face.

'Get on and play something for us, Boo!' someone yelled.

'I will, I will,' Booya responded, still smiling. 'Gonna play the best I ever done for y'all tonight.'

'Play up then!' someone else yelled.

The crowd noisily shushed the second heckler. They looked at each other, grinning, muttering amongst themselves, until someone would remind them that it's Booya Carthy up on the stage.

'I dedicate, here and now, the rest of my life to that girl – she knows who she is. And I ain't shy to tell you in front a this whole room: I love you.'

'Oh my,' Petal groaned.

'Do everthing to keep that man,' Rosie whispered. 'Weren't lying when I say they ain't no one like him.'

'I know,' Labella whispered in return. 'I love him as much as he just say, Rosie. More than that, even.'

Booya began to play *She's A Sunflower*. Some in the crowd jeered, laughing. 'Play some blues, man! Forget the girl; how 'bout us! We want blues. We *need* your blues.' The crowd bustling, lovers cuddling, they were told to "Shut the heck up."

Rosie smiled. 'If ever you need anything, you just come ax me, 'kay?'

Labella nodded.

'Make sure and do that, Bella. I mean it, too. We near 'nough neighbours now!'

'I will. Thanks, Rosie.'

'Love you, little lady,' Rosie said, hugging Labella. 'Boo deserves you.'

'To me he's just Calvin,' Labella said. They both gazed adoringly towards the stage.

As Booya was playing *She's a Sunflower*, three white men walked into Juju.

Unlike some of the southern bars, with their signs above the counter – NO WHITES SERVED. SORRY – white folks were permitted in Juju. Even some of the bars in Chicago still bore those signs, and whites would be politely turned away.

In all-white bars they were not so polite. CALL THIS NUMBER TO REPORT NIGGER-LOVERS, their signs read. And they meant it. Even the "nigger-lovers" would be chased out of town, reported to the local authorities – white men chasing white men because of their tolerance of blacks. Honahee was no such town. In recent history, blacks and whites had mostly lived in harmony, except for the odd scandal featuring a wayward wife who demanded some "black satisfaction".

Numbers of whites didn't frequent Juju, and those who did were mostly the "po' crackers" who worked by day in the sawmills and on the plantations with the blacks. But more now came by night to Juju than had dared spend time in the rowdiness of Blacks. There were always a few to be seen: the white barber who snipped hair next to his black colleague; those who worked in the General Store; the owner of the smart clothes store just along the street. Some ventured in simply because they liked the sound that seeped out in to the street – and they'd stay, if they could tolerate the irreverent rowdiness and the stench.

So no one paid any special attention to the three whites who walked in that night.

Strangers they may be, but they were welcome strangers. Almost unseen, they procured drinks and wandered around the crowd to watch the popular performer playing on the stage. No one noticed that they were looking about the place as if seeking out a bad smell.

As with all nights that Booya played, the crowd called out popular radio favourites for him to play. Any performer worth his guitar strings would be able to play most requests. It just so happened that Booya Carthy could play most of the songs better than the original composers. In between his own songs and improvised numbers, Booya would happily fulfil the crowd's requests. Tonight he was in a playful mood, happy to talk to the crowd from the stage, his broad smile forever on his face as he sang. Tonight was a celebration.

'Hey, man,' someone called out, 'play *St. Louis Blues*.'

'You think that up all by yourself?' Booya asked, the crowd still laughing as he tore into the song.

'*Sweet Home Chicago!*' yelled someone else when he had finished.

'Yeah,' Booya said, tuning his guitar. 'I'll do that. Just remember that I ain't Bobby.' Now knowing the man and the lore, Booya imitated the sweet voice of Robert Johnson perfectly. And the crowd loved it. Then they adored the cover of Blind Lemon Jefferson's *Broke And Hungry* that he bounded straight into after it.

'Play *Kumbaya*,' one of the white men called out.

Booya sought out the face of the caller. Squinting through the light, he found the white face in the crowd down to his right. 'That your request, brother?'

'Just play it,' the man said, smiling at Booya. Either side of him, his white friends were just staring, their lips thin straight lines. 'I wanna hear it.'

'This a *blues* man up here, man. Hear what everone else is calling for?' Booya opened his palms to the crowd. 'You wanna hear gospel, you gotta go to church.'

The crowd laughed and cheered.

The man's smile vanished. 'Said I wants to hear Kumbaya. You play requests; I'm requesting it. Play Kumbaya.'

'Tell you what, man.' Booya chuckled. 'Got a great idea; you gonna like this . . .' Grinning, he launched into Son House's *Preaching Blues*. As ever, the crowd greeted Booya's performance with glee, dancing and singing along. Laughing, Booya allowed them to take the lead vocal, just accompanying them on guitar.

Immediately after, he played and sang *Lift Every Voice* – the anthem for blacks in the south. Every person in the building knew the words and sang along as if their lives depended on it. So compelled by the display, Booya stopped playing guitar just to listen to the rippling chorus. Behind the bar, it made him laugh to see that even Maluch was singing along, head facing the rafters and huge hand over his heart.

Looking over, he saw Petal and Rosie standing on their table in the booth, arm-in-arm, swaying and lolling their heads in time. Even above the electric buzz in his bones, he was glad that Labella wasn't on the table with them. He winked at Petal, smiling when she threw the back of her palm to her forehead, then picked up the pace with his guitar.

To finish the improvised trilogy of songs, he spontaneously created a new piece: *The Woods Is Full Of White Men*. Booya had never known a reception like the one he received when he finished. He even saw white faces in the crowd applauding, cheering through their smiles, cherishing their local star.

Booya turned to look for the reaction of the *Kumbaya* white man, expecting to see him down there in the crowd laughing with the rest of them. But the white man and his friends were no longer there.

'Looks like he gone to church, after all,' Booya said, shrugging his shoulders.

When the laughter of the crowd died down, a single man was screaming at the top of his voice in two-second bursts. Shielding his eyes, Booya could see him through the crowd. He had a completely bald head, with a large and misshapen parietal bone; the remaining teeth rooted to his gums jutted out at angles; his skin was tight and lined as black as a lightning-struck tree; his sharp shoulder bones visible through his shirt. The crowd quieting, he continued screaming; his shoulders and back stiff; his head pointed up at the rafters; his eyes widening with each harsh emission. The people beside him moved away. So stiff and straight was he, the man could have been stuck in swamp mud, calling for help. But there was no emotion on his face as he screamed, a wooden mask. The face as impassive as in prayer, but the sound painful as it ripped through the atmosphere. He screamed and screamed.

'Thank you, brother,' Booya said.

The crowd laughed nervously, before someone carried the man away, still as stiff as a fencepost, still braying his harsh scream as he went, muffled as he met the street outside.

With the crowd at first a little subdued, Booya finished his set trying to show that he was at least still having fun. But on his mind all that time was the screaming man.

'Hey,' he said to Rosie and Petal when his set was done. 'Where's Bella?'

'Virginia say she was tired, so Labella walked home with her. Say that she wants to make your new house look special for when you come home.' Rosie stuck her tongue in her cheek. 'Say that she was feeling kinda sore today, huh, Big Boo?'

Booya could feel the heat rising into his dark cheeks.

'Well . . .' Petal said. They both looked at her, sure that she was about to add something. 'Well . . . you had the crowd in them big hands tonight, Mister Big Handsome Blues Man. You quite the funny man when you get going, ain'cha?'

'Left them screaming,' Booya replied with shallow humour. He raised his eyebrows and spoke to Petal, glanced at Rosie. 'You staying around here for awhiles?' He looked over at Maluch, encouraging people out through the door as the crowd thinned.

'We gonna turn in early tonight, too, Mister Handsome. Ain't we, miss?' Petal said, linking arms with Rosie, tugging her close.

Rosie rolled her eyes. 'I promised you I'd be up in the morning.'

'We is having a girl's day in Clarksdale,' Petal said, nodding at Booya, bearing her teeth to the gums. 'Pick us up some fabrics.'

'Can't wait,' said Rosie.

*

Leaning against a stack of fruit crates in the storeroom, chinking cups with Tiger and Maluch, Booya whistled. 'Man, that was *crazy*!' Placing his hat on a broken lampshade, he began to slug down the whisky. Easing it from his lips like a bottle of milk to an orphaned lamb, he sipped around the edges. 'So crazy, almost forgot I waked up in my own house today for the first time! So just this one cup, boys.'

'Man,' Tiger said, smiling beneath his Fedora, 'ever time a fella has a warm girl waiting in his bed at home he turns like you, Boo.'

'What you mean?'

'Usually you is staying down here 'til the sun's nearly up! Staggering home in the early daylight. Man in your new situation, he forgets his friends!' Tiger raised his hands, sucking in one side of his mouth. 'Ever time.'

'Oh, I . . .'

'I is kidding you, man,' Tiger said, punching Booya's arm. 'I'll drink to your new place *and* your girl.' He raised his cup. Maluch raised his, in turn. 'You done well, my friend.'

Booya twisted his lips. 'Uh . . .'

'Yo' done drunk yo's a'ready, Boo?' Maluch asked, his cheeks swelling.

'One more cup,' Booya said. 'Seeing as it's a drink on me, I'll stay for one more cup.'

Lifting a stack of crates as if it were a pillow of feathers, Maluch dipped all three cups into the hidden barrel.

'Yo' got mo' dan one occasion to toast wid dis cup,' Maluch said, handing a cup each to Booya and Tiger.

'I do?' Booya was raising his cup anyway.

'Dere was a man in 'ere tonight who want to meet wid you. Go by de name of John Harper. Know? He de man dat own an run da Stanza Studio down da street. He impressed wid you, man. Better dan dat. He say for you to go down dere tomorrow wid yo' guitar, wants to meet wid you dere. Say dat you can even skip right pas' dat never-endin' queue. I say dat's a reason to drink to, ain't it?'

*

By the time Booya decided to go home, two more cups later, there were only fallen bodies left. He stepped out of Juju and patted down his hat. Swinging his guitar, he whistled as he walked.

'Hey, brother,' a voice out of the darkness called when he was off Main Street, out behind the General Store.

'Hey,' he replied. 'Who that?'

In the darkness, Booya could just make out the shadow of a man. No. He could see three dark outlines. They stepped out of the dark and into the gloom.

'Who is that?'

The three white men walked slowly towards him.

'Want me to sing Kumbaya now?' Booya asked, smiling.

'We'll make you sing more than Kumbaya, *nigger*. You had your chance.'

'Ah, man, I was only messing. We have a time in Juju, you know. Come back tomorrow and we'll all join in.'

'You had your chance,' the man repeated, the middle one of the three.

'We don't take too kind to devil music,' said the man on the left.

'We're Christian's,' said the last. 'We don't like hearing the Lord mocked, as you done.'

'I's a son of the Lord, too,' Booya answered. 'Ain't no devil music, I just play to entertain. My Mammy say the same thing as you all the time.' Tipping back the rim of his hat, his smile disappeared when he saw the glint of a blade. Hiding his guitar behind him, Booya held out a hand. 'Hey,' he said. 'Didn't mean nothing by it, I swear.'

'Don't think that Lord sees it that way, *brother*,' drawled one.

'I think that he knows how to forgive me,' Booya responded, stepping back a pace.

The middle man snorted a laugh. 'You can arkse him to forgive you when you meet him . . .'

They came at Booya from three sides. Withstanding a couple of blows to his body, his head was knocked to the right by a punch; up and to the left as another connected with his jaw, making him rock. Something harder than bone struck him across the back of his head. As he went down, he heard his guitar moan out of tune.

Pulling his knees to his chest, he cradled his head with an arm, trying to keep the protection of Roots' hat close, trying to keep the boot heels from connecting with his skull. Crying out with each kick and punch that landed on him, his head was swirling, pounding, as if hands were reaching out from the solid ground and trying to pull him down.

'See how you welcomed the devil into that room?' one of the men said, kicking Booya. 'See how the devil picked on that weak-souled nigger, *infected* him?'

Booya felt the bar that had struck him on the head come down on his back, making him straighten out. Toes of the boots kicked at his stomach, the shock and pain leaving him unable to breathe. He curled again, retching for air, reaching for help.

'Ain't gonna sing that devil music no more if you can't play, are ya?'

The bar was repeatedly smashed onto his right hand. It felt as though it were being eaten from within as the bones broke in pieces.

'Ain't gonna be able to sing nothing but moans when we string a rope round his neck.'

A fist smashed into Booya's eye. Seeing it coming at the last moment, he managed to close the eyelid. The blow echoed in thuds around his brain. Another fist punched his face. Blows from the bar hammered on his back. He heard another snap of bone as a booted foot stamped on his arm.

'Kum-ba-ya, my Lord, kum-ba-ya . . .'

And then the other men joined in as they continued to beat him:

'*Kum-ba-ya, my Lord, kum-ba-ya . . .*'

Booya could only vaguely hear them. It felt as though, as once warned, he was being stomped into the earth. Every inch of his body was yelling in agony, screaming insults of pain. He wasn't sure if they had stopped beating him.

'Got the noose?' he heard one of them ask.

'Hey, boys. He ain't gonna be able to play without this.'

Booya heard his guitar pleading as one of them picked it up. Managing to look through his already-swollen eyes, he saw the boots of the men facing away from him as one pair walked towards a truck, swinging his guitar. Mister Henry's guitar. He heard the terrible clang as the guitar was smashed against the fender, shattering to pieces.

Booya closed his eye. He could hear their laughter.

Pain rippled the length of his body. It felt as if numerous smouldering rocks were burning into his skin; demons jabbing fiery pikes at his organs.

'Hey!' he heard a voice yell. 'Hey! Stop there in the name of The Law.'

Booya Carthy dropped away into unconsciousness . . .

*

Coming round, he could feel a presence above him; could hear the heavy breathing. With dull pain, felt a boot nudging his head.

'We're the Knights of the White Camellia. Can ya hear me, nigger?'

He could hear.

'We've been sleeping, just resting awhile. But we're back now, to act out God's will on Earth. Next time the Knights are in town, nigger, just know that you're a dead nigger.'

Then he heard the heavy boots running away and an engine start up.

'Come back here!' A different pair of boots came to a stop near to where he lay. More heavy breathing as the man caught his breath.

'A nigger,' the voice said.

Trying to open his eyes, Booya could feel dirt against his eyeball; the other eye too swollen to open.

'If you can't move home, son,' said the voice, 'I'm going to take you to the jailhouse for inciting violence. If you can't walk, I'll drag you there.'

Booya tried to speak but could only groan.

'You been drinking al-key-hole?'

He blacked out again . . .

*

'Booya?' At first he couldn't place the voice, the West Indian accent. 'Jesus, Booya.'

'You know this man? And watch your blaspheming.'

'Yeah, su', deputy,' Maluch answered.

'That Booya?' Tiger asked. 'Shit, man! He *alive*? Who in hell –?'

'I told both of you to watch your language,' the deputy warned. 'You get him home now, or I'll take all y'all in. If you've been drinking the al-key-hole I'll take y'in anyroad.'

Booya felt himself being lifted, sure that some of his limbs had been left on the ground. There was too much pain to feel. He just felt numb. 'Missur Henry,' he mumbled. 'Gi . . . ar.'

He blacked out.

5

His first thought was: *Man, I sleeped horribly!* His second was: *Hangover* . . . And then the pain reminded him why his head was in agony. He didn't have a hangover – at least, that wasn't most of his pain; this was pain unknown. He felt like a burned wreck. It felt as if a forest had fallen on him. He couldn't move. He was broken.

Booya felt a tear splash onto his swollen eyelid, like healing water. *Must be how a drink feels for a man in the desert*, he thought. Not being able to look upon Labella through more than a water-filled slit of an eye added to his hurt. Again he tried to move, but couldn't.

'Who would want to do such a thing?' Labella was gasping between sobs. 'Who would hurt you like this?'

'Christians,' Booya mumbled.

Labella ran a cold cloth over his forehead. 'You awake? Did you try to say something, Calvin? Oh, Calvin.'

It hurt to keep his swollen eye open. It hurt less when it was closed.

Lifting a small jug to his mouth, Labella tipped in a little water, making him splutter and choke. Slowly, he licked his lips. 'Tha . . .'

'Shhh. Baby, don't talk if it hurts.' She gave him a little more water.

'Ain gon be . . . ab'e to mah . . . love wi you . . . fo . . . day, mayb two, baby gir.'

Crying freely, Labella kissed him on the forehead.

*

The next thing he knew, Booya could see Mammy leaning over him, blocking out the light. She was crying, wailing; repeating his name over and over. Her voice was shrill and unpleasant to his ears – especially as his head felt as though it was filled with sharp-edged bricks.

'That little Frankie say in his broadcast today that someone was lynched on the edge of town last night. He say that The Law thinks the Knights of the White Camellia was here. They find a little flower in the mouth of the . . . Oh, my Cal, I thought . . . Sorry . . . Bu . . . bu . . .'

Mammy dropped heavily to her knees and held Booya's hand – mercifully his fingering hand that he had somehow tucked beneath him when he was attacked, protecting it, and not his picking hand, which was broken to pieces.

'I can't lose you, Cal,' Mammy wailed. 'I can't. Come home. Please come home to me. Labella, you can come live with us, too. Cle won't mind. He needs you both nearly as much as I do. Oh, Cal. I can't lose you. I won't. I won't. I . . .' She clutched his hand to her face – if she gripped it much harder he'd have two broken hands – and cried. 'What do you say, Bella? Say you'll come to us.'

'We only been here two nights, Adeline. It ain't . . . this horrible business ain't nothing to do with us living where we do. I lived in this neighbourhood for all my life. Ain't never heared of nothing like this.'

'You think it ain't that,' Mammy replied in a different, deeper tone. 'But I tell you now that it is.'

'I don't think that Calvin's going to be able to move anywhere for a time,' Labella replied. 'This is the best place for him.'

Booya was proud of Labella, to hear her talking sense to Mammy. He loved her dearly and deeply, but Mammy had been used to only hearing what she wanted to hear for too many years.

'Adeline, do you know who the best doctor in town is?' Labella asked. 'Calvin ain't been seen to yet. I is scared he's got a concussion, but I don't know if I can keep him awake, or whether he should be sitting up or lying down. Will you go?'

Sniffling, Mammy eased herself up. 'Best thing for him now is just to stay resting. Yep, I'll go downtown,' Mammy agreed. 'But keep him awake, Labella, like you say. Do that. And try not to talk too much, Cally. Not with that . . . that . . . swelled jaw.' Mammy turned away. 'Oh, I can't even look no more.'

With just enough vision available to him, Booya could see the two women he loved embracing. He tried to smile.

It hurt like hell.

*

Booya was sitting up in bed, swaddled all over, sipping on a blurry cup of tea. Mammy tried to talk once more of having them both come to live with her and Paw. But there was no argument.

'We stayin ere, Mamm. We li . . . it ere. S'our ome.'

They had been through all this just two days earlier, when he had moved out.

Like then, Mammy had tears standing in her eyes. 'If ever you is a stranger in your own home – the home you help build – I . . . well, you hurting enough, just now. Don't be a stranger, neither of you. And here I was, planning on cooking chicken, rice and peas and all . . .'

'We'll see y'a . . . da sto,' Booya said, trying to smile, resting his cup of hot tea on his arm, cast and in a sling. 'Bu de Genul Sto's our loca sto now!'

Standing behind Mammy, Labella put a hand to her mouth to stifle a giggle. Mammy pointed at Booya. 'You don't even joke 'bout such things, Calvin. I ever I catch you in that place . . . just say I'll make you wish you wasn't catched.'

Mammy said that Paw would come down and see him later, after he had picked her up from Huck's. Before having to almost be forced out of the door, Mammy stayed to talk over every little detail of their lives, including repeating what the doctor had said: that Booya mostly needed rest to help him recover.

All Booya could do was stay sitting or lying on the bed with an arm around Labella. Moving his toes, his breathing increased. Saliva was swilling around his mouth; bracing himself for the pain, he swallowed. 'I got' go see Harper a' Stanza Stud'o. Was they las' nigh'. Wan' see me play, Bella!'

Chewing her cheek, Labella shook her head. 'Nuh-uh, good news as that is, he's gonna have to wait.'

'Bu' Bella –'

She leaned over him. 'Don't talk crazy, Calvin. Rest your jaw. The studio will still be there when you better, huh?' She kissed him on the forehead. Looking over him, she forced a smile. 'You ain't thinking of still playing, is you? I mean, you hear what Mammy say 'bout some man *hanging* last night?'

Looking away, Booya glared towards Roots' hat, sitting on the bedside table. 'Where 'Mis'er 'Enry gui'ar?' Booya asked, the memory ploughing additional pain through him.

Labella put a hand on his stomach to settle him. 'That man from Juju –

the young one, not the bald one. Tiger? – he say that he's gonna have it fixed up. Say he knows someone.'

'He sho tha' he can? I mean –' Booya tried to sit upright, but gave in to the pain.

'*Shhh* . . . You ain't got to worry 'bout that right now. I is sure it's in safe hands.'

6

Fists pounding the front door woke Booya from his slumber. The thuds were shaking the windows and walls.

Throughout that day – if it even was still the same day – he had begun to feel better and better, able to discern the breaks from the bruises and the aches from the pains. His face was bruised all over. He had a cleanly broken arm, fractured ribs and a badly fractured hand. Every time he moved his back it felt as if he was lying on a bed of spikes. If he stayed in one position it was bearable. But there was no way that he could protect Labella if this was The Law at the door, or worse, the Knights of the White Camellia come to finish what they'd started. In his current condition, he wouldn't even be able to protect himself from an elderly woman with a stick.

'Take a break!' Labella called. 'I is coming.'

Booya mumbled, and began the process of lifting his weary body.

Surprised that she had bothered to knock at all, it was Mammy who came bounding in.

'Adeline,' said Labella, 'what is it?'

Her eyes wide and her lips tight, still wearing her Huck's pinafore and apron, Mammy looked around the room. From his bed, Booya saw her disappear into the kitchen. In a moment, she reappeared at the foot of his bed. She hadn't looked at him once. He watched her take two quick breaths. Her lips began to tremble. Booya rolled his eyes.

The deep orange light of the westering sun coming in through the window was shining on Booya's face. Moving his head, he used the curtain to blot the embers of its rays. The unwashed scent of his body filled the room.

Standing behind Mammy in the doorway, as if unable to enter the room, Labella was standing with her hand halfway to her mouth; her other hand clutching a handful of her pretty floral dress. She looked so scared. Booya just wanted to be able to hold her against his smelly, broken body.

'Has Paw come to see you today?' Mammy asked. 'He ain't here, is he? Now?'

'Mammy, calm down,' Booya managed to say. 'One word at a time. What 'bout Paw?'

'He ain't come to meet me from the store. I waited for a half hour, he still ain't come. And I didn't see him on my way here, neither. Was thinking that maybe he stopped by to see you. He ain't been here at all? Has he been here?' The sunlight turning the hem of her blue apron to deep red, Mammy continued looking around the room.

Labella's hand had made it to her mouth and her eyebrows were lowering. She looked ready to cry.

'Go put some tea on, Bella,' Booya said, as calmly as he could.

'You seen him, then?' Mammy asked.

Remaining where she was, Labella did begin to cry.

'No,' Booya said, his voice echoing in his ears. The beating of his heart had begun to quicken, bringing new life to his pain. 'I ain't seen him. I is sure . . .' His forearm cramped; trying to move it was hell, the sound of the bone breaking snapping through his mind. 'Sure that he must just be held up someplace. Here, sit down.' Not without pain, Booya shifted his legs so that Mammy could sit on the bed. 'When you last see Paw, Mammy?'

In little, shuddering gasps, Mammy breathed in deeply. 'He walked me to the store this morning, same as ever day. And same as ever day, I expected him to meet me when I was done. Sure, he's been late collecting me 'fore now, but . . .' Mammy's lips were turned downward; her eyes were moistening. 'He ain't never been *this* late. And he always comes; never misses a day. 'Til now. He sh-should . . . He should a been there nearly *a hour ago*.'

'Well he's just held up then, most likely,' Booya said. 'Talking with someone he meet, or something.'

Mammy pulled a tissue from her bag and patted it beneath her eyes.

'He knows that if he late without a reason I'll box his ears. Only . . . it's just . . . with . . .' Mammy sobbed into her tissue. Labella sat down beside her, putting her arm as far around Mammy as she could. Booya tried to move. He felt tied to the bed. Slowly and painfully, pushing down on the sheets, he lifted his feet.

'Sorry, sorry. I ain't usually this way, but . . . Oh, Cle!' Mammy breathed a staggered breath and sniffed. 'Just with the li'l man's news of them Knights of the White Camellia being in town, and that man what was . . .' Mammy broke down. She could speak no more, bouncing the bed with her grief, bringing yet more pain to Booya's body.

'We'll walk back together. All of us. You'll see, Mammy. He just forget the time, is all.'

*

Every step of the walk home was as terrifying as it was painful. Booya hobbled; Mammy waddled. She wasn't crying, but her face was a mask of her

212

fear and pain. Her bottom lip hanging, with every few steps she sniffed. None of them had barely spoken a word since they had left the new house. The road seemed too silent. Not a single motorcar had passed them. Even through his pain, the pattern of their footfall sounded a warning to Booya: *Turn back now. You won't like what you find. Turn back . . .*

'Is it even safe?' Mammy asked.

Nearly falling over, Booya's heart lurched. Leaning on Labella, who was helping him walk, he nearly toppled them both to the ground.

'Is we safe out here?' Mammy continued. 'Should we a spoke to The Law first? Do you think we safe?'

A bird chittered in the tops of the pines. A cold air fell over them as the shadows of the trees covered the road, no longer cared for by the dying sun.

'Cle better be safe,' Mammy said to the chill dusk. 'Say he safe, Lord. Say he just lost time.'

Booya looked at Mammy to see tears streaming over her round cheeks. The sound of her voice was an unsettling accompaniment to the mischievous warning-tone of their footfall.

Turn back now. You won't like what you find. Turn back . . .

Turn back now . . .

Easing his weight away from her, Booya squeezed Labella's shoulder. She had never felt so small to him. Now he was helping her to walk.

'Lord,' Mammy prayed to the deep blue sky, 'you brung my boy back to me once. I is a good Christian lady, Lord: you know that. Please let me keep my Cle. Please, Lord, I ax of you, keep him safe. I ain't ready to lose him, Lord. I *need* him.'

Mammy continued to pray. The closer they came to home, the less it comforted Booya.

*

They huddled just off the blacktop. Even though the light of the day had already passed over, hidden by the silhouette of the coming night, the house looked as it always had. The deep-green magnolias had lost their flowers, littering the floor of the threshold they must pass over.

'I can't go in there,' Mammy bawled into Booya's chest, grabbing clutches of his shirt. 'What if it's true, Calvin? What if them evil Knights did get him? I can't. I can't see.'

They held each other – Booya wishing that Mammy would remember not to squeeze him so hard. Labella waited behind them, her golden cheeks pale.

'I'll go,' said Booya. 'Just stay here. Together. Come away off the road.'

'We all go,' Mammy said, sniffing, trying to hold up her head.

Booya held Labella's hand; she was looking at the ground. Next to him, Mammy was mumbling to the Lord.

Stepping onto the silken bed of fallen flowers, Booya saw Paw.

He was slumped in his chair; his head lifelessly hanging to one side. Mammy wailed to the treetops, scattering roosting crows. Letting go of Labella's hand, Booya began to walk slowly towards Paw. His legs were numb, someone else's, treading upon air. Still wailing, Mammy followed him. She let out an almighty scream: '*Why?*'

Paw snorted, jumped and snapped awake.

Unseen in his hand, hidden by the chair, his cup poured Moonshine onto the ground.

'What! What happened?' He spilled whisky onto his crotch. 'Shit!'

Booya exhaled and with it a single tear fell. He couldn't remember when he had last breathed.

'What? What this?' Paw just looked haggard and bewildered. 'Who lost a shoe? Huh? What you doing here, woman? Ain't fetched you yet.'

Mammy bounded over to Paw. Leaning back in his chair, he held out his hands. 'Wah! Woah! You just hold on now, wom –'

Climbing onto Paw, she grabbed his ears and shook his head. 'My old heart just can't deal with you no more, you old drunk fool. How can you do me like this?' She continued to jerk Paw's head in every direction.

Holding her wrists, Paw attempted to ward of Mammy's beating. 'Hey! What'd I do? What's going on? I don't –'

'You drunk!' Mammy spewed. 'You didn't meet me at the store 'cause you sitting out here, by your own snoring self, getting drunk!'

'I must've just fell 'sleep,' Paw yawned. 'Hey, quit beating on me, woman.'

Mammy fell onto Paw's knee, smothering him, bawling and nearly tipping the chair over.

'Don't do me like that,' she bawled. 'I can't do without you, you old fool. Don't you do me that way.'

'What the hell happened to you, Boo?' asked Paw, looking around Mammy, his frowning face horizontal to the ground.

'Hell is what did happen to him,' Mammy said, nose-to-nose with Paw. 'And hell is what you put us through since.'

'Huh?'

Staying on his knee, Mammy allowed Paw a little light.

'The Knights of the White Camellia was in town, that's all,' she said. 'They nearly killed your son, and we thought they took you, too. And all you can do is sit out here getting drunk.'

'I was *sleeping*!' Paw remonstrated. Mammy hit him around the head. 'Would you quit, woman? Gotta sleep sometime with your snoring through the whole night like a sick bison.'

Even as she called him all kinds of names, Mammy slathered kisses over Paw's head.

'That right, Boo?' Paw asked. "Bout who . . .? Thought they stopped their warring long ago. Jeez, son, you look messed up!'

'Don't know who it was,' Booya said. 'Didn't see them real well. I was jumped. They . . .' Holding his broken arm across his ribs, Booya hung his head. 'They smashed Mister Henry's guitar.'

'They done *what?*'

Biting his lips together, Booya nodded.

'Want me to fetch up some my old buddies?' Paw asked. 'They can raise hell like you ain't never seen. They'll find out who done it and . . . Ouch, Adie, that hurts! Just . . . just quit it!'

'Don't you talk that way, fool. That ain't the teaching of the Lord. We can just be thankful . . .' Smothering Paw, she began to cry again.

Struggling to keep his head free, Paw looked at Labella, standing there, watching from her tear-stained face.

'Hey, how you, young pretty?'

Booya went to her and wrapped his uninjured arm around her.

'Don't you two look the prettiest sight ever these old eyes seed.' Paw smiled. 'You sure you wanna be part a this family? You too sweet for a piece of this, ain't you?'

'My boy ain't gonna end up nothing like you, you old drunk fool, so watch what you say.'

'Ouch! Stop *doing* that, woman.'

Mammy eased herself off Paw. He was grinning, between yawns.

'Damn! It's still daylight,' he said, winking at Booya. 'Just. Could a fooled me.'

Mammy glared at him. 'Don't you listen to him, sweetie. He a one off, I is telling you. But now you here . . . you can't be walking back to town now, can you? Not now. You gotta stay with us. Did I tell you I is making chicken, rice and peas?'

CHAPTER
EIGHT

1

Silver-toned by the glow of the moon, Mister Henry's guitar swung towards the fender of the truck. Smash, clang, and it slumped into a pile of broken pieces.

Kum-ba-ya

Jerking awake, a spasm of pain shot through Booya's back. Seeing it happen again in a dream most nights still made him feel sick to his sore bones. Itching beneath the cast, he could still not move a finger on his fractured hand. Feeling as it did, he wasn't sure if he would ever be able to play again. Out at the homeplace for three weeks, he had found it hard to care.

Now back home in Honahee, hard as he tried, Booya couldn't recall the three white faces in his audience that night. But he could clearly remember the silhouette of the man, enough to be able to pick him out in the brightest light or deepest black should he ever see him again.

Using all the time in the world that he now had, Booya dressed, pulling his plain picker's shirt over the cast and slithering into the trousers that The Free Riders used to joke were made from a potato sack. He found a note from Labella on the kitchen table saying that she had gone to visit her mama. He shook his head to rid the thought that entered his brain; her mammy was only around the corner.

Restless as he was, there was only one place for Booya to go. He had to walk past the scene of the attack to get there. And there was the truck, without a scratch on it. Even though it was as innocent as a river swollen by heavy rain, Booya couldn't help but sneer at it.

With a thick cloud of potent smoke swirling around his head, Maluch was standing behind the bar. The thin shirt draped over his huge frame was a swirl of colour, clashing with the bright purple neckerchief tied at his throat. Beneath his eyes, a deeper purple blended with the dark skin. Red and green lights lit up the wooden-clad wall behind him, suffocating in the smoke of the cigarette as thick and long as Maluch's fingers. He offered it to Booya. Booya shook his head.

'It from da islan's,' he said. 'Good fo' da pain.' Maluch twisted the bone in his ear.

Pursing his lips, Booya again shook his head.

'Whe' yo' been, man?' Maluch asked. He slammed a jar of pickled pig trotters down on the bar counter. 'I been knockin' at yo' house, an' nothin'. Been worried fo' yo', man, after fin'ing yo' dat way.'

Holding the cast with his good hand, Booya inhaled a puff of the green cloud and sneezed. Dull pain teased his aches. 'Been resting up back home for a few weeks. With this,' he raised his cast, 'ain't had much else to do! While I was away, you hear anything else 'bout them men what was in here?'

'All I hear is rumour goin' round dat dey is goin' from town to town, incitin' ruckus. Brothers' gettin' scared of ever white stranger dey bump into. Some folkses been sayin' dat dey reckon dat's what dey want: to start a kind of uprisin' of black 'gainst white, find a excuse to lynch as many brothers as de trees will fit hangin'. Someone tole me dat it happen befo'. An' it's happenin'. A few of de boys from de ol' plantation in 'ere de other mornin', shootin' craps, I overheared dem say dat dey gon' do just dat. Dey say dey know who dese Knights is, de same ones; say dey see dem in 'ere dat night an' smell somethin' rotten 'bout dem. If dey see dem anyplace, man . . .' Maluch slowly raised an invisible knife and drew it across his neckerchief.

'I know I was lucky, man, even with this.' Booya looked at the cast, covering his right arm from the first knuckle of the middle finger to past his elbow.

'Lucky? Man, yo' dance wid da devil an' on'y burn yo' toe.'

'Believe me, man, I know it,' said Booya, puckering his lips. "Specially hearing what they is capable of. Seems that they never even cut me; just stomped me. And my guitar,' Booya finished, clenching his teeth.

'Mmm. Hey, dis on da juke now: yo' heared it?' Maluch asked.

'Don't think,' Booya replied. 'But I like it. It's got a vibe.'

'Some new blueser, go by da name Sonny Boy Williamson. Already he too big to come to a town like Hon'ee.'

'When you think 'bout who played in this very room in the past, ain't no one what's bigger than Honahee.'

"Cept for Booya Carthy,' Tiger said, stepping out from the storeroom, pulling the door closed behind him, 'if you heared what folks is saying.' He was wearing a new brown chalk-stripe suit, complete with his Fedora. His smile told that he was obviously very pleased with himself. 'Mister Outlaw Blues. The man whose reputation stretches further than the borders of this sorry town. You mended yet?'

'Getting there,' Booya replied, again showing off his cast.

'You looked a sight that night,' said Tiger, 'I gotta say. They done you over good.'

'Yeah. Not as good as the other man.'

'Sorry, Boo. What I mean to say is not many men could take that kind of a beating and be walking around talking 'bout it a set of weeks later, that's all.'

'Yeah. Thanks.'

'Maluch tole you yet?'

'Oh, man!' Maluch slapped his forehead. 'It wen' clear outta my head.' He looked at his cigarette with a quizzical expression. 'John Harper – dat man from Stanza dat see yo' play – 'e was back in 'ere axing 'bout yo'. He somethin' desperate to meet wid yo'.'

'Really? I was thinking 'bout going down there today, but . . . Well, you know.' Booya twitched his throbbing fingers. 'Not much you can do with six strings and no hand to hammer them.'

'No, man,' Tiger said. 'You missing the point, Boo. John Harper don't just go round axing for bluesers – 'specially axing twice – that ain't how he does. *You* ain't gotta audition. He wants to cut you on a disc! I'd give my nose to be in your big shoes, man. And I like my nose.'

'They's still the fact that I can't play with a broke hand and no guitar.'

'Oh, yeah. That's what else I was wondering if Maluch tole you. Got something for you . . .'

With his heels clicking, Tiger swaggered towards the storeroom; hands in pockets, swinging his shoulders with each step, wearing his new look well.

Even as his bones throbbed, butterflies were tickling the insides of Booya's stomach. An itch was bothering his brow.

Tiger returned, whistling. He had a guitar in his hand. Swaggering along he played a smart little lick. Every regular man was for women, but some men were also for motorcars and shotguns – Mister Henry had been for both of the latter. Booya Carthy was only for that guitar. He cared for it and polished it with the same care that like Mister Henry polished their cars and shotguns. Before a white lady and the city train had come rolling into his life.

Tiger laid the guitar down on the bar counter. 'This, my fortunate friend, is your very same guitar.'

The smile wouldn't quite break through Booya's lips. There were the same scratches on the face; the same wear-marks on the fretboard and neck from the hours, days, weeks, months and years of fingering and hammering. It was shining; the highly-polished surface of the face glowing, reflecting the light in the rafters. It looked heavenly, otherworldly, washed in the Water of Life.

'I say it's the same,' Tiger continued, 'but that ain't the exact truth. The neck here and the face, they's the exact same. Don't know how he does it, but my man somehow spliced in new bits to the old. Black magic, if you ax me.'

Maluch laughed in his throat.

'Even some of the sides is made up of the original pieces. The back and this side is where most of the damage was done.' Tiger flipped the guitar over. 'Here and the entire back had to be made up of new pieces. Even the best known doctor in all the world can't bring a dead man back to life, right?'

Chuckling within, Maluch's cheeks swelled as if he knew different.

Booya ran his finger over the back of the guitar. The wood was slightly darker and it had no scars of having lived. From the back it could truly be a new guitar. But its aura remained. And it would live on.

Tiger and Maluch watched as Booya ran a finger over the old wood, staring at his guitar. His face was impassive, a forest man discovering a woman for the first time – he knew he liked the way she looked, would like to touch her and wanted her, but he wasn't quite sure what for.

'You ain't gonna have to put rattlesnakes or graveyard dirt in her,' Tiger said, smiling. 'And it sounds amazing. Didn't think you'd mind if I checked her out for you. I know that –'

'No . . . it's fine. Fine.' The reflected light, red and green, was shining on Booya's face.

Tiger and Maluch looked at one another. Tiger grinned; Maluch shrugged. 'Well?' Tiger asked.

'Yeah. Amazing. Faultless,' Booya replied. 'It's . . . beautiful!'

'*Well?*' Tiger urged.

Snapped from his trance, Booya looked up. 'Sorry, man. How much do I owe you? Your friend? Whoever done the fixing?'

'My friend counts hisself as one of your fans. He won't accept a dime from you. Was done *au gratis*, and he won't hear no different. So you can take your hand from your pocket.'

'Do I get to meet him, to say thank you?'

'I'll pass it on for you, man.'

'*So?*' Maluch was grinning at Booya, rotating a hand.

'What?' he asked. 'Is I missing something? I don't really wanna cup, thanks, man. Not right now. I . . . *What?*'

With another look shared, Tiger and Maluch burst into laughter. Maluch's laugh was deep and controlled; Tiger laughed shrilly as a hyena.

'*What?*' Booya asked, grinning, but still not sure why.

'You just gonna stand and look at her for the rest your life, or you ever gonna actually pick her up?'

2

Booya wasn't looking where he was walking. He was staring at his guitar, as if maybe he took his eyes from it for one moment that it would disappear – despite the fact that it was snuggled tightly under his arm, rather than in the usual position up on his shoulder.

'*Ouff!*' the person he had just bumped into emitted. 'Sorry, didn't see you there.'

It had been quite a heavy collision Booya had dealt. Whoever had received it had done well to keep to their feet.

'No, I's sorry,' Booya said. 'Was my fault. Was me who wasn't looking where I was . . .'

Booya ceased his apology. Grinning a vague smile, the familiar pale, vacant eyes of the blind Indian were staring through him. He rattled his tin cup.

'Spare a dime for a old blind man?'

'Sorry, brother,' Booya said, glad that his mended guitar and healing bones weren't involved in the collision. 'Got nothing on me.'

Booya watched him go, veering across the street, caring not for the horn of a motorcar.

And then he continued on his way.

He stood away from the window of Stanza Studios, looking in. There were the usual hopefuls slumped against the wall. A couple of them looked up at him, no excitement in their expressions; they were all wearing the nervous and afraid look of waiting to see the doctor. Booya couldn't know that same expression was on his face.

Not being able to see past the first few feet inside the door – the heart of the building separated by a dividing wall – was disorientating. It looked as though this building could be fake, a false façade, only consisting of the few feet where the musicians were gathered together so sullenly.

He pushed the door open and stepped into the waiting area.

'Hey, Booya Carthy!'

A young man crouching down against the wall, spinning a guitar by the neck between his legs, was looking up at him, smiling. He had obviously attempted to dress smartly, but his suit had tears in the elbows and dried mud on the knees. He had skilfully shaved to leave a thin line of beard running the length of his jaw.

'Why's the mighty Booya Carthy walking in through the slave entrance with the rest of us mortals?' the young man asked, running his thumb along his beard.

'I come down to meet with Mister Harper,' Booya replied.

'Me too. And this sleeping fool next to me. And him and him and her. But why, man? I see you playing in Blacks and Juju both. Even see you one time in Chi when I follow a girl that way. Booya Carthy ain't gotta audition with *us*. You a *legend*, man. 'Cross the whole state, at least! Into Tennessee, Missouri and Illinois, most likely by now, I's guessin'.'

Booya shrugged. 'Thanks.'

'It's the truth, man. We was saying it in Juju just the other night. But we ain't seen you there for *time!*' The young man was eyeing Booya's sling. 'Guess them rumours is true, then,' he said. 'You still able to play with all that shit on your arm?'

'Can't barely move my fingers,' Booya replied. 'And only halfway done with wearing this yet. Still won't be able to play for at least another month after it comes off. And even then I still gotta build up some strength in my fingers.'

'You need someone to play guitar for you, man? I can do it. My name's Scratch, by the way.' He offered his right hand to Booya, then grinned and retracted it. 'Guess that you ain't in the shaking way, just now.'

Sitting on the windowsill or slumped against the wall, Booya noticed that most of the sombre crowd were eavesdropping the exchange between him and Scratch, watching one then the other as they spoke, looking away when he made eye contact. None of them looked like the potential "next big thing." Surveying them, Booya saw mud under their nails, buckteeth, the stub left by a missing finger tapping on a harmonica. There was a man who looked older than the town, and a boy so small that the shorts he was wearing were nearer to being trousers, hiding his bony knees. The sleeping man next to Scratch snored with a nasty, rasping wheeze. One boy was wearing a pair of dungarees without a shirt, every one of his ribs showing through the skin. An impoverished-looking woman in a Mother Hubbard dress, whose long face followed her sad eyes upward, her skin seeming to fall further down from her long skull as she looked up, almost appealing to Booya for aid. At least Scratch looked as though he had washed in the last month, even if his suit may never have been. Booya wondered if he too should have dressed in his suit.

'Thanks, man,' Booya answered to Scratch's offer, 'but I is just out the game for now. Recently got married and I is aiming to settle down, just while I recover. If ever you gonna pick a time to get your arm and hand broke, just when you first get married ain't it.'

Scratch laughed. 'Scratch understand what you saying. If ever you do though, man, just ask for Scratch.'

'What do you play?'

'Me? I play this easy rider in the style that folks say is your own outlaw blues. Wanna hear some?'

'Yeah, man,' Booya answered, raising both eyebrows. 'Sure.'

'Feel like Moses playing craps with God,' Scratch replied with an impish grin.

'That's blasphemy, young man,' said the oldest man in the room, suddenly coming to life, pointing a shaky finger at Scratch. 'You take that back from where it come.'

Ignoring the old man, Scratch began to play. Booya was astonished. He immediately liked what Scratch was playing – he was more than proficient, there was no questioning that. But not only was he undoubtedly playing in the style of Booya's so-called "outlaw blues", he had chosen to play (Turn My Soul) Black As Coal – one of Booya's lesser-known songs. He couldn't ever remember playing it more than once live, but, laid out before him, Booya could see just why the outlaw blues style had earned such a broad appeal.

Before Scratch started singing, the door behind Booya opened. With recognition clearly dawning through his egg-shaped head, the small white man looking up at Booya had greased hair slicked back from his wide forehead, making his thick-rimmed glasses the main focal point of his unremarkable face. Over his starched white shirt – as white as the piece of paper he was holding – he wore a buttoned-up waistcoat. Smiling at Booya, showing his oddly spaced teeth, the man wrinkled his nose to lift his glasses, then used his index finger to push them in their place. Booya noticed that the man was about to hold out his hand by way of greeting. After quickly looking Booya up and down, he instead wiped both hands down the front of his waistcoat, crinkling the paper. Then he cleared his throat.

'Mister Carthy, you came,' said the face far below Booya. 'I was sorry to hear about your unfortunate . . . accident. Seems that fate has been conspiring to keep us from meeting. I'm sorry: you probably don't know me from Adam. I'm John Harper, owner of this studio.'

'Pleased to finally meet you, Mister Harper,' Booya replied, wondering how this unremarkable little man inspired such a nervous reaction from the waiting hopefuls. 'Sorry I ain't been able to come sooner.'

'Like I say, it's our fickle friend fate who's to blame. You could say that fate is a great friend of the blues though, could you not?' Harper's smile formed in awkward stages: nearly vanishing, before coming bolder, only to disappear as soon as it reached somewhere near to peaking.

'Sure has been through my days, Mister Harper,' Booya replied, thinking of his darker days in Blacks and in the city.

'Please, call me John.'

'And my name's Booya.'

'Then please do come through, Booya.'

'Hey!' the old man croaked. 'I sit here all day yesterday, and was first down here today. When you gwine make time to see me, Mister Harper?'

'I was here 'fore you, old man,' Scratch interjected.

'Young man, we both know that's a lie.'

'Gentlemen,' Harper said, 'sorry, and . . . miss? I shall endeavour to see you all today. Please have your chosen piece ready to perform. And I have to remind you that I can't see you unless you have the required five-dollar fee ready to pay in advance. Thank you.'

Harper let Booya through the door before following, closing and locking the door behind him. The room was a tiny office. File cabinets were lined on every spare stretch of wall. The room had no outside windows, making it feel industrial and business-like. On the back wall was a wide window, showing a slightly larger adjacent office. In one corner, on the angle where the walls would normally meet, was a heavy looking door, painted black. In white lettering on the door was the word STUDIO. Above the door were two light bulbs: one red and one green. Neither was lit. The only noises in the room were the lonely sound of a fan buzzing and the tapping of typewriter keys coming from behind a desk. A smartly-dressed woman, wearing glasses with rims thick enough to rival Harper's, was peering at a page from inches away.

'Mister Carthy . . . Booya, this is Sally, my secretary. Sally, please meet Mister Booya Carthy.'

Sally looked up, wrinkling her nose to lift her glasses, just as Harper had done. 'Oh, so he came then, Mister Harper. It's nice to meet you, Mister Carthy. We've been quite excited about you coming down here to see us. From what I hear you are a very talented man.'

'Well, I don't know.' Booya scratched the returning itch in his eyebrow and smiled.

'It's funny, we've said before that it's the truly talented people that deny their skill, where the amateurish are always ready to declare that they are the best thing since pickled trotters!' Sally said, before bursting into shrill, rapturous laughter.

Harper laughed along. 'That's right. It's an inside joke of ours. And congratulations, you have passed the second test.'

'What was the first one?' Booya asked.

'The Sally Test – another inside joke.' Harper chuckled. 'If she doesn't like you, this is a far as you go, no matter for your talent – if you aren't paying, of course.'

Sally cackled. The fan whirred and Sally continued tapping at her keys, as if the conversation had never taken place. *Just like Mister Harper's smile*, Booya thought.

'Please do come through to my office, Booya,' Harper said, opening the next door.

In Harper's office more file cabinets, and shelves loaded with twelve-inch cans, covered all of the space from floor to ceiling and every inch of wall, all except for a slim path to walk to the chairs positioned on either side of the desk. There were piles of the black discs, just like the one Mister Henry had shown Booya. Bundles of thick black wires, microphones and dissected pieces of recording equipment were strewn amongst the debris. Standing in the middle of the clutter on Harper's desk was a dead plant.

'I apologise for the mess,' Harper said. 'It's an organised mess, though, believe me. I know where every last thing is in this room. Please, do sit.'

Resting his guitar against the side of the chair, Booya sat down.

Harper opened a desk drawer and pulled out a pad of paper. Sliding his hand beneath a stack of paper on the desk, he retrieved a pen.

'Now,' he said, 'your injuries. Mister Beale at Juju told me all he knew about the incident.' Harper lingered a look at Booya's guitar, jerking his head in a vulturine manner. 'You aren't able to play, are you?'

'Not 'til this recovers, Mister Harper.'

'Hmm . . . I assume that you have your guitar with you by a force of habit, or the like. Believe me, like I mentioned previously, the callous timing of fate is what we have come to expect in this industry. Bessie Smith, Robert Johnson, Blind Lemon Jefferson: fate certainly conspired against them, and in such a cruel manner.' Harper frowned. 'So when do you expect to be recovered enough to be able to play, Booya?'

'Month, at least.' His hand was tingling and, beneath the cast, his arm was itching.

'This might sound a foolish question, but I assume you can't play at all at the moment, then?'

'Right,' Booya confirmed, again wondering why he had decided to come today at all.

'I will cut to the chase, Mister Carthy. I have heard you play and would like the opportunity to record you. It's not often a talent like yours happens to a small town such as Honahee. If anyone knows that, it's me. I would like to record you and I believe that, with the right selection of, say, eight to ten original compositions, we can auction those recordings to the most major recording labels in the country.'

Harper steepled his fingers, leaning his elbows on two uneven stacks on his desk.

'I'm sure you understand, Mister Carthy . . . I am sure you understand, *Booya*, that even though I do all this for a love of the music, I do it also to make a living! It is a business. Such is my faith in your talent that I will waive the five-dollar fee I usually charge to record the farmers and the luckless that you saw out there. But in exchange for my production I would want you to sign a pre-recording contract in which we agree I will take a percentage of any monies your recordings may earn – say, ninety-five cents of a dollar,' Harper mumbled at pace into his overbite. He looked up and clapped his hands. 'Business! I will take care of the work required: cut the discs; approach the recording labels, organise the contracts . . . Basically, I manage your business affairs so that you are able to concentrate on creating and performing. You need not worry about the paperwork. All you have to do is perform your songs!

'I predict big things for you, Mister Carthy. Even though the country blues has been replaced somewhat by jump blues, the urban blues, the boogie-woogie, I predict that, nationwide, folks will clamour to see Booya Carthy play. *Everyone* will want to see you, to hear you play. Even the response of a small town like Honahee can gauge the reaction of the nation, believe it or not. And the response that I have witnessed – on top of word-of-mouth – has been astonishing. Would you agree?'

Booya had been struggling to keep up with the whirlwind of prophecy the unassuming man hidden behind the cluttered desk, now blinking his eyes behind the magnifying lenses of his glasses, was predicting.

'Uh, yeah,' Booya replied. 'Folks been kind to me, I guess.'

Behind the lenses Harper narrowed his eyes, his voice dropping to a lower pitch. 'You wait and see what the United States of America has to say about you.' As quick as it had arrived, the monstrous look vanished from Harper's face, returning him to the wispy little man that he was. Picking up his pen, Harper started to scrawl on some paper.

'So in, say, a couple of months from now, I'll close the studio and we'll book in a session for an entire day – depending on how your recovery goes, of course. Mister Carthy, I think that we can form a relationship that we will both find mutually agreeable.'

Finished writing, Harper began to offer his hand over the desk, again retracting it and wiping it on his waistcoat. Booya noticed that sweat had appeared on the glistening dome beneath Harper's receded hairline.

'Come, Mister Carthy; I'll show you the studio. Where the magic happens!'

Wiping a handkerchief over his forehead, Harper chuckled and led Booya from the room.

3

'Local performer, known 'bout as Scratch, has died in bed at the age of seventeen,' Frankie announced towards the end of his broadcast weeks later. Men, including Booya, took their hats from their heads. Women pulled their children close. 'The doctor confirmed that Scratch died by unlawful poisoning. News has been brought forward that he survived long enough to hear a song of his own composition played on the wireless. It is said that he smiled and died the moment that his song ended. You may still hear his song, *The Trouble With My Girl*, cut down at Stanza Studios, playing.'

Eyes that had been looking downward looked over at Booya; his stare remained trained on the ground. It seemed like it was only two minutes ago that he had first met Scratch in Stanza's waiting room, listening to a rendition of his own outlaw blues.

Labella rubbed Booya's arm. 'You okay, Calvin? I only met him that one time in Juju, but I know he was your friend.'

'Huh?' Booya looked at Labella through the tears standing in his eyes. He wiped his cheeks with the back of his sleeve. 'Yeah.'

'Wasn't that your song, that *Trouble* song – not that I like the title.' Still rubbing his arm, Labella smiled at Booya. He tried to smile back at her. Closing his eyes, a single tear escaped from between the lids.

The scent of the honeysuckle growing above the stoop drifted over the crowd as they began to wander away. Mothers called for their children to come. Some folks stole a last look at Booya, standing there holding his hat like a sad statue.

Opening his eyes, Booya smiled, just staring. 'Yeah, it was mine, that song' he said. 'They can have them all, whoever wants them.' He rubbed his cast beneath his plain shirt. 'Ain't no use to me. *The outlaw blues.*' Booya wrinkled his nose. 'Wish I never even heared that word. You know, I heared he was sick, Scratch. Some was saying that his mammy catch him in bed with a girl, say he had to stay home.' Booya chuckled. He swallowed the lump in his throat. 'Others say he slipped shaving his little beard and wouldn't be seen again until it was back to being neat; or that a hoodoo had been put on him and he was living up in a tree!' Prickles tickled Booya's arm beneath the cast. 'Some say he was catched by the White Knights. But no, was *the outlaw blues* what catched him. Poisoned over a girl.' Staring at a broken branch hanging from a hydrangea, the weight of a huge sky-blue flower pulling it to the ground, Booya shook his head. He looked down at Labella. 'He only wanted to play, Bella. He wanted to play because of me, and my *outlaw blues.*'

Labella gripped one of Booya's hands with both of hers. 'You can't blame yourself, Calvin. I heared myself that he weren't being too discreet.'

'That's just it. I could've tole him. Warned him.' Putting his hat back on his head, Booya relaxed his shoulders. 'Well, I can't now.' He sighed. 'Let's go inside.'

With a solitary nod to Frankie, Booya and Labella walked up the steps and into Huck's.

Labella wanted to talk with her mama – something about cooking pork that Booya cared not to understand. He sought out Mammy. When he found her she glared at him.

'Ain't been out to see me and your Paw in a while,' she said.

'Got a new home and wife, Mammy. It'll take time, I guess, getting used to both.'

'That's the order you put them in: home then wife?'

'That ain't fair, Mammy. You don't get to judge how much I care for Labella.' Booya looked around to see who might be eavesdropping. And then he noticed: this was the exact place in the same aisle when first he set his eyes on her.

'You don't fool me, Calvin.' Mammy said.

He pressed the heel of his hand to his forehead. 'You gonna tell me what this is 'bout? Ain't fair that ever time I see you, you tell me that I ain't doing things right, Mammy.'

'*Do* you feel you *is* doing things right?'

'*Please* . . .' Booya's hands bid his plight. 'Please will you just tell me what's buzzing in your ear? Or don't tell me nothing at all. You is talking in riddles. I ain't getting it and I really don't need it right now.'

Mammy breathed in long and hard, inflating her chest to massive proportions. 'Will you come out to the house tonight?' she asked.

'If that's what you want. If you actually tell me what's *bothering* you – if it ain't just not having been out to see you – course I will. But I if you start on me again when we there, then I is coming straight back to town. With my wife.'

Mammy lowered her eyes. Placing a hand gently on her upper arm, Booya said, 'Look, you wanna step outside a second and tell me what's getting at you?'

'Okay,' she replied. 'Sure.'

Booya narrowed his eyes, pondering whether she looked secretly triumphant.

Mammy leaned on the doorframe, her arms crossed. Booya noticed that the twinkle in her eye had, thankfully, been joined by the sparkle. She smiled a little smile. 'You is handsome, you know. Even with them shadows of bruises. Now, I know that ain't your fault, but where's that sweet little boy I used to know, used to mother?'

Booya rolled his eyes and grinned. 'Now you just sounding like all the other ducks in that pond,' he said, nodding towards the store.

'Did you know that your Paw used to be just like you when he was young? And he used to give me that look, too,' she said, pouting and nodding. 'He'd give it to me whenever he knowed he's in the wrong. Still gives it to me now.'

'So . . . you finally gonna tell me what I supposed to have done?' Booya asked. '*Is* it 'cause I ain't come out to see you and Paw in a week, even when we stayed with you for more than three weeks just a while back? Mammy, stop! I just don't know what I done!'

'It ain't nothing you done wrong by me, Calvin,' Mammy replied, continuing her riddles. 'You remember when I tole you that time that you need a good woman to fish you out that Fool's River when you catch the tide?'

'Uh-huh. I remember.'

'*Uh-huh*,' she repeated. 'Your Labella's a good little lady; gonna be a fine woman one day soon, I see that. But can't you see how you is doing by her? Only telling you this 'cause I is afraid that, in part, I is to blame by what I say that time 'bout Fool's River, 'bout needing a good woman. Tole you not to be like your old fool Paw, but you is heading exactly that way. I can see it in you, Calvin. See it the second you was coming towards me looking all like a sad sack. I've seen it once and - oh-ho, don't be giving me them lost puppy dog eyes – I see the same look that I've seen time and again in your Paw. You've seen for yourself how bad he's done by my old heart all them times. Only the will of the Lord keeps us both alive through them. And they is plenty more times that you, thankfully, know nothing of – and I ain't telling them, 'cause I is still trying hard to forget myself. He gets it from his fool daddy. I'd as soon stitch the devil a new pair of britches than see you get the same from yours.' Mammy straightened the creases in her apron, glancing through the door of the store.

'Ain't saying your Paw's a bad man. Is just saying I know how it feels to be the wife at home. And that sweet Bella's gonna be feeling that way whether she tells you or not. Even if she don't actually know it herself! Maybe not yet, but if you go 'bout life in the same way you doing, she'll know it soon enough. She ain't never had no daddy of her own – that's by account of the mammy that the Lord give her, poor girl. That woman's enough to make any man paddle for his life down Fool's River, I don't doubt it. Probably even put rocks in his own pocket and dive right in.

'Calvin, you gotta ax yourself what it really is you want from this life. We only got the one life to live. And no matter what I spend my life bleating 'bout, I ain't done bad. I ain't. Just always remember that the devil stirs them waters on that Fool's River. Don't never forget that. Don't let his pull be stronger than that good girl standing on the riverbank, silently watching you drift off. Don't forget that I needed to be the big, strong woman I is to pull your Paw back. Think how much bigger than you is than that little girl of yours, Calvin. Okay?'

Booya was nodding when he saw Mattie – Labella's mother – approaching the door, her raptorial beak heading directly for them. Wearing the same sky-blue pinafore and white apron as Mammy, she was half the size. Her tight lips were bracketed by deep lines in her cheeks, in the same place where Labella's dimples appeared when she smiled. A shudder ran through Booya.

'Hi, Calvin.' Mattie looked at the cast and sling and offered a pitying expression normally reserved for a poorly child. 'You'll be back to normal soon, lovely. Bellie say to tell you she won't be long. She just gotta pick up some molasses.' Looking as though someone had given her a boiled sweet to suck, but it had turned out to be a sour animal dropping –which, out of politeness, she continued to suck anyway – Mattie turned to Mammy. 'Adeline, sweetie, I need some lifting done, remember? That sugar ain't gonna move itself now, is it? Hope you better soon, Cal, darling.' And with a gay flutter of skirts, Mattie was away.

'See what I mean?' Mammy whispered. 'That's the other devil you fighting. Row away down the first river you can if Bella wakes up one morning anything like that hellish woman she got for a mammy. The devil might've been a good man 'til he fetched hisself a wife like that old hag.

'Coming, Matts!' Mammy hollered. 'I gotta go now, Calvin. Good seeing you. And don't think for a second that I want to have to be saying them things the first time I see you in a week. Don't mind me, just mind my words.'

Booya stooped and kissed Mammy's cheek. 'I do love her, Mammy,' he whispered when he was by her ear. 'More than anything.'

'There you go now: that's your guilt coming out. Don't think that I ain't tole your Paw the same. He knows that river. Hate to say, but he's learn to tame it, some way. Don't waste your breath telling me you love her more than anything. Tell her! It ain't just the *good* Lord what moves in mysterious ways. And don't forget that neither.'

4

At first Booya couldn't figure out why it should feel so wrong when he woke up beneath the bridge the next morning. He must have been walking home to Mammy and Paw's and fancied sleeping there. He must have done that fifty times in the past; more probably. So why did it feel so wrong this time? Whilst Paw chuckled heinously, Mammy would just look at him and know.

Booya reached for his guitar. When it was not there beside him he began to worry, cursing his careless stupidity. Maybe he had left it in Blacks?

Juju

Booya lifted his hand to scratch his eyebrow, trying to get at the throb between his forehead and his muddled, drunk mind, and saw the cast on his arm. No wonder moving it had felt so awkward. His guitar wasn't with him because he couldn't play! And he didn't even live at Mammy and Paw's any more . . .

Labella!

Glancing at the clear blue water, Booya scrambled to his feet, up the bank, and began the journey back to his true home.

*

The shadow of the chinaberry tree in the street cast a low shadow, pointing mocking fingers at him as he stood by the front door, trying to figure out what to say. Instinctively he knew that it was still early in the day. But Labella was an early riser.

The door opened for him.

'Been standing out there all night?' Labella asked. She was still in her nightdress, a gown pulled around her.

Booya's head was on his chin. 'Bella . . . I . . .' He didn't look up.

'Going to stand there all day yet?'

With his head still lowered, Labella holding the door open for him, Booya took off his hat and stepped inside. Before closing it, she looked outside to ensure that no neighbours had been watching.

Following Labella through to the kitchen, after she had breezed past him, Booya watched her put the kettle on the stove. He looked down at the morning light on the wooden floor. Water on the underside of the kettle hissed on the flame. Labella turned, leaning her back against the countertop, hands on hips and head tilted to one side.

'You going to tell me where you was?' she asked, her voice even. 'Or should I be axing who you was with all night? You don't even know her name. Is that right?'

'You got it all wrong, Bella.'

'Oh, I got it all wrong,' she repeated.

'I is here now, honey.' Booya started advancing towards her, offering her his arms to snuggle into.

'Keep . . .' She raised her hands, pulling her head back in disgust. 'Keep your hands off me, Calvin. You is a mess! Keep away from me. Don't know if I can even look at you. Been lying awake half the night thinking 'bout . . . You know how it was with Paw? Yeah: that's what I been thinking all night long. I thought . . . Thought you was at least in the *house*, Calvin! Can you even imagine how that felt? In the state you in, do you even care? You can't even tell me you're sorry.'

'I am sorry, honey.'

'Tell me now, sure.'

'It ain't like that, sweet honey.'

'Don't tell me it ain't like that.' Curling her lips, her dimples stood out on her cheeks. 'You weren't even here. It was exactly like that.'

'That ain't what I mean. I –'

Gripping the counter behind her, Labella leaned forward, her lips pinched together. 'Tell me what it is you mean, then. No. Don't. I don't want to hear it.' Labella turned away from him and sobbed into her hands. 'Just leave me alone. Go back to whoever it was you was with.'

Looking at her slim shoulders jolting with sorrow, Booya could feel the sting of tears rising into his eyes.

'I weren't with a girl, Labella. Weren't with no one. I just fell asleep under that bridge on the way out to Mammy and Paw's place. Don't even know what I was doing there 'til I wake up. Don't know when I made the decision to go, Bella. Don't even know how I got there! But that's where I was, all night.' He sighed; phlegm sounded in his throat. He coughed. 'I'd been drinking. Was drunk. Didn't know what I was doing and just fell into the old routine – I know how that sounds; and I ain't proud. On the way to the homeplace I sometimes used to sleep under that bridge, the one just past the town sign. 'Cept for Mammy and Paw, no one really knows 'bout that. Me and that bridge, we got a kind of . . . kind of bond.' Booya huffed a humourless laugh. 'But it was the drink what led me there.'

Booya looked out the window at the quiet street, the chinaberry's branches moving on the breeze. With the heat already dripping down, today was the kind of day when it felt like the fall was never going to come.

'When we got back from Mammy and Paw's last night and you went to bed, I weren't tired yet. And 'cause I can't play no guitar right now, and you was sleeping, I went out to see some friends, just for having nothing to do and . . . I was only gonna go for a little while, but . . . We was having some drinks for Scratch – my friend what was poisoned? – just a couple of drinks, and . . .' Curling his hands into fists, Booya punched at the side of the kitchen table. 'I know now I shouldn't a gone but . . .' He shook his sore head.

He could remember Tiger stepping from the stage, the crowd loving him and his suit . . .

"Okay,' Booya said soon after, "one cup. To Scratch. Bella's at home sleeping and . . ."

"You say that ever night," Tiger said, smiling, spinning his guitar in his hands. After offering it to Booya, Maluch passed his potent cigarette to Tiger. "Whoo-ee," Tiger said, blowing an endless line of smoke to the red and green light in the rafters, clouds wafting around the thick leaves of the plants. "How many times you have to say to folks tonight that you ain't fit to play, Boo?"

Puffing out his cheeks, Booya shook his head.

"Yo' wan' me to fill dat fo' yo', man?" Maluch asked.

Booya looked into his empty cup. "Uh . . . one more can't hurt none."

Tiger laughed. "Say that ever night, too!"

"Yo' woman know dat yo' here ever night, Boo?" Maluch asked, his eyes smiling from within the dark-blue paint around his eyes.

"Like I say, she sleeping. What she don't know can't hurt her," said Booya. "Just while I'm fixing, can't play, don't know what more I can do. Anyway, this the last time."

"Say that ever night, too!" Tiger and Maluch chorused, Booya laughing with them, tipping back his cup and drinking from way beyond the edges . . .

He dug his fingernails into the wooden table top. 'I is so sorry I hurt you, Bella.'

'But you would rather be out drinking with your friends than be home with your dull wife.' Holding herself, she turned around to face Booya. Strands of her hair were sticking to her wet face. 'That's it, ain't it? That's it all, right there. So long as I is home for when you need me, you don't actually care how I feel.'

'That ain't how it is at all.' Somehow he kept his voice even, though tears began to prick behind his eyes, similar to the feeling in his repairing bones. 'I promised that I'd always tell the truth to you. Why would I make up something like sleeping under a bridge? Ain't that too crazy a thing to imagine up?'

'But you never thought 'bout *me*! You didn't think 'bout how I might be feeling for one *second*!'

'You're right. I wasn't thinking at all. A friend died, but that ain't a excuse to get drunk – seeing it, that's what I done: used it as a excuse. It's unforgiveable, now I can see how you feel. And I *is* sorry, Bella, like you can't imagine. Didn't plan it, none of it. I just weren't thinking! I'd do anything in the world to change it if I could. They ain't –'

'I don't believe that one bit. You is only saying all that 'cause I catch you.' Labella spun and dropped her elbows to the counter, her head into her hands.

'Last thing I wanna do is hurt you, Bella. I love you. I hate the thought of you here all alone. That's what's making me cry now, too. I hate it! But I knew when I left that you was safe in bed.'

Quietly placing his hat on the kitchen table, wiping his face, Booya stepped over to her. When he lifted her hair and placed his hand on her shoulders not a single nerve in her twitched.

'Don't know what good I ever done to deserve you in the first place. I'd do anything to be with you for all my days. You can't know how you is the only thing I need: above friends, above drink, even above ever playing again. I'd do anything . . .'

Turning, Labella buried her face in his chest, wrapped her arms around his waist and squeezed as tightly as she could. Gently embracing her, Booya could feel her weep. He kissed the top of her head.

'Sorry, Bella. Sorry I made you feel that way. Truly. More sorry than anything. Care 'bout you more than for the love of the whole world. Ain't got nothing without you. I'd do anything.'

'Not sleeping out all night under bridges would be a good place to start,' she mumbled into his chest.

Booya could feel her sobbing and softly laughing as one.

'Done,' he said. 'Deal.'

'Calvin?'

'Yeah, Bella,' he whispered into her hair.

'I don't mean to be harsh on you.'

'How's you apologising to me!'

''Cause . . . You know . . .' As it warmed his chest, her voice was quivering. 'You know how I say like it was with your Paw? All alone, my mind got to wandering where I didn't want it to. I know you sometimes go down to that place after I gone to bed, but, lying awake, I couldn't work out no real reason why you wouldn't be here in the house for all the night. Unless . . .' Her voice crumbled.

'Shhh . . .' He gently swayed her. 'Bella, don't cry.'

'Thought that I *lost* you, Calvin,' she mumbled into his chest. 'I'd never see you again.'

'You ain't never gonna lose me, honey.'

'Seeing Mammy, when she thought she'd be forever without Paw . . . After them knights . . . When I see you coming up the road . . .' She broke down.

Whispering to her, he swayed and hushed her. 'Don't even think it, baby girl. Ain't gonna happen. Never. I love you more than anything, Bella. I is here to stay.'

CHAPTER NINE

CHAPTER
NINE

1

Sitting in an armchair, Booya itched and scratched beneath the new bandages on his arm. He checked the movement of his fingers. It wasn't good. The muscles felt tight and the bones throbbed and tingled. His hand wanted to stay half-closed like a claw, as if it was constantly halfway to picking something up, not at all keen to open or close. Despite being cleaned, it smelled bad.

The doctor had told Booya what to expect. The doctor had been correct.

Ignoring the doctor's advice for further rest, Booya slowly picked at the strings, every movement of each finger tugging reluctant tendons over the tender bones. At least his fingering hand was able to do its usual work. How it boasted, a sprinter teasing a lame man. After surveying again how well the guitar had healed, Booya placed it by the side of the armchair.

Labella and the doctor came into the room together. Of recent mornings Labella had looked pale and had felt sick. Even her hair had become like a greased mane. But despite Labella's sickly appearance, she had a little smile on her lips, slightly parted – just as they had been when Booya first saw her.

She was carefully rubbing her stomach low down.

Tipping his hat, the doctor smiled. 'Hope you heal well, Mister Carthy. Unless you need me, I'll visit with y'all in a month.' He looked at Labella and raised his eyebrows. 'If not sooner. Good day to you both. I, ah . . . I'll see myself out. Take care now.'

'What's he 'bout?' Booya asked as soon as the doctor had left. 'What's given colour to you, Bella? Here . . .' Labella came to him and sat across his knees, snuggling into his chest, the smile never leaving her lips. He wrapped his bandaged arm around her. 'What? What is it? Something sure is up. You gonna tell me, or do I gotta chase after the doc?'

'You is going to have to guess . . .'

*

'See, Tiger,' Booya explained, standing in the doorway. 'I was gonna stay home with my baby mama.'

'You in the family business now, my man?' Tiger asked.

'Doctor come say this morning,' Booya beamed. 'Still early days, but that's the size of it, yeah.'

'Hey, congratulations, man. Here, Bella.' Tiger hugged Booya and kissed Labella. 'Congratulations, baby mama.'

'So that's it from now on, man. Gonna just live the family way. My late nights is done.'

'Got more than seven months to go yet, Calvin,' Labella said. 'Why don't you go?'

'Don't you need me here with you, though? Looking after you?'

'What can you do: make me cups of hot water and come to bed early? That's all I is aiming to do. All I can do. And all I *want* to do. Bed can't come soon enough! Go and celebrate. It's fine by me.' Labella was smiling.

Like Booya, she had been smiling ever since she had shared their news.

'I don't think I wanna celebrate without you there, Bella.' He kissed her again. 'I just wanna stay here and celebrate with you.'

'You mean to say that you'd rather stay home with me, stroking my hair and listing to the wireless, than visiting a frolic?'

'Yeah. Think I would.'

Labella giggled and wiped a breadcrumb from Booya's lip. 'You really *have* changed.'

Tiger was laughing. 'I ain't *hearing* this! Lah-lah-lah,' he sang, spinning his hands around his ears. 'If I hear this, the whole of 'Hee gonna know that Big Boo Carthy is a old lady. I ain't hearing a word of this. Lah-lah-lah.'

They both watched Tiger's crazed gesticulations. Labella picked up Booya's hat and patted it onto his head.

'*Go*, Calvin. I want you to.' Labella rubbed her stomach. 'When he comes you ain't going to get another chance.'

'He?'

'Just a feeling.' Resting both hands over her stomach, Labella looked up at Booya. He bathed in the beauty of her eyes.

'Be a better blueser than his old man,' said Tiger. They both turned to look at him. 'Sorry,' he said. 'I ain't *listening*.'

'Just *go*,' Labella said.

'But . . .' Booya turned to Tiger – still pretending that he wasn't listening and enjoying the exchange. 'Tiger, don't think I will tonight, man. My arm is fresh out the cast and, you know . . . don't wanna make it no worse.'

'That sound like a excuse to you, Tiger?' Labella asked.

'Sure does, Bella; the excuses of a man old 'fore his time.' Tiger thumbed the lapels of his suit and looked towards the falling sun. 'And ain't no one wants to hear old Boo Carthy no more anyway; not now they got Tiger.'

Booya and Labella stood looking at each other: he looked confused, pleading to stay home whilst also appealing to go; tears of joy were welling in her eyes.

'Go and enjoy yourself,' she said to break the moment. 'I can see in your eyes that you want to really.' Labella continued to rub her stomach. 'You been a good boy recently, and good boys get what they deserve. *Go!* I'm letting you. We'll both be waiting here when you get back. Just go for an hour, if you want. Some of your followers is waiting to meet you, remember? Imagine if that Blind Lemon man —'

'Blind Lemon Jefferson,' Booya said.

'Yeah, imagine if he never come to a frolic you was at 'cause he felt like going to bed early.'

'She got a point, man,' Tiger said. 'This is a big one, one you definitely ain't wanting to miss. Only comes but one time a year . . . Uh, sorry. I just ain't getting involved in no . . . you know.' Humming to himself, hands in his pockets, Tiger began to swagger away from the door, kicking his inch-high heels.

'Go, would you?' Labella said, pushing Booya in the chest. 'You ain't no slave.'

'Could fool me,' Tiger muttered with his back to them, chuckling.

'Tiger, if you don't drag this man out of here, I is coming to the frolic with you.'

'Damn! You'd be better company that this sack of old man's clothes, Bella.'

Booya punched Tiger's arm. 'Don't cuss in front of my baby mama.'

'Cuss 'til I turn white unless you move your big black ass.'

'Quit cussing, man!'

'Then quit acting like Methuselah.'

Before Booya could hit his arm again, Tiger skipped out of the way.

Booya took Labella in his arms. 'One hour: that's all I is gonna be gone for.'

Holding each other, they kissed.

'Ain't that how y'all got in the family way in the first place?' Tiger asked, leaning on the chinaberry tree.

'You learn 'bout that one day, boy,' Booya said. 'But first, I's gonna whup you when I catch you.'

'Your big black ass ain't never gonna be able to catch me, *Methuselah.*'

*

By the noise alone, the house frolic could be located easily enough from more than a mile away. The familiar sight of the furniture from the house sitting on the lawn outside was like an arrow pointing the way. Some bold chancers might try their luck, but it was rare for anyone to take a chance stealing any of the furniture from this particular frolic. Anyway, most of the night there would be someone who had come out for air, cooling down on an armchair in the frisky night air, or with a partner.

The furniture in this house was more desirable than would usually be seen outside an average frolic, apposite to the grand design of the house. It was one of the older houses in town, in the same style as Huck's Place: with stoop, a veranda perfumed with strongly-scented climbing flowers, big bay windows, hallway, reception rooms and multiple bedrooms. With the house situated on the same side of town as Mammy and Paw's, it was curious that Booya had never noticed it before, though it was somewhat hidden by tall, looming pines.

'See,' Tiger explained, 'Walter Carini throws this huge frolic each year on the anniversary of the death of his wife, a celebration of her life more than her death, understand?' Booya nodded, looking along the width of the broad wooden house. 'Carini make most his money through bootlegging, feeding Chicago. He got connections deep in the underworld of the city. It's even tole that the Dillinger gang once hid out in this same house. Even as a white man, he just loves to wave his backend in the face of authority. Hence,' Tiger said, pointing both index fingers at the house, 'the annual frolic that the whole of Hon'hee is invited to. Everone knows when Carini opens the doors of his house, both frolickers *and* The Law.'

Picking his fingernails, Booya looked at Tiger. Looking up at the big house, then back at Booya, Tiger smiled. 'Gets busted near 'bout ever year,' Tiger continued. 'But by the time the revenue man barges they way in, evidence of any liquor having ever been on the property is long gone. And Carini, he knows how to charm the revenue man; he knows he can't be busted. Guess that's how bootlegging got him such a big ass house!'

By way of consolation, the sheriff and his deputies would be out in force in the early hours, sweeping up any drunks from the streets, Tiger explained. It was also a night for looting and criminal damage in the town; a few frolickers always had to spoil it for the many. But that was after the party, and of little care to the host. Rather, it amused Carini that The Law would have to, in a way, tidy up after his party, his celebration.

Folks saw Booya coming, pointing him out to friends as he approached the house.

'Tiiiiii-gerrrrrrr,' one called, hands in the air like a chimp.

In recognition, Tiger raised a hand, greeted like a returning hero. 'And with me I bring one Mister Booya Carthy. Y'all may a heared a him?'

What Tiger had said about Booya being an old man he began to feel. Even though they looked dapper in their sharp suits, regarding him in their presence with wide-eyed awe, they all looked so young.

'You gonna play tonight, Booya?' asked one, smoking on a rolled cigarette. It looked like it was maybe the first time that the boy had ever smoked. The smoked climbed cruelly into the smoker's eyes, making them water. He swallowed the smoke down, managing to suppress a lurching cough.

Booya raised the soft bandages encasing his hand. 'Out the business for the time, man.'

The boy looked delighted that Booya had spoken to him.

'How long for, man?' asked another.

'Month maybe. Maybe six weeks.'

'Must be going *crazy*, Booya.'

'Yeah, but he finded him other things to keep busy,' Tiger interrupted, grinning. 'This man standing 'fore y'all find out today he's gonna be a daddy for the first time.'

The little crowd of Tiger's friends and admirers whooped, clapped and cheered.

'Get the man a drink!'

'When's it due, man?' someone asked.

'Woah! Woah!' Tiger waved his arms in front of him. 'Stop interrogating him. He's here to have a time, not have his life history documented.'

Now that they couldn't ask Booya questions, they seemed not to know what to say or do. They drank from their cups in an uncomfortable silence, wondering what else they could talk about. Someone quickly returned with a cup of liquor. Booya stared at it, as if trying to surmise if it was friend or foe. As Paw had taught him to do, Booya sipped. He took another sip. This could quite possibly be the finest whisky he had ever tasted, in town or city. It was liquid fire, molten gold. It gave life to his tongue.

'All you play?' He took another sip; it wasn't enough so he took another. Carini clearly knew how to brew his liquor. No wonder the city had rewarded him so richly.

The boys all nodded.

'We all *try* to play,' said the first one who had spoken to Booya, peering out from beneath a hat too large for his head, his arms hidden up somewhere in the sleeves of his suit. The group tittered nervously. 'Tiger's the best.'

'Too right,' Tiger agreed, tracing a half-circle around the rim of his Fedora.

'All 'bout practice,' Booya said. They turned to him like hungry chicks to a returning mother. 'If you practice for a hour you'll become skilful.' Booya nodded, looking at each entranced face in turn. 'But if you play your guitar at any spare moment you find each day, you can be good as you wanna be. Was tole that by . . .' He was about to say Roots, but that wasn't true. Mister Henry, the very last time Booya had seen him, had told him that. It had been one of the conditions of his gift. He could still remember that day so clearly: as ever, Mister Henry had looked as splendid as his room . . .

It had been a miserable grey overcast day, Booya remembered. Paw had taken him in through the front doors of the mansion, to thank Mister Henry for his guitar. And then, in the corridor, the man with the pockmarked face, the deputy, the grin. His thin lips had mouthed a single word . . .

Boo

'Who tole you, man?' Tiger asked.

'Huh?'

'Who tole you to practice that way? You was halfway to telling us when you slip from the face of the Earth.'

Booya looked at the eager faces gazing at him, searching his face for an answer.

'My Paw,' he answered. 'Paw tole me that.'

'So if we practice we can be as good as you, Boo? That what you saying?'

'If you practice you can be anything! That's what I's saying. Take inspiration, but you gotta go your own way.' Booya took another sip, a beautiful sip. 'Was my Mammy what tole me that.'

The crowd laughed.

'Shall we?' Tiger asked Booya, tilted his brim towards the house.

'Rude not to, right?' Booya replied. 'Hey, you know where I can get me another cup?'

The boys all looked at Booya with astonishment. A couple of them tried gulping a mouthful of the fiery brew, swallowing, wincing, and immediately regretting it. As Booya and Tiger sought out the stash of whisky, the line of Tiger's disciples followed them over the stoop and into the house.

It was a frolic deserving of its reputation, the likes of which Booya had never known outside of Blacks, Juju, or the various barrelhouses and juke-joints in the city. Levee Banks and the Ol' Creek Stompers – the band Booya had first seen at the picnic – played a session. It was all blues: electric and acoustic, soloists and bands, men and women.

Booya frolicked. He danced and he drank. The whisky gave him his fuel – which he soon realised just how much he had missed; the music put a smile on his face. When requested, The Ol' Creek Stompers even played a jumped-up Cajun version of a Booya Carthy song. With his whisky tongue, Booya cursed the outlaw blues.

If it wasn't for Mammy . . . doing something . . . he would have missed this! Mammy said, or done . . . something? Something about spending more time . . . somewhere . . . ?

The quality whisky blurring his memory, Booya vaguely he knew that it couldn't be important. Not when there was dancing to be done and whisky to be drunk.

*

When the inevitability that was the revenue men came through, Booya was in the kitchen. Whispered warnings travelled through the house, but Booya hadn't paid attention. When he did see them, he quickly tipped his drink into standing soapy water in the sink. For some reason – his drunkenness – he re-filled his cup with the dishwater. A revenue man, officially dressed and officiously keen, barged over to him.

'What's in that cup?' he shouted at Booya, spinning him round. Booya tipped the cup to show him. 'Is that dishwater?' the revenue man asked with sick disbelief.

'Yep,' Booya answered, and he tipped the cup back and drank the lot.

The revenue men consulted with each other.

'It obviously was here,' they said. 'The floor is swimming in booze. And *he's* obviously crazy drunk,' – the revenue man indicated Booya – 'but they all are. And we can't hardly take them all in.'

Curling his lips at the abuse being hurled at him, another of the revenue men agreed. 'We ain't going to find it now. We'll get Carini next year, for sure.'

'And watch yourself, all y'all niggers and crackers,' the first revenue man addressed the assembled. 'Ya might be safe up in here, but if you're drunk anywheres out on the street, we're going to take your ass down quicker than you can holler Goose.'

'Goose,' one laughing man nearby cried.

'*Goose!*' they all joined in. '*Goose! Goose!*'

Led by the band, the frolickers serenaded the revenue men as they exited the house.

A couple of the boys from Tiger's crew had been following Booya ceaselessly all night. If Booya went into a room, they would appear a few moments later; if he was dancing, they were dancing too. He didn't mind: he was used to having people's eyes on him all night. It's what he had once aspired to. Perhaps inspired by Roots, he couldn't be sure, his original intention for performing in public had been for girls to look longingly at him. There were no girls to speak of at this frolic tonight, though he wished that Rosie, Petal and Virginia were here to party with him. And what a party! The whisky was doing some non-stop work on his body and mind now, even though an exhaustion had taken over his bones.

Just one more cup, and then . . .

The boys were again by Booya's side. 'Go on, ax him,' he heard one say.

'Ax me wha'?' Booya slurred.

'Well . . .'

Booya tipped back his hat and leaned on the kitchen counter, finding it at a second grasp.

'Go on,' he said, the booze making heavy his tongue. 'If sumin need tuh be say they ain't no use constipatin' yo'seff.' He didn't even notice that he was speaking the same way that Paw often did.

'You hear 'bout that time in that one town when the Knights of the White Camellia set light to the back of a house at a frolic? They was waiting out the front with guns, shot all the men and womens like ducks when they was trying to escape the flames.'

'Yeah. I heared.'

'They is some talk about the Knights hearing 'bout this frolic here tonight. Some even say that they seen them earlier outside town. You don't think that will happen here, do you, Boo? I mean, you think we safe, with word going 'bout like that?'

'Ain't gon' 'appen 'ere, man. Yo' perfully safe.'

'But you was attacked by them was . . . n't . . . you?' the boy asked, seeing Booya's frown intensifying.

'So wha'f I was. Say that yo's *safe*, didn' I?'

'Hey,' Tiger said, walking in. 'What going on?'

'Nuth'n, man,' Booya said, eyes and head rolling. 'See'y later. Go'n 'ome. Need tuh get my head down someplace.'

As Booya staggered away, they watched him leave. Tiger stared at the boy who had spoken so foolishly.

'Bye, Booya,' the other boy called.

'Y'all never done leaving him alone?' Tiger asked the two boys. 'What you say?'

'Only mentioned the Knights of the White Camellia, Tiger. 'Bout how I heared they –'

'You . . . *huh*? What'd you do that for?' Tiger asked, exasperated. 'Didn't you figure he might be quite sensitive 'bout them, seeing he's still wearing the evidence of what they done?'

It might have been the smoke from the cigarette he was smoking that made the boy's eyes water.

2

After the bell and after the hour he walked alone. He had travelled far, from town to town. People weren't so friendly in some towns once they knew that he was a stranger stopping for the night. They would do well to find out anything from him. He was only there for a drink and something to eat, maybe a girl. Nothing else. No talk. Then he would be on the road again, walking until the next town slowly came into view.

He was the walking man. He needed no one and nothing.

On the road there were always little games to play. Passing through a town and looking for the sign:

BLACKS ARE NOT PERMITTED WITHIN THE TOWN BORDER
AFTER SUNDOWN. ANY CAUGHT WILL BE PROSECUTED

Always made him laugh when he saw that. Prosecuted must be the white
man's word for lynched-after-being-beaten-to-Heaven's-gates. Unless by
force, he never left a town before sundown. Knowing that he was breaking
the laws of racism stirred the blood that pumped through his heart. That was
the best game for the walking man.

"Might change my mind the day I is caught." That was one of his
favourite jokes. "Have plenty things to think 'bout hanging from a branch or
the back end of a stood-up crop wagon," he would tease himself.

He never had answered his own question: Do I want to somehow be
caught within them borders after dark comes? He wasn't sure. He guessed
that the answer would come to him when it was too late to do anything about
it.

Until then, he kept on walking.

To his disappointment, he hadn't seen that sign so far. There was only
one more sign left to read, right up ahead. The back of the sign was facing
him. It looked to the walking man like it was only a town sign. He liked to
read the name of the place that he had just left, just the same. Mostly so that
he remembered never to go back to the same place twice.

WELCOME TO HONAHEE, he read in the dancing flicker of match-
light, gold print on a black background, fading magnolias embracing the
words.

'That's the wrong thing to say to a man leaving town,' he said to the sign.
'Should name that greeting on your ass, sign. Looks like you been round
many years enough. Should know that by now.' With a foolish grin at his
mouth, he waited, as if expecting an answer. 'You welcome yourself. Heh-
heh-heh. Thanks all the same.' He spat, tipped his hat to the sign, and
continued walking down the road.

Walking made the walking man thirsty. Drinking Moonshine and walking
made him even thirstier, mostly for one more drop of whisky. In his
gunnysack, he had some whisky left in his canteen. The best way he had
learned to make a drink last the miles was to set the reward of a sip after a
hundred paces, and then push on for a hundred more before having that sip;
or maybe a hundred more after that. It could be tens of thousands more
paces before he would take his reward. It could be just ten.

'See how we's looking in another hundred,' he said aloud. 'We ain't got
far to go, now.'

The walking man often assured himself that he didn't have far to go. It
was always between not far and a long way off when there was nowhere in

particular to head for. And then, through the darkness, he spied a bridge.

Bridges were a rare treat. They were somewhere to rest a while, maybe even spend the night if the weather was wild. Tonight there wasn't more than a gentle breeze on the balmy air. Now that there were so many motorcars on the road – always more than the day before, it seemed – it had become dangerous to sleep by the roadside. Could wake up with tyre tracks printed into your flattened face. Bridges; forests; old barns. Even in forests and old barns there was always a chance of a clan meeting happening upon a sleeping black man. That was a predicament akin to a worm sleeping in a bird nest. Bridges, though. Nothing except for bugs had any interest in what was beneath a bridge.

He flicked a match down the bank.

In the flash of flame, the bank hadn't looked so steep. One hand on the bridge to steady himself, he walked down the bank upright. At the bottom, he pulled his canteen out of his gunnysack. A quick sip; maybe a smoke; maybe a sleep. One hand feeling the way beneath him, he crouched to sit.

'Fire in hell!' he said, jumping with surprise.

Not much fazed the walking man, but stiff bodies in the darkness beneath a bridge was an imaginative prank by his old adversary, the dark.

'Spill some of my Moonshine! Thanks friend.' He capped the whisky and pulled out a match. 'You asleep or adead, friend?'

The match-light revealed to him a bloodied face, one eye closed – if there was an eye in the socket at all – and one staring absently. He put two fingers to the man's jugular. The flesh was warm, but there was no blood pumping through the veins. The walking man flicked the match away and lit a fresh one.

He squinted his eyes at the grotesquely deformed face. 'Seeing as you is adead I 'scuse you for not answering. Heh-heh.' He tipped his hat. 'Y'all claimed this place first. I ain't one to argue with no dead man, so I leave you here to your dead self. Sleep tight. Heh-heh-heh.'

The walking man walked up the bank and he carried on down the road. There was a river, so perhaps there would be another bridge. One that the dead didn't choose to shelter beneath.

He would have his next sip of moonshine in a hundred paces . . . A hundred more.

The walking man could hear the distant rasp of an approaching motorcar before he saw the headlights. That gave him time to think about whether to duck into the fields on one side, or the bulrushes growing alongside the river on the other. Instead, he thought that this time he would see what happened by keeping on walking, allowing the motorcar to pass him by. After all, this was just a simple little town without his favourite sign. This place was a duck pond, not an alligator swamp.

But maybe this was the killers of that dead man coming up the road. That would be interesting. What if they stopped and tried to kill him, too? If he scuttled away into the bushes like a scaredy spider he would never know. This was another of the tests of the road. Life and motorcars could pass you by. Or you could stare them in the eye and walk right on.

'Sip in a hundred paces if it just pass me by,' he said. 'And ain't sharing a drop if they stop.'

The pale round headlamps of the car were approaching. Rabbits scattered from the dim glare and harsh noise. Scaredy spiders scatter like rabbits. So maybe he was more like a rat. A rat might run at the last second, but you had to admire the bravery of that particular diseased little rodent. He scrunched his nose and lowered his brow. He became the rat.

The closer the car came, the quicker it seemed to be travelling. Doubt crossed the walking man's mind. He scared it away with the rabbits. Even so, he was surprised when the motorcar did stop. Just one of life's little challenges. When he saw the sheriff and his deputy dismount he wished that it were the killers of the dead man.

'Perhaps it still is,' he whispered beneath his breath.

'What you doing out here?' the sheriff asked.

'Growing corn, sheriff,' the walking man replied. 'Heh-heh-heh.'

'Walking in the dark,' said the sheriff, 'a nigger can get run down by a motorcar, ya know?'

'Be sure and careful then. Thanks for the advice, boss.' The walking man tipped his imaginary hat to the sheriff and turned his back on him to walk on.

'Don't you walk away from me when I'm talking to you,' the sheriff shouted.

The deputy moved to block off the escape route up the road. The walking man turned around – a Law man either side of him. The cars red rear lights lit up his face.

'What I'm saying,' the sheriff continued, 'is that *accidents* happen to smart niggers like you when they're walking all alone in the dark.'

'Don't know what more I can say except for thank you the advising, sheriff.'

'Does it sound to you like this nigger is being smart with me, Deputy Betts?'

'Sounds that way to me, Sheriff Toms.'

'It's a nice night, sheriff,' said the walking man. 'Was just out walking. Didn't mean no offence. Was showing that I understood your advice. If I's on my way, I ain't no concern to you no more. That's why I was just walking on.'

'If you're out my way for good you ain't never going to be no concern of mine, ever,' the sheriff drawled, eyeing the walking man. 'Didn't think it that way, did you, nigger?'

The sheriff shone his flashlight directly in the walking man's eyes. 'Where you from, ugly nigger?'

'Um . . .' The bright light in his eyes momentarily startled the walking man. He clawed in the dark for a name of a town he had walked through. He had read the names of hundreds of towns, but none would come easily to him. 'Boss, I's from Covington.'

'Covington, huh? That's over a hundred miles from here, ain't it, Deputy Betts?'

'Hundred or more, Sheriff Toms.'

'Hundred or more, says Deputy Betts. So what's a nigger like you doing just outside of Honahee, a hundred or more miles from your home?'

'Visiting relatives,' the walking man replied.

'What's their name and where they live at?'

'What's they name and where they live, you ax?'

'That's what I arksed you, nigger.'

The extra seconds had bought the walking man time to think. 'Rupert and Crystal Steeles; that's my uncle and his wife. They living out on Hardacre Lane on the far side of town.'

The sheriff squinted his eyes. 'You and I both know there ain't no Rupert and Crystal Steeles, 'cause we both know there ain't no Hardacre Lane in my town.'

'Hardacre? Ain't real great with names, but I is sure it's Hardacre where Unca Rupe lives, sheriff. Telling you 'cause that's where I just come from!'

'Well, even if that is true – which it ain't – why are you leaving town in the middle of the night?'

'Just wanna get me a start on the sun. Heh-heh-heh.'

'So you don't know nothing about a big frolic tonight at Walter Carini's place, not two miles from here?'

'Can honestly say I don't, boss.'

'You expecting me to believe the word of a nigger? Nigger's lie to their own ma's. If you can't respect your own mother, you ain't going to tell the truth to The Law.'

The walking man held the sheriff's glare.

'What do you say, Deputy Betts?'

'I say that sounds about right to me, Sheriff Toms.'

'See, nigger? That sounds about right to Deputy Betts.' The sheriff sniffed around the walking man's face. 'See, I can smell a liar, and I smell that you're that same man. I think that you're a vagrant, a drifter, in the town to do no good. And then travelling on to bother the lives of the good folk in the next town along. We don't look kindly upon vagrancy in this town, you know that? We're a tight little community here in Honahee. We don't like outsiders messing with what we've got here in our quiet and tidy little town. We're happy just the way we is.'

The sheriff's nose was centimetres away from the walking man's face. He could feel the sheriff's spittle landing around his mouth, hot as acid.

'So, y'ain't got nothing to say now you're found out, nigger?'

'Don't think he's so keen to talk back now, Sheriff Toms.'

'That's right, Deputy Betts,' the sheriff agreed. 'Deputy, will you please do me the favour of searching through this nigger's gunny. Drop it down by your side,' he instructed the walking man. 'Step away from the bag. And I wouldn't advise you in stepping no farther than that.'

The walking man slid the gunnysack from his shoulder and let it slip to the floor. He heard the clank as his canteen hit the road.

'What am I going to do with you?' the sheriff asked, his teeth grinding as Deputy Betts searched the bag with his nose turned in the air, away from the emanating waft. 'That's what the question is: what're we going to do with you?'

'Just a bit of bread and mostly stinking filthy dirty clothes, Sheriff Toms. But I found this, too.' Deputy Betts handed the canteen to the sheriff. He opened it and sniffed.

'Whisky.' He took a sip; spat it out. 'Tastes like shit-water. Typical of a nigger.'

Deputy Betts laughed.

The sheriff wasn't laughing. 'Where'd you get this?'

'A white man give it me in town.'

The sheriff hit the walking man across the ear with his flashlight. The deputy winced.

Instinctively, the walking man reached for his ear. It was still stuck to the side of his head. That was good enough for him. He lowered his hand, his eyes never leaving the sheriff's glare. He could feel the warm flow of blood trickling from behind his ear and down into his shirt.

'I'll arkse you again: where'd you get this shitty whisky?'

'A black man give it me in town,' the walking man replied.

The sheriff again smashed the flashlight over the walking man's ear. Now there was a steady stream of blood. Half of the walking man's head was throbbing. But he was used to sheriffs like this. They could cut him to pieces, if that was what they wanted to do. But he would never let them know that they had hurt him. Never. That infuriated them. It made them hurt him more, which only further stiffened his resolve. They got madder and his blood turned to ice, colder still with every furious red blotch that appeared on the sheriff's face. They could hurt themselves hurting him! *Heh-heh-heh*

It was clear that this sheriff wasn't as dim as most of them. He was eyeing the walking man, trying to seek out some kind of weakness. It was obvious that this sheriff enjoyed sheriffing.

'What do you say we do with this here nigger, Deputy Betts? Leave him out here for the crows to clean his bones? Or take him back to town?'

'I say we take him in, sheriff,' Deputy Betts replied.

'Lucky for you Deputy Betts' a God man, nigger.'

The walking man smiled, showing his yellow-black teeth. 'How 'bout if I tell you a little secret I finded out, sheriff, boss?' the walking man asked. 'You let me go on my own way then?'

'Guess that depends on what that secret is now, don't it.'

'I know where you can find a dead man near here.' The walking man's smile remained.

Sheriff Toms rolled his fingers around his flashlight. 'If you're being smart to me again, nigger, I'll carry on with this 'til either your head or the casing of this flashlight is broke. And I don't care which happens first, I swear. I can always get me another casing.'

'Telling you the truth, sheriff,' the walking man replied. 'You'll see. If I show where that dead body is will you let me go? I mean, ain't much of a deal if I is going back into town nohow. I need something back for that, boss.'

'I'm sure we can come to . . . some kind of agreement,' the sheriff replied. ''Til then: Deputy Betts, cuff this man and put him in the back of the vehickle. Where we to, nigger?'

'That bridge. Just down the way there.'

3

'Mother of Jesus!' said the sheriff, shining his flashlight over the mangled face. 'What's happened to you?' He placed a hand on his thigh, leaning in closer.

A moan came from out of the darkness beneath the bridge. The sheriff leapt in the air, bringing his flashlight around to the sound. Through the moisture in the air, the beam of light shook over the rocks and grasses beneath the bridge, speckles and bugs drifting in the yellow light.

'What is that?' he yelled, unable to conceal the fright in his voice. He slid his gun from the holster and pointed it toward the waving circle of light. 'Who's there? That someone there?'

'Who's that?' a voice from the darkness answered. 'Where am I?'

'Identify yourself, now!' The sheriff could see only the man's raised forearm, covering his eyes from the light, and the occasional glint of whites as the man peered around the shielding arm. He could see that it was another black man.

'What's going on?' the man repeated from beneath the bridge.

'You armed?' the sheriff asked.

'Huh? No, I ain't armed,' the voice replied.

'Come out. Slowly. Hands in the air. Make a false move and you're dead as meat.'

'What is it, Sheriff Toms?' Deputy Betts asked. 'You see much?'

'Shut up, deputy. Put the prisoner in the vehicle. Then get your flashlight and shine it down here, with your pistol trained on the light. Think we got us another nigger.'

'A dead one?'

'Heh-heh-heh.'

'Was you born yesterday, Betts? No, not a dead one. The dead one is a white man. Shut that crazy nigger up, now! Hurry and put him in the car and help me out here.'

Booya stepped out of the darkness. Suddenly there were two lights shining in his eyes. He was sleepy and still drunk. He felt sick. He could taste whisky and he could taste soap, both sitting uncomfortably in his stomach. He wanted to lower his hands to shield his eyes, but was terrified that the next thing he would feel would be lead punching a hole in his heart. Behind the quivering light, he could see the beige uniform of The Law.

'Hands right up in the air. That's it. *Slowly.*'

Booya stumbled on a rock, yelped, and fell to a knee.

'Woah, woah, nigger! Almost just got yourself a new hole in your head. Step . . . *careful.* And keep them hands way up.' The sheriff stepped back to allow Booya to stagger past the heap on the floor. 'Up that bank. Real slow. Keep your hands in the air. See the deputy's flashlight there? It'll guide you. Never step out of its circle. *Slow.*'

'What's this 'bout, sheriff?' Booya asked. 'Was just sleeping.'

'Shut up, nigger. Don't give me that ignorant shit. Right now, you've got to concentrate on keeping all your blood on the inside. Keep on moving.'

As the sheriff directed, Booya walked up the bank. He couldn't remember making the decision to sleep beneath the bridge. Seeing what he had of the body, waking as he had, he was too terrified to try.

Following Booya up the bank, one of the sheriff's feet slipped under him and he fell forwards onto his knees. 'Shit!'

'Y'all right there, Sheriff Toms?' the deputy asked.

'Don't shine the light my way, you dumb-ass. Keep it on the nigger.'

The sheriff inspected his gun. Dirt was around the breach and inside the barrel. Cursing, he sucked his finger, which had caught the sharp metal of the trigger-guard. He crested the top of the bank, walked around to the driver's door, and turned on the headlamps, slamming the door closed. 'Stand him in the lights.' Pulling the walking man from the backseat, the sheriff dragged him along on his knees to stand next to Booya. 'I'll keep these two here,' he said. 'Bring that body up here, Deputy Betts.'

The deputy gulped. He went about his work quickly, frequently glancing up the bank as he did.

Wiping congealing blood from his fingers, Deputy Betts placed the body where the sheriff directed him to – in the glow of the headlamps, next to the two pairs of feet of the still-standing prisoners, careful not to step between them and the barrel of the sheriff's gun.

'Knew this would be a good night for catching some niggers up to no good,' said the sheriff. 'Always is. It's like Carini's in the employment of The Law, gathering all that vermin together in one place. Wouldn't you say, niggers? Good: quiet niggers. My second favourite kind of nigger after a dead one. Speaking of dead ones, let's have a looky at this body.'

With his hands in the air, his weary eyes looking down at the body, the soap suds in Booya's stomach rose into his throat. It was even more horrifying in the light. Not only for the face, with its grisly, staring, lifeless single eye, the entire body was covered in scarlet blood. The clothes were torn and sliced. A thick wound in the stomach had started to weep blood in juddering bursts, the flashlights picking out more details of horror.

'I recognise him!' the deputy cried. 'This is one of them Knights of the White Camellia. I heard a rumour that they might be back in town tonight. But I thought they was supposed to be the ones doing the killing.'

'Heh-heh-heh.'

'Shut up, nigger,' the sheriff warned the walking man, stepping forward with his gun level, 'or you'll be just as dead as him.'

The deputy looked up from the corpse to Booya.

Booya fathomed the same thing at the same time: this was indeed one of the Knights. It was the one who had almost terminally smashed Mister Henry's guitar against the fender of that truck.

The deputy's face was youthful beneath his high forehead and receded hairline, a pink flush on his cheeks from the exertion. Breathing heavily, he pointed at Booya. 'Him. With the bandaged hand and arm. This dead man's one of the men that done that to him, nearly two months ago now, the first night the Knights was about town. Saw enough of this man that night to recognise him, even in the dark. Even dead. And that nigger there . . . Well, that's Booya Carthy.'

'Is that right now?' the sheriff said, looking Booya up and down, settling his glare on Booya's wide eyes.

'Heh-heh-heh,' the walking man cackled.

'Nigger, you just shut your mouth up. Don't want to hear that laugh from you again, ya hear?' The sheriff stepped in front of the walking man. Then he peered up at Booya's face, stark in the headlamps. '*Booya*. Sounds stupid enough to be a nigger name. Carthy, though; sounds like your nigger granddaddy stole him a good Irish name. Niggers and their thieving, it's going to be the death of many-a-man.' The sheriff turned on his heel. 'What we've got here, Deputy Betts, is a obvious case. This is a lesson for you in summarising a crime scene before the evidence gets away. We was just fortunate enough to catch them in the act of doing, weren't we?'

'Sure was, Sheriff Toms.'

'Sure, Sheriff Toms,' the sheriff repeated. 'Seems to me the situation is this: we've got two niggers trying to take the law into their own hands, revenging a little beating – like you observed yourself, Deputy Betts, which won't go unnoticed in my report. That original beating was done by this man, alleged Knight of the White Camellia. We caught this one,' said the sheriff, indicating with his pistol the walking man, 'just as he was fetching to leave town, to escape what he'd done. And we caught this big nigger still right beside the body. Catched 'em both red handed. That what it looks like to you, Deputy Betts?'

'Sure does to me, Sheriff Toms,' the deputy replied.

'"Sure does," says my jury. "Guilty," says the judge.'

'He's the judge,' the deputy pointed out to the prisoners. 'Sheriff Toms.'

'That's right, deputy. Good lawing to say.' The sheriff walked back to Booya. 'You're a mighty big nigger. You ain't going to cause me no trouble, make me use my firearm, are ya?'

Even though it all still seemed like a crazy nightmare, even though every time his eyes looked at the bloodied corpse he felt sick, Booya understood that he and this other man had been tried and convicted out here in the dark. But this would only last a few days. Better to be guilty until proven innocent than be dead. For now he would comply. But he couldn't control his shaking body.

'Y'all got anything you want to say, just while you got the chance?'

'I didn't do nothing wrong, sir. You just waked me up and here I is. All I was doing was sleeping.'

'I ain't never even seen this big man before now,' the walking man said, smiling. 'Even if his name sounds familiar from somewheres. Heh.'

The sheriff swung his glare on the walking man. 'You could just as easily be brothers though, ain't it? All y'all look alike. He might just have sucked your mama's titties dry before you got a turn. That's why he turned out big and you turned out dumb.'

'Ain't got no blood on my bandages, sir,' Booya said, holding out his hands. 'I couldn't have done what you say without getting no blood on me. Honestly, I ain't got nothing to do with this. Had nothing to do with it 'til I waked up.'

'And I tole you already,' the walking man added, 'I just finded the dead man dead. Heh-heh.'

'Them's merely details,' the sheriff replied. 'We'll see to them. See, someone always has to pay for murder. Both of you is someone. And two someones is always better than just one. But I've got to say I'm glad that you pointed that out to me.

'Deputy Betts, will you see to it that both these men have a little blood on their hands. Don't want it to look like a false arrest now, do we?'

4

It was still dark outside the jailhouse when Booya awoke. The fluorescent light bouncing from the whitewashed walls made his waking feel all the more dreamlike. He sat up with a jerk, his sore head following seconds after. Within a blurry second or two of waking, the cold brick cell, the line of thick black bars and the encased fluorescent lamps on the ceiling all quickly reminded him of the trouble he had found himself landed in.

The walking man was staring directly at him, grinning.

'Call you Booya, does they?' he asked, showing his rotted teeth.

Booya swung his legs off the wooden bench he had been sleeping upon with neither blanket nor pillow. Shivering, he rubbed his forearms through his shirt. His back and neck ached. His repairing hand and arm throbbed. But his eyes were open and clear. 'Yeah, they call me Booya.'

'Heh-heh-heh.' Like a laughing, fixated rodent, the walking man didn't take his eyes from Booya. He had a growth of some kind on the tip of his wide nose, his skin as deep-black as a forest. Other random spots and lumps covered his face, though his smile seemed strangely trustworthy; his face saying with no boast that he was familiar to all experiences. But the strange, mad humour in his dirty-green eyes shot wicked electricity around his irises.

'What's your name, friend?' Booya asked.

'Me, I's called Alf. Folks 'bout called me that when I was just a chile, on account of rolling in the Alfalfa. So that's why I's Alf. Could say they ain't no sense in having a name at all 'less it tells folks what it is you do most, like Cook Man or Nigger Catcher. Heh-heh-heh, lucky I ain't never rolled in shit.' Alf's laughter was as infectious as he looked. 'Heh-heh-heh. Guess both us names will be changed to Murder Man right now.'

'They put me in here with murderers?' enquired a voice from behind Booya. 'Confined in darkness for all my life and put here with nothing to bump off but walls and iron bars and *murderers?*'

Separated only by the thick bars, Booya looked at the blind Indian in the adjoining cell. His pale, hypnotic eyes were spinning in their sockets. He was wearing the same sleeveless buffalo poncho that Booya had bumped into on occasion; his blue denim shirt, faded almost to white, buttoned to the top. The wispy grey hair was untucked from behind his ears, framing his lined face, yellow in the florescent light. Rocking back and forward, the blind Indian was holding the bars between the cells so tightly that his fists had turned as white as the walls.

'Heh-heh-heh.'

'If you is murderers then state your intentions towards me now. I ain't got no fear of dying, no I don't. If there be such a person as God, He ain't got nothing left to deal me. But the devil . . .' The blind Indian became more animated with each pained word he spoke, increasing with each of Alf's cackles. 'Tell me now!' he demanded. 'Stop that hellish laughing! Unless . . . you *is* the devil!' The blind Indian let go of the bars and staggered backward, wailing until he hit the bench in his cell and sat down. Immediately he stood up and stumbled forward toward the bars.

'Stop that hideous laughing, you devil!' He clutched his hands across his heart. 'You can't take my soul. I declare it to be the Lord's alone, no matter how bad He treated me in this life. Devil, take what you want of my earthly body; Lord, lift up my soul!'

The unearthly pleas of the blind Indian, coupled with the ceaseless laughter of Alf, devilish indeed, made Booya wonder where exactly he had been imprisoned, if it really was still earthly. The bright glare of the fluorescent lights contrasted the dark outside. Within the resonance of laughter and wails, Booya turned and kneeled on the bench, put his hands through the bars and closed them around one of the blind Indian's hands.

The blind Indian gasped. 'He is come! His hands so big and cold, he is come to take me! Leave my soul, you devil!'

'Hey, man, I ain't no devil. We in the jailhouse; all in together, brother.'

The blind Indian stared absently ahead. 'You have a duty to announce yourself if you is here for my life, devil. It is your covenant!'

Alf cackling wildly, the blind Indian began to raise his voice once more, yelling out his irrational pleas. 'Announce your intentions! You must –!'

'Hey! We in the jailhouse, man, like I say. My name's Booya Carthy. I live in Honahee, just outside. Don't know what I is doing here, 'cept for that I ain't done nothing wrong.'

'What devil is it you've brung with you who makes such laughter, that laughter, that . . . evil laughter?' The blind Indian was gripping Booya's hands tighter and tighter.

'Heh-heh-heh,' Alf offered.

The blind Indian's grip yet intensified.

Booya gently peeled his fingers back and removed his hand – one broken hand was one too many. 'That's Alf making that noise. He's a prisoner here, too.'

'And is he innocent, too, like you say you is?'

Booya turned and looked at Alf's vague, smiling face. Rubbing his hands together, he saw the dried remnants of blood on the bandages. Alf looked down at his own hands. Rather than being amused, he seemed more confused or bemused by the blood he found.

'Yes, sir,' Booya said. 'We both innocent.' The blind Indian was still gripping the bars, but not with the same intensity. 'You innocent of something too, friend?'

'I is guilty,' the blind Indian replied. 'But only of being blind. I is guilty of the crime I is accused of. But only if it is a crime. Was walking down the road, not knowing where I was going. See, being blind you tend to bump into things and off a things. It's other people who stand a better chance of missing me, seeing as they can see, unless we is two blind people bumping together.

'But that weren't what happened. No. I was walking along with my darkness, minding my own business, when I bumped into a lady. I couldn't know that she was a white lady, and I couldn't know that what my hands finded all by theyself was that woman's titties within her dress. I guess my hands might've stayed a second, maybe two. I couldn't tell what they was before . . . I guess a second. And then she raised hell, start screaming "Rape! Assault!" Know what kind of chance a blind Indian stands in that kind of situation?'

''Bout that same kind of chance a black man being finded by The Law nearby a dead white man, even if he ain't done nothing.'

The blind Indian's vacant, unseeing eyes looked directly into Booya's. 'Then yes, you do know, brother. They take my cup away from me. Don't s'pose you got a spare coin? A nickel, even?'

'Sorry, friend. Had nothing on me when they find me. And they is fetching to take all that away from me, too.'

'They take everthing I got,' Alf said. 'Got my gunny. Got my *Moonshine*, man.' For the first time Alf's face became sincere and sober.

'In all my years, however long that may be, I've never been in a jailhouse,' the blind Indian said. 'If I could see my mama's face – if she was living and I weren't blind – she'd be as disappointed as the flowers if the sun refuse to shine. I ain't never done nothing wrong. I don't know who would ever think that getting a touch of a white woman's titties through cotton is worth anything like this frozen hell! You ever been in a jailhouse before now, brother?' the blind Indian asked. 'Sorry, I don't recall your name. But brothers in hell we is.'

'No, man. No way. Was nearly killed by that white man I see dead tonight. I wished him dead. But seeing him that way, I wish he weren't. And now I is accused of doing his killing.'

'Yet it's all right for them Knights of Wherever I keep hearing mention of, going round stringing up – 'scuse me, brother; I can hear the blackness in your voice, but – niggers,' the blind Indian said.

'The dead man we see tonight is . . . *was* one of them Knights of the White Camellia. That's who was aiming to string me up; ended up hanging some other man.'

'So an innocent black man has to pay for the life of a serial murderer,' the blind Indian said. 'Ain't that justice.'

'Two black men,' Alf interjected. 'Heh-heh-heh. Two niggers gotta pay. Heh.'

'You innocent, then?' the blind Indian asked Alf. 'Innocent even with that devil laugh of yours?'

'Guilty of a few things, I 'fess. Wandering town to town the most of it. But I ain't never killed no one. Not when I was sober 'nough to remember, nohow'.

'You ever been in the jailhouse, Alf?' Booya asked.

Eyes searching the walls, Alf curled his lips and wrinkled his nose. 'Night here; night there,' he replied. 'Being honest? I prefer life at night under the stars rather than any roof above. The stars they twinkle like they is friends. They sleep out all night. I like feeling how they feel, twinkle right back at them. Heh-heh-heh. Trouble, trouble, trouble. It don't follow me round as such, but it finds me up to no good from time to time. Normally no good involving some homebrew liquor, heh-heh-heh.'

The steel door beyond the bars of the cells crashed open. A tanned, white deputy with shoulders as wide as Cole or Maluch, arms as thick as a pillar, bowled through the door with chains draped over his arms. They crashed as he dropped them to the floor.

'Come here to the bars, niggers. Both you. Stand with your backs to me, right up close. Try anything stupid and I'll break every bone in you, from the toes up and down again.'

'Where is God in this town?' wailed the blind Indian. 'Why does He forsake us like – ?'

'Shut up that mouth, y'Injun nigger,' the deputy shouted. 'I hear you again there'll be some new charges against you.'

The blind Indian found his way to the bench and slumped against the wall. 'May God keep you safe, innocent brothers,' he spoke.

'Don't you understand a fucking warning when one's told you?' the deputy shouted, tightening a manacle around Booya's wrists.

To allow a little bit of air to pass between the cold steel and his bones, Booya wished that he had somehow clenched his fists before the manacles were tightened. But there was nothing he could do about the equally tight manacles around his ankles, nor the short length of chain that bound them.

'Your transfer's here,' the deputy said.

'Transfer where?' Booya asked.

'The White House,' the deputy replied.

'Heh-heh-heh.'

'Shut up, nigger,' the deputy spat. 'Ain't nothing to laugh about where you're going.'

'Where?' Booya asked again.

'Find out when you get there. And then you'll wish you was anywhere on Earth except in that place or in hell. Consider yourself lucky you ain't already in hell. Some thunk we should string you up for killing one of their own. See, there's some . . . *sympathisers* in The Law, and tonight you niggers killed one of their kind.'

Booya felt panic rising in him. 'Sir, I swear by the Lord's name that I ain't got nothing to do with that dead man. Ain't never seen him 'til–'

'You're the blues man,' the deputy interrupted, pulling on Booya's chain, pinning him tight to the bars. 'They say that you was revenging a beating dealt out to ya,' he growled hotly in Booya's ear. 'It's already been decided, see: you're as guilty as a fox with a chicken bone stuck in his mangy teeth. Make whatever deal you like with the Lord, but it ain't gonna change shit. You're one guilty nigger. Guilty of murder. See that blood on your wrists? You'll be lucky if the state don't hang you before the Brotherhood of Knights does.'

'Wait! Wait.' Booya rattled his chains. 'I gotta right to trial, ain't I?'

'You ain't got a right to nothing but smelling your shit. Say a single 'nother word to me and I'll break your wrists.' The deputy squashed Booya's bandaged arm against the bars, making him cry out in agony.

'You scream again, nigger, and I'll break your teeth.'

Booya could feel Alf looking at the side of his face. Could sense that it was humourless, maybe even scared. He bit his tongue. When the deputy again squashed his bandaged hand against the bars, he almost bit through it.

A couple more deputies came through the open door and unlocked the bars of the cell. Booya took one last look at the blind Indian. Unseeing through the darkness of his pale eyes, he stared back at Booya with shared pain.

*

Outside, a dark van with gauze over the windows was idling. The first birds of the day had begun to sing; the sky was toned heliotrope.

'Twinkle has faded from the stars,' Alf said.

They were thrown into the van. Their chains were padlocked to the floor. A deputy armed with a shotgun climbed into the back with them.

The van pulled away from the jailhouse and drove from Honahee, past Mammy and Paw's hidden home. Through the trees, Booya could just make out Paw's empty chair.

As the van bumped along the road, jolting the manacles viciously against the skin covering his anklebones, Booya hung his head, numb to the painful sensation. Across the van, Alf sighed. Booya almost wished that Alf would laugh, in a strange way reassuring him that there was still humour to be found in the world, no matter how flailing a mind needed to be to find it. Blinking was the only movement on Alf's face.

'Where we going, man?' Booya asked him. 'You know?'

Alf turned to Booya and smiled. 'Going down the river would be my guess.'

'Where? What river?'

'To The Farm.'

'What . . . farm?'

'Parchman,' Alf replied. 'I'd put money on it, only I ain't got nothing to bet with. Heh-heh-heh. Not even a pebble or stone. Heh.'

'We going straight to the pen?'

'Sure looks that way,' Alf said.

'But we ain't seen no qualified judge yet. Don't know much, but . . . Oh man, it ain't right! I know that we can't be sent to the pen without first seeing no judge. That sheriff ain't no real judge, no matter what he say.'

'You wanna tell his face that? Ain't no use telling me, brother. Looks like some crackerjack is making some bread off us, is my guess. We was two niggers catched in the wrong place at the wrong time. We ain't the first or last, believe it! I think the only thing what saved us was the fact that we was two. That, and they is some bread to be maked out of us.'

Booya looked to the guard. He was staring at Alf, his brow lowered, looking like he was contemplating violence.

'Hey,' Booya said to him. 'Ain't they someone I can talk with?' Booya asked. 'Ain't done nothing, man.'

Shifting his shotgun, the guard continued to stare at Booya in the same threatening manner.

'Can you at least send a message to my Mammy and Paw when you get back to Honahee? Huh? Can you do that? They names is –'

'Hey, man.' Booya looked at Alf; his eyes now mad and wild, Alf's sad and thoughtful. 'Ain't gonna do no good talking at that man, man. Might be able to talk with someone when we get where we going . . . but I doubt that. I see you's a good man, catched sleeping some place and you ain't supposed to be here. But you's here, sure 'nough.'

CHAPTER TEN

1

The van carrying the two prisoners left the blacktop road behind. The new road hissed beneath them as gravel and dirt licked the chassis of the van, answered by the appreciative purr of the engine. There was nothing except fields, burgeoning plants hiding the dry earth from the sky. On the far horizon, where the sun was wakening into the brightening blue sky, grew copses and woodlands of trees. The road was long; the ride bumpy. For the entire journey, the world had been sleeping, time frozen whilst Booya was being was being stolen from his life.

This was Parchman Farm. The sign welcoming them to the Mississippi State Penitentiary told them as much.

Against the window, Booya was leaning his head on his hand, too numb to cry any more. He could have stayed home last night. He could have stumbled on back to Labella and his unborn child. Like the day, she would have woken by now, to again find that he was not there in bed beside her. His emotions were paralysed.

Beyond the road they travelled, Booya barely noticed the lines of men in the fields. The rising sun was blinking from the heads of their tools as if they were splashing in water. A man on a horse was riding alongside the line, a shotgun resting across his legs. Then Booya saw small packs of more armed men, some with dogs.

'Never once wished I was wrong like I wish I was wrong now,' said Alf, picking at the growth on his nose. 'Shit, man. Suggest you try and forget 'bout what you leave behind. It ain't gonna help you none out here; will drag you down. It's just like what I heared it tole. Folks say they'd rather cast iron in the devil's fire than stay a week here. Shit, man. Try and learn to forget.'

'I was made to sing the blues,' Booya mumbled. 'Wasn't made for this. Ain't saying I never done nothing wrong, but I ain't never broke the law to end up in this place.' Until he drank again, his tears would have no spring to draw from.

'You gotta know that blues to sing the blues, brother,' said Alf. 'If you didn't know it 'fore now, you gonna be friend of the blues soon 'nough.'

They drove through field after field along the dusty road. Booya noticed that the men never once looked up from their work; the van driving through them was no distraction. This was a different country, a law unto itself. The van kept on moving through the fields.

They passed through a fence, barbed wire coiled thickly along the top, into the yard beyond it. Having meandered and honked through broods of chickens and gaggles of geese, carefully maintained allotments and numerous water troughs lined up against the wooden fence of the yard, they pulled up beside a row of long, low brick barracks with tiled roofs, chimneys, and bars over the windows.

The driver killed the engine, came around the truck and opened the side door. The guard who had stared at the two prisoners wordlessly for the entire journey climbed out of the van, his shotgun ever ready. The driver entered the rear of the van and unclasped the prisoner's shackles, allowing the chains to crash to the floor.

Booya's ankle breathed into life. Such was his numbness, he hadn't realised how worn the skin had become. Now it cried in agony, exposed nearly right through to the bone.

'Out,' the armed guard instructed.

Alf looked down at Booya's ankle. 'Shit, man. After you.'

Careful to land on his uninjured foot, Booya limped out of the van. Looking down, he saw that the bottom of his trousers were covered in blood. He found it hard to care. The guard took a quick glance at Booya's ankle. Sight didn't change the sneering expression his face. The driver was looking, too.

'Bracelet rubbed your ankle raw, buddy. You're going to want to get that treated, so it don't get infected. You'll lose it if it does – if you don't end up chopping it off yourself first.' The driver laughed.

The door of the nearest barracks slammed closed. A man wearing a white shirt, khaki pants and a Stetson walked over to the group standing by the van. He had an athletic but hungry-looking bloodhound held on a short-chain leash. The bloodhound growled at the driver and guard. The man yanked the dog's chain.

'Quit it, Washington. You're growling at the wrong men,' he said. 'Growl at them niggers, if you've got to growl at anyone. That's who you'll be eating.'

The driver laughed; the guard continued to sneer.

'So, boys, eight hundred dollars a nigger we cleared last year on The Farm, near enough. You and your sheriff are both standing to make a fancy little pot come Christmas if these niggers come good.' The man finally looked Booya and Alf up and down.

'That big nigger there got hisself a bust ankle, boss,' the driver said.

'So I see,' the man replied. 'And a bust wrist. What've you brung me!'

'That there on his hands ain't his blood, far's I know.' The driver removed his hat and wiped his sweaty brow.

'That right?' the man asked. 'He good to work?'

'Look at the size of him! Soon as he's fixed, he'll make number one squad, for sure.'

'You want to be right, or else Washington here'll get a big old pile of bones to chew on, huh, boy?' The dog barked in agreement. 'That's right! But I don't know what you're laughing at,' he said to the driver. 'You boys ain't going to get paid if that happens.'

The driver shrugged. 'The sheriff sorted it all out with Long-Chain, boss. We've got to get back – just as soon as I piss in them bushes, that is.'

'Come with me, niggers,' said the man. 'I'll show ya to your cage.' He turned and began to walk towards the barracks. Washington stared at Booya. The man jerked the leash and the dog jumped to his side.

'Have fun, boys,' Booya heard the driver call out.

Biting his dry tongue, his mind and body aching, Booya hobbled forward. Alf walked close by his side. If he was found to be useless, Alf knew that Booya would spend the rest of his short days floating face down in a swamp.

It was bright and clean inside The Cage. Inside the door was a foyer, separated from the dormitory beyond it by thick floor-to-ceiling bars. A door in the bars was standing open. There were two-tier bunks stacked along both walls and single bunks in two rows along the centre. At the foot of each alternate bunk was a standing wooden cupboard, alternating with low chests – a shared wardrobe for each pair of beds and a drawer in each chest per man. A bright white sheet was laid at the foot of each bed, as clean as could be seen anywhere in the State, folded to perfection. Panelled lighting in the suspended ceiling lit the long, wide room. In the harsh light, Booya noticed that all of the low chests had a Bible sitting atop.

The man pointed at a bunk against the outer wall, third in from the near-end of the room. 'You, top,' he pointed a finger at Alf. 'Big man, you're bottom.'

Washington barked. The man pulled him to heel.

'From now on you are officially prisoners of the State. But, in here, you're my slaves. You do as I say. You listen to me, you get privileges in return. You think for yourself, or try to escape, you end up with buck shot inside of your guts. And you're dog meat for Washington here.

'Your feet want to be touching the floor as soon as the whistle sounds in the morning. See how these beds is made? That's how you do, before leaving for work. You work the fields or the woods – hoes or axes – dark-to-dark. Come back here, feed yourself, do whatever it is niggers do. Dirty your pillow with field dirt and you clean it then and there and spend the night with a wet pillow. You've got a responsibility to keep yourself clean, otherwise you'll be scrubbed with yard brushes and dried with a whip. Spit on the floor, I'll make you lick the whole place clean, twice over.' He pointed to the end of the room. 'Showers and shitters in the rear of The Cage. If you've got to piss in the night, you holler "Alley Boss", wait 'til whoever's on duty to give you the word. Until he says so, your bladder stays full.

'I'm the picket boss. You call me Sir and Boss. You do as I say, and as your captain and sergeant says. You move where the trusty-shooters tell you to. And we'll all get along just fine. My advice is to not ever find out what happens if you don't do as you're told. Wait here.'

The picket boss walked through the bars and out through the front door by which they had entered. In his absence, Booya and Alf said not a word to each other. Within a moment, he returned with striped overalls piled in his hands. Washington's chain clinked as he strode towards them.

'Change into your stripes and give me your clothes. Don't be telling me they don't fit 'cause, believe me, they fit. You.' The picket boss threw a pack of bandages to Booya. A tube of anti-infection cream fell from the bandages, onto the floor. 'Fix yourself up. I ain't your nurse maid. Tomorrow morning you're on the squad, same as everyone else.'

'Boss?' Booya was holding the overalls and pack of bandages in his arms; even the weight of those felt too much to bear.

'What's it, nigger? Mighty soon to be arksing questions. But I guess I'll allow you one, seeing as you ain't got the rules in your big head yet.'

'I ain't done nothing, Boss. I was wrongly accused.'

'*Boo, man . . .*' Alf whispered.

'We both was,' Booya continued. 'Alf and me. Ain't they someone we –'

'I've got to say that that's a good question, right there.' The picket boss grinned, baring his tobacco-stained teeth. 'I almost forgot.'

He walked to the end of the room, into the barred foyer, and returned with a four-foot length of broad leather, swinging it as he and Washington strutted back towards them.

'Sit!' he instructed Washington.

Washington lowered his hind to the floor, never relinquishing his stare from the prisoners. The picket boss slapped the long length of leather against his hand. The harsh sound of the slap echoed around the empty dormitory. Washington turned his head, watching.

'Meet The Bat. Or Black Annie, as I know you niggers *affectionately* call it.'

Booya noticed that holes had been drilled through the end that the picket boss had slapped against his palm. They didn't look like belt-extension holes – unless this belt belonged to a twenty-five foot tall giant. The picket boss again slapped the leather against his palm, answered by the striking sound.

'This is the answer to any questions like that that you might have. You can arkse The Bat as many questions as you've got bothering you. But this is the only answer you're ever going to get. And, believe me, she's always happy to answer.' The picket boss narrowed his eyes, stroking a thumb over the Bat. 'You want to arkse again, nigger?'

Booya shook his head.

'That's right; you don't. Go tell it to Roosevelt; see if he gives a shit less. Best thing to be thinking is how quick you can work a hoe; how hard you can swing a axe. In the field you'll find all the answers to any questions you've got. Just remember that The Bat – Black Annie, whatever you want to call it – is always keen as a dung beetle is for shit to give you a lecture.

'Both your asses are mine for the rest of your days – want to tell you that now, just so you understand and don't fool yourself thinking any different. Your life means nothing except the amount of work y'all do out in the fields. Keep your head down and we all live our lives as one big happy family.' The picket boss grinned, a sneer rising on one side of his lips. 'Any questions?'

Silence answered him.

The big new inmate looked long at the leather strip and then looked up at the picket boss.

'That's what I thunk.'

2

The turnkey – a man so fat that his guts hung out over his belt, looking half-roasted from the sun, somewhere between white and swine – dragged his key along the bars at the end of The Cage. 'Plough squad one fetching home, Boss,' he hollered, his voice high and sweet, belying his size. If hogs could talk perhaps that's how they would sound.

The picket boss was dozing with his feet propped up on a chair, his Stetson covering his eyes. 'Call 'em in,' he murmured beneath his hat.

The turnkey walked out of the door, his wheeze trailing behind him.

Booya had heard the sound of the returning men from a long way off, the pounding of feet and low sound of chanted song. He leaned up on an arm, half-curious, half wanting to hide. A few minutes later, the turnkey returned. He leaned on the doorjamb, sweating like boiled meat.

'Plough squad . . . number two, Boss,' he squealed between laboured breaths.

'That's it, call 'em in,' the picket boss replied.

The turnkey rolled outside. After unlocking The Cage, the picket boss followed him.

Over the next fifteen minutes, Booya heard the routine repeated. Everything would begin to quieten, and then that sound of pounding feet, the low hum of voices, a far-off whinny of a horse, the turnkey hollering and the picket boss confirming. He heard drumming feet and the clattering of metal against metal as the men from the next-door barracks were called home.

They had been plough squad five.

And then came the sound of pounding feet, closer, spinning the world on its axis.

'Sounds like this is us, Boo. Heh-heh-heh.'

'Plough squad . . . six, Boss,' the turnkey wheezed.

'We're open,' the picket boss replied. 'Let 'em come straight.'

Like an approaching storm, it was obvious that some of the squad had now arrived outside The Cage. There was clanging in the tin water-troughs, the low hubbub of activity building; laughing, lots of sighing and a few moans. The first convicts began to enter The Cage.

'Catch you one day, Chase,' said the second man who walked in.

'If you tie my ankles together, Zona, p'raps you will.'

Zona hacked a laugh. 'When you's getting a itchy leg from rope burn, just remember it was you what give me the idea.'

'Was your sister what give me the idea of tying feet together.' Chase slapped a filthy hand to his head. 'Shit! Just 'membered: when I was sent down the river I clear forgot to untie the bitch. Sorry, man.'

'When I tie your jaw closed maybe I forgets to untie you.'

They headed for their separate bunks and began to get undressed, dropping their stripes to their feet. Other men were entering the building: talking, joking, undressing and speeding to the showers. None of them had yet noticed their new fellow inmates.

Booya saw how all the men were covered head-to-foot in dirt, reminding him of the white men from the travelling minstrelsy shows who painted themselves and sang like black men. White eyes peered from faces plastered in sweat and dust, even the eyelashes balancing a plateau of dirt. It was as if the earth had risen in the form of a man. Until they stripped off their clothes, sweat-covered from the ears to the tips of the toe.

Throughout the day, Booya had guessed that the other inmates would appear as he felt: desperate, inconsolably sad, beaten into resignation. But from within the caked faces, all pairs of white teeth that he saw were gleaming. They joked, slapping one another's backs, smiling over the bellowing exchanges. Although some moaned over their aches, these men weren't acting like prisoners at all.

Booya's bunk was shaking, and not just from his heart hammering in his chest. He tried to turn around, but it wasn't easy whilst being shaken. Moreover, he could do without his ankle being torn about. Above him, Alf was obviously enjoying the ride. *Heh-heh-heh.*

'This weren't a engaged bunk when we leave for the field this mo'nin,' a voice said, continuing to shake the bunk.

'Hey, quit it!' Booya said, his ankle screaming. Applying light pressure to the bandages, he looked up at a set of big white teeth and brown eyes. When the shaking did stop, it became a dirty brown face with a smile.

'Ooooo,' the smiling man cooed. 'Got a big ol' yellow gal, do we?'

Around the barracks, the words received a loud chorus of laughter. Booya looked around the room in a daze. Strange faces all staring at him; hardened faces broken into laughter. His head, or the room, was spinning. In pain, he felt like crying. He felt like hopping away and hiding. Closing his eyes, head in hands, he took himself back to the orchard in Mister Henry's grounds, sitting amongst the fruit trees. Everything was so simple then. What if life had never changed? If he never removed his hands from his face perhaps he could stay there forever. He could feel the rapid pulse of his heart beating through his forehead. Electrical pulses rippled behind his eyes, tickling his fingers. His palms wet, Booya lifted his head.

However distant, he could still hear the sound of activity, but nothing more was being directed towards him. The sound of laughter had slowly died way. Grimacing, he moved his ankle.

'Ah shit, man.' A hand appeared on the bed beside him. 'Sorry, man. I didn't realise that you . . . Ah shit, I's sorry. Wouldn't done it if I knowed. Ouch!'

Not looking up, Booya examined the thick yellow-and-red mess beneath the bandage. Layer-by-layer, he could see where the skin had worn through.

'The bracelet done that on the way up in here?'

'Uh-huh.' Booya breathed in sharply through his teeth. He reached for the anti-infection cream and smeared it on thickly – it stung like an attack by a platoon of red wasps – before resealing the bandages. Instantly, the cooling relief of the cream replaced the stinging sensation.

'Man, that looks sorer'n hell!'

'Yeah,' Booya replied, trying to repair the smouldering bridge as well as his ankle. 'Say that's 'bout what it is.'

The pursed lips and gentle, concerned eyes beneath the lowered brow offered genuine regret. There were boulders of dirt in the convict's tear ducts. His eyelashes were blond with dust. Beneath the dirt, Booya could see the wispy shadow of a moustache above the man's thick lips. Though he was a boy, really – he could be the fourth member of The Free Riders.

'Shit, I feel bad, man,' he said.

'Really, it's okay.'

'You know,' the boy plonked down beside Booya on the bunk, a sift of dust landing on his white sheets, 'they call me Two Cell. Know why?' Booya shook his head. 'They say I only got two brain cells. Say that I don't even work them two what I got hard 'nough. See, here we all got nicknames we's known by. Ain't none of us here knowed by the name our mama give us.'

'That right?' Booya looked around the roomful of strangers.

'Yep. Everone here; and everone come and gone 'fore now. Tell you a few them: see that nigger there with the whip scars on his back? He called Rump Steak, or just Rump. Know why? Look at his big naked ass. Bigger'n a cow! The nigger there with the big shoulders, he's Ox, on account of how strong he is. Ox is number one in our plough squad. Bari, nigger next to him, 'pparently they's a word called "baritone". Bari sings in this big deep voice when we's out on the squad, so he's Bari. Meatyore – that other big nigger over there – he pounds the earth to pieces like them rocks what come from space.'

Two Cell examined the side of Booya's face. 'I ain't never named none a them, understand? I just got to learning what they is and what they's standing for. Follow?

'Rabbit always hopping round like a crazy buck with the rabies. Stub Toe, he a clumsy nigger. Big Lip . . .' Two Cell turned to Booya, a serious expression on his face. 'Need me to explain that name?'

'I get it,' Booya answered, managing to smile.

Two Cell continued pointing out inmates, their nicknames and the reasons behind them – most of them obvious. There was Pop Eye: he had bulbous popping eyes. Double Span: his sentence was twenty years – two hand spans. Cliff Top had apparently lived forever on the edge of death. Steamie Horn had a voice that sounded like the horn on a steamboat. Tied Eye was cross-eyed – 'They got a mind of they own, them freak eyes, always pointing whatever direction they is; over your shoulder when he's looking direct at you!' Mauler liked to fight; he was inside for repeatedly assaulting civilians. Vicksburg came from Vicksburg. Patch Hair: 'You see that other naked nigger over there, towelling his sack? See how the hair on his chest is in patches? See him turn, his back just the same?' Hygiene was considered absolutely disgusting, even amongst prisoners. Clod Ear was as deaf as a piece of earth. Hind was as pretty as a mule's ass – at the moment that Two Cell pointed Hind out to Booya, Hind smiled. 'See? Even when he smiling it looks like a mule bending over and showing you his guts through his asshole,' Two Cell pointed out, leaning into Booya.

'That naked nigger coming from the shower: that's Chase. He always first out to the fields and first back to The Cage. Say that no one can catch him. So far, he right! Zona, behind him: he's from Arizona.

'Just one more nigger I wanna show to you. This little nigger with his head in his hands. That's Li'l Big Heart. Right now he having a hard time. Misses his ma and his li'l gal. He only in for stealing a hog. Stealed the wrong man's hog, is all. Stupid li'l nigger stealed one from a judge hisself! Even I know you don't steal but a piece of sunlight from a judge. *Everone* know that. He was only hungry, trying to feed his family and his li'l gal's family. Was more'n a forty pound hog what he stealed. Judge say that when he can afford to pay back the hog he'll let him out The Farm. This is it, see: judge wants sixteen dollars for the pig – which even that is way too much. But that ain't it all: Li'l Big's ordered to pay eighteen dollars court cost; twenty-five dollars judge fee; ten-fifty fee for the officer what catched him. Even three dollars forty jail fee! They's more costs than that, but that's the most of 'em. In squad six, we get paid seventy cents a day for working in the fields – or slaving, as we like to say; the guards liking to hear us say. Nigger can make more, but we's on basic – that's the word: basic, right? They tole you how much they be charging for boarding here?'

'No, man.' Booya was watching Li'l Big Heart's skinny rib cage lifting up and down. He couldn't be sure, but Booya thought he was sobbing.

'Sixty cents *a day*! I may be Two Cell, but even a dumb shit nigger like me know that seventy less sixty ever day don't add up to no hog and all them costs in a lifetime. See, whitey thinks that it's a privilege for a nigger to be banged up here. That we ain't got nothing better to do; like we's *wanting* to be in here. I don't know, for some niggers I guess they does. But how's Li'l Big ever gonna get free of The Farm, now that he in? Skinny nigger like him ain't gonna never make it to the real earning squads. I know the answer to how that li'l nigger's leaving the pen: if he dead. Or he ain't never gonna leave 'til they earned ten thousand bucks off his skinny ass, however much that is, poor li'l nigger. He only wants to go home. Judge know 'cause of his size he ain't *never* gonna be on the number one squad making dollars. Judge knows a li'l nigger like that would never make it home in a hand of years. Did you know that any white man catched doing the same hog rustling gets hisself ninety days in the jailhouse?'

'How'd he get his name?' Booya asked. 'Li'l Big Heart.'

'Huh? Li'l Big Heart? First day he was in the field he rescued a mole from beneath a hoe blade 'bout to come down on it. He fetched a whipping for disrupting the line, but not 'til that mole he finded was safe. That's his big heart. Happy to fetch a whipping since then, too, to save whatever animal's in danger. And Li'l 'cause he's only a li'l nigger.'

'How long's he been here for so far?' Booya asked, noticing how tiny Li'l Big Heart really was. His legs not yet grown into his knees; the bones in his arms thicker than the muscles.

'Year?' Two Cell replied. 'Year'n half? Something like that. For stealing a hog to feed his starving people. And the hog got away from him! Most crazy part of his story. It's tole that the judge got the same hog back unhurt. But like I say, man, he struggling now. He don't like doing the field work more than anyone I ever seen. He falls to his knees, like, once ever hour, just 'cause his li'l legs can't take the strain of the work and the sun. Cut back his pay more'n any other convict I ever see. You hear a li'l whimpering at night: that's Li'l Big crying for his family and his li'l gal. Poor li'l nigger, Li'l Big. Tears up the heart of even the biggest men in here. But not the guards. Never them. And 'specially not our sergeant.

'See how Ox puts his hand on Li'l Big's shoulder, whispering to him? Even Ox ain't gonna get between Li'l Big Heart and sergeant. Not even Mauler's dumb enough to do that.'

They sat on Booya's bunk and watched Li'l Big Heart sitting in his shorts, barely able to lift his head from his bony hands. Ox's hand covered his shoulder like a water lily over a raindrop.

'Hey, man,' said a long, thin face with an extended chin from a few bunks up, pulling a shirt over his head. 'What you in for then?'

'He's Corn Never right there,' Two Cell said loud enough for everyone around to hear.

Booya noticed how the prisoners were already grinning. 'How come Corn Never?' he asked, ignoring Corn Never's question.

Already laughing above them, it was obvious that Alf understood.

'His full name's Corn Never Been Shucked!' Two Cell replied.

Everyone – including Booya and Corn Never – laughed along.

'Gonna tell what you's in for?' Corn Never asked again. 'You gotta, man.'

'He obsessed with knowing what ever new nigger's slammed for,' Two Cell whispered.

Looking at Booya, it was quite obvious that most of the convicts were interested.

'Didn't do nothing,' Booya answered, picking at his bandaged hand.

Even Alf laughed when he said that.

'Me too,' someone called out.

'I ain't never done nothing, neither!' another yelled.

'I mean it, man,' Booya appealed to those listening. 'I ain't done nothing wrong.'

'How 'bout you?' Corn Never asked chuckling Alf. 'What nothing was you accused of not having done.'

'Guess I done as much of nothing as Boo down there,' Alf answered. 'But what we is accused of was killing a man. Heh-heh-heh. A *white* man.'

Convicts around them whistled and called for air. Two Cell stood up from the bunk so that he could see Alf tell their tale. He sat down on an opposite bunk, spreading more field dust on to someone else's sheets.

'Really. We ain't done what they say,' Alf continued. 'Was just near 'nough for them to say we done it. Big man down there, he was just sleeping nearby and they say he done it. Me, I was walking down the road and they say I done it, too. Heh-heh-heh.'

'How long they give you?' Corn Never asked with a keen smile.

Everyone around was watching Alf; no one else was smiling anymore.

'Don't know,' Alf answered. 'So I can't tell.'

The eyes were all wide, looking from Alf to Booya.

'You niggers never went to no trial, man?' asked one man, introduced by Two Cell as Pop Eye, staring at Alf and the ceiling above his head at once. 'Not gived you no sentence?'

'Nuh-uh,' Alf replied. 'We was carted away in the night. And some of this morning. Heh!'

'Shit, man,' Bari boomed. 'Know what that means, don't you?'

'Yeah,' Alf said. 'Heh!'

The men who had been listening to Alf's story began to go about their business of drying and dressing, or undressing. It was clear that their story had touched a nerve in The Cage. Booya had heard men in the city boasting of the length of their jail sentence as if it was something to measure their manhood by. And here they had been smiling and joking until they heard Alf's testimony. Being reminded of what his life was now, Booya's mood sunk to depths deeper than he had ever known.

With a sigh, Two Cell repeated what the picket boss had told him and Alf: 'Don't happen often without no judge involved, but it happens. Sorry it happened to you, man. You might as well believe you don't exist no more. Welcome to The Cage.'

Turning away, Two Cell started to undress.

Booya could only sit on his bunk, transfixed on Li'l Big Heart. He couldn't recall the name of the burly convict who came by and discreetly whispered to him, 'You wanna make sure that dirt's gone from off your sheets, nigger. Just saying.'

3

Still dark outside, Booya was already awake when the steam whistle blew. The dormitory quickly came to life. Sitting on the edge of the bunk, he tentatively lifted his bandage. In the night his ankle had continued to weep a clear liquid. In places the clotted scabs broke away. Two Cell was kneeling next to him, inspecting the damage with a pained expression.

'Should a gone to the pen hospital and gotten that seen to,' he said. 'Shit, man, that's the worsest one I ever seed!'

'Boss just give me the bandage and the cream and say to fix myself up,' Booya replied.

Two Cell drew his lips together and grimaced. 'You gonna get used to life on The Farm pretty quick, man. But if you get a infection in that, you tell Boss straight off. Ain't gonna be no good to him if you only got one leg to stand on, hear me? They got enough yellow gals in the laundry room already. No doubt he'll give you a little talk 'bout Black Annie, but a injured nigger – 'specially one big as you is – is fighting against his interest. Ever heared 'bout niggers knocking-a-Joe, like most them laundry room niggers done?'

Standing, towering over Two Cell, Booya shook his head.

'Knocking-a-Joe's when a nigger gets so tired of working in the fields that he'll do anything he can to get outta working. Takes a hoe or a axe to hisself and cut off his own fingers and toes; even a foot or hand! Make sure he ain't never going back out there. Escaping The Farm without escaping, know I'm saying? Ain't never gonna be able to work out in the fields again. If not in the laundry room – staying back and cleaning sheets – they get a job in the kitchen. It's hot in there, but it gets them out the heat a the sun.

'If you think you know how hot Ol' Hannah can burn, think again, brother. Today you'll see for yourself how bad God can be on a nigger. See, God's a white man: that's what I come to understand. That's why they all got hats and we get the diseases. If the mean bastard ain't already sended you to be fixed up, Boss say you gotta work out today?'

'Uh-huh.' With his foot on the bed, Booya added some cream and resealed the bandage. The cream wasn't so soothing this morning.

*

In the gloomy darkness of the predawn, six armed men on horseback were waiting outside the low, split-rail fence that enclosed the barrack's yard. Eager to run, the horses were kicking up dust, eyes wild as the riders pulled the reigns to steady them. The mounted men were all wearing Stetsons; six images of one of the two men who had haunted Booya's oldest nightmares.

A breakfast of biscuits, syrup and coffee awaited the convicts on a table in the yard. Booya had forgotten about eating and drinking all together. Nothing had passed his lips since . . . he couldn't remember when. Probably since drinking perfectly distilled whisky at Walter Carini's house frolic. Eating the prison food was a sweet and bitter experience, almost confirming that this was his family now. Before Booya knew what was happening, the convicts left their cups and broke into a run, chased from the yard by the men on horses; hooves pounding the earth to the side of the running men and driving behind them.

'Git, git, git,' they yelled from their snarling horses, yanking the reigns to encourage the stomping hooves.

Booya could only limp, dragging his injured ankle to the side as he hopped along, feeling the liquid oozing out of the cracked scabs. Watching Chase speeding away, Booya was attempting to run with the rear of the pack. Their feet skimming over the dirt, it looked as though those trying to keep up with Chase were having fun.

Glancing to his side, Booya saw the fierce determination on Li'l Big Heart's face, his short and bony legs pumping as hard as they could. The huge frame of Ox jogged next to him, a barrier between the fearsome, snarling horse and the tiny boy.

'C'mon, Li'l Big,' Ox encouraged. 'Keep on going, li'l brother. Doing *good*.'

Just in front of Booya, Alf was cackling wildly.

'You shut your noise, motherfucker,' yelled a man riding beside him, cracking his whip in the air. 'Or you'll fetch a whipping soon's we're at the field.'

Alf cackled with glee. The man spat a jet of tobacco directly in Alf's ear. After that, Alf didn't laugh so much. But he grinned like a maniac, just the same.

The boughs of the faraway trees on the horizon were still holding down the morning sun. Even so, the heat of running through the humidity of the early dawn was making Booya sweat.

'Don't fall, man,' Two Cell advised. 'Whatever you do, don't do that.'

Turning to look at Two Cell, Booya stumbled on a rock. Grabbing Booya's arm, Two Cell helped him to regain his balance.

'Sorry, man. But I's just warning 'cause that's what theses Cholleys want you to do. It's all just a game to them; they loves to see a nigger in pain. That's what they think they real job is, torturing us niggers. They getting paid to do what they love!'

With Ox encouraging Li'l Big, and the guards hollering all kinds of abuse and obscenities at them, Booya hobbled on until they arrived at their destination. The inmates fell directly into line, knowing their place of work on the near edge of a field littered with weeds and grasses. Except for the clattering of hoes and the heavy breathing after the run, a silence fell over the line. Holding the splintered shaft, Booya looked along the line.

'See my gleaming blade,' Bari called out in a voice as deep as thunder.

Every squad member lifted his hoe. Bari's voice was only a distant peal of thunder when the combined voices of the squad answered mightily:

'*Bring it down. Bring it down.*'

The hoes clicked against rocks and stones, in unison lifting and digging the earth. Reflected light flashed along the row and back again.

'Say, see my gleaming blade.'

'*Bring it down. Bring it down.*'

The singing of the men began to overlap Bari's calls, skilfully in rhythm with the clinking of hoes.

'When God me made.'

'*I was just a babe; was just a babe.*'

'Say I'll never be no slave.'

'*'Til I'm resting in my grave; resting in the grave.*'

'Say, see my gleaming blade.'

'*Bring it down. Bring it down . . .*'

The sound of field song that Booya could still remember from his youth was of men separated by plants, working alone together, answering the calls they heard like a tide lapping the shore. The singing of the convicts was a tidal wave crashing time and again. Heartening him, Booya could even hear Li'l Big Heart singing in as deep a voice as he could muster. Working next to Booya,

Two Cell had a pleasant singing voice and was in tune with the rest, but kept stumbling over his tongue in trying to repeat the line. But it slowed his hoe down none.

'See the sheriff riding.'

'Keep my head down. Keep my head down.'

'Say see the sheriff riding.'

'Keep my head down. Keep my head down.'

'Looking for someone to blame.'

'Tied rope by his side; rope by his side.'

'What the spirit's been a-saying.'

'Hang me high. Hang me way up high.'

Mind-weary from his sleepless night, Booya was desperate to join in with the singing. Recognising the pattern, he repeated every second echo with the convicts. Hoes clinking in time as the magical wink of the sun reflected, playing alone on stage was nothing compared to this. Work came second to the chorus; led by Bari, it was all about keeping pace with the next man. It did not pass Booya's notice that the songs he had heard sung in his youth were of other men's lives, telling of their hardships and troubles. This was the very heart of the blues. For the first time since arriving on The Farm he didn't feel alone.

Before he noticed that the sun had climbed upon their shoulder, they stopped for lunch. The men dropped their hoes where they stood and made tracks to a white man on the nearest path, leaning against a wagon, his mule patiently waiting to draw the wagon on to the next squad along.

The water provided was warm, but welcome. But the lunch was without doubt the most revolting that Booya had ever laid his eyes upon. The corn bread was dry and crumbly, as tasteless as a stick; the beans, peas and sweet potatoes were raw as rocks; and the salted meat – whatever meat it was supposed to be – was discoloured and crawling with bugs. Until he saw some of the others chewing on it, Booya wasn't sure if he was supposed to eat it at all. He tried some corn bread and it dried his mouth – there was no way that he could work out here until sundown with a dry mouth. Leaving the bread and meat, he sucked on beans and peas until they had softened enough to swallow.

Seeing Li'l Big slumped in a drainage ditch, trying to shade his head from the sun, Ox sheltering him as best he could and feeding him sips of water, was a desperately stark reminder to Booya of where he was. Looking enviously at the Stetson on the head of the man perched upon a horse who had remained with them throughout the morning, stalking the line, Booya wished that he had Roots' hat.

With work and singing to focus on, Booya had been able to concentrate on something other than Labella and the baby, Mammy and Paw. Booya's troubles, forgotten for that morning, came rushing along the road to greet him.

Two Cell slumped down next to him. "Kay, man?"

'Yeah,' Booya answered. He took a sip of the warm water.

With the sound of the chorus temporarily resting, the day was quiet and tranquil. Two Cell had been right about 'Ol' Hannah'. Booya noticed that the black men with rifles who had watched over them from a close distance all morning hadn't taken a break. They were patrolling along the ranks, their eyes black and cold. Unlike the mounted guard, these men were wearing the same convict stripes – though the lines of their stripes vertical – but with a rifle as their hoe.

Booya nodded towards them. 'Who they?'

'They trusty-shooters,' Two Cell replied, spraying corn bread. 'They convicts, just like you and me, but they been specially selected to guard us. Notice how they stand off from us, never getting close? Look in the dirt down there just past Li'l Big and Ox, and over behind us to the other side, past Hind's big ass. Each time we stop, they draw a line: that's the gun line. Don't cross that, man. Don't even get near. All they waiting for is a excuse to unload they rifle. You cross the gun line, they say you's trying to escape. You even get near it . . . Man, I see it happen! They's just hoping, *willing* for us to step over that line. See, if a trusty-shooter guns down a convict that they say was aiming to escape they get a pardon from the governor. Don't matter if we is truly trying to escape or just walking off our aches and pains. Don't matter to a trusty. Or the governor, neither.

'You need to piss, just holler "Getting out, shoot." They might let you. Trusties, they mostly is just as worse as the sergeants and the captains – captains is the ones what ride us out to the field. No way none a them is as bad as the sergeant we got, though. He quiet today, up they on his horse.'

They both looked towards the tree that the sergeant was sheltering beneath, away from the convicts, standing as still as the cloudless sky.

'No one on Earth is worse a man than him. It's a rare day when he stays quiet all day long. It's like he's thought a something bad for us, but is wondering how to make it worser.

'The captains like to beat down niggers just for fun. But trusty, he wins his freedom back by stealing another nigger's whole life from him. The sergeant: he's the devil's own.'

'What 'bout them, coming along with the dogs?'

'Them's the trusty dog boys. Ain't as bad as a trusty, but they business is catching niggers, just the same. Telling you, man, escaping The Farm is impossible. Don't even be thinking 'bout it. Ain't gonna happen. Even though they all act like sergeant's pet, you ever get selected to be a trusty you's as dead on the outside as we is on the inside. Niggers don't take kind to other niggers shooting down they own kind for they freedom. Just keep your head down. Don't never give up on the idea you might get out one day – if that's what it takes to keep you going – but don't dream too far ahead of yourself.'

'My girl . . .' The words stuck in Booya's throat. He had thought about Labella so much, but saying her name on The Farm whilst wearing the ring-arounds was somehow like cheating on her. If there was only some way that he could just see her, a picture, her likeness in a passing cloud, *anything*. In his mind's eye, he could picture her on that first day in the store: half-stooped, stacking shelves; himself stunned to a pause. He had got his girl eventually. He had lost her, won her back; almost lost her again, been accepted back. And then she had been stolen from him; him from her.

Two Cell put a hand on Booya's shoulder and rubbed. 'Take time, man,' he said. 'You feel you gotta talk, then talk. I 'member what it was like when I's first slammed.'

Booya looked out over the field, at the earth they had ploughed that morning, the knee-high scrub awaiting them, the trees in the far distance, the sun burning a hole through the rich blue sky. He watched crows hopping over the clods of earth they had turned, their fearsome eyes scouring the dirt.

Booya turned to face Two Cell. 'Can I ax what you in for?'

'You mean Corn Never ain't tole you yet? Damn! Nah. I see a fight happening one day. Was two niggers beating on a white man. Niggers say whitey's pa had kicked them off his land for being lazy niggers. This whitey was only a kid, little and sappy and all. I went over to get them to stop but they was wild with liquor; they eyes like a coyote with rabies. If I never pulled my blade, I kept guessing with myself after I was catched . . .' Two Cell slapped his thighs. 'Maybe you be talking with one them now, 'stead of me!

'If I just leave them to kill that white boy – looking as that's what they was doing – or if one them niggers hadn't fell down dead . . . See, quick as they come at me, I sticked them both. Judge taked less than ten minutes to find me guilty of murder and attempting to murder. White boy disappeared and never did come forward to tell it like it was.' Two Cell sighed. 'Don't see why a white judge got any business sentencing a nigger for sticking a nigger anyways. Well, two niggers.

'Judge give me a double fan and a fan: fifteen year.' Two Cell drummed his hands on his legs. 'But I done half that already. Ain't got no doubt I is gonna see my days.' Two Cell saw Booya hang his head. 'Sorry, man, don't mean to be . . . Hey, you was saying 'bout your girl. If you still wanna say . . .'

Booya breathed in the dusty air.

'The day that The Law accuse me, I just find out I was gonna be a daddy. Just went out for one celebrating drink, my girl staying home . . .' Picturing Labella smiling in the doorway of their new home, him turning and chasing after Tiger, Booya could feel the tears building in his eyes. 'I can't miss that, man. She don't even know I is here. Probably thinking I's dead . . . Had a dream last night 'bout my unborn boy. Was dreaming I was in Mister H –'

'Lunch done, six squad,' a trusty-shooter called along the line of convicts. 'Back to work.'

'Gotta piss, shoot,' Tied Eye called, hand in the air.

'Piss your pants.'

Some of the men laughed, even as they glared at the trusty.

In the afternoon the work seemed harder. Over the lunch break Booya had stiffened up. His shoulders were aching. His hand and wrist were hurting. And the sweat seeping over and into his raw ankles stung the wounds with a new-found aggression. Just standing on the injured ankle was agony. In spite of the glorious song, the first hour passed as slowly as the morning had gone quickly.

In struggling, Booya could see that he was not alone. Li'l Big Heart was hardly able to lift his hoe from the soil. It waved around; it stuck and dragged. Ox continually whispered encouragement to the tiny figure next to him. Booya sneaked a glance at Li'l Big: his legs were barely able to hold his frail little body erect; his head was lolling around sleepily. Booya had been awake to witness how sparsely Li'l Big had slept.

'Slacking on the line!' a hoarse-voiced trusty-shooter yelled. 'Pick up your hoe or have pay held, convict.'

Ox glared at the trusty-shooter with a hatred deeper than Booya had ever witnessed in another black man's eyes.

'Keep on going, Li'l Big,' Ox said. 'Just keep pace. Don't let them beat you, brother.'

Li'l Big moaned. 'Hannah . . .' he mumbled through his cracked lips.

For a few more moments he continued to work, his hoe bouncing on rocks and slipping over the earth. When Booya saw Li'l Big's eyes roll he knew what was to come next. Lil' Big Heart fainted, first to his knees and then face down in the earth.

'Li'l Big!' Ox yelled.

'Get away from him convict,' the trusty-shooter shouted, approaching with his rifle aimed at Ox.

Ox gently slapped Li'l Big's face. 'C'mon, brother.'

'Away from him, nigger,' the trusty said. Ox looked up at him like a tiger protecting his feed.

'He fainted clean away. Got sunstroke. He *needs* shade.'

'Get away from him now or I shoot.' Rolling his shoulders, the trusty-shooter sighted his crow-like eyes along the barrel.

Ox looked down at Li'l Big's seemingly lifeless body, the fainted boy's mouth open. He put his hand over the thin rise of Li'l Big's chest. 'You'll be okay, li'l brother.' Sparing another hateful glare for the trusty, slowly Ox moved away.

The trusty approached Li'l Big. 'Stand away from the boy, convict.'

Ox did as he was told, spitting, 'Judas, nigger,' at the trusty.

The trusty grinned. He took his eyes from Ox, picked up one of Li'l Big Heart's bony legs and began to drag him away from the line.

Perhaps it was the advance of his huge shadow that gave him away. But if Ox hadn't yelled before he went for the trusty-shooter he might have covered the ground in time. The trusty swung round and, in one movement, landed the butt of the rifle square on Ox's snarling jaw. The ground shook as Ox landed, turning clods of earth to dust.

'Driver!' the trusty yelled. 'Two niggers down!' He picked up Li'l Big Heart's leg and quickly dragged him over the rocks and earth and out of the field, the rifle hanging from his shoulder.

On his huge black stallion, the sergeant was already pounding along the cracked, dry path, noisy as an approaching freight train. Rocks scattered from the horse's hooves, striding as if carrying the Galloping Hessian from the depths, leaves falling from the bushes as it brushed past. Standing in the stirrups, the sergeant's hand was at his hip. 'Get back to work, convicts,' he yelled along the line.

With his back to the action, Booya tried to glance beneath his armpit to see what was happening. He could only see the legs of the stallion and Ox groggily rubbing his chin in its shadow, leaning on one elbow in a pile of dug weeds.

'You're going in the sweatbox 'til the sun goes down, nigger,' the sergeant said to Ox. 'Get up. Try anything else and next time you'll be dead. Get up, lazy nigger.'

Standing and watching, in the near vicinity no one had sung a word since Li'l Big Heart had fainted. Along the length of the line, the clink of hoes against stones absent, word passed of what had happened.

The sergeant turned in his saddle. For the first time, Booya saw his pockmarked face, the toothpick clicking against the gleaming white teeth.

'Get back to work all you lazy niggers!' the sergeant shouted. 'Else I'll have y'all in sweatboxes. Three to a box if I have to.'

Booya couldn't move. In the blazing heat, he was frozen.

Like a raptor, the sergeant locked his fierce eyes on Booya. 'Got something you want to say, nigger?'

The sergeant squinted his eyes, two shiny bullets. A glint within them shimmered as the sun reflected from the revolver on his hip. Beneath his hat, the diagonal scar across his forehead ploughed through the wrinkles. The stallion stomped its feet and jerked its huge head, baring its teeth and crying out as the sergeant yanked back the bridle. He was nearly on top of Booya.

'Tell me, nigger,' the sergeant said, 'are you stupid, lazy, or thinking of trying to make something?'

Nauseous, as if he might be sick at any moment, Booya could hardly breathe. Nose-to-nose with the stallion, he felt a snake rising in his throat, its tail squirming deep inside. He felt faint. Still frozen, he stared up at the pockmarked face. The mouth split into an evil grin, and there again were those gleaming white teeth, shinier than the head of an axe. The sergeant's hand was moving now to the revolver at his hip.

Booya's head continued to spin. He was sure that he wobbled upon his feet. The stallion lifted its feet and readjusted them on the earth, shifting from the tickling weeds beneath its hooves. The sergeant clicked the toothpick against his teeth and stretched his fingers as they hovered above the holster. His eyes narrowed as his grin widened.

Booya felt a hand pull at his shirtsleeve. It caught him, to stop him spinning off balance.

'*Work*, fool,' Two Cell growled through gritted teeth.

In the shadow of the sergeant and his horse, Booya worked furiously. No one in this length of the line was singing any longer. He was sure that at any moment he would hear the bang of the hammer on the revolver, a second before a bullet shattered his skull. His heart pounded in his ears. His eyes watered, trying to blink the image of that pockmarked face from his sight. An itched plagued deep within his eyebrow.

Eternity broke, and the shadow disappeared. The sun again lit upon the dry earth that Booya was turning.

'Man, you *crazy*?' Two Cell asked. 'Thunk you was dead, for sure. He the toughest sergeant on whole a The Farm. The one I tole you 'bout; *warn* you 'bout at lunch. Hates niggers. Hates whites. Son-of-a-bitch . . . hates . . . rabbits! Hates the sun and the moon; the sky and day and night. Man, he hates everthing what God maked. No, sir, Sergeant Helland ain't a cholley to mess with. He killed niggers in cold blood in front of a audience for less than what you just done. Not yet but one day on The Farm, could've swored you was dead.'

CHAPTER
ELEVEN

1

Finding Booya sitting in the shade of a tree, sucking grass, Alf sat down on the floor next to him. Sweat was pouring from Alf's face, over the violent violet boil on his wide nose and the white welts on his face. Wrinkling his nose to shake free a drip of sweat, he drew back his lips, baring his rotten teeth, and sniffed. On the Sunday breeze, Booya could smell puffs of foul, stale aroma steaming from him. Beneath the ancient boughs of the oak, he yanked a fresh piece of grass and began to suck.

Pulling up the legs of his pants, Alf began to chuckle. He had been skipping and cackling around the outfield, obviously with as much understanding of the baseball game as Booya had. Alf had fast become unpopular with his squad six teammates. When the ball had arrived at his feet for the third time, laughing, he had hurled it at the line of men waiting to swing the bat, rather than to a member of his own team. It was clearly an important and intense game to all of the six squads involved. The humour had worn thin for Alf when Mauler had chased him around the pitch, squared up to him, and pushed him on to his backside. Still, he had chuckled himself all the way over to Booya and lay down next to him on the grass, grinning up at the mighty boughs.

'Hear them saying Li'l Big's Ox's gal boy?' Alf asked, scratching his armpit as he watched the game. 'Not to his face, heh-heh.'

'Nah, man.' Booya could remember how helpless Li'l Big had looked, his tiny convulsing frame lying on top of his sheets after he was discharged from the infirmary with 'mild sunstroke'. His eyes had been closed, sweating so much that there was visible dampness around him on the sheets, but his body still jerking and jumping from shivers. Booya remembered thinking that it looked as though scampering demons were carrying him through an invisible waterfall. That was after he had seen Ox's black skin slapped as red as a summer rose; blisters on his back at the head of shapes like a snake's forked tongue. Booya now understood what the drilled holes in the Black Annie's business end were for. 'Corn Never tole me that Ox had a little brother who died, called Benjamin. Say that Ox looks out for Li'l Big 'cause he never could save Benjamin.'

'Yah.' Alf pulled out a clump of grass, chewed on it and swallowed. 'They just don't want Li'l Big slowing up the line, y'know? Ain't gonna have our pay cut 'cause of the weak baby.'

The two men sat in silence, watching the game, Booya still picturing how Li'l Big Heart couldn't even lift the water jug that he'd been sent with from the infirmary. Clod Ear was galloping round the outfield, approaching second base. A convict from squad three pinged the ball to the second baseman as Clod Ear slid in to the base. An argument ensued, until guards arrived to separate them. Clod Ear trudged back to the end of the batting line. Trusties roamed beyond the outfield, rifles in hand. Booya looked beyond them, past the flat landscape to the far, hazy horizon.

'You gonna go to The Tonk, man?' Alf asked, waking Booya from his reverie.

'Huh?'

'Tonk the Tonk,' Alf said, gyrating on the ground.

'Uh . . . don't know.' Booya frowned. 'What's The Tonk?'

'The Tonk House.' Alf was now thumping his mid-quarters up and down. 'Heh-heh-heh.'

Booya understood. 'Oh. Ha! Nah, man, don't think. Got a girl back home, remember?'

'Yeah . . . back *home*, man. Ain't here.'

'Yeah, but . . .' Booya curled his lip. 'Nah, man.'

'Your girl, she one them big-hip mamas?' Alf asked. 'Beautiful and black?'

'She's . . . just perfect!' Booya answered. 'She's like . . . like a sunflower: I tell her that. When she smiles it's like a sunflower opening up. She's the best day you ever had. A bright sun. A day by the river . . .' He bit his lips. 'I miss her, man.'

'Heh-heh, already guess that.'

Booya couldn't help but smile with Alf.

'In the Tonk, girls from the city come up and offer they services. So it ain't hardly like cheating! That's why the guards let us have womens in here: they think the promise of pussy's enough for us to give some more in the field. They pay the womens from our pay. Man, can't wait to go back to The Tonk and pay all I got! Heh-heh-heh.'

Alf had begun to gyrate again. For such a wasted-looking man he was surprisingly lithe.

'Serious though, don't need nothing more but one them girls from the city. Take it from me, man, it's some fine pussy, blacker'n a coal hole, heh-heh-heh.'

'Where's The Tonk place at?' Booya asked Alf, watching a passing bird.

'Heh-heh-heh. It takes a man to know a man and I is a man and knowed that you is a man, man. Heh-heh-heh.' Alf told Booya the directions to the little wooden shed with the tin roof. 'Can't miss it: smell the lingering pussy like you can smell where a fire's been at. I got the fire right here!'

Booya left Alf happily thumping in the dirt.

*

Alf had been right about smelling the girls from a way off; the sweet perfumed scents were drifting through the air like butterflies. It was Alf's taste in girls that could be questioned. It mattered not to Booya. Five girls were leaning up against the Tonk House, scantily dressed, breasts spilling from tops, stockinged legs otherwise uncovered, smoking tobacco or chewing gum.

'Hey, honey,' they cooed.

'Hi, big boy.'

'What you fancy, sweetheart? Wanna taste?'

They lifted the hems of their skirts or pushed their breast together in their tops as he approached them. Up close, one of them had a surprisingly sweet face – a young girl who looked barely weaned from her mother's breasts offering Booya her own. He smiled at her, recognising a vague resemblance to Virginia.

'Hi, honey,' she said, offering Booya her hand. She led him into The Tonk.

Waiting outside the main door was a single trusty. He winked at Booya.

It was muggy and humid inside The Tonk, exacerbated by the sun beating on the tin roof. The dank darkness reminded Booya of the shack from the Harris plantation before he and Paw had patched it up. Behind three of the four doors, Booya could hear low voices, bunks rattling, and the sensuous sounds of lovemaking. Inside there were no guards.

The fourth door was open. The girl led Booya inside.

Immediately, she began to remove her clothes. Booya grabbed her wrists. She looked bewildered, even frightened.

'What you want, honey?' she asked, wide-eyed. 'I don't do no freaky shit like some them want. You know you'll get in trouble if you try something I ain't letting you do.'

'No. No, it ain't like that,' he said, letting go of her wrists. 'Sit down.'

She dropped onto the bunk, bouncing springs. 'What's it you want then, man?'

Booya swallowed. 'I got a girl back home –'

The girl chuckled, running a hand through her lank straight hair. With her mouth open, she shook her head and clapped her hands on her thighs. 'Ah shit, man. I don't need to be hearing this.' She crossed her legs. 'Everone here is guilty, right? But they don't need to be feeling guilty over they woman back home. I ain't a priest, in case you ain't noticed. Can't give you no absolution, before or after. I is only here to give one thing.' She uncrossed her legs, holding Booya with her dark eyes, blinking her long lashes. Not at all innocent. She looked down, then back up. 'You want some or not?'

Booya picked up the girl's hand. At first she tried to pull away; and then she sighed, cocked her head and stuck her tongue impatiently in her cheek.

'Listen,' he said, sweat beading on his forehead, the metallic scent of the air foul to breathe, 'I was sent here by a sheriff what said I done something that I ain't. I was taken in the night and never even got the chance to tell my girl and folks where I was being took. They don't even know that I is up in here. I shouldn't be here. Just wanna ax you to send a message to them, tell them where I is and that I ain't dead – like they's probably thinking. That's all. My girl back at home . . . I just find out that she's having my baby 'fore the sheriff catched me and send me here.'

Pulling her hand out of Booya's, the girl sighed again. 'What's your name?'

'Booya . . . Uh, Calvin Carthy.'

'Say, you ain't that blues man everone in the city's talking 'bout, is you?'

'No,' Booya replied, standing and turning his back to the girl. 'No. That ain't me. Must have the same name as I do, is all.' Facing the girl, he leaned against the inside wall. 'My girl's called Labella; my Mammy is Adeline Carthy – she works down at Huck's Place in a town called Honahee. Heared of it?'

'Think I heared of the town,' she laughed. 'But I ain't never heared of no Huck's Place.'

Booya smiled at her.

'Need you just to do this one thing for me. I know it's a lot to ax, but you don't know how you'd be saving my life. Make sure you let them know I was brung here without no trial. And make sure you get the message directly to Adeline, too; that's important. I mean what I say: I ain't s'pose to be here.'

She lit a cigarette and raised an eyebrow. 'No one is, right?'

'What's your name?' he asked.

'*Really?*' Blowing out the smoke with a sigh, leaning her elbow on her knee, she rolled her eyes. '*Jesus.* My name's Clara Mae, 'kay?'

'Will you do it for me, Clara Mae?' A shadow passed over a crack in the wooden wall. Booya couldn't be sure if he'd seen an eye peering in through the crack. Beneath the sound of bouncing springs and moaning, he lowered his voice. 'I'd owe you forever.'

'I aint making no promises.' She flicked a stump of ash on the floor and looked up at him. 'Sure they ain't nothing I can do for you, here?'

'If you do this one thing for me, Clara Mae, I would do anything for you in return. And make sure and tell the trusty we did whatever you want, so they pay you.'

2

Monday morning began with the sun yet refusing to rise on The Farm, their world. Darkness from the outside seeped in through the grills on the windows. The door to The Cage was locked. Beyond the bars, the alley boss was sitting on his chair, shotgun by his side and dozing bloodhound by his feet, reading by soft lamplight. Lying awake, Booya listened to the snores, whistles and wheezes.

The painful throb in his repairing arm and hand were still with him. His ankle was healing without infection, though with an ever-present stinging pain to remind him of his injuries. In the fields the dry cracks in the scabs kept opening, weeping fluid and itching like hell. Beneath his sheets, eyes on the Boss, Booya applied cream to the tingling wound. Unlike most mornings when he opened his eyes, his pillow was dry. Like most mornings, the steam whistle sounded long after his waking.

Li'l Big Heart had stayed in or on his bed for all of Sunday, still too weak to move any further. It was a Herculean effort for him to even peel back his damp sheets. He hadn't eaten for more than twenty-four hours, though he had drunk twice his body weight in water.

'You can't work, li'l brother,' Ox said with a nasal hiss through his broken nose as Li'l Big was getting dressed. 'You ain't strong enough yet.'

'I gotta work,' Li'l Big replied. His voice sounded barely broken, even as his body appeared so. 'Gotta get back to my girl and my family. Dreaming 'bout them all the time, even when I's awake. It's driving me crazy.'

Li'l Big slipped on his boots and looked up at Ox, startling him: Li'l Big's bulbous eyes looked like they were popping out of his head.

'Gonna work harder'n ever. Ain't no other way; ain't no one else gonna save my skin. I can't stay here. Buy that mean old judge five hogs, if that's what he wants. But I ain't staying here. I can't. I's feeling strong, man, really.'

'Li'l Big . . .' Blinking his bruised eyes, Ox rubbed his huge hand over the vest hanging from the little back. 'When I get out, brother, if it's 'fore you – and it ain't gonna be long now, if I keep my head down – I gonna get me a job and buy them five hogs for you. Whatever it takes.'

Standing in the doorway, with Washington the bloodhound on a short chain, the alley boss unhitched Black Annie from the wall. Wheezing and sweating, the turnkey opened The Cage. With his tanned, muscular arms tensing, the alley boss watched the turnkey pull open the barred door with something like disgust on his face.

'Clear out The Cage convicts,' the alley boss called out. 'You got thirty seconds.'

The turnkey wiped his forehead, sweat rings wetting his shirt from his armpits to his sagging waist.

On the way out to the field, the merciless pounding of horse's hooves drowned out all other noise. Ox jogged by Li'l Big's side. The convicts in front kicked up dust, all running into the air behind Chase.

'I'll keep up with the line,' Li'l Big reassured Ox between puffs, a scowl-line of determination between his eyebrows. 'Was just feeling funny the other day.'

'If you start feeling dizzy, just pull out the line, Li'l Big, 'kay? Just call over the trusty and say you ain't feeling right.'

'I'll do that.'

'I got you, li'l brother.'

*

Booya was impressed by how much of the infinity of the field they had worked in the days before Sunday's rest day. He watched a bird fly over the field. As he sang with the line, he even allowed his mind to wander. He thought about The Three Free Riders, if they had forged their reputation in the city – a small part of him wished that he had asked Clara Mae if she knew of them. He wondered whether Roots had finally sailed on down to the delta of Fool's River. Even George Wilmington crossed his mind. Booya hadn't thought of Mister Henry's son in such a long time. He now knew the truth of what had happened to George's father. Surely George still had everything in the world that he wanted, but he didn't have a paw.

'Stop daydreaming, ya lazy nigger, or you'll feel Black Annie's kiss,' Sergeant Helland spat on cue, as the devil always is.

Daydreaming postponed, Booya dug the earth, digging and weeding with the rest of the squad beneath Ol' Hannah's well-stoked furnace.

Further along the line, Li'l Big Heart was hoeing like a crazy gardener, his face a mask of the same fierce determination that he had worn when they ran to the fields that morning. Like a Chihuahua running to keep pace with a Great Dane, Li'l Big had to work his limbs twice as hard to keep up.

'Slow up, li'l brother. Just stay with the rest. With the song. In time.'

'Well I ax my captain what's the time of day?' Bari called.

'Say, captain, what's the time of day?'

'He looked at me, good pardner, threw his watch away'

'Oh Lord, he threw his watch away.'

Li'l Big slowed down his hoeing, singing to the earth.

'Well, I ax my captain how long's my stay?'

'Say, captain, how long's my stay?'

'And he looked at me, good pardner, threw his key away.'

'Oh Lord, he threw his key away.'

The thunderous sound of the men singing rippled in the pale blue sky. Lining the path behind them, waiting for the earth to be turned, a muster of birds watched on.

The sun was nearly at its midday peak. The hoes clicked rocks, flashed, and quieted the soil. The trusties clutched their rifles, glared and scowled, wandering along the line beneath their hats. Sergeant Helland, on his horse, padded up and down, his revolver on one hip and Black Annie strapped to the other.

Li'l Big's hoe began to stab aimlessly at the earth, prodding and jabbing with a combination of gravity and the weight of the implement, the blade hardly lifting from the earth as the other men picked, dug, lifted.

'Brother, you okay?' Ox asked. 'Call on shoot to get out. Take a rest, man; you need it. Must be lunch soon anyway. Just get out the sun.'

In reply, Li'l Big groaned. For a minute he resumed pace, keeping up with the line. Sweat poured from him. His meagre biceps and triceps pulsed. Ox stopped working.

'Pick up your hoe in line, nigger,' Helland yelled, bringing Black Annie down on Ox's shoulder.

'Li'l Big ain't right,' Ox said, ignoring the pain. 'You gotta get him out the line.'

Helland slapped Black Annie across Ox's cheek. 'Boss! You call me Boss! You never just talk to me, you indolent nigger!'

'And I's telling you he ain't right!' Ox yelled into the sergeant's face. 'Get him out the line now!' He threw his hoe to the ground. 'Boss!'

Helland slapped Black Annie across Ox's other cheek. Ox grabbed the end of the strop and tugged, making the sergeant wobble in his saddle. In a flash, the sergeant pulled out his revolver and pointed it between Ox's bruised eyes. 'Want me to tickle your brain with lead, nigger?' Helland grinned. 'Say you do.'

Li'l Big moaned and fell forward in the dirt. Crying out his name, Ox let go of the leather and dropped down next to Li'l Big.

'Take him out the line,' Sergeant Helland yelled to the nearest trusty-shooter, who was standing and watching with the rest of the squad. The trusty looked at Helland, then back at Ox. 'I said take him out!' Helland repeated, turning his revolver on the trusty.

With his rifle aimed at Ox, the trusty-shooter began to walk forward.

Ox turned Li'l Big over.

Li'l Big's eyes were open just a slit. When Ox put his hand on Li'l Big's chest, this time it wasn't even rising shallowly. Fever and sunstroke had nibbled at him like teeming rats. Li'l Big Heart had fainted dead.

Lips slightly parted, his eyebrows hyphenated, Ox looked up at Helland on his stallion.

'He's dead,' he said. 'You killed Benjamin.'

Other convicts watching the spectacle frowned at the name.

'Get back to work, nigger, else you'll stay in the box for a week.' Sergeant

Helland turned his horse away from Ox. 'Get back to work, niggers, or else pay is held for a day for all y'all!'

The trusty had stopped in his steps.

Helland drew alongside him. 'You don't get that little dead nigger out my field in the next minute, I'll see that you spend a night in The Cage with the convicts, understand?'

The tight skin above the trusty's high cheekbones flinched; a white scar in the dark skin pulsing. 'Yes, Boss,' he growled.

Still glaring at Sergeant Helland's back, Ox picked up his hoe. And then he screamed a sound as loud as the earth splitting and charged at Helland.

High upon his horse, revolver still in his hand, Helland turned in his saddle. With a click of the toothpick, his gleaming white teeth reflected like a hoe blade in the sun. His black stallion swished its tail, brushing flies aside. Leaning back in his saddle, he shot a bullet straight between Ox's bruised eyes, stopping Ox dead in his tracks.

Metres away from Ox, Booya looked down at the bloodied face, the lips pulled back from the teeth in a cemented snarl. A splinter of skull was sticking from one of Ox's tearducts. Gripping the hoe, using it to hold himself upright, Booya retched. In his throat he could taste the syrup from breakfast. Clinging to the hoe, he dared to glance up at Helland.

Holding the barrel level with his chin, closing his eyes for a brief moment, Helland sniffed the cordite in the air. He put the warm barrel against the trusty-shooter's temple. 'Take both these dead niggers out the line,' he said, his eyes as dark and his voice as cold as the metal alloy of his firearm. '*Nigger.*'

3

'What's the matter with you?' Meatyore appealed in his deep voice, his dark, sunken eyes travelling over the circle of convicts gathered beside two of the bunks. Meatyore tapped a finger against the bristles of his shaved head. As he sneered, lines travelled from his small nose to the sides of his mouth. Breaths steamed from his nostrils like a caged bull. 'How long you gonna let them get away treating us like this? They have illegally murdered your brother, after *allowing* your li'l brother to die!'

Sitting on a low chest at the foot of a bunk, watching Meatyore's boulder of a head turn, Booya rubbed his healing hand. Looking past the cardpool games, he saw the alley boss sitting in his chair, hat tilted, paying attention only to his Tijuana bible. Folding his arms across his chest to stop himself from shredding his nails, Booya stared at the reflection of the fluorescent lights on the floor between the shadows of the conspirators.

'Keep your voice down, Yore,' Steamie Whistle warned. 'Getting too loud, man.'

'No, man,' Meatyore protested. 'What if a man done that to your family on the outside? Huh? You carry on digging *his* earth, obey *his* orders? Or you run and get your weapon? Well?'

'Ain't no use in more of us dying that way, Yore,' Tied Eye replied, looking towards the front of The Cage. 'That's what they *want.*'

Meatyore punched a fist into his palm. 'Then let them have it. But only let them have seconds to live after it.'

'What 'bout the sergeant, though, Yore?' asked Vicksburg. 'He'd see us all killed. Then Long-Chain will just go out fetch some mo' convict niggers to take us place.'

'I ain't gonna die inside, man,' Big Lip said, joining in, his big lip downturned and shaking his head. 'I got a family and less than a span left.'

'Anyone else too scared to do nothing?' Meatyore asked, his eyes growing smaller still. 'Just let Sergeant fucking Helland and the motherfucking Judas trusties do you how *they* want?'

'Huh?' Clod Ear asked, leaning in. 'What's gwine on?'

'Big Lip's right man,' Vicksburg said, stroking his beard. 'I ain't gonna give that mean cholley the satisfaction of killing my black ass, no matter how much I hate what they done.'

'I's with you, Yore,' said Mauler, Patch Hair and Hind, and a few other convicts whose names Booya didn't know.

'That it? All the rest you too yellow belly to do nothing, too? Huh, big man? Even with the way you was put in here?'

Booya was saved from answering by Vicksburg's interruption:

'Don't do it, Yore?' he warned. 'You ain't never gonna get even halfway to them 'fore they make you dead.'

*

Upon arrival at The Farm Booya had assumed that the biggest threat to him would be fellow prisoners – murderers, thieves, brawlers and rapists; the lowest form of human. These would have been the men in Blacks to be constantly wary of. Just to look at them was to see their aura of danger. Like a pack of wild dogs or fighting cocks thrown together in a pen, he had been surprised by the lack of fighting. It was true that nearly every game that took place in The Cage, no matter what it was they were playing or how trivial the quibble, was interrupted by more than one shouted row – most times with a player accused of cheating – but it would always quickly be quashed. On the outside, Booya had seen similar situations end in attempted murder, or worse.

Looking around the room, Meatyore and Mauler's auras were glowing red. They looked mean, full of murderous intent. When Mauler stared directly at him, Booya looked away. He felt uneasy, the same as when he had stepped from the stage and into the crowd in Blacks.

Towel in hand, Alf was striding back from the showers, the forever-manic grin plastered over his face. Naked, he dropped down next to Booya on his bunk.

'They give you a name of your own yet?' Alf asked.

"Cause of my size some was calling me Trunk,' Booya replied. 'Say that they ain't just gonna call me Booya. Say that weren't a nickname – even though it's been my nickname for all my life! But now some is calling me Revelation instead, on account of the damage I do to the earth, kinda like Meatyore.'

'Heh-heh-heh, I like that. Revelation.' A frown line appeared between Alf's eyebrows, and then vanished, replaced once more by the grin. 'Heh-heh-heh. They calling me Squealing Demon, or just Squealing. Heh, or just Demon. Guess 'cause a my laugh.'

'I guess.' Booya smiled.

Alf scratched between his naked legs. 'Ain't so sure 'bout being called Demon, but I be called a lot of names in my days. Things a lot worse than Demon, too. Heh-heh-heh.'

'What the hell's Squealing chatting 'bout, Reva?' Two Cell called over from a game of craps. 'He bothering you?'

Booya shrugged and Alf cackled.

'Squealing puts the nigger in snigger,' Two Cell said, before resuming his game, accusing Tied Eye of cheating in the seconds that he had been turned away. 'You looking at my cards, man, even now. I see you, fool.'

'I's all-seeing, my friend,' Tied Eye replied. 'But I ain't no cheat. You just can't count, s'all.'

'You keep your wonky, cheating, tied motherfucking eyes to yourself,' said Two Cell, pulling his cards to his chest. 'I'll mind my own counting. And Hind, you can shut that hole in your face too.'

Alf laughed, bouncing the bed. Booya wasn't watching or listening – he was resting his head on the heel of his palm and massaging his eyes.

'You close to that boy what die in the field, Boo?' Alf asked, nudging Booya. 'Reva, I mean, heh-heh.'

'Huh?' Red, yellow and white dots danced before Booya's open eyes. He rubbed his stomach. Li'l Big's empty bunk was directly in front of him. The sheets were pristine. 'In the sense that I was close by to him in the field, yeah. See him go down. You know, I was thinking the sergeant was gonna kill us all.'

'Man, he *crazy*. If I's a demon, then he sure is the devil. Hard to imagine the real devil being worser than that crazy son-of-a-bitch.'

Again Booya checked on the conspiring of Meatyore and Mauler; the alley boss further down The Cage, still in his chair.

'I know that deputy,' Booya said to Alf.

'What deputy, Boo?' Alf asked, readjusting his parts. 'What you talking 'bout?'

Looking at the two empty bunks, Booya shook his head. 'Nothing, man.' Leaning his back against the wall, he sighed. 'You know, I was thinking that we was lucky not being lynched, with what we was accused of having done. Then I think back to what happen today . . . And the sergeant . . .'

'You still don't get it, does you, Boo? Reva, I mean. Heh-heh-heh. This ain't 'bout justice. Ain't even 'bout crime. Us being here is all 'bout *money*. Why you think we come in the night and weren't even signed in at the front? Whitey's making dollars off our black asses, just like it's always tole. That's the only crime what taked place, and it's on us; we is the victims. We ain't never going to the chair or gallows. Can't make no money off us if we is dead!

'Judge never wanted his hog money from Li'l Big,' Alf continued. 'Judge knowed that a li'l nigger like that ain't never getting out this place. But once he was inside you can bet that judge is getting a few extra dollars a month. Probably enough for two hogs by now. And leftovers to buy a shed for them to shit in! Well . . . was. Don't be thinking otherwise no more, Boo: this *is* death row that we's on.'

As Booya's head filled with heat, feeling like it was swelling, his body went cold all over.

Alf sighed. ''Nough to make you wonder if they's anyone left in the entire world what cares, if they ever was. I know all that a long time ago – that's why I always stay just me on my own self, heh-heh-heh. Whitey, he stuck in his old ways. Always will be, far's I can tell. And he keeps drugging us back down with him. Heh-heh-heh, ain't never gonna be just me on myself again, is I? Heh-heh-heh.'

Leaving his wet towel on Booya's bed, Alf started to get dressed.

As his body shivered, Booya's head was becoming hotter. All of his past was drifting further and further from him; miles of infested, impassable swampland separating him from those he loved. He didn't notice the loud argument coming from the game on Two Cell's bunk, nor the alley boss threatening to bring Washington and Black Annie to join their party.

Booya lay back on his bunk. He covered his eyes with his hands, trying to recall faces and places familiar to him, to escape this place, however fleetingly. Since being inside, he regularly closed his eyes to picture Mammy and Paw, Labella, Rosie and the girls; trying not to think of how they might be dealing with life with him gone, but of happier times. But without seeking them, the images that came to him now were faces of those who had left his life: Roots Cryer kneeling in the picking fields; bandanaed Cole Kitchens wiping a rag in a dirty cup; The Free Riders out on the stoop of Huck's, teasing each other; Mister Harris and his wife handing out bread. George and the diddly-bow. Mister Henry and his roomful of gold . . .

Booya could even summon voices, background noises of music in Blacks and Juju; the smell of flowers and grass at Labella's favourite place by the river; ducks splashing in the water beneath the bridge. He could hear a guitar being picked; could smell fruit, and the dangerous perfume of whisky . . .

But then, unwanted, came Sheriff Toms and weak-hearted Deputy Betts, Maisy and Lenut Colden; the Knights of the White Camellia singing *Kumbaya*.

Shadowing them all was the deputy in his new guise. Sergeant Helland.

The bright light was blocked out from Booya. He removed his hands from his eyes.

'Got a minute, brother?'

Meatyore was leaning over him. From the years spent exposed to the sun, his skin was darkened to forest-brown. Booya hadn't noticed previously the deep scars adolescence had left in Meatyore's cheeks and on his forehead like blight on a diseased leaf. Earlier he had barely been able to look at Meatyore. Like earlier, Meatyore's small, stony eyes were looking everywhere at once.

Meatyore flicked his eyes again to the alley boss, currently distracted by watching over a game of dice, even laughing at what he was witnessing. Meatyore's glare was of pure hatred.

'Ain't going nowhere,' Booya answered, shifting his feet.

'You might yet, man,' Meatyore replied. 'Got a plan to break out this place. We gonna pay revenge to that nigger-hater sergeant and all his trusty boys 'fore we gone. He ain't gonna get away with what he done to Ox and Li'l Big.' Meatyore glanced to see where Mauler was – he was trying to recruit Bari.

'You a big man, Revelation. Second or first biggest here. We can use you. This is *our* revelation. 'Less you got something better to stay for, that is.'

'Tell me what you got in mind,' Booya said.

4

'I heared what Yore say, Reva.'

Alf's head was hanging down from the top bunk. Upside down his eyes were even more raving. With the numerous skin disorders scarring his face he looked like a bat affected by a fungal disease. Booya rolled his head away from Alf.

Wearing just his pants, Alf dropped down next to Booya. 'Heared what he say, Reva, man,' Alf repeated. 'Revelation. Heh-heh-heh.'

'Yeah?' Booya replied, still facing away. 'You in then?'

'Nah, man. I ain't in. Telling you, it might seem like a good option now, but it ain't. You can't never win running from The Farm. Don't care how far you get, it'll catch up to you and bite you on the ass – and that's if you a lucky one. Greased up bacon got a better chance in the pan. Telling you, man, won't do no good running.'

'Spending a life on someone else's time ain't no good neither, Alf.'

'*Squealing*, Booya,' Alf corrected. 'Shit! *Reva*, I mean. Damn! Heh-heh-heh.' Alf waited for Booya to respond. He didn't. 'I's Squealing now, Reva.' Alf crab-walked round the bunk and hung on to the bars by Booya's head. Booya could feel Alf's bad breath, like a breeze carrying the scent of a garbage dump.

'You might stay escaped for three months, four. Even five, if the wind's blowing the other way, even if you get free a The Farm in the first place. But they bloodhounds is the best in the country at finding a man what thinks he free. 'Cept you ain't never gonna *be* free, only loose, even if you think you finded yourself somewhere real good to hide away at. That difference right there is like heaven and hell. Think it: always wondering 'bout them hellhounds on your trail. They find you even if you was dead and in a box underground – that's what I heared – even if it weren't them what you put you there first!'

Booya raised his eyes to Alf, half-dressed, hanging from his bunk. Those wild eyes always betrayed his expression, which was now serious. 'I'll take my chances,' he said.

'You ain't got no chance, Booya man . . . Reva, I mean, heh-heh-heh. That what I been telling you just now. Ain't no chance never! You think in here them trusties is mean, you wait see who fetches you back from the loose. I'd just as soon take my chances bargaining in hell with the devil and all his demons while wearing a suit of kin'lin'.'

Booya rolled away from Alf and cushioned his head on his hands, staring at the whitewashed walls. 'That's it, ain't it?' he murmured.

'Think it,' Alf continued, leaning his elbows through the bars. 'Think 'bout your girl and if you lead them hellhounds to her door. Say it one last time: got a better chance of staying alive in here than if you's loose. S'all I gotta say, now. Just promise me that you'll think it over 'fore you's decided.'

*

The routine was the same as every morning. When the steam whistle blew the men were quickly unshackled from their sleep. The smell of coffee drifted in through the open door and through the locked bars of The Cage. The blue of the horizon beyond The Farm still hours from creeping over the trees. After visiting the bathroom, clean ringarounds were pulled over lean frames.

As was planned, Meatyore stayed in bed beneath his sheets.

The convicts drank their coffee and crammed as many syrup-smothered biscuits as they could into their hungry mouths. For Booya, the taste of syrup now reminded him of the fragment of bone in the corner of Ox's eye; the stony snarl he carried to the grave. But that was not all. He chewed on just dry biscuit.

It was obvious that, after the events of yesterday, the captains on horseback, with their shotguns in their hands, were alert to any insurrection. Like piling stacks of storm clouds, Helland stared each man down through his narrowed eyes.

Booya's empty stomach was churning. His knees were shaking. His heart was thrumming. An itch started teasing his eyebrow. He wasn't sure which was the angel on his shoulder and which one the devil. With Alf's words still ringing in his ears, even the impossible chance of returning to Labella could not calm him.

The turnkey was leaning against the outside wall of the barracks, sweating in the early morning humidity. A rifle was leaning on the wall behind his rotund leg. As the convicts spilled out of The Cage he counted their heads.

'Going back in, Boss,' he called out, picking up his rifle. 'One count short.'

Booya watched the turnkey disappear through the doorway. He stole a glance at the trusties standing beyond the fenced yard, chatting amongst themselves, waiting for the trek out to the fields. Washington and the alley boss were wandering over to the next plough squad along. Looking over his shoulder, Booya saw Sergeant Helland still hovering over the convicts, Black Annie strapped to one side, his revolver the other. A pair of the larger convicts were standing dangerously close to Helland. Commanded by the devil on his shoulder, Booya's feet began to move towards the captain nearest to him.

Inside The Cage, all remained quiet.

The convicts moved around the yard, the same as any morning, but moving around in tight crowds of four or five. Vicksburg moved from one crowd to Booya's. Booya peeled away and joined Hind's crowd, further from prowling Sergeant Helland. Tied Eye knocked the breakfast table to the ground, sprawling over it, knocking coffee cups and plastic plates into the dirt. 'Shit! Sorry, Boss.' The captains grinned, muttering through their sneers. As if tied by a short length of rope, Cliff Top and Hind splintered from the group they were standing in. With a sharpened stick hidden within the cuff of his shirtsleeve, Mauler slipped back into The Cage.

Alf scampered over to Booya, who tried to turn his back on him. Grabbing Booya's shirt, Alf peered up at the big man. He kicked the side of Booya's foot.

'Get away from me, man,' Booya growled from the side of his mouth. Through the corner of his eye he looked up at the captain nearest to him – a few big steps away. His own sharpened stick slithered in his sweaty palm. 'Let go.'

'Boo, just listen to me one more time,' Alf said, digging a finger into Booya's side. 'Just hear –'

A high-pitched squeal bled through the open door of The Cage. In the second before the squeal was muffled, all heads turned. In the arranged crowds of convicts, gripping their sharpened sticks, feet began to side-step towards the mounted guards.

From The Cage came the sound of spraying bullets, thudding into the walls and breaking glass. Conspirators glanced up at each other, lips parted, eyebrows raised. They looked to Cliff Top, his lips pulled tight, his brow lowered with furious intent. He glared to each who gained his eye. 'Now, motherfuckers,' he growled through his teeth.

Shocked into action, some convicts tried to manhandle the shotguns from the captains, trying to plunge sticks into their hands, arms or legs. All were either kicked or butted in the face before they could get a hold. Sprawled on the floor, convicts scrambled to their feet. The captains backed up their horses towards the perimeters of the yard, encircling the convicts.

Booya looked up helplessly at the captain on the horse next to him. From two feet away, a shotgun was pointing directly into his face.

'Go ahead and make my day, nigger,' the captain said. He spat in Booya's face. 'Get the fuck away from my horse.'

Behind his back, Booya allowed the stick to slither from his hand to the floor. With careful steps, staring into the muzzle of the shotgun, he moved towards the gathering huddle of convicts. Some of the other convicts were shaking, pushing together as close as possible, trying to worm deeper into the huddle. Tied Eye ploughed in, trying to hide in the throng. Standing shoulder-to-shoulder with Vicksburg, Booya watched two of the captains dismount and creep towards The Cage.

'Look out Yore,' Hind shouted. 'Captain's coming at The Cage.'

One of the mounted captain's moved his horse to the edge of the huddle and pointed his shotgun directly at Hind. Convicts clamoured to move from him. The shotgun was shaking in the captain's grip. 'Say one more word. *Nigger*.' He skimmed his shotgun over the heads of the huddle. 'Any of y'all.'

The first captain peered around the door of The Cage, jumping back just in time to avoid a pair of bullets tearing through the wooden doorjamb, skimming the air above his head. More bullets zinged as they ricocheted off the bars of The Cage. Behind him, the second captain dropped his rifle and fell back through the doorway, putting his hands over a seeping wound in his gut. Resting his head against the wall, he cried out in pain. With the convicts now all penned into a chaotic crowd in the centre of the yard, shotguns trained on them, the mounted captains drew closer, pushing the convicts further inward.

Yelling, Cliff Top broke from the crowd and ran towards the two captains prone on the floor. Before he could reach the discarded rifle, one of

Meatyore's spray of bullets travelled directly through his heart. His blood began to pool around him, lapped up by the dry, grateful ground.

Any hope of an insurrection and escape was falling apart as soon as it had begun.

Having witnessed Cliff Top's back exploding into a red mist, some of the convicts were already lying on the floor, covering their heads.

Four dog-boys appeared with their snarling bloodhounds. They separated and helped the captains in encircling the convicts.

Within the group, a head taller than most, Booya looked for Sergeant Helland. Second to escape, it was he that the conspirators most wanted to fall. But Sergeant Helland had disappeared.

In the barracks doorway, ignoring the fallen man's screams of agony, the uninjured captain picked up his and his colleague's rifles.

All gunfire had ceased.

'All you white men put down your guns!' Meatyore shouted from inside The Cage. The moans of the injured captain were all that answered him. 'We got a weapon!' he called.

Protected by the pack, the braver of the huddled convicts began to shout uproariously in support.

The captains gripped their shotguns tighter, their fingers licking over the triggers. The dogs barked furiously, straining on their leashes.

'C'we let 'em loose?' one dog-boy asked a captain. Above his vertical stripes, he was wearing a cloth hat. His pupils were dilated, black next to the bright white of his popping eyes. The leash attached to his jumping, barking bloodhound jerked him forward, skidding his feet. 'C'we sic 'em on these nigger convicts?'

'Wait for the sergeant,' a captain called. 'Or I'll see that you get the chair, nigger.'

Meatyore was again shouting from inside

'Holler when they done what I say!' he yelled.

'Ain't one of us is going to drop our weapons,' one of the captains shouted in return. 'We have the convicts out here surrounded. Come out now with your hands up and you might only get the sweatbox for a week.'

Booya heard two quick *pops*. Penned in, the convicts looked at each other.

'Yore?' Vicksburg called out from the edge of the huddle, stepping back from a bloodhound barking at him from feet away, foaming at the jaw, skittering his dog-boy owner over the dust by his pull. 'Hear me, Yore?'

Still mounted on his horse, his revolver holstered, Sergeant Helland trotted around the side of the barracks. 'All you niggers work today without no lunch,' he said to the huddled group. 'Lucky if you get a drink. Any others of you niggers what thinks you might have a plan, just know now that you're already dead.' He glared over the convicts, spitting fire.

Close to Helland, Booya dared to look directly into that face of evil. He was not a man, he truly was a devil, a nightmare that had somehow found a way to haunt his real life. Helland was the living, breathing manifestation of The Farm.

'See, man?' Alf said. 'Like I tole you, Booya, ain't no way out. *Booya!* Alf slapped his forehead. '*Reva*, I mean to say, heh-heh-heh.'

Sergeant Helland whipped his head round and glared down at the back of Booya's head through narrowed eyes, glinting with malice and sick humour. With recognition. A small smile crept over his thin lips. A twinkle of his gleaming teeth shone through. The line of scar ploughed a deep furrow in his forehead. Looking down, he mouthed a single word, a name . . .

Boo

5

Every time the shadow of Sergeant Helland and his horse passed over them, the men shivered in spite of the burning heat. The trusty-shooters were all dreaming of freedom; even the tiniest excuse would suffice to put use to their rifles. Those who were assigned shotguns had been ordered to switch their birdshot cartridges to buckshot. Every one of the convicts knew that a trusty with the smell of freedom in his nostrils was as dangerous as diving into shark-infested waters with a bleeding wound. Overseeing the line, the tails of the bloodhounds were wagging. Heatwaves poured up from the earth. The fires in hell were heating up.

As they worked, the men sang in a mournful bass.

'*If I die and my soul becomes lost, ain't nobody's fault but mine . . .*'

Today some of the convicts chose to simply hum.

The shadow of Sergeant Helland cloaked Booya, smothering him. Even as Booya continued working his chest tightened, his stomach cramped, his thoughts ebbed and flowed, frequently breeching the levee. They all knew that Helland was just begging to know who the conspirators were, but, to him, all of the convicts were guilty of the insurrection.

The sinister shadow stayed. The ghostly outline of the horse's head bucked and nodded.

'You know they used to string niggers up by their thumbs?' the voice drawled behind Booya. The horse sprayed air through its nostrils. 'Sometimes they used to hang niggers in that fashion 'til their thumbs come clean away. Can you imagine that, nigger?'

With the low hum of the chorus drifting around him, Booya continued to work the soil with his hoe.

'For shooting practice they sometimes used to let loose a couple of niggers, training their aim, y'know? Even at this very place they done that. Yep, more fun shooting running niggers than rabbits and deer.'

Booya could feel his fellow workers moving away from him – washing blood out of the ringarounds in the metal laundry tub outside The Cage added an unnecessary workload, which no one liked to have after a day in the field.

'Come with me, nigger,' Sergeant Helland said.

Booya stopped hoeing. He had no doubt that it was he who Helland had spoken to; fellow convicts neither – the sergeant liked most of all to cut the biggest of them down to size. Booya could feel relief washing from his Cage buddies in waves of empathy: no one wanted to see a convict die, but few of them wanted to be killed. Half-stooped, Booya was rooted to the spot, his hoe waiting to kiss the earth.

'Don't make me arkse twice,' Sergeant Helland growled. 'Up on that path; out the field.'

Booya lowered his hoe to the ground and turned. Sergeant Helland was no longer grinning. As if wading through swamp mud, Booya staggered up the bank and onto the path. Looking down at his long shadow, he saw the shape of the horse and rider blot his figure from the sun as Helland drew up behind him.

'Walk straight on, nigger,' said Helland. 'Don't deviate; don't dally; don't stop. I'll be behind you all the way. I tell you to turn, you turn. I hear you say a word, I'll cut off your head with The Bat. If you try and break 'n' run, you're already dead. And Diablo here will dance the jitterbug on your bones.' The horse whinnied. Helland flicked his toothpick at the back of Booya's head. 'Why ain't you walking, nigger? Fucking *walk!*'

Booya moved forward on wobbly legs. Each time his shadow breeched that of the horse behind him he was smothered in an instant. The sound of song remained in the field behind him, until it faded completely. With a pulsing beat in his temples, making him dizzy in the heat, he plodded on.

They came to a road and followed it for a quarter-mile, alongside the infinite horizon of fields. At a junction they turned left and continued straight, alongside another vast field, further still from The Cage. The fields around him looked just like everywhere else on The Farm, but it was all unknown territory to Booya.

It was the hottest day that he had ever known. From her position just above the trees, the sun was already blazing relentlessly, her heat melting and dripping to the earth.

Since giving the last direction, Sergeant Helland hadn't spoken. The only sound behind Booya was the clip-clop of hooves, and the sound of his feet scuffing the dirt somewhere beneath him – a reminder that he was not yet dead, just a dead man walking. Out here there were no squads working. There was no one.

Booya saw sunflowers growing alongside the road. He needed no reminding of Labella; he thought about her all the time. He wished that the rest of her life without him would be joyous, full of pleasure and laughter. He prayed that their son would bring her happiness. Faith promised him that he would see her again, but not upon this earth.

As soon as he saw the coffin-like box from the edge of the road, Booya knew where Sergeant Helland was leading him. The field it was resting in was untended, growing wild. Gliding above, a buzzard cried out twice.

'Down there,' Helland directed, sure enough. 'Lift off the lid.'

Booya did as he was told.

A thin and grimy tube extended from a hole in the dirt-covered lid. There was nothing else to it. It was a rectangular wooden box, long and thin, cut from thick pine. The other end of the filthy tube was sticking out through the underside of the lid.

'You wanna make sure y'ain't too big,' Helland said. 'I got no problem hacking bits off you if ya is.'

Booya just stood looking up at Sergeant Helland. Beyond Helland, he saw a trusty swaggering down the road.

'Ain't gonna know you fit if you spend all day gawping. Get in the box, nigger,' Helland growled, lifting Black Annie from his belt. He swung the leather through the air, a heavy *swoosh* following her flight. 'Get. In. Now.'

Booya took one last look at the sunflowers and climbed into the sweatbox. His head touched one end of the box, his feet the other. His back wasn't quiet flat and he couldn't straighten his legs.

Helland removed his hat, showing his pale, scarred forehead above his tanned, pockmarked face and glared down into the box. 'Saw it in the way that you looked at me that first time. And ever since. Thought there was something familiar about you, too, but couldn't place it – after all, niggers do look alike . . . It was the fright in your eyes.'

Helland's expression turned a tone fiercer. His brow, with the thick scar dissecting diagonally across it, became as wrinkled as his face was pockmarked.

'I never did forget your dumb, nigger name. Then I started to hear it again, spoke by folks about, people who really should know better. Heard all about your reputation, playing that "poor me" nigger music. Every time I heard it spoke, I wanted to cut out the tongue that said it, thinking back to that day when Colden and I could've saved the world from ever hearing your shitty name spoke. *Boo-yar.*' Helland spat on the ground. 'I never did think that there would be a day when I would get another chance to erase that name from the face of the earth.' Those gleaming white teeth appeared between his lips. 'And here we are.'

Desperately needing to stretch his neck and shoulders, too terrified to blink, Booya saw Helland's hands turn to fists, twisting the rim of his hat.

Helland's smile had retreated, to be replaced by scowling fury.

'Hated everything about that stuck-up white English nigger; thinking he could do whatever he wants, no matter what no one who actually owns this country he's a immigrant in says. Then I got busted way down here just for doing what was right to be done. You and your nigger parents was too dumb to realise that you was slaving for him. Would've had old Abe Lincoln turning in his grave to see you washing that white nigger's asshole.'

Helland replaced the hat on his head and slipped down from his horse, his eyes never leaving Booya. He stood on the road up above the sweatbox, his thumbs tucked under his belt. He was sucking his cheeks so hard it looked to Booya that Sergeant Helland might soon eat his own face – perhaps to repay a disposition to its ugliness. But his look was of pure and evil hatred.

Squashed into the sweatbox, stuck, Booya had never felt so helpless, or afraid. Death, and soon, would be mercy.

'I should've let Colden stomp you when you was just a shootling. But now you're *my* slave, boy, don't you never forget that. I don't never want to see you laughing, even smiling. You're back in this box in a second if I even hear of you doing either. I ain't fond of your dirt black face; reminds me of looking at horseshit.' Helland shook his head. 'I don't like looking at horseshit.'

Approaching the sweatbox, he picked up the pine lid.

'You think about trying to get out this box and you'll find yourself shot trying to escape; not dead, just shot up bad, understand? You wanna think about that and the good it done them three dead niggers this morning. That first look you give me when you come here told me that you was afraid. You're right to be afraid, nigger.'

Helland slammed the lid down, blotting out the day.

Booya tried to twist his feet and move his knees out of the way. He was too slow. Helland banged the lid down fiercely on them, sending shots of pain running through Booya's legs, ringing around his knees like electrified halos. The sound of nails being hammered down echoed around the box in dull thuds, through his shoulders and head.

Immediately he began to sweat. The heat and humidity was immense, pressing down on him. It felt that he was sinking further and further down into the earth, closer to hell as the heat rose with each gasping breath. He felt buried alive. Pain flared in his knees; his neck was at an awkward, painful angle and his feet were twisted uncomfortably. There was no way of readjusting. His head was pounding, desperate to escape the thickening air. In the dry, hot atmosphere he tried to steady his breathing, mites of dirt like glass in his dry throat. With his lips, he fumbled for the air tube. He could feel the rough, sharp edges where previous occupants had nibbled at the end. Booya wondered if this was the very box that had held Ox, whether he had nibbled on this same tube, and where Ox might be now; whether it was a better, more peaceful place, or a hell just like the one Booya now found himself in.

After first blowing through the tube to remove any visiting bugs, Booya could draw only a thin stream of air through the filthy tube. But it was of some comfort to breathe slightly cooler air, enough to calm his initial panic. He could see no light at all. It was as black as the bed of the Mississippi river.

Booya closed his eyes and tried to imagine that it was just a dark night in a hot room. With his head spinning and in pain it felt like trying to sleep after drinking too much whisky, except for that his stomach was spitefully empty – that morning, as a conspirator to Meatyore's plan, he had been too nervous to eat more than a single biscuit. As promised by Helland, the convicts had not stopped for their regular drinks break that morning. Booya was thirstier than he had ever known.

The sun was soon to be at the peak of her powers.

Measuring his breaths, calming him, Booya inhaled through the tube . . .

Exhaled . . .

Inhaled . . .

Exhaled . . .

The only sounds he could hear were his scratchy breath through the tube and the steady beat of his heart in his ears, but he could feel every contorted nerve and squashed artery in his body. His blood was twisted.

Inhale . . .

Exhale . . .

Inhale . . .

*

When the lid flipped open, the nails screeching as they were plied from the wood, the rushing light of day stung Booya's eyes, making them water. He could make out only a red-ringed silhouette standing above him. He had expected to be released from the box only when the day's work was done, but the sun was clearly still in charge of the sky. Somehow he had managed to fall asleep.

The blurry outline was waving, gesturing, like someone was shaking a stick at him.

Blinking, Booya's eyes started to adjust. It was a trusty-shooter, his rifle urging Booya to get up.

The day swirled into the box, washing cool air over him like a baptism.

Curling his fingers over the sides of the box, Booya lifted himself into a sitting position. He couldn't straighten his knees, nor massage the hot pain from his neck. His ringarounds were sticking to him all over. He felt sick.

'Up, nigger,' the trusty repeated.

Booya lifted himself to his feet. He felt groggy and weak, in a dreamlike state, a dream in which pain could be felt. His ankles felt like they had when he had stepped out of the prison van on arriving at The Farm. They were on fire. With the threatening barrel of the rifle, the trusty indicated to Booya to climb up the soft bank to the road. Like he had on so many mornings after a night beneath the bridge, Booya staggered up the bank.

'Run!' the trusty ordered when they were upon the road. 'Back to the field, nigger. Run!'

Like a marionette with tangled strings, Booya could only plod along the road on his tortured ankles. His mouth was dry and he felt more nauseous with each painful step. Stumbling along, his ankle, hips, knees and neck were aching with stiff agony. The trusty jogged twenty paces behind him.

Again that feeling of death approaching, unseen from behind, swept over Booya. The trusty could tell Sergeant Helland that Booya had been shot trying to escape, no questions asked, out here all alone. Each plodded step fell with a tense anticipation of the shot that would surely come.

When Booya heard the mournful song of his squad, saw them along the road, further along the field than when he had left them, he knew then that Sergeant Helland had obviously instructed this trusty differently.

Even Helland wouldn't be able to torture a dead man.

The squad had already stopped for the brief drink's break that they were afforded in place of lunch. Plenty of hours of work were still left in the day. With a spiteful grimace, Helland permitted Booya a small cup of warm, muddy water. Beneath the earthy taste, it had a bitter tang.

'Welcome to your own personal hell,' Helland growled down to Booya, the violent smile once more across his cruel face. 'Get back to work, nigger.'

6

The group of convicts, huddled around the table in the centre of The Cage, stood up. They were all laughing. Alone on their bunks reading the Bible assigned to them, or gathered around a cardpool or game of jacks, most of the convicts looked up at them. Booya put his Bible down on the pillow and swung his legs round. Reading the Bible only made him curl his lips and shake his head these days anyway.

"Kay, everone, listen up,' Bari announced from his position standing on a chair. He tucked his shirt over his stomach and into his pants. Lifting his arms out like a preacher, he puffed out his barrel-chest. 'I said, *listen up*! Thank you. Our new inmates . . . have names!'

Those who hadn't been paying attention now were. Every convict in The Cage was watching Bari with interest. Some cheered. From around the table,

Corn Never had not yet stopped laughing.

'You wanna shut that ass-shaped hole in your face a second, Corn?' Bari asked, glaring at Corn Never.

'I's a sorry, man,' Corn Never said, dropping down onto a chair and wiping a hand over his cheeks. 'I's done, I's done.'

Bari popped his collar and cleared his throat. 'Now, in no particular order: meet Hoghead!' Bari stuck out a hand in the direction of a man with no neck, who shrank even deeper into his jowls upon hearing his new nickname. 'For the man who axed if The Farm's on the same timezone as Arizona soon's he walk in the door, we got Tucson Time!' Tucson stood up and took a bow, the convicts laughing, clapping and cheering. 'For the man wound up so tight upon finding himself incarcerated in a state pen, rather than his preferred accommodation of a jailhouse, ready to spring on any convict who speaks with him, we got Coil!'

'Go fuck yourself,' Coil answered, sticking fingers up to anyone and everyone who looked his way, slumping his shoulders and diving onto his bunk. When he hit his head against the wall, he sprang up again. 'Fuck off, all y'all.' Answered by a chorus of 'Ooo-ooos.'

'And this ugly fool here,' said Bari, holding his arm out in the direction of a convict with a forehead that sloped all the way to the bridge of his nose, his eyes impossibly close together and his squat face as wide as a watermelon turned on its side, 'well, I's telling you ladygals, this fool's Ugly, or Ug.' Even Ug laughed along with the convicts. Hind brayed with delight.

The fifth new recruit, a tall, slim black man, was standing in a shadowed corner near the bathroom, observing the proceedings. He ran a hand through the tight rings of his greased-back hair. Chewing a piece of gum as he surveyed his new home with fiery eyes, he looked over his Cagemates with disdain. He tugged the vest beneath his assigned ringarounds, his narrow eyes daring any convict to even look at him. Lowering his brow, he stroked his hand over the side of his face that was caved-in, a broken jaw never properly healed.

'Where is that slippery nigger?' Bari called. 'Where he at?'

'Huh?' Clod Ear asked. 'What you say now?'

'Over they, Bari,' Patch Hair said, bouncing his bunk, pointing towards the bathroom. 'Scowling away in the corner.'

With his broken jaw moving as he chewed, the fifth inmate glared at him until Patch Hair had to look away. Spraying his malignant stare at others like a scent, he weaved his arms across his chest.

'The final member of our squad,' Bari announced, arms raised high in the air, 'is from this day to be known as . . . Slack Jaw!'

From his darkened corner, Slack Jaw watched the mouths and their laughter. Narrowing his eyes until they were nothing but slits, he surveyed the faces, as if marking them. Even after they had returned to their card games and private time he watched them. Chewing his piece of gum until it was hard.

'Man, they should just call you Lucky,' Two Cell said, sweeping the cards from the table into his hand as Alf gathered up the dimes. 'Y'always seem to win. What else did you learn from your life on the road, huh, you ugly snoose?'

With the change clattering in his pockets, his yellow eyes manic and wild, Alf laughed at Two Cell.

'Damn,' Zona said, 'you *would* be called Lucky if it weren't for that laugh, Squealing Demon.'

Alf laughed some more.

'Play me out, man,' Two Cell said, stretching and yawning. He rolled his head around his neck. 'I ain't playing no more, 'specially not with Squealing.' Pushing back his chair, Two Cell swaggered over to Booya. He found him lying down, staring at the bunk above, picking at his fingertips. Sliding onto the bunk, Two Cell waited until Booya looked up at him, about a minute later. 'You 'kay, man?'

Biting his bottom lip, Booya stared at Two Cell, then looked away and nodded. He resumed examining the bottom of Alf's bunk.

Stroking the wispy hair of his moustache, Two Cell watched Alf clearing another bunch of dimes into his dirty paws. Though Two Cell's cheeks filled out, he didn't laugh. Cleaning out his ear with his pinky, he looked back at Booya. 'Never heared back from that ho, huh?'

Booya sighed, rubbed his eyes, and swung his feet over the edge of the bunk. He saw Hind push Alf in the chest, could hear Alf's laughter. 'Nah, man. Been back up to The Tonk, but I never seen her to ax. Three months passed now. If they ain't no word in all that time . . .' Booya let the words hover . . . and fall to the floor. 'Axed others, they just roll they eyes. With the little amount of bread we earn on the squad, ain't got nothing to give them, nohow. Ain't no one here can afford to loan me nothing but a laugh or shout.'

Twisting his lips, Two Cell nodded. 'And they try and win that back after.' He turned his face to Booya. Their laughter broke simultaneously. Two Cell wrapped an arm around him.

With his knees jolting up and down, Booya tapped his feet together. 'Last time I went up to The Tonk, trusty wouldn't even let me close. Say that I weren't earning a wage more than my board no more.'

'Helland?' Two Cell asked.

With a slight movement of his head, Booya nodded. 'He promised me hell, man, and he weren't lying. No one else gets put in the sweatbox three, four times a week without having done nothing. But he ain't dumb, when he beats me with Black Annie, on my back, my legs, even the soles of my feet, it's never enough so I can't work. Helland, he ain't no amateur. All I have to look forward to is the day when he hangs me up on my own personal cross. Probably a burning one.'

'Hey, man,' Two Cell said, gripping Booya's shoulder. 'Don't say that. That's just the way the wind blows on The Farm, huh?'

Along the walkway between the bunks, Corn Never tumbled over to Booya and Two Cell. His long face was full of bubbling excitement. With both his eyes and his mouth smiling, he looked from Booya to Two Cell. 'You know what Slack Jaw's in for?' he asked, watching their dull expressions. 'Done for raping,' Corn Never continued regardless. 'Tole me that he would even rape old womens and baby chilun. Didn't care if he needed to plug it with dough or cut it some first, neither, he say. Even say that corpses was all even game to him, long as the corpse was warm enough to feel it. Didn't mind the stiffness, he say. Only thing he say he didn't like 'bout the corpses and the real small chiles is that they ain't never trying to fight him out. 'Cept Slack Jaw weren't just accused of what he done, he was as pleased to do it as a fox with a bloody jaw and a rag of meat. Tole anybody what would listen all of what he's done. Surprise is that he ain't tried to rape one of us all!'

'With a face as sick-looking as the one he got,' said Two Cell, raising his eyebrows, 'it ain't no surprise he can't get womens without taking them.'

Corn Never cackled. 'Uh-huh. That what I was guessing.' He looked over The Cage towards Hoghead. 'I's gonna go find out what he was slammed for. Let you know soon's I know.'

'Be sure and do that,' Two Cell replied without enthusiasm.

Looking straight ahead at where Corn Never had been crouching before he sped away with a chuckle, Booya was staring directly ahead at the bunk just across from him, the one that had been vacated by Li'l Big. Its new occupant was lying with his dark-lined eyes mostly closed. Asleep or not, the sight of Slack Jaw alone made even the biggest of convicts jittery. Booya was sure that he could see the ghost of a smile creeping over Slack Jaw's twisted mouth.

CHAPTER TWELVE

1

1943

'Looky, man,' said Two Cell, spreading out papers on Booya's bunk. 'Looky what I got!'

The legs of Booya's pants were pulled up, showing the scars around his ankles. They had healed into ugly, gnarled and discoloured patches of skin, four inches long, all the way around his ankles. It looked like a bacterial canker plaguing the bark of an ancient tree. But there was no longer any pain in Booya's ankles; the bandages had been discarded long ago. Covering his scars, he joined Two Cell in kneeling on the floor next to his bunk. A broad smile crossed Booya's face. He ran a hand over his close-shaved head. 'What you got, man.'

'Um . . . what to show you first?' Two Cell scattered the pages. 'This! Check this.' Two Cell handed Booya a scrap of plain paper, with barely legible handwriting scrawled over it.

Deer Guvnor,

I neva dun no rong fo I wos sent to de farm ef the wite man wot I help save that day cud be axd then I sho he wud say the same I beliv in the time I dun I workt hard an neva dun nuthin rong stil an I lern wot hapun to a man ef he dun rong. Ef yu pardon me sir I lurnd now to work hard fo the res of mi lif. Pleez pardon me sir.

Frowning, Booya looked up at Two Cell's smiling face. His moustache was now thick; it straggled over his top lip. His face was leaner than when Booya had first met him, no longer with the rounded flesh of youth. Two Cell's hair was shaved only around the sides, creating a fuzzy mop on top of his head. There was a twinkle in his eye. 'I writ' that,' Two Cell declared.

'What's it?' Booya asked, still frowning.

'The letter I writ to accompany my petition to the governor.'

'And?'

'*And* . . . we'll get to that,' Two Cell answered, scrabbling amongst the

315

other pieces of paper. 'See, first time I sended a plea for release, they advertised it in the newspaper in Pascagoula – my hometown; or the sight of the "attempt to kill and murder" as they say it. Folks, they sended letters back to the newsman, saying things such as *"we is sick to the teeth of seeing the bodies of dead Negroes on the streets of our town,"'* Two Cell said in his best white voice, making Booya smile. 'And that I was lucky to escape with my neck in the first instance. Even the sheriff, 'pparently agreeing with the general opinion of the public, writ: *"That ill-intentioned boy stirred enough sand in my town to make a island. If the convict gets his pardon it will undo all the hard work that the law force has undertaken to tidy up this town of the violence that has for so long suffocated Pascagoula. He is clearly too high-tempered and too dangerous to set loose. The penitentiary is the safest place for Negroes such as that nigger."* Make up that last bit myself,' Two Cell said. 'It's all here.' Two Cell lifted up a handful of papers and newspaper clippings and threw them in the air.

'On my second appeal, the angry cholley's weren't so nice. Even the D.A. writ the governor, saying things such as, *"It would be an insult to the entire State of Mississippi if this pardon were to be granted. The safety of law-abiding citizens in any town the offender happens upon could never be assured. May it not be forgotten that this man is a convicted murdering nigger."* Again, I added that nigger bit. But that's what they was saying, man. Hate mail, they call it. Saying how my they hate *me*!' Two Cell prodded himself in the chest, his forehead comically wrinkled.

Shaking his head, Booya laughed and clapped his hands together. 'Must be a crazy town, man. After all, it's your hometown. But I still don't get why you telling me all this. And where you got all these papers from.'

'Well, my friend, I petitioned a third time. All I thought I'd get was more a the same – and they did in the local paper, more of the same hate mail. But!' Two Cell waved a piece of paper in the air, a cream-coloured paper, thicker than any of the thin, wrinkled sheets on the bunk. 'For my *third* appeal, with the help of a attorney and my own letter I writ, this landed on the governor's fat desk.' Two Cell handed the piece of paper to Booya.

Not only was it thick, it was textured, as if it had been made out of solid cloud. Booya had never seen anything like it. He ran his fingers over the fine surface, liking the feel of it in his hands.

'You gonna actually read?' Two Cell asked. 'Or just touch it up all day?'
'Sorry, man.'

Sir, I fear that a travesty of justice has been meted upon a man innocent of the crimes for which he has served. I regret that his appeal was not brought to my attention sooner, and that such a brave and vigilant citizen has been for so long unjustly incarcerated. For the fifteen years since the terrifying attack upon my person . . .

Sparing a glance at Two Cell's eager expression, Booya stopped to read the beginning of the line over again.

. . . For the fifteen years since the terrifying attack on my person, I have searched for my saviour that day to reward him for his selfless actions. My conscience could never reimburse the years that this heroic citizen has lost, to the State's worthy benefit, but I feel that it is my duty and, moreover, it would pleasure me greatly to offer the accused employment in my sawmill, under my strict observation and guidance.

Booya's eyes travelled up to Two Cell, who was chewing on his lip. 'It really is from him, the man you saved?'

'Man, I don't give two spits, and I don't understand half what he writ, neither. But what I do know is . . . I's getting outta here, man! Governor say Yes! Ain't you happy for me? By the look on your face, 'bout say you ain't.'

'I . . . just stunned, man.' Booya held up his hands. 'Congratulations!' They embraced. 'Gonna miss you, man, is all,' Booya whispered into Two Cell's ear. 'Ain't gonna be the same without Two Cell.' His long-broken heart throbbed at the thought.

'Hey, man, Two Cell ain't leaving just yet, only tole that I will be. So quit the moan-moan.'

So little hope remained in Booya, he almost couldn't summon the conviction to ask Two Cell. And it was not with hope that he did ask. 'You do me a . . . favour when you get on the outside, man?'

Parting from one another, Two Cell was grinning, rival even to Alf. 'Do anything you ax me to, man. But I ain't doing nothing 'til I gets the end of my thing wet.'

Head down, Booya smiled. The bustle of fellow convicts around him, fighting to be the loudest voice in The Cage, might not have been there at all. He was a vessel, all but numb of emotion. These days he only breathed as part of the squad. His body had become muscular and toned, but inside he remained hollow and empty. He had thought of asking other pardoned convicts before now, but there was no way that he could have trusted any of them to go to Labella's door, no matter how much it would ease his troubled mind.

'You try and find my girl?' he asked. 'Just tell her where I at, where I been at for all these years? Tell her . . . they ain't no way that I is leaving here, not now, but just . . . just . . .'

Two Cell placed a hand on Booya's shoulder. ''Course I do that for you, man. She still never know yet where you been at, huh?'

Booya shook his head. 'Never even seen my son.'

'Keep the faith, brother,' Two Cell said. 'Don't let them beat you in here. One day you gonna take me down to the riverside you tole me 'bout. I feel that, man. And after everthing you tole me, I definitely gotta share a cup with your Paw! Sip round the edges, right?'

Booya looked up at Two Cell. 'Do that, man, yeah. Sit down and talk with him a while. Tell him . . . Tell him I is okay.' Booya laughed, holding back his tears, blinking his toughened eyes. 'Tell him I been having a time!'

Two Cell nodded and smiled. 'You got it, brother.' He watched as Booya chewed his lips. When he saw Booya swallow, it looked as though it was painful.

Booya ran a finger over his eyebrow, and then picked at his tearducts. He looked into the darkness through the grilled window and exhaled heavily. 'When you see her, tell my Bella I love her, man. And that ever day I miss her like crazy. Just tell her that for me, yeah?' Booya turned his face to Two Cell. 'And tell my boy I ain't never seen the same. Whatever happens, tell them that I always will love them.'

'You been in here, what, three years now?' Two Cell asked.

Again staring out of the window, Booya scratched the itch beneath his eyebrow. 'More than five.' When the day came, long-since-passed, when he guessed was the day that his child would be born, he had been unable to speak with anyone. It was hardly noticed in The Cage; the big man was just a piece of furniture when he returned from working each day. But even in his solitude, Booya's emotions were as alive as ever, just hidden, as he tried to control the cascading memories. If felt to him as if he had counted every second of those years.

'When you first come here,' Two Cell said, frowning, 'you say that your girl was just fallen pregnant, right? So how you know it's a son you got?'

'Labella say she knowed, even when he was first growing inside her.' Thinking of that day and night of Carini's house frolic once more, Booya held his breath. 'I dream of him all the time, man; what he might be like now, with me stuck up in here. See, Labella got this . . . Labella, she . . .'

'Hey, hey. Take your time, man.' Gripping his shoulder, Two Cell pulled his friend close. Lifting his gaze, he glared at the bunk opposite. 'What the fuck is you looking at.'

Lying on his bunk, Slack Jaw rolled over, that pretty name tingling through the length of his body. *Labella.* Pretty name.

2

Beneath the burning Mississippi sky, the convicts worked the line with a feeling like standing on an edge of an ice cliff. Not just for the sun, a new nefarious blaze was smouldering upon their shoulders. As they worked, they sang their new song, with euphemism veiled by the clear blue sky, a tribute to the one of their number who had recently been promoted to trusty-shooter. It was called *Snake In The Grass.*

Standing on the path behind the line, clutching his trusty rifle, Slack Jaw's broken face split into a smile as he watched the line of ninety convicts. Running a scaly palm over his slicked-back hair, his teeth chattered as the words he wished to yell mumbled from his mouth. Beneath his vertical stripes, his skin turned to goose flesh. Glancing along the path at Sergeant Helland, seeing him trotting to the other end of the line, Slack Jaw's free hand played at his groin. Lifting his rifle once more to his shoulder, he lined the sights on the backs of the convicts, still smiling as he moved from man to man.

'I is glad that evil bastard's left The Cage,' Two Cell said to Booya, severing a weed with the tip of hoe, then lifting the blade. 'But part of me will always wish that one of us all had killed that nigger when he was sleeping. Gives me shivers, man, him watching over us, rodent-looking motherfucker.'

'Like we say 'fore,' Booya said, 'if he was given a chance to plot with the devil, he'd even return in death to do the devil's work. Ain't surprised it was Slack Jaw that Helland picked.'

Two Cell laughed. 'Yeah, man. I's just glad that this my last day in the field.' Two Cell glanced at Booya. 'Sorry, man, but when I walk out them gates I ain't never coming back.'

'Why's it took so long?'

Spinning the hoe is hand, bringing it down, splitting a dandelion in two, Two Cell shook his head. 'You know that hate mail? Well, they even start up a petition against my petition. But I ain't going back to Pascagoula, Boo. Ain't never going there. I's going straight to that white cholley's sawmill. And that's fine by Two Cell. He picking me up from the gate in the morning.'

'That's good, man,' said Booya, bringing down his hoe. 'Can't say I won't miss you.'

'Keep the faith now, brother,' said Two Cell. 'Keep on singing, and keep your head down. I got you, man. I just know s'all gonna work out.'

'Yeah,' Booya said.

'It's kind of funny, how you never lead the singing,' Two Cell said, a half-smile cresting his lips.

'How so?' Booya asked, digging the soil with the sun on his bare back, showing the recent kisses from Black Annie.

'You know . . . with you being a blues man.'

Booya stopped working. He looked up from the ground to Two Cell, his mouth dry, to see the smiling face. Two Cell indicated the hoe with his eyes. Booya continued to work with a new weight on his shoulders.

'How long have you known?' he asked after a moment.

'Near since you first arrived. Was Hygiene who first say. Say he just knowed your name from someplace. Say you was good, too – that's what he heared.'

'Who else knows,' Booya said into his chest.

'Just a few,' Two Cell replied. 'See, when you never go for the guitar when it's being passed round The Cage – when Bari *lets* anyone else play – we see how you don't never even look at it.'

'I don't play no more, man,' Booya said, swallowing over the lump in his throat, licking his lips.

'That's what we thunk. Ain't no sense in axing a man what ain't supposed to be here in doing what he don't wanna do. Most us been here so long, we ain't never gonna know what goes on outside the gates. In here, everone's just convicts knowed by a different name. And Corn Never don't know, so I think you's safe.'

Without breaking pace with the line, Booya dared look in Helland's direction.

'What's that serpent got to say?' Bari sung.

'*Ain't gonna listen, watch him slide away.*'

'And what's that serpent gonna do?'

'*Gonna eat the dust, while we eat our food.*'

'And what would be that serpent's name?'

'*Spit in the dirt, ain't gonna say.*'

'Oh Lord, they's a snake in the grass.'

'*Snake in the grass, you can bite my ass.*'

Behind the line, Slack Jaw's teeth chattered, looking from the sergeant to the backs of the heads working in the field in front of him. '*Turn around,*' he mumbled. '*Let me see your eyes 'fore I bag you and my freedom. Turn around, motherfucker. But keep on singing.*'

Working at the end of the line, just along from Booya and Two Cell, Chase and Zona were the only convicts not singing their hatred. Lifting their hoes in time with the song, jabbing the blades into their shadows, even with his top tied around his waist Zona was sweating more than on an average day.

'You might be fast, Chase, man, but you ain't that fast. You ain't gonna be able to outrun the hounds.'

'They can bring me back just as soon as I see my mama,' Chase replied. 'Don't care what they do: give me another span or spend the rest my life in the box, if that's what they want. Don't care if I is denied petition for a hundred years and more, long as I get to see her one last time. Mama's too sick to come way out to the Yazoo. And they say she ain't gonna survive another winter. The Super denied me compassionate leave when I petition.' Chase scoffed. 'Know what he say? "This ain't the fucking army we training out here."' Bringing down his hoe with a grunt, Chase stabbed the earth up to the shaft of his hoe. 'If I can get free of The Farm – and I know I can – I can run as far as the railroad and hitch home. Run day and night to get there.'

'And if they catch you 'fore you get there?' Zona asked, his face grave.

'I'll know that I tried,' Chase answered. 'And I'll try again 'til it's done, either way. Just create the distraction I need to get to the road, man, and I'll be gone.'

Tightening the shirt around his waist with one hand, Zona looked around. Up on the path, Slack Jaw was firing hatred from his eyes, the rifle rubbing over the front of his stripes. A couple of far-off trusty's were kicking earth. A trusty dog-boy was sitting in the shade, scratching between his bloodhound's ears. Sergeant Helland was facing away, bothering the far end of the line.

'Don't do it,' Zona pleaded one last time. 'Write your ma and tell her you love her. But I's telling you, man, don't do it.'

'You know I gotta,' Chase replied and then spat in the dirt, sparing a glare for Slack Jaw, his lean body tense. He curled his fingers tight around his hoe.

'If you gotta run, run faster than Jesse in Germany. Faster than a hurricane.'

'Be seeing you again, brother,' Chase said with a wink.

'Kinda hope you don't,' said Zona. 'Ready, man?'

Eyeing the road behind them, the litter of trusties, Chase laid his hoe carefully on the ground. Then he turned and fled in the opposite direction.

'Oh evil snake, tell me what you see?'

'*A boot heel coming down from Galilee.*'

'And evil snake, how does it feel?'

'*When your head is crushed by that boot heel.*'

Singing the line into his shoulder, Zona looked around again. Sergeant Helland was still facing the other way. As soon as Helland turned, even if it fetched him a whipping from Black Annie, Zona would do what had to be done. Returning to the earth, he began to hoe. If only Helland would stay plaguing the other end of the line forever maybe no one would notice that Chase was gone until dark. He was desperate to look, to see how far Chase had run. He could run like a hare, Zona knew, from years of trying to keep up with him. He had faith in his brother convict. Perhaps he did have a chance. If anyone could outrun The Farm, it was Chase.

He looked up to check on the trusty-shooters, evil fools that they were.

He saw that Slack Jaw was staring straight back at him.

Run like a hurricane, brother.

Zona cried out and dropped to the floor, grabbing his calf muscles, acting out a charley horse. With the thunder of the field song drowning out Zona's false cries of agony, as he rolled around he dared to check on Slack Jaw's hateful face. He was slowly approaching with his rifle trained on Zona, muttering to himself.

Closing his eyes tight to sky, rolling in the dirt, Zona gripped his calf. He could hear Slack Jaw's footfall now, crunching clods of dirt.

'Runner!' he heard Slack Jaw shout. 'Boss, we got a runner!'

Slack Jaw was running, his rifle and his spiky hackles up. With Black Annie swinging, Helland galloped down the line. One of the dog boy's let loose a hound, its head level, sighting as it gave chase. Slack Jaw was pointing his rifle into the field beyond the line. Zona rolled onto his front and chanced a look at Chase. Halfway to the far-off treeline, he was kicking up dust . . . but not as far away as Zona would have wished. Leaning on his elbows, he began to lift himself from the dirt.

Slack Jaw used Zona's head as springboard, pounding it into the ground, and landed in the dirt in front of Zona's face. He ran on a few paces. Stopped and took sight along the rifle, his teeth clicking.

The hound was at the head of a dust cloud, following his speedy advance over the field. Chase was approaching the tree line, skimming over the earth.

Grabbing his hoe, Zona scrambled to his knees. He lifted it up in the air, swung it back in an arc behind him.

Helland's horse was storming over the field. Black Annie was swinging.

Before he could bring forward his hoe, Zona heard the pop of the rifle. He saw Chase fall down, smothered by a cloud of dust. The hound was upon him in seconds.

With the full force of the galloping horse, the slam of Black Annie knocked Zona clean unconscious.

With the last words of the song dedicated to him drifting up into the clear sky, Slack Jaw was still staring through the rifle sights. '*Show me your eyes, motherfucker,*' he muttered. '*I want to see you know it was me. Show me your eyes.*'

CHAPTER
THIRTEEN

1

It was a wild and wet night. The wind was howling around the tightly-knitted houses. Shutters banged and windows rattled. Rivers of rainwater were running downhill. Nobody was out on the streets. Labella looked out through the curtains. There was little to see beyond the spattering rain on the glass.

'I is frightened, mama,' came a small voice from behind her.

The room lit by candlelight, flickering in a draft, Labella pulled the curtains closed and walked over to the child.

'Come here, little one. Don't be scared. Ain't nothing to be frightened of. It's just a nasty storm, but it will pass.' She picked up and cradled the child. 'How 'bout you sleep in with me tonight? Would you like that?'

The big brown eyes blinked and the child nodded. 'Why did Granmammy Adeline go home?'

'She wanted to get home 'fore the storm started,' Labella replied. 'You wouldn't want to be caught out there in this, would you?'

After a pause, the little head shook.

Walking through to her bedroom, Labella lowered the child down onto the sheets. They rubbed noses. The child giggled.

'Why don't we go live with Granmammy Adeline, like she always axing us to?'

'Oh, sweetie –'

A knock came from the front door. At first Labella wasn't sure if it was a loose dustbin lid, or some other thing blown loose in the storm that had made the sound. Then the knock came again, no mistaking it as anything else.

'Stay here, honey.'

Labella walked to the front door. Pulling back her hair, she eased the door open.

The dim light from the candles peered around her and lit upon half of the face. She didn't recognise the man. She was sure that she had never seen him before in her life. You don't forget a face with such a horrendous injury. It looked as though half of his face had been broken. If anyone were to be, he was definitely the sort of person who would be out in a storm as violent as this. Water dripped from the end of the greased-back coils of his hair.

Labella managed to batten down the hatches of her gasp. 'Can I help you?' she asked.

The stranger smiled. It was a pleasant smile, in a face that must have once been passably handsome.

'I apologise, ma'am,' said the stranger. 'Don't mean to startle you, coming to you on such a wild night. 'Cept I made a promise to deliver a message to you. See, 'til recently I was a inmate of the penitentiary known as Parchman Farm. Anyone else come visiting you from that facility?'

'No,' she replied, clutching her hands to her chest. 'No one else has come.'

'Then it'll be my pleasure to deliver the message,' he said, his smile broadening as the name that he had heard spoken tingled through his bones. 'And to a pretty lady like you.'

'Please, what is your message, sir?' Labella asked. 'It's late and I is trying to put my little one to bed. With the storm, and all . . . The penitentiary, did you say?'

'I apologise, ma'am,' the stranger drawled again. 'But the reason I've come to you so late, even on a stormy night such as this, is that I bring news of your husband.'

'What? What is it?' she quickly asked, wringing her hands.

'Your husband . . .' The stranger frowned, his eyes leaving Labella's for the first time. With rainwater slithering over the sunken jawline, he looked up to the left at a picture on the wall as he tried to recall the name that Helland had instructed him to use. 'Boo-yar?'

'Yes!' Labella tried to steady her voice, as well as her nerves. 'Yes, Booya or Calvin.' She grabbed Slack Jaw's wet, slippery hand. 'Please, sir, what do you know of him?'

The feel of that small, soft hand sent a jolt of ecstasy all the way through Slack Jaw. It had been a while since he'd felt the touch of a lady as pretty as this. That one woman earlier who had been closing up the post office was almost a waste of his juice, if ever there was such a thing. As if his thoughts had transmitted through his skin, Labella let go of his hand as quickly as she had grabbed it.

'He – Boo-yar – he's been a inmate up there at Parchman these past five years or so gone by. As I understand, you ain't had no idea he was there, that right?'

'No! I thought . . . You mean he *is* alive?'

'Alive as this storm,' Slack Jaw replied, his smile slipping so easily past the deformed bone of his jaw. His grey eyes travelled past Labella's shoulder to the little girl peering around a doorframe, then ducking back behind, just leaving her big pair of eyes showing. 'Hey there, precious.'

Labella turned around. 'Oh, honey, I won't be long. Why don't you just go back to bed now? I'll be through soon, I promise.'

'I is frightened, mama,' the little girl replied, stepping from the doorway, still clinging to the jamb. 'Is you frightened, too, mama? That why you crying?'

'No, sweet sugar; I don't think I ever have been happier. I'll tell you later, in a minute. Got some good news, honey! Just go back to bed now and I'll be through.' Labella turned back around to face the man. Slack Jaw's eyes flicked quickly upwards.

'Please tell me what else you know. He *is* alive! My Calvin! I just knew he was. Been such a long time he's been gone, and I was beginning . . . I wasn't, but . . . With them wicked Knights terrorising the town that time, and with what everone in Honahee was saying . . . It was hard . . . But I . . .'

Now the stranger chanced to take hold of Labella's hand. For another touch . . .

She felt him shiver.

'Can I come in, ma'am? Tell you all what I know.'

'Well yes! Of course. I was 'bout to ax.' Labella turned to see her daughter still peering around the doorframe. '*Melody!* Come on now, get to bed. The storm ain't going to come and get you through the window.'

'I want you, mama.'

Labella returned her eyes to the stranger. His eyes were a little slower travelling upwards this time.

'I just got to go put this little one back to bed. Why don't you go through to the kitchen here and sit down. You is wet through, poor soul! I won't be a minute. Come on you,' she said, walking to Melody, doing what murderers and thieves wouldn't dare by turning her back on Slack Jaw.

Once Melody was wrapped beneath the blankets, Labella once more rubbed noses with her daughter. Her nerves were numb, but buzzing.

'Why you crying, mama? What you sad at?'

'Sometimes we cry from good news, honey. And I just had the best news they ever was! How 'bout I tell you in the morning when I know some more, huh, and you ain't so tired?'

'I wanna know now.'

'Well, all right, I'll tell you. But don't get excited, now. Promise?' Labella held out her little finger.

Melody linked fingers and smiled. 'Promise!'

'This man's come to tell us that daddy is working up on a farm. If that's right, I think that soon we'll be able to see him.'

'The one I ain't never seen?'

'Your daddy, honey. You only got one.'

'But I ain't never seen him.'

'Well that ain't going to last much longer, sweet pea. Honey, mama's got to go see what else this man knows. Promise I won't be gone long. Will you stay in bed now for mama?'

Within the confines of the thick sheets, Melody nodded.

'I love you so much, precious girl.'

'And I love you, precious mama,' Melody said, and then yawned.

'Go to sleep now.' Labella kissed her daughter on the forehead and turned to leave the room. She almost fell to the floor when she bumped into the man, standing in the doorway, one hand on the jamb.

'What you *doing*?' she exclaimed. 'You frightened me, standing –'

'I was just thinking . . .' the man interrupted. One hand pulled at his belt. 'Why don't we all stay in bed for mama?'

Pushing his words aside, Labella saw the man's eyes lingering on Melody.

'Don't worry, honey. You just go to sleep now,' she said. 'Mister, get out of my room right this second,' Labella said to the smiling face, a harsh whisper that betrayed little of her fear. 'If what you say is true, then thank you. But I think that you should leave right this minute.'

The wind shrieked through the house. A thick sheet of rain clattered on the window, battering the roof.

'Believe me,' Slack Jaw replied, 'I ain't going nowhere for quite a while yet, lady.'

Labella backed towards Melody. The back of her legs bumped the bed, forcing her to sit.

'I'll shout this house down, I swear. I'll scream 'til everone in the neighbourhood is at the door.' Labella's hand covered her open mouth. 'What do you think you . . .?'

Slack Jaw finished unbuckling his belt and began to pull the leather through the eyeholes on his pants – a poor man's Black Annie. 'Ain't no one gonna hear a thing 'cept the storm,' he replied. 'Scream all you like. I want you to. I *like it* like that.'

'Please, mister,' Labella pleaded. 'Don't hurt my little girl.'

'Honey . . .' Slack Jaw pulled the last of his belt from his pants, folded it in two, and pulled the pieces together with a vicious crack. 'I can't promise I won't.'

2

Footsteps splash in puddles. A dark, wrapped figure was walking, looking from house to house. The lights are in the house he seeks. Because of the arrival of the storm, his journey had taken longer than he had hoped. In a town without an obvious whorehouse, he feared that he would have to wait until the next morning.

It was exactly where his friend had described. Even for a convict, he could see the appeal of living in a place like this. But then anything was alluring in contrast to more than years spent on The Farm.

The heavy rained had ceased, replaced by a gentle spray, whipping from blowing leaves. The air smelt fresh. He was excited for his brother.

With his fist about to knock, Two Cell was standing at the door. But then he heard a squeal of pain. It sounded feline, but it was definitely pained. Perhaps it was a tom having his mischievous way.

But cats don't then plead and sob.

Stepping away from the door, Two Cell walked to the nearest lighted window. Looking through the waterfall of rain and the thin curtains, his eyes widened, and then narrowed. Licking the rain dripping from his moustache, he saw the convict who had guarded him with a rifle until two days ago pulling back on the belt around a naked woman's neck. Another agonised cry, muffled by the storm, broke through the curtains.

Two Cell returned to the front door. As he turned the handle and eased the front door open, he pulled a knife out of his pocket and clicked it open in his palm. His lip, turned up on one side, twitched. Quietly as he could over the rug on the creaking floorboards, he stepped to the bedroom doorway. The door was ajar. He slowly pushed it open. Above the spoken obscenities and whimpering moans, the slight squeak could not be heard. Rain thudded on the roof, as loud as ninety hoes breaking rocks. Candles flickered in the fireplace, whisking dancing devils around the white walls. The thin curtains he had looked through were flapping against the glass. The bed sheets were pooled on the floor at the foot of the bed, a vest and a pair of blue denim jeans, a red frock dress and skirts strewn over them. With his hand on the door handle, Two Cell stepped forward into the room, onto a thick, patterned rug.

At first glance Two Cell hadn't noticed the little girl wearing a nightdress pressed into the corner of the room, holding her knees to her chest, shivering wildly as her wide eyes stared up at him. He put a finger to his lips. The little girl looked too shocked to even move. Two Cell recognised those pained eyes.

'Don't quit moaning, bitch,' Slack Jaw puffed, slightly loosening his grip on the belt. 'Don't quit me yet.' Thrusting forward, he pulled up on the belt.

Labella whimpered.

A floorboard creaked.

'I tole you to wait your own turn, you little –'

The look that Two Cell saw on Slack Jaw's face took a moment to turn from puzzlement to fury. He stabbed the knife into Slack Jaw's arm that was gripping the belt, twisted, and pulled it out. Immediately Slack Jaw released the belt, screaming louder than Labella ever had. Still on her knees, she slumped forward face-first into the pillows. The belt buckle clattered against the serpent's tongue prong. Flailing backward, kicking out, Slack Jaw reached the edge of the bed. Glancing at Labella, he mumbled, '*Just show me your eyes, bitch.*' With his lips drawn back over his teeth, he growled at Two Cell. Blood pulsed from his wounded arm, pooling with the blood already on the sheets. His injured jaw caught the shadows, but the candlelight reflected the fire in his eyes.

Holding the bloodied blade in front of him, Two Cell breathed in through his nose, out through his mouth. Slack Jaw was still closer to the woman than he was. The little girl was safe in the corner. He saw Slack jaw look towards her.

'After that little girl, think I'll rape you too.' Slack Jaw said, knees up, gripping the edge of the mattress behind him. 'I'll kill you, mother –' He sprang forward.

Two Cell grabbed the naked ex-convict by the head, using the force of Slack Jaw's lunge to throw him to the floor. Slack Jaw flailed for the knife. A rivulet of blood poured from the wound on his arm. Grabbing the greasy coils, Two Cell smashed Slack Jaw's broken face into the rug and plunged the knife into the top of his neck to the hilt. He put all of his weight on the bone handle, pushing even harder when it would move no further. The body of the ex-convict beneath him pulsed just once.

He sat back and breathed in through his nose, out through his mouth. Covering his eyes with his bloodied hands, he thought of his friend. And then the room rushed back in on him.

The little girl was screaming. Jumping up, she ran to her mother, limp on the bed. Looking into the little girl's eyes, sucking her thumb as she held her mother's head, Two Cell slowly climbed off Slack Jaw and covered the dead body with a rug. With his sleeve, he wiped the blood from his face.

CHAPTER FOURTEEN

1

The noise of dice games and gambling filled The Cage. Somewhere in the room, involved in a game, Booya could hear Alf laughing, squealing. Booya was lying on his bunk, staring across the barracks at the rag that had been stuffed into the broken window – never repaired since the day Sergeant Helland had poked his revolver through it and felled Meatyore and Mauler. As he was thinking of Helland and how he had lately left him be – relatively – the grizzled face of the alley boss suddenly filled Booya's view.

The alley boss spoke quietly within his vile breath, his authority absent. 'Someone in the Mess Hall to see you, Reva.'

Booya swung his feet off the bunk and followed the alley boss past the open bars and out through the door. A captain was waiting with his rifle raised. Away from the building, another captain was standing in the shadows, guarding the path. He stepped aside for Booya. As was his qualification, the captain looked fierce, but his countenance also appeared solemn. Light spilled out into the yard through the open door of the Mess Hall.

'Go on now, Reva,' the captain said. 'Go on in.'

Measuring his step, Booya lifted his foot. His heart cramped. After a quick look over his shoulder at the captain, the rifle pointing at him, Booya stepped inside.

The door of the Mess Hall closed and locked behind him.

Only the central strip of the florescent lights was on, the corners of the room remaining in darkness. A man was sitting at a table in the centre of the room. He was wearing a smart grey suit, leafing through papers. The sound of Booya's slow approach was hardly enough to summon any noise in the vast, otherwise-empty room.

Booya looked over his shoulder, sure that he would see a big net about to enshroud him, or ten men with daggers step out from the shadows. But as there had ever been, there was only the walls and the door. His knee bumped into a plastic chair, shifting its feet with a screech. The man looked up. Booya stopped.

He knew this man. For all these years he had thought of him more than anyone else. It couldn't be, but it was. Booya was staring at a ghost.

It had been so long. He no longer wore the fine line of moustache that Booya remembered crowning his top lip, and he was somehow much younger, but he was certain that it was him. The man staring back at him was most definitely Mister Henry.

Mister Henry stood up and walked around the desk. Noticing a speck of dust on the cuff of his suit jacket, he wiped it off and cleared his throat. The harsh light of the central strip created shadows beneath his eyes, his nose and his mouth. Booya could see the recognition in his eyes and, for some reason, the slight blush. Offering his hand, Mister Henry smiled easily at Booya. Only now Booya was the bigger man.

'Calvin.' That unmistakable English accent Booya remembered so well from his youth. Mister Henry nodded. Though he still appeared to be uncharacteristically nervous, his smile was genuine and true.

'It's good to see you again after all these years, Calvin. Though I would rather it were in different circumstances. I'm sure that both of us would.'

With his muscular arms limp, Booya shook the hand offered to him. He found that he could not utter a response.

'I apologise,' Mister Henry continued. 'Of course it's possible that you don't recognise me after all these years gone by, now that we're both grown men.' As they moistened, Mister Henry's eyes twinkled. His voice became as soft as butterfly's wings when he continued: 'I, however, recognised you the very instant I saw you as the same boy I played with as a child. George Wilmington, Calvin. It is my delight to say: at your service.'

Stilled stunned by shock, as soon as he had spoken his name Booya recognised George, his little blond friend from a different life. The twenty or so years that had passed since Booya last saw him vanished in a breath.

'Um . . . when we were younger your parents used to work for my father, Henry Wilmington, as servants –'

Booya pulled George close and embraced him, his grip strong, forcing George to become a part of his reality.

'Oh!' George exclaimed. And then he hugged back.

'I missed you, man,' Booya said. 'I miss them old days. Think a them all the time.'

'I'm sorry, Calvin,' George whispered in Booya's ear. 'I'm so, so sorry.'

To feel the solitary tear drop from his cheeks didn't feel at all foolish, as it never does child-to-child. 'What you sorry for, man . . . uh, Mister George, sir, I mean to say?'

Sniffing, George lifted his head sharply. 'Please, Calvin, please do sit down.'

His expression becoming stern, business-like, George cleared his throat. 'First I'll tell you how I came to learn that you were being kept here. I have been seeking you out – yourself and your family – for many months. On that horrific night that your father saved my family, he could have just fled with you and your mother, tried to save himself. That mob would have . . . To make an example to other would-be sympathisers, none of my family would have survived. Thanks to your father, we were able to travel back to England – of course, without my father.

'Father always said that he would do anything for the plight of your nation. Through reading all that he could, I came to know that he idolised Lincoln, which, I believe, is why he started his investigations into civil rights in the first instance; though he would have been disappointed to see so little change. Remembering how father was, he would by now have expected to help engineer a complete reversal! But I know also that a significant part of father's interest began with your family. With you, Calvin.

'I sought you out and found that your family had moved on to a town called Honahee. But it was completely by chance that I happened upon your mother in the county store – whatever the name of it is now, I forget. To my utter surprise, your mother recognised me in an instant. So I –'

Scattering papers, Booya reached across the table and grabbed George's hand. He instantly withdrew it and looked at it with reproach.

'I is sorry, Mister George, for interrupting and grabbing at you. But please tell me is they all right, Mammy and Paw? You see Labella, too? See my son, Mister George? He okay? They all right?'

George breathed in deeply, and then smiled. A finger twitched at his moustache.

'Your mother is fine, Calvin. She is the same virtuous lady that I remembered her to be. Your father: his health is a little frail and I regret to say that he is not well, at present. But he, too, is just as I recall: polite and witty. I saw to it that the best doctor in the county will be visiting him regularly. Money cannot buy better medical aid. And I have been assured that your father's condition is treatable.'

'And my girl, Labella?'

Looking ever like his father, George's lips drew into a thin line. 'There is no other way that I can say it, and it would be dissonant of me not to tell you truthfully.'

'Tell me what, Mister George? Please . . .'

George again inhaled, preparing what he must say. 'She was viciously attacked by a recently pardoned ex-convict of this institution. I must quickly add, Calvin, that she is okay now, getting better with every day. She has been treated by the same doctor as your father.'

Booya clenched his fists on the tabletop.

'They catch him? They catch Two . . . the man what done it?'

'It was another ex-convict of this facility who caught the aggressor, Calvin. If he hadn't appeared when he did . . . As I understand it, I fear that your wife's injuries would have been much worse.'

Booya frowned. Suddenly his clenched fists felt weak, as if they were trying to hold sand.

'A serial offender was pardoned from Parchman Farm at around the same time as the man who saved your wife. It was he who committed the atrocity. I believe he was known within these walls as Slack Jaw. It is understood that he was tasked to stop a message from you reaching your wife, who unfortunately found herself caught in the middle of this vengeance. It isn't yet known who exactly challenged the convict, this Slack Jaw, to intercept your message. The man who saved your wife, Taylor – what is the name that he said you would be familiar with? Two Cell? – murdered your wife's attacker, Calvin. I am so sorry to have to be one to inform you of all this. Believe me when I say that it is not a welcome undertaking.'

'You see him then, Mister George? Two Cell?'

'I visited him at the local jailhouse. In Honahee, he had already gone to trial for the murder. As it was his second such offence of which he has been convicted . . . I regret to say, Calvin, that he had already been sentenced to execution.'

All air deserted Booya. Again he had wished death upon a man. Again death had accepted. He wondered if Sheriff Toms had again been the judge.

'If it wasn't for that man Two Cell I fear that we would never have found out that you were being kept imprisoned out here.'

'Ain't they nothing no one can do for him?' Booya pleaded. 'Ain't they nothing you can do, Mister George?'

'I certainly will try to do all that I can. You see, I am a solicitor these days; an attorney. Which is how I demanded to be permitted to come and see you. Taylor told me all about how you came to be incarcerated – of which he knew every last detail – and was very intent in repeating that it wasn't merely a story passed through rumour, gossip and conjecture, but was the truth told to him over the years directly by you. Unfortunately what he told me was all too believable, which is why I originally returned to the United States. I felt that, through my qualification, I could continue the work that my father started. Continue his legacy. It was an almost impossible struggle to gain access to you. I'm sure that you are well aware of this already, Calvin, but you are not even registered here as an inmate. It's an outrage!'

Just as Booya had thought that it was Mister Henry in the room with him before, now George morphed into his father once more – the high scarlet rings of rage beneath his eyes reminiscent of Mister Henry's boiling anger the last time Booya had seen him, ignited by the deputy, as Helland had then been.

'When I threatened to bring your case to the attention of the federal courts, they changed their minds soon enough. Though I am ashamed to admit that I had to lay a small bribe. It makes me sick to my stomach to hand money to such wicked men. What they have done is a complete violation of the Constitution, of a man's civil rights! You should never have come here without first going to trial.'

Booya looked down at the shiny grey floor, like a pond in winter. 'Shouldn't never have come at all, Mister George.'

'Agreed! It infuriates me, the ruthless behaviour of men tasked to guard criminals. It begs the question: who is the biggest criminal of all? But your stay here is done, my friend.'

Booya glanced around the walls and at each of the windows. He gripped the table-edge. 'You ain't safe, Mister George, if you try and get me out a here. They's a man, a sergeant here, he –'

'I know all about Jacob Helland, Calvin,' said George, nodding. 'I know his past; his vile reputation. You have no reason to fear him any longer. I already *have* plans for him. You *will* be released from this place. I will see to it personally, have no doubts. And, Calvin . . . don't fear for me,' George finished in a more sinister tone.

George made notes as Booya talked over all of the facts of his case, starting from Tiger coming to meet him on the night of Walter Carini's annual house frolic. He also told George about Alf and his equal innocence, that he had been sent down to The Farm with him. George was particularly interested in how Booya had been treated since his incarceration. His cheekbones pulsed with contained anger, shaking his head as he scribbled.

As he spoke, Booya continually looked over his shoulder, peering at the darkness outside the windows, expecting to see a revolver pointing towards their table. But soon he came to feeling safe in the comforting company of George, after being reassured and calmed by his perceptive friend. Booya found, for the first time in nearly six years, that he could almost relax. And he surprised himself when he managed to raise a smile, forbidden from him for so long.

'Mister George?'

George looked up, his stern gaze softening as he witnessed Booya's tortured introversion.

'You say you was sorry when I first come in here and see you. What you got to be sorry for, if you don't mind me axing? All this what you doing for me and my family . . .'

George laid down his pen. For a long while he stared at the table, with the tips of his fingers pushed together. When next he spoke it was in a heavy whisper.

'I have carried a weight of guilt with me for all these years. I have never been able to forgive myself for the way that I treated you when we were children. I was well raised, Calvin, and had everything that I could possibly wish for, but I was venial. In a way, I was no better than the men who guard you.'

'But Mister George, that –'

George silenced Booya with his sad stare. 'Please, Calvin, you are kind to try and say, but it is my guilt, and it is true. When I broke your diddly-bow that time and father told me off . . .' George exhaled through his fingers, and then thumped them onto the table. 'Because I couldn't take control of it, it couldn't be only mine and I had to share it with you, I didn't want you to have it at all, even though you didn't have much and I had everything that I could ever need, want, more than I ever asked for. That day, my father reminded me of everything that your parents did for our family, how hard they worked for us. He told me that I was your friend, and he asked why I would choose to treat a friend in such a manner. And then he bought you that guitar as an apology for my behaviour. I was furious.

'When I knew that he planned to give you a gift, I stole something from my father. It wasn't even something that I wanted, what I stole, but I didn't want . . . I couldn't bear that he might give it to you, because I knew that you liked it. For all these years, it has been my millstone. Other than to repay and thank your father, my true reason for seeking after you, before I even knew of your story, was to give it back to you.'

George reached down below the desk, into his case. He pulled out something that had been carefully wrapped in brown paper and tied with string, laid it down on the desk and ran his hands over it.

'I carried this with me in the back of the carriage on the night your father rescued my family. It was the only thing that I saved that night, except for a few toys and drawings. For all these years I hoped to have the opportunity to one day give it to you. I, um . . .'

George slid the package across the table.

'I'm just glad that I have been given that chance, Calvin. It's yours.'

For a long time Booya kept his eyes fixed on George, watching as he chewed his fingernails. Booya's fingers were twitching, keen to pull the string that sealed the package. Taking the two loose ends of string between his fingers, with a little friction and a rustling sound the bow gave way. Booya carefully peeled back the paper covering.

He could remember every single moment of that day of so long ago: picking fruit from the trees, chasing the butterfly, the smells in the colourful garden, the beautiful voice leading him, the cool of the dark hallway, and the room where everything shone with golden beauty. And then the record that Mister Henry had played him, the moment when his life changed, forever . . .

'I called him Blind Lemon Jeff . . .' The words caught in Booya's throat. His eyes were as moist as George's. Booya had forgotten that it wasn't only pain and desperation that could make you cry. 'When Mister Henry play me this, I knowed then that was what I wanted to be able to do: play and sing like Blind Lemon Jeff.' He shook his head. 'Thank you, Mister George.'

George smiled. 'You're welcome. Thank *you*, Calvin.'

They both stood up at the same time, walked to each other and embraced.

'I'll get you out of here, Calvin,' George whispered to him. 'If I only ever have one mission in life, it is to see you released from here.'

They parted and George brushed his hands down his suit jacket.

'Oh, Mister George?' Booya said, pinching the wet bridge of his nose. '*Did* you see my son?'

'Your son? Calvin, you have a daughter. A pretty little girl called Melody. She looks just like you did when we used to play in the orchard.'

2

Upon waking the next morning, Booya's feet were touching the floor before his eyelids had fully opened. Looking around The Cage, his home for so long, he grinned to himself. Following the dream he had just awoken from, even though there had never been a steam whistle to wake him on the Wilmington property, only the rising sun, he had been fully prepared to go and chase butterflies in the orchard.

Alf saw Booya chuckling. 'Got a coon in your unders?' he asked.

'Got something to tell you, man,' Booya said to Alf in hushed tones, careful to ensure that they weren't overheard. Alf was sitting on the top of the bunk; standing next to him, Booya was nearly the same height. 'Only you. And you can't tell no one else, 'kay?'

'If you got some spare of whatever put that smile on your face, I want some. Heh-heh-heh.'

Booya laughed freely. 'It's yours, man. *We getting outta here.*'

For a man who wore a lunatic expression to observe a blank ceiling, Alf didn't look particularly pleased. In fact, his response was to hang his head.

'We leaving, man,' Booya repeated. 'Tonight! I guess to wherever it is you wanna go. 'Less you want to come back to Honahee with me, where you was first picked up?'

'How come, Reva? How come we leaving? You just decide we getting and we get out? That why you was out The Cage for half the night?'

'Yeah, man. A friend of mine, a old friend, he a attorney and he threatened the superintendent hisself. Not that I think the Super ever probably knowed nothing 'bout us being here. More than that, he – my friend – done some research into what happened to us. Apparently some crazy brother had been going round killing any white man he even expected was a Knight of The White Camellia. Mister George find out that this fool 'fessed in court to murdering the man what we was accused of killing. Say in court he didn't regret what he done, just stared and snarled and say to the judge,

"Judge, if you yourself is raging a war against me and my brethren beneath one them banners, I'll see that *you* lose your head. Do the same to any cholley what he's fixing to do to us." He was going to be sentenced to the chair anyway, but a mob stormed his jail cell and did The Law's job for them.'

'So they had the fella catched what they knew done it all along, and we still come here?' Alf asked.

'So Mister George say.'

'Oh,' said Alf, fluffing his pillow. 'Motherfuckers.'

Alf jumped down from his bunk and began to dress.

'Ain't you pleased to be . . . *to be getting out of here, Squealing?*' Booya finished in a whisper.

Alf continued meticulously remaking his bed. Wiping his hands over the soft sheets, not a wrinkle to be seen. His shoulders slumped forward. 'Truth tole, Reva . . . not really.'

'Bu –'

'In fact, telling the truth, I ain't coming on the outside with you.'

'Bu –'

'Think I'll just stay here, man. Ain't got it so bad. Not all. Got a bed and a job to do. Don't even need to think 'bout feeding myself no more, 'cept the putting it my mouth. They ain't no one waiting for me on the outside 'cept some nigger in some town who one day will do me for making with his girl, heh-heh-heh. Or his goat!'

Alf's eyes were flashing.

'Making more money gambling than I ever could in the world. 'Nough to pay for at least one ho each Sunday. You know today's ho day, Reva? Hee-hee! Yep. Even *ho*ing on a Sunday, heh-heh-heh. And at my own willing, too! And most them bitches tip me a *drink*! Serious though, ain't no cholley guard giving me a hard time like you. Ain't a place for a man like you: got a family and people what love him and shit. I leave my family once and I thought it done me good. Realise in the time I spended on my own over the years that ain't a way of life at all. Guess if I ever get the feeling to get out one day I can buy my way. But I don't think . . .'

As he often did, Alf stared off into space as if the world around him didn't exist.

'Got but one favour to ax of you, my man,' he said.

'Yeah, Alf . . . Squealing, whatever you want.'

'Wave to the stars for me, Reva. Wink to each one, heh-heh-heh. Don't think they's missing me, as such. They got theyself 'nough other company around, heh-heh-heh. You can do just do that one thing for me. Two things, I guess I axed: winking and waving. Heh-heh-heh-heh-heh.'

*

Booya waited alone in the Mess Hall. He had changed from the ringarounds and into the same clothes that he had been wearing on that fateful night years ago. His muscles bulged at the seams; the waistline of his pants sagged on his hips. Vague orange spots of blood remained on his white shirt. He tucked the cuffs of the sleeves inside to try and conceal them.

He had said farewell to no one.

As the door slowly opened, Booya couldn't still his thrumming heart. With all the splendour and finery of his father, George Wilmington stepped through the door.

'Calvin, are you okay?' he asked. 'You look as if . . . Has someone done something to you?'

'No. No, Mister George. I . . . just got a lot on my mind to think through.'

'I am sure that you do,' said George, nodding. He smiled and patted his pockets. 'Well, are you ready to go home?'

Booya nodded, almost imperceptibly.

'And the other man?'

'He ain't coming, Mister George. Say he wanna stay.'

George raised his eyebrows. 'Oh! Stay here? Right then.'

The two captains watched Booya leave the yard for the last time. No one chased him, forcing him to run. Looking Booya's clothes up and down with something like confusion on their faces, not a single ringaround to behold, they watched as he climbed into George Wilmington's motorcar.

As the car bumped along, Booya tried to keep his gaze within the lighted road ahead. He was sure that if he looked out of the side window he would see Helland galloping alongside, swirling Black Annie in one hand, pointing his revolver with the other. With his body count piled up high on the back of his horse.

They travelled past the dark expanses of fields on each side of them. The road hissed beneath them as gravel and dirt licked the chassis of car, the appreciative purr of the engine as reply. A rabbit darted from the road in front of them. Booya couldn't stop his legs from dancing.

'Are you cold, Calvin?'

'Nuh . . . nuh . . . no, Mister George, thank you for axing, sir.'

They left the road leading from Parchman. George Wilmington steered onto Route 49.

3

With the sun wakening into the brightening blue sky, copses and woodlands of trees welcomed Booya home. Birds flitted from branch to branch, following the progress of the motorcar. Even with his growing nervous excitement wrestling with the beast of his fears, somehow Booya had slept for a long stretch of the journey. But he was awake as they rolled into familiar countryside. He twitched his toes to stretch out his scarred ankles. He felt free, unshackled from everything but the memories.

'Thank you for all you done for me, Mister George,' he said, breaking the long silence.

'I can never fully repay the debt that I owe your father,' George answered, his eyes on the road. 'I only hope that you can learn to forgive me, Calvin.'

'You never done nothing what needs forgiving, Mister George.'

'*Mister*,' George spoke. 'Your respect of me, even after how I treated you when we were young, that alone is more than I could wish for as reward.'

Stones crunched beneath the tyres as the car pulled up to the side of the road. In the years since Booya had last seen home, the trees and bushes had grown to cover the entrance to the little homeplace. A stranger could pass by on the road and never know of the Carthy family living behind there.

'Here we are, then,' George said, turning off the engine. 'How do you feel?'

Booya stared ahead through the windshield. 'Just want my family back and things the way they was.'

They sat there for a moment. The sky was blue; the magnolias were green and flowering.

George managed to smile. 'Let's go to them, then.'

Booya breathed in deeply. Everyone he loved was just the other side of these trees. George opened his door; Booya opened his. And then he breathed out.

The world washed back in. It smelt of nature in bloom, and it smelt good. Booya brushed through the bushes until he could see the little house that he had helped Paw to build. There were Mammy and Paw's chairs – a new one for Paw; the broken bones of the old one were slumped against the sidewall of the house. Most of the vegetable plot was overgrown with brambles, with a few blossoming peas entwined. The grass was long and the house looked aged. Except for the song of birds, all around was quiet.

Booya trod slowly through the browned grass. He could smell bacon frying. The doom of his incarceration was forgotten for that moment, but now this felt like his dreamstate. He stepped up to the front door, rubbed a hand over his shaved head, and walked in. He could hear voices in the kitchen, drifting on the smell of bacon.

'But I ain't hungry, mama,' a child's voice said.

And then a little girl appeared in the doorway. She stood and stared at Booya. To him, she was a perfect miniature of that girl who had been crouching and stacking shelves, and just like then, frozen as they met each other's eyes for the first time.

'Hi,' he said, a word he had never managed with Labella that day. Again he fell in love upon first sight. He placed the Blind Lemon Jefferson record against the wall.

The little girl fled back into the kitchen. 'Mama!'

Labella appeared in the doorway. Booya could see the faint stains of bruises beneath her eyes, the fresh tears trying to wash them away.

'Calvin!' She limped to him as quickly as she could.

They fell into each other. He tried not to hold her too tightly; tried not to kiss her too hard. Her body felt just as he had remembered it every night for the past six years.

'*Calvin?*' As big and healthy as ever beneath the bulges in her soiled apron – just as George had told him – Mammy bowled through the doorway. 'Calvin!'

Mammy smothered him and Labella, raining kisses on Booya. 'Oh, Lord,' she cried. 'I owe you my life, Lord. I owe you like I never owed you. Thank you, Lord, oh God, for answering my prayers – no matter how long it took you. Oh, Calvin. Calvin! My precious boy. You alive! It really is you. You bless me, Lord. My son! Calvin!' Mammy sobbed into his shoulder, and then leaned backwards. 'You feel just like bone. They treat you bad? 'Course they treat you bad. Oh, my Cally. You gotta have something to eat right this second. I fix you something right away. You –'

'Mammy . . .'

'Oh!' Mammy wailed. 'Oh, Calvin.'

'Mammy . . .'

'Yes?' She shushed for a second. 'What's it?' She kissed him long and hard on the cheek.

'Can you please fix me something?'

'Oh, well, 'course. I understand, Cal. Please just . . . Just don't *go* nowhere.' After another lingering kiss Mammy waddled through to the kitchen, looking back at Booya when she reached the doorway, her hands to her bosom.

Labella stared up at Booya, looking just as Melody had in the kitchen doorway. Booya saw how far the bruises had bled. He wanted to tell her not to cry but could hardly see her through his tears. She fell once more into his arms.

'I missed you, my love,' she cried. 'You don't know how I . . . I . . .'

'Missed you too, Bella. I do know. Missed you more than anything.' Through his welling tears, Labella was six kaleidoscopic images. 'I thought I was never gonna ever see you again. Thought of you for ever second. Couldn't live without you, Bella. I couldn't. Most the time I didn't even know who I was, without you. Ain't never gonna be away from you for a second, ever again.'

He lifted her from the floor, he heard her groan and felt her shudder. He let her down.

'You still hurting real bad?' Hatred and anguish stomped over his heart. 'I heared. I is so sorry, Bella. It's all my fault. He –'

'Shhh . . . Calvin, I is mending. And I'd go through it all again to get you back.'

'Don't. Please, don't.'

Booya looked over her head. The little girl was again standing in the doorway.

'Hey,' he said.

'Hi,' Melody replied, twiddling a finger through her hair, unseating the daisy behind her ear, and then looking at it on the floor where it had landed.

Labella sniffed and smiled. 'Melody, come meet your daddy.'

Reaching for Labella's hand, Melody stepped cautiously towards them.

Booya couched down on one knee. 'Hi, Melody. Missed you, too.'

'She knows all 'bout her daddy, don't you, Mellie?'

Melody nodded and then sunk her chin into her chest, looking up at Booya through the top of her eyes. 'You been on a farm?' she asked.

'Uh-huh,' Booya answered through twisted lips. 'But I ain't never going away from you again, promise you that. Not ever for a second. Can I get a hug, Melody?'

Melody looked up at Labella. When Labella nodded a tear dropped to the floor. Letting go of her mother's hand, Melody stepped to Booya and wrapped her arms around his neck. He picked her up and held her. She was as light as a hoe. Gently pulling Labella close, they huddled as a family for the first time.

'Where's Paw at?' Booya asked.

'Must still be in bed.' Labella looked over her shoulder towards the bedrooms. 'Calvin, he ain't been well.'

Booya kissed his girls and stopped at the bedroom door. It was hard to even step away from them; he wanted to tell them not to go outside. The world was outside. He knew what the world was capable of.

As soon as he opened the door, Booya was met by the musty and stale smell of illness. He pulled back the curtains and opened a window. With the sunshine a rhombus on his chest, Paw did look old. He had the first grey hairs that he had been so proud he'd never had. Lying there, he looked small – the man who had once had forearms solid as rocks and could jump as high as a flea. Booya picked up a bony hand at the end of a skinny arm and saw Paw's eyelids flicker.

Paw squinted and blinked rapidly in the daylight. 'Boo?' he said. 'Son? You still a dream or that really you?'

'It's me, Paw.'

'*I* is *Me*,' Paw laughed, becoming a cough.

He couldn't help himself: Booya smiled. After all these years Paw could remember something as insignificant as a joke between him and a barman. 'Easy, Paw. Take it easy.'

Paw stroked Booya's face. 'Young Booya Carthy. Good to see you, son. I missed you so much all these years. Warned you never to trust The Law, didn't I? Here, give your old man a kiss.'

Booya kissed Paw and put a hand on his head. 'Missed you too, Paw. Hated being away from you. Been thinking, Paw – it's important that I say this now, just with you – I ain't never going back to that old life, Paw. If playing guitar and trying to be a blues man, to be somebody, only ever brings so much trouble, not only to me but for everone in my life I love and care for . . . I ain't gonna do it no more. I can't, Paw. You understand? I can't lose everthing again. I say it once, and it happen twice. Folks always tole me it's a gift from God. But it's a gift that the devil wants for hisself – Mammy was always right 'bout that. I see now. I know I's only just back, but . . .'

Paw listened, watching his son until he was sure that Booya had finished. Having watched his son's lips moving, Paw could see how hard it had been to say. 'You gotta do what you feel is right, Boo. If that's what you feel, then that's what's right.'

'That's what I feel, Paw.'

'Cultivating Calvin Carthy, huh?'

'That's it all, Paw.' Booya licked his numb lips; bit them until he could feel it. 'So when you gonna be well again, old man? So good to see you. Wanna share a cup, just as soon as you well?'

Paw smiled. Despite his frailty and the addition of grey to his hair, his big broad smile would never change. 'I's fine, really. Just wanna make a slave woman of your Mammy for a while, heh-heh.' Paw coughed into his hand.

'Serious, Paw, how you doing?'

'Just got some nu-moan-ya or something, say the doc. Got some sick medicines to drink – taste nearly as bad as your Mammy's own home remedy; thank the Lord she never interferes with my homebrew – and I gotta rest. Doc say it should clear up fine. Got young Mister George to thank for that.' Paw smiled. 'We all got a lot to thank young Mister George for.'

'He here with me, Paw! I clean forgot 'bout Mister George and leave him outside. Let me go get him.'

As he passed her, Booya kissed Labella, resting in a chair.

Booya walked cautiously out to the road. George's car was gone. Only the marks in the gravel where the tyres had been remained.

CHAPTER FIFTEEN

1

With a cushion on her stomach, Labella slumped in an armchair with her head in her hands, strands of hair poking through her fingers. She ran her fingers along her eyebrows, beneath her eyes, up the sides of her small nose, and round again. Her breaths rattled in the back of her throat.

The day was bright outside, climbing up the steps and in through the open front door. Insects buzzed in through the window, bothering the fruit bowl on a rickety table. With a chubby palm and a *Shoosh*, Mammy waved them away. Standing on the naked floorboards, folded arms covering her chest, she watched Labella rubbing her face. With a glance out through the doorway, Mammy walked to her. Groaning as she lowered herself, she tucked her flowery dress under her knees and kneeled beside the armchair, rubbing Labella's knee.

'What you gonna do, honey?' she asked.

With her bottom lip curled, hiding her face, Labella could only shake her head. A tear wetted her white dress.

'You know you gotta tell him, don't you? Poor, sweet honey. What more has life got what it can throw at you?'

Clutching the cushion in her hands, Labella lifted her face to Mammy. 'I ain't sure I can, Adie.' The stains of bruises beneath her puffy eyes were joined by faint lines. Her eyebrows were steep arches. 'I . . .' With a sob, Labella buried her face in the cushion.

'Shhh, chile,' Mammy said, rubbing Labella's back. 'You'll know what to say when the time comes. But you gotta tell him.'

*

Out in the clearing, Booya was holding Melody by her hands, spinning her around in circles. With her hair blowing back from her face, Melody clucked and laughed.

'See me flying, mama?' Melody chuckled, noticing Labella standing there.

Labella smiled.

'Again, Paw. Wanna fly again.'

Booya whisked Melody onto his shoulder. 'Don't know where you gone! Hey, *Mellie*? You seen Melody anyplace, Paw?'

Sitting beneath a tree, Paw was sipping around the edges of a cup of milk and honey, with a dash of whisky. 'Huh? I ain't seen her no place, Boo. She prob'ly off flying someplace.'

'Up here, Granpaw.' Melody waved. 'Look! I is up here!'

'Think I hears her, but I still ain't seeing her.' Paw put a hand to his forehead. 'You check up in the treetop? That's where you'll find her, Boo.'

'Up here! I is up *here*!' Melody patted on Booya's hat – the same hat Roots had given him, which Paw had found six years ago, down by the river, near by a large, dry puddle of blood.

Booya span around, always a millisecond too late to see Melody. 'She playing her little tricks on us I is betting, Paw.'

'Just seed her fly by!' Paw said, pointing into the trees. He spilled his drink down his front. 'Ah, shee-oot. Don't tell yo' Granmammy, hear?'

Melody chuckled into her hands.

It was then that Booya saw that Labella was the only one of them who wasn't smiling.

'What's up?' He lifted Melody down to the ground and put his hat on her head. 'Bella?'

'I wanna fly again, Paw,' Melody said, peering out from beneath the rim of the hat.

Booya patted her backside. 'Go see how Granpaw's getting on. You can fly later.'

'Can you make me fly, Granpaw?' Melody asked, skipping over to him.

'Can't even hold a cup without messing myself and you axing if I can make you fly? I know what we'll do: let's go ax yo' big ol' Granmammy if she'll give us some jam. Maybe fill my cup when we there, too.'

Melody helped Paw – Granpaw – to his feet and they disappeared together down the path. Labella watched them go until she could see them no more. Pressing the cushion that she was still holding tight to her chest, she wished that the path were longer, less covered. Her other hand was settled low down on her stomach.

2

Skirting the town, Booya wandered alone on the long route down to the riverbank. All the time that he had been inside, every day the water had continued to roll down this river; ducks quacked and splashed, fishes jumped, insects buzzed, birds sang and cotton grew. Some are born and some die. The world goes on. For all that time Booya's heart must have carried on beating.

Nightmares had found him again last night; a reminder perhaps. Just the thought alone of the child made him feel sick. What if the baby was born with a caved-in jaw, hideous like his father?

Pinching his bottom lip, Booya's eyes were welling. This was his life.

In the meadow on the other side of the river the horses were picking at the grass and the berries in the bushes. The big old willow brushed over the water where the sun reflected in a dull, merciful yellow.

Closing his eyes for a moment, Booya laid back with his arms behind his head where his hair had begun to grow back, trying to unravel the messy knot of his feelings. At the centre of the knot, he knew that he loved Labella more than anyone or anything on this earth. In his heart he had only ever wanted her. But he didn't really know her anymore. He had left her as a grown child and now she was a mother.

For six long, bleak years he had wished every day to see her; every night to be with her. When he had finally been reunited with her, even wearing the remnants of her injuries, she was even more beautiful than his memories of her: smiling, shy, frowning, naked. She was a good mother to a wonderful child. Fighting against fate, she had loyally waited for him – another fate that he had tried to banish from his thoughts in his loneliest hours.

In the centre of that jumbled knot, Booya uncovered his love. There were just a couple of loose strands that needed dealing with.

'Hey, Big Boo.'

Booya rolled over. 'Rosie!'

Wearing a new yellow dress with big white spots, she sat down next to him and pulled her knees to her chest. 'How's you, Big Boo? Heared you was back from the dead for a second time. Thought I might find you down here.'

'How so?'

''Cause you wasn't at home or up outside Huck's with your guitar.'

Booya tilted his head. 'Ain't a musicianer no more, Rosie.'

'On a break or forever?'

'Just at the moment I is thinking forever.' Booya sighed. 'If it was only 'bout the music . . . You know?'

'Yep.' Rosie looked out over the still water. 'Oh, I know. But I never know anyone so missed around town as you was when you was gone. But I guess I understand why you been hiding from the world, and ain't even come out to see me, *Big Boo.*'

'How the girls, Rosie?'

'Yeah, they fine, far's I know. Petal moved into a big house outside of town with a new beau, some business man what's got more money than sense.'

'You kidding!'

'Nuh-uh. He so taken with her, he buy her a pony and all kinds of toys. Go out to see her on occasion. Can't no one argue that they ain't in love. And they talking 'bout starting a family.'

Cocking his head back, Booya frowned, his mouth half-open.

'She *all woman*, Boo. Been saying that all these years to anyone who'd listen. Petal may not be to everone's taste, but all that sweet girl ever wanted to be was a mama. And now she met someone who's gonna make that true for her, Lord willing.'

'Huh! How 'bout that.' Watching the horses, Booya nodded five or six times. 'And little Virginia?'

'She already got a couple kids from a local man; honest man, too. She still found round town most the time, fussing over those two sweet little ones.'

'That's good. Good for both them. Ha!' Booya sucked his lips together, thinking about the girls. The three of them were probably the best friends he'd ever had. 'How 'bout you, then, Rosie?' Booya asked, looking far into Rosie's big brown eyes.

Rosie laid her legs out in front of her, tucking her dress beneath her thighs. She rolled onto her side, propping her head up on her hand. She had not aged a day or changed one bit. 'Ah, you know me: so set for moving I can't keep still long enough to keep one man.'

'How many you got, just now?'

'Well, I, ah . . . is between men just now,' Rosie answered, smiling.

'That right?' He looked her body up and down. She was clearly still that same fine-looking, fun-loving lady. She was most certainly just as he remembered her. And, looking her over, he could remember her all right.

'Booya Carthy, is you checking me out, married man and all?'

He began to reach out a hand. 'What if I is?'

Rosie slapped down his hand and sat up. Glaring at him, she said, 'Thought you was different to the rest of them, Boo. We all did. That's what we all thought was so sweet 'bout you. Bellie's my *friend*, you . . . you . . . *Urrgh!* You changed, man.'

Re-smoothing her dress beneath her, Rosie moved away from him but did not leave. With quizzical disgust, her gaze lingered on his face.

Sitting up, Booya stared at the water. With the heel of his hand pressed against his forehead, he scratched his hair until his fingers began to feel numb.

'You all right, man?' asked Rosie. 'Everthing all right with you and Bellie?'

Booya didn't answer. The river flowed silently by, only the fishes disturbing the water.

'I do love her, Rosie. Sorry. I is so sorry. I . . . I heared how kind you was. Heared how much you done for Melody, how much she loves you.' Booya's lips curled downwards, but he managed to stifle his tears.

Rosie didn't hesitate in putting her arm around Booya. 'Hey, Boo, don't worry 'bout it. None of us can ever imagine what it was like for you up there. But I seen with my own eyes what it was like for Bellie. She cried for you, Boo. Should a seen how she cried. It was like nothing you can believe, 'nough to make the river rise. Thought she was never gonna stop! And when that evil bastard come . . . We can only imagine what you been through, Boo. But don't never forget what Labella's been through for you.'

Booya continued to stare ahead.

'Just don't know what to do, Rosie. Ever direction I is facing, I just don't know where to look or turn. I never dreamed how hard it is to climb out of hell once you been so deep inside.'

'They's only one thing you can do, Boo: you gotta be there for them what have always been there for you — even when you ain't been in the same county. She needs you more than ever, man, however strong she is. Think it's bad for you? It's a hundred times worse for Labella. Forget 'bout your own troubles for a while and you might see how far behind you can leave them feelings. It's all 'bout your girls now, man. Unless God sees fit to make it otherwise, however much you don't like it, that baby's coming. You got time to get used to it, but it's the choice of God alone to decide whether it lives or dies.'

'Will you help out too, Rosie? I ain't done none of this 'fore, remember. I need you.' Blinking rapidly, Booya smiled. '*We* need you.'

'I was gonna help out if you axed or not. But try and touch my good stuff again and you ain't gonna have no lemons left in your bowl no more.'

Booya's trousers had ridden up at the ankle, revealing his deep scars. He quickly covered them.

3

By the calendar they had seven months to wait. As Labella grew slowly outward, they had day after day to bear. Most days, he and Paw sat out in the clearing, cup in hand. Whenever Booya wanted to talk about his issues Paw had a willing ear to listen; a supportive tongue to advise. Often Mammy waddled out to sit with them and they would surreptitiously water the earth with their drink . . . as if she didn't know.

How it would solve their problems if Labella were to lose the baby. But if

Booya lost Labella to the dark force that had so maliciously wisped around his life it would finally have taken from him nearly all that it could.

Labella helped to make Booya's return to a semblance of a normal life as serene as she could. She listened as he spoke through his lingering fears, comforted him when he was confronted by doubt. But when Booya asked how she was feeling, even as her ankles swelled and her stomach stretched, never did she reply with any words of pessimism. It was with Rosie that she cried and told how she dreaded and feared her unborn child; how she was tormented by the memories of that night every time the child stirred inside her.

Playing his guitar could never be as pleasing as it once was for Booya. Words leapt upon him, conjuring unwanted images in his mind. There was even no solace to be sought in the Blind Lemon Jefferson record that George had given him. It wasn't that Blind Lemon didn't sing and play as sweetly as ever – hearing him was to be transported back through time to trouble-free days – but there was a song on that record, *That Crawling Baby Blues*, which always sneaked up on Booya.

"*Many man rocks some other man's baby,*" Blind Lemon sweetly sang. "*And the fool thinks he's rocking his own.*"

How was it that Blind Lemon could croon messages directly to him, through words recorded when Booya had still been only a child?

The doctor who had visited Paw at George's expense became midwife to Labella. Unknowing of the circumstances of her pregnancy, he delightedly reassured her that, as far as he could tell, the child was healthy. With each visit he deigned to coach Mammy her role for when the child arrived – being so isolated outside of town, as they were, it was unlikely that they would be able to call upon any last minute support. Mammy insisted that she was well capable of delivering a child and didn't need the condescending tutorials of the doctor.

'See the size of that boy there?' she said, pointing at Booya. 'I delivered him all on myself when that old fool was elseplace. And I was the one what was carrying then! Don't need to be tole, Mister Doctor. I is perfectly capable and knowing in myself to do the job.'

'I'm sure that you are, dear Adeline,' the doctor replied. 'Whilst my services are available to you out here, I merely suggest that it would be wise to refresh your memory, for my sake only. It would rather sooth my conscience. Please, humour me.'

'Just don't be thinking that I don't know them things, Mister Doctor. I remember them all just fine and well. It's a natural thing for a mother.'

'I would never question that you don't,' the doctor replied.

Through distracted interest he taught Mammy, and was satisfied that she would serve Labella just fine.

And then, one quiet day, the unwanted baby arrived.

Booya had hoped beyond hope that they would be delivered a girl, one he could love as he loved both of his girls. But it was a boy that Mammy so expertly delivered, as Booya always knew deep inside him that it would be. But something strange happened when he looked upon the baby boy for the first time. All nightmares were banished; there was no churning of serpents within him. He saw that his feared enemy, who had been so long approaching, was just a helpless child.

After the family had all looked upon the tiny boy, Mammy and Paw took Melody, against her wishes, for a walk out to the clearing.

Booya sat next to Labella on the bed. The child was fed, asleep, wrapped in a flannel towel on the sheets. Their eyes stayed on the child. In the silence of the room, Booya could hear Labella's jolting breaths. He clearly heard the soft splatter of a teardrop when it landed on the sheets.

'I don't know if I can love him, Calvin,' Labella said, her lips screwing together. 'Just don't know if I can, even though I know that's wrong. Is it wrong?'

Booya ran his hand over her damp hair. His own feelings banished by the sight of the baby, he forgot himself.

'You don't gotta keep him, if you don't want. Someone in town would be happy to take him. Anything you want. You ain't alone, Labella, don't never forget that. Whatever you do I is right here beside you. Always. Whatever you want it's your choice to make, and I'll still be here with you.'

'But if I let him go and something happens to him I could never forgive myself. If I keep him and he turns out to have bad blood then I . . . I just don't think I can win!'

'Nothing happens without reason, I guess,' Booya said after a while of watching the soft rise and fall within the towel. 'Even though I never have been able to see the reason why in so many things, everthing's got a reason. Can't even pretend that I know what it's like for you. All I can say is that I'm right here with you.'

'I think . . .' Labella sniffed, her hand resting on the little bundle. 'Think I'll call him Sebastian. That's what my daddy who ran away from me and mama was called. Then it's like he's coming back to me again, if I call him that. Is that a reason, like you say? Think that could be a reason?'

Booya now understood what the reason resting easily in his heart was designed for. When he had been wandering alone in the wilderness, lost, not knowing which way he was headed, that his life was not worth living without Labella. This boy's biological father might have been the cause of his original hurt, but the little boy had done nothing but confirm how much he loved his wife.

He pulled Labella to him. She rested her head upon his shoulder. 'I think that it could be,' he said quietly.

'I've decided, Cal. I is going to love him. Going to try to love him. I think

I can; look at him, so little and helpless' She wiped her eyes. 'Thank you.'

Looking at the perfect little boy, Booya though that he might be able to love him too.

Like a son.

CHAPTER SIXTEEN

1

The southern man leaned back in his leather chair and ran his hand over his bearded chin. With one eye open, he looked out over the New York skyline, the sun reflecting blue from the windows of the opposite apartment blocks. With the window open and air conditioning unit on, his blue checked shirt stuck to his front; the leather of the chair making his back wet. Sweat even beaded in his bushy eyebrows. Lifting the tumbler from the glass coffee table, he swilled his drink round, ice clinking in rhythm as the record began to play, and closed his eyes.

'Don't you ever listen to anything else?'

A slender, dark-haired woman had joined him in the room. She was smiling at the southern man.

He didn't see; his eyes remained closed. 'Just listen, Antoinette,' the southern man said in his southern accent. 'Ain't it the most beautiful thing that you ever heard?'

'So you really think you've found him, huh?'

'I hope so, this time. Maybe I'll never sleep again if I don't.'

Antoinette walked over and sat down on the armrest of his chair. Feeling her join him, he opened his eyes and wrapped an arm around her waist.

'Other than the usual poison lover theory, over the years I heard rumours that he's here in New York running a club; that he's training to be the first black man to run for Congress; that he's a pilot; that he's a prison guard, a university professor, a trucker, a chicken farmer; that he's really Sonny Boy Williamson – the second, naturally. I heard that his family were washed down the river by a freak flood just after he cut this record. I suppose that would almost be one of the most plausible theories. But!' The southern man waved a finger. 'The latest I heard is that he never left that town Honahee; that he gave up music to live a quiet life and raise a family.'

He turned to Antoinette. 'It might be a long shot, Annie, but I've got to give this lead a chance. If I could find him . . .'

'I know you do, honey. I know. I know you've got to at least give it a shot.' She rubbed a hand through his dark hair, curling a cluster through her fingers. 'Do you think that you'd consider your life's work complete if you do find him?'

'A man's work is never complete. But just seeing his face would answer a hundred-thousand questions.' They sat back to listen. He wagged his foot in time to the music. 'You know, part of the legend is that he's alleged to have created these songs on the spot the day that he recorded them. The man I spoke to in Chicago said he hardly spoke a word all day. Almost didn't record him, saying that he was too drunk to stand, that he sort of . . . *slid* around the walls before climbing onto the stool. But then he heard him *play*. And *then* he heard his *voice*! Then, after that day, he never heard of or saw him again – except for in the regular gossip of folks. The only reason that he left Honahee to go to Chicago was because a white woman raped him – again, allegedly. That's kind of hard to believe, seeing as he was supposed to have been more than halfway from six foot to seven.

'In Honahee I met folks in a barrelhouse called Juju, always plenty happy to brag that they'd seen him play there one time when it was called Blacks, or knew of someone who knew of someone who had. And then he apparently just . . . slipped from the face of the Earth! I was *so close*, Annie. I always felt like I was just around the corner from where he was standing. So I sprinted around that corner, and the next, and the next. Until I was right back where I started.'

'Alan, take a breath!' Antoinette said, laughing. 'I know all this, remember? You've told me all about the reputation of Booya Carthy once a week for more than twenty years. I know his story better than his own family, if he has one; if he even exists!'

'Oh, he exists all right.'

'Why don't you go find him then?'

'Not 'til after *Fool's River* is finished. You know how I love that cut.'

2

Three days, and more than twelve-hundred miles later, sweating in the heat even with all the windows rolled right down, the southern-man-returned-south stepped out of his car. He had driven up this stretch of road a dozen times, looking for signs of life behind the thick green trees and bushes. Each time he had come back to the sign welcoming him to Honahee, and then back again past the bridge – the landmark that is supposed to have been a part of the legend, so he'd heard. He was just beginning to think that maybe he was on the wrong side of town. He had spent many days of hours chasing after this man's long shadow before now, but this was definitely where he had been told to look.

'One more pass,' he said aloud with each failed attempt. 'Just one more.'

The breeze through the open window just wasn't cutting through the heat. Warm waves of air greeted him as he drove a little slower with each pass. But then, through the windows the warm air carried the smell of pork on its blanket.

The car crept along. The radio, blasting out the Rolling Stones, had long been quieted. Someone was definitely cooking some pork. Somewhere. Out here. Nervous excitement fluttered inside him.

Behind the thick bushes came the unmistakable sound of voices, laughter. It sounded as if there must be a hundred children behind there. He repeatedly tugged his white shirt away from his sticky chest, creating a draft, pulled up the brown belt on his cream chinos and reset his straw Fedora.

On the third attempt he found his way through the bushes. Beyond the huge magnolias he could see a house, primitive but of an impressive spread, clearly with bits added-on over years passed. He noticed that there were separate front doors. Separate houses! A large, neatly-tended vegetable plot. This was a regular development they had going on out here.

A little boy was standing in front of him, juice from a pear running down over his chin. With his chin resting on his chest, the big brown eyes were looking up at the southern man. He had the dearest little face.

Pulling his trousers from his sweaty legs, the southern man crouched down. 'Hey, little buddy, what's your name?'

The little boy ran away. The southern man followed him.

There were children of all ages, outnumbering the adults three-to-one. One of the adults was an elderly lady of size, sitting in a chair in front of the most worn-looking section of the houses. She could be the grandmother, thought the southern man; no, the great-grandmother perhaps, or, assuming that they were all related, even the great-great-grandmother.

He noticed that the chair next to her was empty.

There was a very attractive lady with the most golden skin, probably on the front-fringes of middle-age, with children swarming around her. All of them appeared to be attractive and healthy – the most perfect little colony out here, hidden away from the world.

Hand-in-hand with an impressively tall young adult, the little boy was returning to the man.

'Can I help you, friend?' the adult male asked.

The southern man looked down at the little boy again, smiled and the boy smiled back cheekily, showing the gaps in his teeth. He didn't act so timid next to the big man.

The southern man held out his hand. 'Hello there, my name's Lomax.

Alan.'

The big man took the offered hand. 'Henry,' he said. 'Pleased to meet you. Sir, can I help you?'

'Sorry. I'm sorry.' Behind his hand, he cleared his throat. He wiped a handkerchief over his brow. 'My reason for coming out here today: I was looking for a musician by the name of Booya Carthy. I was told that I would be able to find –'

'He dead!' sprang from the mouth of the little boy.

Lomax jumped back a foot, considering himself fortunate not to have fallen over. 'He's, uh . . . ?'

The little boy was chuckling into his hand.

Henry pulled on the boy's arm. 'Cleveland! We don't shout, do we?'

'Is that the truth, uh, Henry? Is this where he . . . ?'

'I's Booya's son,' Henry said. 'He did live here but he's passed, like the little terror say.' Henry yanked playfully on Cleveland's arm.

'Oh . . . well. I was a big fan . . . I *am* a big fan of your father's. I wished for many years to record his music but could never quite make contact with him. And now it . . . seems it's too late,' he said. 'I am so sorry. When . . . ?'

'Few years now,' Henry answered.

'I am truly sorry to hear that. Are you a musician, Henry?'

'Ain't none of us musicianers out here, sir,' Henry answered.

'I see.'

'*Henry!*' a woman's voice called. '*Cleveland!*'

'Sorry, sir, I gotta go. Sorry I couldn't help you. Take care now, sir. Come on, Cle.'

Lomax watched the man scoop up the little boy and rejoin the clan of the family. The legend that never quite was would always remain so. Booya Carthy was dead.

*

'Come on,' Henry said to the children of all different sizes. He had checked that the man Lomax had left. 'Time for the surprise now, you think?'

They skipped and hollered along the path to the clearing, carrying their various instruments: drums and cymbals, fifes and flutes, jugs, harmonicas and violins. The adults followed the brigade, dropping cursory glances towards the road over their shoulder.

Henry let down Cleveland and little boy ran ahead. A butterfly momentarily distracted him. He tried to catch it but it escaped his grasp. As it flitted away, he pumped his little legs, running to the clearing. Despite letting Cleveland down, Henry's arms were not empty: he was carrying the guitar that he well knew had once been a gift to his father from his own namesake.

Little Cleveland ran up to the two men sitting beneath a tree, drinking around the edges of their cups.

'I tole him, Granpaw!' Cleveland shouted. 'A man come looking for you and I tole him, like you say we should.'

Cleveland leaped into Booya's lap.

'*Ouff!* You getting big, Cle.'

'Good name, little man.'

'You always say that,' Cleveland said to Paw, leaning over from Booya's grasp and touching Paw on the nose. 'You only say it 'cause it's your name, too, Granpaw.'

'*Great* Granpaw,' Booya corrected.

'Paw Paw,' Cleveland said, putting his hand over Paw's mouth.

Booya saw that everyone was piling into the clearing. 'What this?' he asked, placing his cup behind his back.

'We been practicing something for you, Granpaw.' Cleveland jumped up and ran off to Henry – or Paw, as Cleveland Junior called him.

'You know anything 'bout this?' Booya asked Paw.

Paw shook his head. 'Nuh-uh. Was 'bout to see if you was gonna go get me another cup? Seems I missed my boat.'

'And I think you'll find that I went last time, old man.'

'Yah, yah, yah. Whatever. Here's the womens; they can do the fetching.'

'Hey, Bella,' Booya called. 'Come sit down with me.'

Labella lowered herself onto Booya's lap.

'Don't you be getting no idea 'bout squashing my bones, woman,' Paw said to Mammy.

'Don't think I don't know what you up to out here, you old foolio.'

'Ah, what the hell. Squash me if you wanna.'

'You going to sit with us, Mellie?' Labella called over to a young woman fussing over children. Melody indicated that she was too busy arranging her children for the surprise.

'You know she got another one on the way?' Labella asked Mammy.

'Think you find that I knowed first, honey,' Mammy answered with a wink.

Beneath Mammy's weight, Paw mocked a wheeze. She elbowed him in the chest and leaned back against him. He rested his head on her shoulder.

'My Calvin,' Mammy said.

'My Booya,' Paw grinned.

'Still calling him by that fool name?' Mammy rebuked.

'It was him what choose it when he was still but newborn, remember?'

'It was a *sneeze*, Cleveland. Maybe a little bit of wind, at best. He never say nothing like . . . *Booya*. He was just a newborn baby!'

'I always just liked Calvin,' Labella added.

'You always was a sensible one, honey,' Mammy said.

Assembled with their various instruments, the children were arranged in a semicircle. With their genes, some of them weren't looking so much like children anymore. The other adults were standing behind them.

'This a regular Carnegie Hall we got going on out here,' Paw said. Mammy elbowed him again. 'Will you quit it, woman? Was just saying! Ain't nothing wrong with just saying.'

At one end, Henry was standing with his guitar. 'Paradise,' he said to a little girl at the front. Playing with her dress, she turned to Henry. 'You gonna . . .' Henry urged her towards Booya.

She walked forward a few steps. 'Granpaw Calvin, this is a present to you from us on your birthday,' she lisped through the gaps in her teeth. 'We been practicing.' She spun and ran back to her place in the line. Her cousin, Rosie, handed her a fife.

'Fifty,' Mammy breathed. 'I never will believe it. My little boy, fifty years old.'

'Hush yo'self, woman. They 'bout to start.'

'Ready, Sebastian?' Henry called over to the man at the other end of the line.

'Ready, brother,' Sebastian replied.

'Ready, kids?'

'Ready, Paw,' they answered. 'Ready, Uncle Henry.'

~ THE END ~

AUTHOR'S NOTE

In researching the history of the blues for this book, I read many biographies of blues singers and references to the times and places relevant to Booya's story, two of which were invaluable.

"Worse Than Slavery: Parchman Farm and the Ordeal of Jim Crow Justice" by David M. Oshinsky tells of an incredible, and often unbelievable, insight into the treatment of inmates and life at Parchman Farm. Conditions at Parchman did not improve until the 1970s, and were, in fact, much worse than depicted in my novel. I recommend Oshinky's book as essential further reading to greater understand the lives of convicts in Parchman Farm.

"The Land Where the Blues Began" is Alan Lomax's intense chronicle of the history of the blues, heartfelt and thorough in its descriptions, it is the A-Z of the subject. Lomax appears briefly at the end of my story, and I hope that he would approve. No single person in history has done more to bring blues music to the attention of the wider world, and he truly did go out seeking real-life Booya Carthy's, who, but for Lomax, would have lived an impoverished life playing on their own front porch.

ACKNOWLEGEMENTS

My thanks to my editor, Gary Smailes at Bubblecow, for his insights, patience and often brutal editing of the original manuscript (my finished draft initially ran to nearly 195,000 words; he's saved us all a lot of time!), the team at Spiffing Covers for their wonderful cover design, and allowing me to abuse their offer of 'unlimited revisions', and to Richard Sanford, singer / songwriter / heartbeat of one of my favourite bands, The Diarys, for allowing me to use the brilliantly titled 'Drunk Smile' (in Chapter Six / 5, Petal refers to Booya's 'Drunk Smile Blues') as one of Booya's songs. And some honourable mentions for supporting me along the way, for reading drafts and offering suggestions and encouragement: Lorna Burton, Peter and Christine Drown, Joe and Jo Drown, Tanya Haslehurst, Geoff Scott, Lucinda Periac-Arnold. And many thanks to you, who have just finished reading it. I hope that you've enjoyed it. Now I think I'm going to go and have a cup. Always sipping around the edges . . .

11760964R00220

Printed in Great Britain
by Amazon.co.uk, Ltd.,
Marston Gate.